KISSING THE RANCHER

"I've got this," Rachel said as he again struggled to pull apart the packaging with his gloves on. "There's a tab right here."

"Thanks."

They were so close she only had to look up to be staring right into his eyes.

"What, no qualifiers about doing it all yourself?" Rachel said breathlessly.

The side of his mouth kicked up. "I know when to quit."

Her gaze fixated on his lips, and the warm scent of his skin. Unable to stop herself she leaned in.

"What do you want from me, Rachel?" he asked so softly she barely heard him.

She knew he was giving her the opportunity to step back, no questions asked, but she stayed exactly where she was, her mouth an inch from his.

With a stifled sound he closed the gap between them and kissed her, the shock of his cold lips swiftly dispelled by the heat of his tongue as he took possession of her mouth.

He kissed with an intensity that stopped her breath and made everything inside her go quiet, and then hot, and needy. She grabbed for his shoulder to keep him exactly where she wanted him . . .

Books by Kate Pearce

Published by Kensington Publishing Corporation

THE
RANCHER

KATE PEARCE

ZEBRA BOOKS
KENSINGTON PUBLISHING CORP.
http://www.kensingtonbooks.com

ZEBRA BOOKS are published by

Kensington Publishing Corp.
119 West 40th Street
New York, NY 10018

All Kensington titles, imprints, and distributed lines are available at special quantity discounts for bulk purchases for sales promotion, premiums, fund-raising, educational, or institutional use.

Special book excerpts or customized printings can also be created to fit specific needs. For details, write or phone the office of the Kensington Sales Manager: Attn.: Sales Department. Kensington Publishing Corp., 119 West 40th Street, New York, NY 10018. Phone: 1-800-221-2647.

Zebra and the Z logo Reg. U.S. Pat. & TM Off.

First Printing: December 2018
ISBN-13: 978-1-4201-4475-8
ISBN-10: 1-4201-4475-8

eISBN-13: 978-1-4201-4476-5
eISBN-10: 1-4201-4476-6

10 9 8 7 6 5 4 3 2 1

Printed in the United States of America

ACKNOWLEDGMENTS

Many thanks to Keri Ford and Sian Kaley for reading the book and pointing out all the mistakes before I turned it in to my editor. Any mistakes left are definitely mine. If you want to keep up with the Morgans, please check out my website at www.themorgansranch.com and join my newsletter for updates and unique excerpts.

Chapter One

Cauy Lymond stared at the gate blocking the road and reluctantly stepped down from his truck into a teeth-chattering wind. The rusting five-bar gate leading up to the main house was closed with a chain and padlock he didn't have the key for. With a soft curse, he went to find the tool-box he always carried in the back of his truck. By the time he located his wire cutters and work gloves his hands were blue with cold.

After leaving the ranch at sixteen for the sunnier climate of Texas, he'd forgotten how cold it got in Morgan Valley during the winter months. It took him just a second to snap the chain, but far longer to persuade the gate to move past the accumulated muddy ruts so he could get his truck through.

He didn't bother to shut the gate behind him. He'd probably have to replace the damned thing anyway. It wasn't as if his father had left him any livestock that could escape. He turned the heater higher and drove up the steep slope toward the single-story house, barn, and ramshackle livestock sheds arranged in a circle at the top of the slight incline. The sides of the rutted track were piled high with abandoned farm machinery, metal and plastic drums, and the odd rusting domestic appliance.

"What a dump," Cauy murmured as he turned off the engine, and stared at the unwelcoming house. He didn't remember it looking like this when he was a kid, but he hadn't returned for almost fourteen years. At one time his father had taken a lot of pride in the place.

"Welcome home."

The trouble was, it *was* now his home. He didn't have anywhere else to go. Cauy felt in his pocket for the house keys his mother had mailed him from Florida where she'd lived after dumping his dad's ass. He hadn't brought much stuff with him so he hoped the place was still habitable. He blew out a long breath, and watched the wind bend the trees in a graceful scrabble of desperation as if even they wanted to get away.

He didn't want to get out of the truck. . . .

Eventually, he forced himself to brave the frigid temperature and went around to the side door that led into the mudroom and kitchen. To the right of the door was the old chicken coop. Even though the wire had long gone, three chickens stuck their heads out of the dilapidated wooden structure and glared at him like *he* was the intruder.

He found himself smiling as he wrestled to turn the key in the lock. It took a hefty kick with his booted foot to persuade the warped door to open. Cauy paused with his back to the wall and attempted to work out what he was looking at. Someone had helpfully closed the blinds so the room was in complete darkness. A faint smell of damp, bleach, and used cooking oil wafted across his nose, and he swallowed hard.

"First things first." Yeah, so he was talking to himself now. If he didn't he might just run back to his truck and never return. "Open the blinds, check the electricity."

Apparently, his mom's cousin, who'd married a Turner, had come over on horseback and checked that everything was still connected and paid up. Without much hope, Cauy flicked on the light switch and was rewarded by his first clear view of the kitchen in all its dilapidated glory.

Jeez, for a second he contemplated plunging the place back into eternal darkness but as he already felt like he was in the middle of a horror flick it might not be a good idea. He made himself take stock of the space. The kitchen table with two chairs sat against the far wall. A recliner facing a flat screen TV was crowded in one corner where they had once kept the dog's beds.

"Weird . . ." Cauy wandered over to check out the TV. "Same old kitchen appliances and tablecloth, but Dad managed to afford a new screen." As he'd never seen eye to eye with his father, he wasn't surprised at their differing priorities. Not for the first time he wondered where the money he'd regularly sent his mother had gone.

After the shock of finding out his father had left him the ranch, Cauy had discovered things were worse than he'd imagined. Mark had run up huge debts and blamed his neighbors the Morgans for destroying his livelihood.

He checked out the refrigerator, which was running but empty, and tried the range. Water flowed into the deep sink and didn't back up. Whatever else he found, Cauy wouldn't starve or be driven out into the cold.

If he remembered correctly, there was a parlor, a farm office, and an official front hallway on this side of the single-level structure, and three bedrooms and a large bathroom on the other side. Turning lights on as he went, Cauy opened every door and peered in. Nothing much had changed. He kept expecting his father to walk through from the mudroom at any moment complaining about his day.

He ended up in what he remembered as the master bedroom to find someone had added an en suite onto the side of the house. The room had an unused feel, and he wasn't surprised when he went into the second largest bedroom and found all his dad's stuff in there. Cauy took in the ashtray on the arm of the old recliner, another TV, and a queen-size bed covered in a quilt like the ones his grandma used to make. The room still smelled of leather, stale smoke, whisky, and his father's spicy aftershave.

Cauy shuddered and shut the door. He and Jackson had originally shared that room. Their sister, Amy, had the smaller space next door. He clicked on the light in the bathroom and was pleased to find everything working just fine. He'd have to thank Jean Turner when he went back into town. He suspected she'd done a lot more than just ride over.

Retracing his steps to the kitchen, Cauy rinsed out the ancient coffeemaker and set it to work. He'd stopped off at Maureen's store in Morgantown to get the basics. No one had recognized him, which was hardly surprising seeing as he'd left home so long ago.

There was no microwave, so he dumped a can of beans and sausages in a pan and set them to warm on the stove. A couple of bread rolls and he'd be fed and watered for the night. If he was lucky, one of the guardian chickens might lay an egg for his breakfast.

The house felt wrong without his mom . . . like the heart had gone out of the place. Maybe that was why when she'd finally left, his dad had stopped caring and let everything go to shit. On impulse, Cauy pulled out his cell and checked for coverage, amazed when he got a few bars.

He waited as the phone rang, mentally trying to work out the time difference and failing miserably. He was just about to give up when his mother answered.

"Hello?"

"It's Cauy, Mom. I just wanted you to know I got here safely."

"Cauy! I'm so glad you called. I was just taking the dogs out for their last constitutional before bed."

His mom, Anita, had two Pomeranians she spoiled rotten. Cauy pictured her in her cozy kitchen and couldn't help but compare it to where he was now. Had she ever been happy at the ranch? She'd always made an effort for him and his siblings, but he'd heard the fights. They all had.

"Is everything okay up there?" Anita asked.

"Yeah. Do you miss it, Mom?"

She took her time before she answered him. "Some of it. We had some good years before your father made some bad choices that changed everything. I miss the place, and the people in the valley. They were always kind and supportive of me."

"That's not what Dad said."

"Cauy, your dad was an alcoholic. He went out of his way to set up the backs of the very people he needed to help him survive. Ranching isn't a solitary occupation, and he forgot that."

Unwilling to argue with his mother, who was the only person in the world apart from his two siblings who were still talking to him right now, Cauy decided to shut it. While he was at the ranch he intended to investigate his dad's claims and hopefully lay them to rest. He also had no intention of handing the ranch over to the Morgans.

"Anyway, I'm here, and I'll report back on the state of things when I get a chance, okay?"

"Okay, but promise me you won't tire yourself out, or do anything stupid. You're still not a hundred percent."

"No, Ma. I promise." Cauy crossed his fingers like a five-year-old. "I'm just going to take a look around, and see how things are hanging."

Anita snorted. "Whatever that means. Take care, Cauy, and call me if you need anything."

"Will do."

He ended the conversation, got himself some coffee, and took a grateful sip. There was no use crying over spilled milk. His mom had always loved to tell him that. Unless he wanted to give up entirely, he had to find a way forward, and at least the ranch offered him an opportunity to do something positive with his life.

It had been in the Lymond family for almost a hundred years and had once rivaled the next-door Morgan Ranch in size and prosperity. If what he'd heard about the Morgans was true, there was no longer any comparison between the two places.

Cauy yawned so hard his jaw cracked and smoothed a hand over his stubbled chin. He'd get the rest of his gear out of the truck, find his sleeping bag, and make use of the single bed in the master bedroom. Tomorrow was soon enough to take stock of the rest of the place. In the mean-time, he had shelter, water, and food, which was enough for any man—especially one who'd reached the end of his rope. His future was just as messed up as the ranch. He finished his food and took the plate over to the sink. Maybe they deserved each other after all.

Rachel Morgan dumped her bag in her bedroom, took off her shoes, and went right back down to the kitchen where her grandma was waiting for her. The smell of roasting pumpkin floated up the stairs, and Rachel sucked it in like oxygen. Ruth was the best cook in the world. When she wasn't at Morgan Ranch, Rachel often dreamed about her food and woke up with drool on her pillow.

"Rachel, darlin', come here and give your grandmother a hug."

Rachel went willingly, bending down to kiss the wrin-kled cheek of her grandma Ruth and holding her tight. She smelled just like the pies she loved to bake—full of good-ness, with just a kick of spice.

Rachel sat at the table and Ruth pushed a plate toward her. "Have a chocolate cookie while I get on with dinner.

They'll all be milling around in here like sharks in an hour or so."

"I could help you cook," Rachel offered. "It doesn't seem right that you still do everything."

"I don't do it all," Ruth smiled. "I've given up cooking for the ranch guests. Avery found someone to take that on and Billy's a qualified chef as well. Now I just cook for my family, and that's just how I like it. If I need any help I'll ask for it, so don't you worry about me."

Ruth was in her seventies, but had the wiry strength of a much younger woman and the determination to match. She'd single-handedly run the cattle ranch until her son and grandsons had come back to help her. Rachel was still in awe of her and hoped one day to be half as strong and capable.

After a few minutes of preparation, Ruth closed the oven door and took the seat opposite Rachel at the table.

"So how's your stepfather these days?"

"Oh." Rachel hastily swallowed a mouthful of cookie. "He got married again."

"*What?*" Ruth put down her coffee mug. "When?"

"Just last month. He married one of the professors at his college. She's very nice, and also a widow." Rachel tried to shrug. "I had no idea until he asked me to go with him to the wedding to act as a witness."

"Good Lord." Ruth shook her head. "How do you feel about that?"

"I'm very happy for him, but it was a bit of a shock," Rachel confided. "They've gone on an extended honeymoon to explore ancient Greece. That's Jane's specialty, and they won't be back for several months."

"Then I hope you'll stay here with us for a while." Ruth patted her hand. "You can't want to be going back to an empty house."

"He's putting our house on the market. Apparently, Jane's place is closer to the Humboldt campus. I haven't lived there full-time for years, but it's still home." Rachel sighed. "I tried to say all the right things, but I feel like such a kill-joy. I *know* he's been lonely, and that he misses Mom, but—"

"It still feels like a betrayal." Ruth nodded. "You just need some time away to come to terms with it, and what better place than here among your other family? We'll all enjoy your company over the holidays—especially Billy."

The last thing Rachel wanted to think about right now was her birth father, Billy. When Rachel was a baby, her mother had taken Rachel and walked out on her husband and four sons never to be seen again. The discovery that she even had a real father and four siblings was still new and, despite their warm acceptance of her, still filled her with uncertainty.

"I've finished at college now, so I suppose it doesn't matter about the house that much." Rachel picked up another cookie. "I don't think I would've found an engineering job in Humboldt."

"Probably not. What do you plan to do with that fancy degree of yours?"

"I'm not sure." Rachel considered. "I could go abroad and work in the mining industry, or I could stay here. There's always a demand for engineers. It just depends what comes up first."

Some part of her longed to travel, but the new uncertainty of her adopted father's unexpected marriage had shaken her complacency. After the first years of her life when it had just been her and her mom moving constantly around she'd always craved stability. When her mom had married Paul she'd been in heaven.

"Well, while you're here you can start looking for new opportunities," Ruth said. "Chase knows everyone, and I'm sure he'd be happy to help." Ruth finished her coffee and got to her feet. "I've just got to make this pie. Would you slice the apples for me? I need them really thin, mind."

Rachel gratefully took on the task while Ruth retrieved her pastry from the refrigerator and rolled it out on a floured board. Soon the kitchen would be filled with noisy Morgans and other family members. Rachel still felt like something of an outsider, but as she planned to stay awhile she hoped to remedy that.

"January and Chase are in San Francisco, and Blue's at the marine base in Bridgeport teaching horsemanship, so we won't have everyone," Ruth observed as she cut out a lattice top for the pie. "Chase says he's buying me a bigger table, but I'm not sure where he thinks I'm going to put it."

Rachel handed Ruth the bowl of sliced apples and watched her work her magic with sugar, spices, and all things nice.

"HW's here?" Rachel asked.

"Yup. Driving everyone mad as usual—especially Ry."

Rachel had liked Ry on sight, but getting to know his twin, HW, had taken longer. He was as wary of her as she was of him—for very good reasons. She sometimes suspected that he felt like an outsider in his own family as well.

"I feel like everything in my life is up in the air right now," Rachel blurted out.

"That's because it is." Ruth covered the pie with pastry and added egg wash. "Change can be painful you know."

"Yeah . . ." Rachel tried to smile. "I'm really lucky to have somewhere to go while I sort myself out."

"Take as long as you need," Ruth said as she added the pie to the bottom shelf of the oven. "Fresh air and hard work can help you think things through. Or, to put it another way, you'll be so tired that you won't have time to worry about anything before you fall asleep."

"I'll need to work on my riding before I can be much help around here." Rachel sighed. "Ry said I'm getting better but I'll never—"

Ruth smacked her gently on the arm with her wooden

spoon. "How about you start by thinking more positively about yourself, young lady?"

"You're right," Rachel said, grinning. "I've got to stop putting myself down." She flung out her arms. "I'm young, I've got great prospects for a fulfilling and interesting career, and I have a family who loves me."

"You filming a commercial for the guest ranch, Rachel?"

She turned her head to find Ry Morgan smiling down at her. She never had any problem telling him apart from his identical twin.

"Nope." She stood up and accepted the hug he offered her. "Just giving myself a pep talk."

Ry kissed her cheek. "I was worried that you were going to burst into song or something."

Ry had the same blond coloring as she did, but his eyes were hazel while hers were exactly the same blue as Ruth's and Billy's.

"Mirrors crack when I sing, Ry. How are you, and how's Avery?"

"I'm good." He kissed his grandma, and then took the seat next to Rachel. "Avery's doing great. We got engaged."

"That's awesome!" Rachel squealed. She really liked Avery, who was low-key like Ry and had a dry sense of humor that appealed to Rachel. "Is she living here now?"

"Nope." Ry grimaced. "She's still at the Hayes Hotel where she says she's staying until we get married. She *says* I need to find her a house to live in, and I'm working on it."

Ruth got up to check the pie, and Ry lowered his voice. "I'm getting pretty sick of creeping around here and the Hayes place at night, so I'd appreciate any help you can give me on the house building front."

"It's not really my thing, but have you thought about buying some kind of modular house to speed things along?" Rachel asked. "You can always replace it later or use it as an office or a guesthouse when you build your real home."

"That's a great idea." Ry sat back. "All I'd have to do is get the services in, lay a flat foundation, and stick the house on it. Avery doesn't want stairs, and she'd love something new, seeing as she's had to put up with that historic hotel her whole life."

"I suspect it's a little bit more complicated than that," Rachel said. "But Chase has offered you land on the ranch to build on so you've got that covered."

"I'll talk to Avery and see how she feels about that idea." Ry grinned at her. "Thanks, Sis. I don't have a lot of rodeo money stashed away like HW does. I was thinking I'd be offering Avery a tent to live in for the next ten years."

"I can see why she might prefer the hotel." Rachel shuddered. "It gets so cold out there in the winter."

"Yeah. Mom hated it." Ry's smile faded, and he gave Rachel an awkward glance. "You probably knew that already, right?"

"She was never happy when she was cold," Rachel answered as diplomatically as she could. The subject of their mother was never going to be an easy one when Annie had walked out on her family after trying to drown her own baby and then five-year-old Ry in the bathtub. "I think that's why she preferred the coast of California."

Ruth opened the oven, and a cloud of steam rose up. "The pie's not done yet. Everything else looks good to go."

Rachel jumped to her feet, eager to get away from poor Ry, who looked as if he wished he hadn't started down that particular path of conversation. If she was to make any real progress getting to know the Morgan side of her family, Rachel was going to have to keep probing those difficult subjects. Part of her wished she could just walk away from it all, but what would that accomplish? The Morgans were good people, and part of her desperately wanted that honest connection with them.

As Ruth said, sometimes life wasn't easy, and compared

to most people in the world Rachel had nothing to complain about. A burst of laugher in the hallway alerted her to the fact that more Morgans were approaching, and she braced herself for impact. After her small family of three, the size of the Morgan family was sometimes overwhelming.

"Rachel!" HW came over and clapped her on the shoulder. "Good to see you again. Are you staying for Christmas?"

"I already told you that three times, HW." Sam, HW's better half, rolled her eyes as she came up beside them. "You never listen to me, you big dope."

HW side-hugged his girlfriend and winked at Rachel. "The thing is—ninety-nine percent of what Sam blathers on about I can take it or leave it. There's just that tricky one percent when I should be paying attention."

Rachel found herself grinning back at them both as Sam thumped HW, and allowed herself to relax a little more. She could do this. They all wanted her here. Now she just had to convince herself to believe it.

Chapter Two

It was even worse than he'd imagined. . . . Cauy shook his head as he looked up at the leaden sky through what had once been the roof of the pigsty. He was good with his hands and could repair the outbuildings eventually, but it was going to take him a long while to bring the ranch back to what it had once been.

He picked up some of the wooden planks and stacked them against the door, as if that would make a difference. He'd grab a coffee and take the truck out to check the perimeter fencing. It was a job all ranchers hated, but was also the most important one. Not that he had anything to keep within the boundaries of the property except some old memories. But he had plans for the place, and some money set aside for stock when he needed it, which was why the fence had to work.

The sound of an engine laboring up the hill made Cauy step out into the yard. As far as he knew, no one was expecting him, but that didn't mean his arrival hadn't been noticed. Small towns were the same wherever you lived.

The white truck belonged to the sheriff's department and he relaxed his stance. He'd forgotten how to look friendly, so concentrated on looking like a dependable citizen as the uniformed man got out of the driver's seat.

"Hey," Cauy called out. "Can I help you?"

"Good morning." The guy came toward Cauy. He looked slightly familiar. "I'm Nate Turner, the deputy sheriff. I had a call that lights were seen up here, and came to check it out."

Morgan Valley was obviously still not a crime hot spot if the sheriff had time to investigate every call he received. Cauy stuck out his hand. "I'm Cauy Lymond. Mark's son."

Nate shook his hand. "I thought you looked familiar. Long time since you've been around here though, right?"

"Yup, about fourteen years."

"Where were you based?"

Cauy didn't normally like answering so many questions, but Nate Turner was the law around these parts.

"Texas. I worked in the oil industry."

"Yeah?" Nate smiled. "I just came back from a wedding over there. It's beautiful cattle country."

Cauy didn't allow himself to get distracted and focused on the present. "I *think* we were at school together."

"Possibly, or it might have been one of my siblings. We're a big family. Like the Morgans." Nate looked around at the dilapidated buildings, his expression dubious. "You planning on staying here?"

"I came to take stock of the place. My dad left the ranch directly to me. I'm not sure whether it's worth saving right now."

Nate took off his hat and scratched his head. "Yeah . . . it looks like you have a bit to do." The deputy sheriff was obviously a born diplomat, which probably helped in his job. "I thought the Morgans offered to buy it from your father, but I might be wrong. You should check in with Chase. He's the one with all the money these days and he's a great guy."

"So I hear." Cauy kept his opinion of the Morgans to himself. "Thanks for letting me know."

"No problem." Nate handed Cauy his card. "If you need

anything, or have any problems with vandalism, or pot growing on your land let me know."

"People grow weed out here?" Cauy asked. "And I thought this place was still living in the past."

"You'd be surprised." Nate grimaced. "It might feel remote, but we're not that far from some of the biggest cities in California. We don't get a lot of violent crime, but it's definitely on the increase."

"Good to know." Cauy nodded. "Thanks for stopping by."

"You're welcome." Nate hesitated. "If you ever fancy having a drink there's a group of us old-timers who meet up in the Red Dragon Bar every Friday night. You'd be more than welcome to join us."

"I doubt I'll have much time to socialize, but thanks for the information."

He didn't drink anymore either, but that wasn't something he shared with just anybody. He'd managed to sound like a regular human being for at least a few minutes. His mom would be proud. . . .

"You're welcome. Have a great day." Nate got back into his truck, backed up, and set off down the road again, leaving Cauy to the blessed silence. He watched the truck until it disappeared from view, and wondered who'd ratted him out. His only neighbors were the Morgans. Seeing as they were after his land he wouldn't be surprised if they were already keeping tabs on it.

He decided to carry on with his plan to inspect the fence line. After that he'd probably be forced to go back to Morgantown for more provisions and gas, which meant two interactions with other people in one day.

"Whoop-dee-whoop," Cauy murmured as he found his truck keys. "Next thing you know I'll be hosting a ball."

* * *

"You sure you want to do this, Rachel?"

Blue Morgan checked the horse's saddle girth for the fifth time and turned toward her, a frown on his face.

"Yes. I can take a picture of anything that looks broken and text it to you." Rachel put on her gloves and allowed Blue to boost her up into the saddle. She gathered the reins and looked down into her brother's worried blue eyes. "Seriously, I'll be fine. You and Roy have enough to do today dealing with the last of the guests without having to check out those fences."

He still looked concerned, and she carried on talking.

"I've got my phone, my backup phone, and more warm gear than I'd need to climb Everest. It's a straight ride up to the mine, and if I follow the fence line I can't get lost."

"As long as it doesn't snow. That can turn you around real quick," Blue countered, and then sighed. "Just call me if there is even the slightest problem, okay?"

"Will do, Big Brother."

She grinned down at him. As a retired marine he hated things happening out of his control. If she'd known him growing up she figured she would never have had a boyfriend because he would've scared them all away.

He returned her smile. "Yeah, I know I'm a mite over-protective. It drives Jenna nuts. I'm working on it."

Rachel blew him a kiss as he untied her sweet-tempered horse, Petunia—named by Roy—and stepped back.

"I'll be careful, BB. I promise."

She headed out into the weak winter sunshine and followed the ranch road upward toward higher ground. She could've gone by the creek, but the water was freezing and picking her way through the boulders while worrying about falling off would not have made her journey very pleasant. It was nice to be out of the house in the crisp, clear air.

Roy thought someone had been tampering with the fence

surrounding the abandoned silver mine so Rachel had volunteered to go and check it out. The fence had only recently been put in so there was no reason to suppose it had simply fallen into disrepair. Chase was terrified that someone would get into the old mine and end up dead, which Rachel knew wasn't exactly unheard of.

She was dying to take a closer look at the mine works herself, and had added her hard hat and safety gear to her saddlebags when Blue wasn't looking. Chase had already asked her advice about the structure and safety of the place so she wasn't trespassing or anything. She had a map of where the family thought the shafts were located, and of each branch of tunnels, but no one was really sure what was down there.

Chase said it was too dangerous and was checking into new technology that could go down the shafts, and allow him to take a look without human involvement. Although Rachel knew he was right, she still wanted to see the place for herself. It was part of the town's history. Most of the families who settled in Morgantown had been involved in the mine at some point, and local interest in the place was high. Which was probably why people constantly tried to break in. . . .

Determined not to get lost, she obediently followed the fence line up to the high plateau where the mine buildings had once stood. There wasn't much to see anymore in the barren landscape. The original pioneers had stripped out the forest, losing the topsoil and creating their very own California dust bowl in the process.

From what she could see so far, the new fence looked fine, but there was at least another half a mile of it to examine on the far side of the mine.

When she reached the boarded-up entrance with its huge DANGER DO NOT ENTER signs she couldn't resist stopping and dismounting. The door was still padlocked and appeared in good shape. Rachel closed her eyes and tried to imagine what the place had looked like a hundred years ago. She'd have to ask January if there were any old photos.

She walked around to the left side where the foundations of a building remained and stopped. There was an almighty crack in the ground, which she was fairly certain hadn't been there when she'd visited in the spring. It was about two feet across at its widest and stayed that way as far as she could see it. The valley did have the occasional earthquake so it was possible the shake had unsettled things down below.

"This is not good," Rachel murmured as she followed the zigzagging line toward the boundary fence she was supposed to be checking. The crack was narrowing rapidly. "I guess this might be why the fence is down."

She considered going back for her horse, but it wasn't raining, and she wasn't planning on going farther than the fence. She'd take some pictures, text Blue, and leave it at that. Keeping her gaze on the fracture she walked through the thin grass toward the wire encircling the area of the mine. The crack was definitely getting smaller, but it was still worrying.

"Ah. There it is."

One of the fence posts had collapsed sideways into the fault, pulling the coils of wire down with it. Rachel dug out her cell phone and took a few quick pictures, stepping over the fence to where the fault line continued off into the next field.

"Hey!"

Rachel almost dropped her phone as a shadow fell over her. She clutched it to her chest and glared at the idiot who had shouted at her.

"Who the hell are *you*?" Rachel gasped.

The unknown cowboy raised an eyebrow. "You're trespassing."

Rachel glanced down at her booted feet. "I'm about a yard over the boundary line, and I'm obviously checking out the damaged fence."

"You're still on my land."

Rachel took a step back and elaborately climbed over the downed wire. "Happy now?"

"Yeah."

She still couldn't see much of his face under the brim of his brown cowboy hat and upturned collar. Not that she wanted to as he obviously had the major grouchies.

"Tell the Morgans to fix this fence, okay?"

Rachel rolled her eyes. "Why do you think I'm here?" She hoped he got the silent *dumbass* she'd added to her question. "It will be fixed as soon as someone can get up here and do it."

"You didn't come prepared?"

Rachel considered his question, which she supposed was a valid one, but still made her feel inadequate. "I don't know how to fix a fence."

He snorted and half turned away from her.

She pointed at his pickup, which was parked reasonably close. "I suppose you've got all the right tools in your truck?"

"Yeah, sure I do. But I don't work for the Morgans, and I can't afford the time to do it for free."

"Wow. That's very neighborly of you." Rachel was getting cross now. "I'll tell Roy not to bother with the rest of the boundary with your land that we've been 'fixing' for you for the last two years."

"I didn't ask anyone to do that."

"No, but you didn't have to, did you?" Rachel gave him her sweetest smile. "We just did it because we're nice. Have a lovely day, won't you?"

She stomped back the way she'd come. What a rude, ignorant slob! She had been about to apologize, but his grumpy attitude hadn't exactly encouraged her. She supposed she should be glad that he hadn't pulled a gun and shot her like in the good old days. As far as she knew, the ranch next door to the Morgans was not only empty, but up for sale, so who was the guy who'd claimed the land as his own? She hadn't been at Morgan Ranch long enough to know everything going on, so she'd check in with Ruth, who was totally up on all the local gossip.

She sent a text to BB with the photos attached and warned him to be careful around the mine. After managing to mount the patient Petunia without a block or a boost, she put her phone away and made sure of her bearings before setting off back the way she'd come. Behind her, she heard the distant sound of a truck, and assumed it was the cowboy going off to make someone else's day miserable.

The fence line wasn't going to be a problem. The real issue was what was going on below the surface. The cracks carried through into the next ranch, and the mine workings probably did as well. She tried to imagine telling Cowboy Grumpy Ass that if he wasn't careful his precious land might disappear beneath his feet.

Mind you, being there when that happened and watching him disappear in a cloud of dust did have some appeal. . . . Rachel grinned and clicked to her horse. She'd tell Chase about the condition of the mine when he came back and let him decide what he wanted to do next.

"Some dude told you to get off their land?" Blue repeated Rachel's statement, his blue eyes narrowed, his fingers flexing as if he was looking for a handy weapon. "Who the hell was it?"

"I don't know. I didn't ask him." Rachel sipped her iced tea. She was sitting at the kitchen table surrounded by Morgans who were all finishing up dinner. "He wasn't exactly being pleasant about it."

BB half rose from his seat. "Well, we'll see about that—"

"Sit." Ruth hauled him down by the elbow. "Let Rachel finish the story."

BB did as his grandma said, but he obviously wasn't happy.

His daughter Maria shushed him with a reproving glance. "Be quiet, Dad. I want to hear what happened next."

BB sighed and folded his arms across his chest. "Go on, then, I'm all ears."

"What did he look like?" Billy asked Rachel, his expression troubled.

"It was hard to tell. He was all bundled up in a big coat, and his hat shaded his face." Rachel considered the image in her head. "He definitely wasn't old, and his accent wasn't from around here." He'd had a slow drawl that reminded her of Texas.

"I wonder if it's one of the Lymond boys?" Billy turned to Ruth. "There were two of them, right? Cauy and Jackson."

Ruth nodded. "That's right. They had a little sister called Amy. Amy moved to Florida with Anita when she left Mark, and the older boy went earlier when he was a teenager."

"I thought Mark Lymond put the place up for sale?" BB asked. "Chase was all set to buy it, but his lawyer said no thanks."

"Mark Lymond never liked us," Billy reminisced. "He was always complaining about something. Sounds like his son is just the same."

"Remember when Mark called out Jenna in front of the

whole town?" Blue said. "He was afraid of a female vet doctoring his livestock, and tried to make out she wasn't properly qualified."

BB scowled at his father. He obviously wasn't prepared to let the matter go, and knowing how protective he was of Jenna, Rachel wasn't surprised. In fact, considering Blue's military career it was amazing that Mark Lymond had survived speaking ill of BB's fiancée at all. . . .

"If the poor boy is stuck up there all by himself, no wonder he's miserable." Ruth put her mug down on the table. "Jean Turner goes over there every month to check the house is still standing, and she said it's a bit of a dump. We'll have to go and welcome him home."

"*Welcome* him?" BB raised his eyebrows. "He was rude to Rachel, and his father sucked ass. I'm more inclined to go over there and tell him to keep a civil tongue in his head or he'll have me to reckon with."

"Which is why you're not invited," Ruth said firmly. She looked at Rachel. "How about you and I go up there this afternoon and give him a proper welcome home?"

"If you really think it's a good idea." Rachel made a face. "I'm not sure he'll want to see me on his land again, but I definitely don't want you going up there by yourself."

"Which is why I should come with you," BB interrupted again. "I'll make sure he behaves himself."

"I'll come," Billy said quietly. "I haven't got anything to do this afternoon. If it is one of Mark's sons, he might remember me."

"Great." Ruth stood up. "Now let me see what I have in the freezer. . . ." She disappeared off into the pantry still talking to herself.

BB leaned in toward Rachel and lowered his voice. "If he steps out of line, you let me know, okay?"

"Will do." Rachel nodded. "But I think Ruth and Billy will handle it."

She also rose to her feet and started clearing the plates. Going to see the grumpiest cowboy in the valley wasn't her idea of a fun afternoon. Knowing Ruth and her low tolerance for bad manners, she suspected that if he stepped out of line he might not enjoy the encounter much either.

Chapter Three

Cauy stared glumly at the limp chicken sandwich sitting on his plate and wished he'd bought some chips to go with it. He was trying to eat healthier, but sometimes all he craved was a huge bag of barbecue chips to shove in his mouth. His fingers were aching from twisting wire to mend the boundary fence, and he wasn't even a quarter of the way round the property. He *had* checked out the fence bordering Morgan Ranch and found it well maintained and secure.

Which meant he might owe the beautiful blonde an apology. He winced as he recalled her response to his territorial paranoia. She'd hardly been cattle rustling, just taking a picture of the downed fence, and he'd treated her like a terrorist. The thing was, he hadn't expected to meet anyone out there, and she'd surprised him. He'd forgotten how to talk to people, and it showed. . . .

Outside, the guard chooks started clucking, and he tensed as a vehicle swept into the yard. Had the woman set Nate Turner on him? Leaving his uneaten lunch on the table, he went to the back door, braced himself, and went out. The sight of a diminutive elderly lady being helped out of a huge blue pickup truck made him blink.

"Howdy, neighbor!"

He took an involuntary step back and collided with the door frame as she advanced toward him with a smile.

"Welcome home." She searched his face. "It's Cauy, isn't it?"

He nodded like an idiot and helplessly held open the door as she swept past him.

"Jean Turner told me you were coming back home, and I didn't like to think of you up here all by yourself."

Cauy opened his mouth and then closed it again as she kept talking. An older man with a lined face, graying hair, and very blue eyes came through the door and offered Cauy his free hand. His other arm was loaded with plastic boxes.

"Hi, I'm Billy Morgan." He pointed at the woman and half smiled. "That's Ruth Morgan. My mother. She's something of a force of nature."

Cauy shook his hand, as Ruth turned back to him.

"Is that your lunch?" She pointed at his limp chicken sandwich.

"Yes, ma'am." He felt like he was five again.

She tutted and headed for the door. "That's not going to keep you fed. Rachel? Bring that covered dish in first, the hot one, and then we can start on the rest."

"I'm coming. Just getting something to protect my hands. This thing is *hot*!"

Cauy knew that voice. . . .

The tall blonde he'd met that morning came through the door carrying a covered dish in a cloth. She slowed as she went past him, her vivid blue gaze meeting his with a distinct challenge.

"Hello again, *neighbor*."

She was definitely a Morgan. And apparently, her name was Rachel. She looked young enough to be Ruth's great-granddaughter, which meant that one of the Morgan brothers must have married young and started producing early.

Ruth took the dish from Rachel. "Thank you, darlin'.

Now, why don't you and Billy bring the rest of the stuff in while I have a nice visit with Cauy?"

Nice visit? Cauy's stomach rumbled as the smell from the foil-wrapped dish reached him. This was not how he'd planned on meeting the Morgans again, not at all. He'd intended to find a local lawyer and meet them on neutral territory.

Ruth pulled out his chair and put the dish on the table. "Sit down, and eat up."

Cauy thought about telling them all to get out, but the allure of a proper home-cooked meal and being treated like a human being was way too strong. He also had a suspicion that if he didn't do what Ruth Morgan said she'd be on the phone with his mother, and then he'd really be in the shit. So much for his tough-guy image.

"I'll make some fresh coffee," Ruth called out to him. "You seem to have that, at least."

He sat and uncovered the dish to find a large slice of chicken pie, mashed potatoes, and carrots. He swallowed hard. Was accepting food from his father's sworn enemies a concession of defeat, or could he class it as keeping his enemies close?

His stomach clenched with longing and he gave in to the desire to eat. He picked up his fork and dug into the pie, almost moaning at the buttery pastry and creamy chicken sauce. At this point, he didn't care if the food was poisoned, it tasted so good.

"Dessert." Ruth Morgan placed another plate on the table along with a fresh cup of coffee and a glass of water. "Now, slow down, or you'll give yourself colic."

"Yes, ma'am," he managed to mutter before noticing the stewed apple and ice cream in the bowl beside him. Where had the ice cream come from? He was pretty sure there was nothing in his freezer.

By the time he'd cleared both his plates, Billy and Rachel

Morgan were back in the kitchen and the door had been shut against the cold air. Cauy tried to make sense of all the boxes Ruth Morgan was emptying. Did she think he'd brought a small army with him?

He took his plates over to the sink and discovered he now had a new sponge and washcloth to go with the last of his dishwashing liquid. There was also a plastic bowl in the battered sink.

"I put the meals in the freezer." Ruth came over to him, wiping her hands on a towel. "They are all marked with the contents, how to cook them, and an eat-by date. Do you have a microwave?"

"No."

"We have an old one that used to be in Roy's kitchen. I'll get someone to bring it over for you."

Cauy cleared his throat. "That's very kind of you, but—"

"It's no trouble. There's no point you wasting money on something when you don't have to, is there?" She patted his arm. "I put some cleaning supplies under the sink, and cans and dry goods in the pantry. There are a few essentials in the refrigerator as well. Do you like cooking?"

"Not really."

"If you change your mind, come and see me, and I'll sort out some proper pans for you." Ruth looked at Billy. "Is there anything I've forgotten?"

"I don't think so, Mom."

"Good, so we can sit down and chat." Ruth guided Cauy back to the table, her hand firmly on his elbow. "How is Anita doing these days?"

"She's good." Cauy kept a cautious eye on Rachel, who was perched on the arm of the chair, and Billy, who was leaning up against the wall next to her. "I'll tell her I saw you."

"Are Jackson and Amy going to stop by and visit you for Christmas?"

Cauy hadn't even thought to ask them. "I don't think so."

Ruth frowned. "Then you'll have to come to us. We can't have you sitting here all by yourself on Christmas Day."

Cauy wondered why not. It wouldn't be the first Christmas he'd spent by himself, and probably wouldn't be the last.

"Cauy might have plans of his own, Ruth," Billy intervened, and winked at Cauy. "Don't mind her, she just can't bear to think that anyone might prefer to be alone during the holidays."

Ruth raised her eyebrows. "I'm not asking him to move in with us, Billy. I'm just saying that if he wishes to join us for Christmas lunch he's more than welcome."

"That's very kind of you." Cauy finally remembered his manners and stood up. He had no intention of going anywhere, but his mom had brought him up right. Ruth Morgan wasn't at all how he thought she'd be. His father had never had a good word to say about her, insisting she was a pushy woman who thought she ran the whole town.

From what Cauy could tell Mrs. Morgan had been born into the role, which would have infuriated his father, who had a low opinion of women generally.

He went over to the back door and grabbed the handle like a lifeline. "It was nice of you to come all the way out here. I appreciate it."

"It was no trouble at all." Ruth Morgan looked at him, and then at her family. "Billy, give Cauy that card with all our cell phone numbers on it. Roy, our foreman, will be coming up this week to see if he can help you out with anything."

Cauy opened the door. "There's no need for him to put himself out."

Ruth sighed and rose from the table. "Stubborn as your father, I see."

"My father—" Cauy couldn't think how to finish that sentence without saying something rude about the Morgans and, despite everything, he knew Ruth Morgan had come with the best of intentions. Rachel and Billy were now looking at him like he was some kind of worm.

"Come along, Mom." Billy wrapped his arm around Ruth's shoulders. "Cauy's probably got things to do."

Cauy waited until they came alongside him, and cleared his throat.

"I do appreciate you coming by, Mrs. Morgan."

She smiled at him. "Don't be a stranger, okay? I've known your family for seventy years, and we always helped each other out in times of need. Just call if you need anything."

"I will. Thanks again."

Billy nodded to him as he went through the door. Cauy let out a breath he didn't realize he was holding and then found himself face-to-face with Rachel, who didn't look any happier to see him now than she had earlier.

"Nice to see you are an ass to everyone you meet, and not just me," Rachel said. "What did my grandma ever do to you?"

"Your grandma?" Cauy asked before he even thought it through.

"Yes." She frowned. "Billy's my dad."

"That can't be right." Cauy slowly shook his head. "He had four sons. We went to the same school."

Rachel raised her chin. She was tall for a woman, and easily met his gaze. "You're saying I can't be a Morgan?"

"I'm saying . . ." Cauy stopped mid-sentence as some long-forgotten memory stirred deep in his head. "You're the baby that *disappeared*?"

"Got it in one, which still has nothing to do with how you just treated my grandmother," Rachel said.

Cauy was still trying to get his head around who Rachel was. "Everyone thought you and your mom had died. *My* dad thought—" He abruptly shut up when he remembered that his father believed Billy Morgan had murdered his own wife and child and had taken some unholy glee in the notion.

"Rachel?" Speak of the devil. Billy had come back to see where his daughter was. Seeing them next to each other there was no denying they were related. Billy looked way too kind to ever hurt a fly. "You coming?"

"Yes, sorry."

Rachel smiled apologetically at her father, and Cauy almost swallowed his tongue. He'd never seen her smile before, and the beauty of it hit him low in the gut. If she was Billy's daughter, she wasn't as young as she looked, which made him feel slightly better about appreciating her charms.

Billy turned to Cauy, his smile wry. "Ruth can be a little . . . managing. But she means well."

"I'm very grateful to her for coming," Cauy reiterated.

"Well, you know where we are if you need anything." Billy nodded. "Have a great day, son."

"Thanks."

Rachel walked away with her father, and Cauy watched them leave before closing the door and locking it. He felt like he'd had an early visit from the Christmas fairy—not that Rachel Morgan would appreciate being called that. Hopefully, they'd realize that he didn't need their help and keep away.

He sat back at the table and rubbed his hands over his stubbled jaw. He'd been polite, hadn't he? He'd let the Morgans into his house and said thank you for everything Ruth had done for him. So why did he still feel like a heel? It wasn't as if he cared what they thought of him. For a brief moment, he'd remembered what it felt like to be part of a happy family who wanted to see you and welcomed you home. He hadn't expected that from the Morgans, whom his father had ended up hating. . . .

* * *

"He's very quiet," Ruth said as Billy drove them down the hill toward the lower gate. "And he definitely needs a haircut and a shave."

"Cauy?" Billy chuckled. "You didn't give him much of a chance to get a word in edgeways."

"He certainly looked a bit shocked to see us, didn't he?" Ruth said. "How he was expecting to live out there all by himself with no company at all, I don't know."

"Maybe he likes it." Billy stopped the truck.

Rachel got out to open the gate as Billy continued to chat to Ruth and drove through. She got back in and did up her seat belt. Without his hat and coat on, Cauy Lymond had light brown hair that curled into the nape of his neck and warm brown eyes that weren't far off level with her own. He was lean for his height and tanned like most people who worked outside year-round. Despite what Ruth thought, Rachel quite liked his stubbled chin.

"How old is he?" Billy asked.

"He's a similar age to BB, I think, so around thirty. They were in the same year at school, but Cauy left home when he was around sixteen. His mom wasn't very happy about that. She told me Cauy and Mark didn't get along, and the house was a lot more peaceful without all the yelling."

"Sixteen is still very young to leave home and go to Texas," Billy countered. "At least my boys waited until they graduated high school before hightailing it out of here."

"That was because I would've whooped their asses if they'd tried to do anything different." Ruth smiled.

"What did he do in Texas?" Rachel joined the conversation, her curiosity overcoming her.

"He was in the oil industry, I think." Ruth frowned. "Anita was always worrying about him, I know that."

"It's dangerous, dirty work," Billy agreed. "I hated it."

"You worked there, too?" Rachel studied the back of her father's head from her seat in the rear.

"Yeah. The money was good, but the working conditions and hours could be killers." He shrugged. "And I wasn't exactly an exemplary employee. I only worked to pay for my addictions, and then moved on."

His blunt honesty about his lost years was sometimes hard to take. But when Rachel studied her father's lined face she saw those forgotten and desperate times etched there and in the startling blue of his eyes. Sometimes it made it hard to look at him. He'd caused so much heartache in the Morgan family and managed to not only save himself, but also come back to the family home a different man willing to face his past and apologize for it. Rachel still shied away from the complicated emotional mess that represented, and how her parents' actions had defined and changed her life. She suspected all Billy's children did the same.

"Maybe I'll call Anita and tell her I've seen Cauy." Ruth was speaking again. "She might be able to fill me in on a few details."

"You are a terrible gossip, Ruth." Billy turned onto Morgan Ranch land and the electric gate slid open.

"I just like to know what I'm up against," Ruth replied.

"Why?" Rachel asked. "He was rude to you. Why would you care what he's doing here?"

"He wasn't exactly rude, Rachel. He thanked me very nicely several times."

"Yeah, he did," Billy chimed in.

"*I* thought he was rude." Rachel sat back in her seat, arms folded over her chest. "He made it look like we were a nuisance he wanted to get rid of."

"Maybe he's just shy?" Ruth suggested.

Rachel snorted. "Right. That wasn't the vibe I was getting."

"Your grandma can be a bit overwhelming sometimes, Rachel," Billy pointed out. "Cauy's just got back, the ranch is in ruins, and some bossy old lady comes in, takes over his kitchen, and asks him all kinds of intrusive questions."

Ruth laughed. "I suppose I am a bit nosy. I just wanted him to feel welcome."

"You did a nice thing for someone who didn't appreciate it," Rachel said firmly. "That's on Cauy Lymond. Not on you."

"Wow, you're a tough audience, Rachel." Billy pulled up in front of the ranch. "He's obviously got on the wrong side of you." He winked at Ruth. "You remind me of your grandma more each day."

"Nothing wrong with that." Ruth opened the passenger door and stepped down onto the ground. "I've done pretty good with my life so far."

Billy came around to Rachel's side of the truck and waited until Ruth reached the house. "Are you okay? Did Cauy say anything to you after I left?"

"No, I was just telling *him* off for being rude," Rachel sighed. "Maybe I overreacted."

Billy patted her shoulder. "Just like your grandma. She was quite the firecracker back in the day. Ask Roy."

They went up to the house and discovered Chase and his wife, January, already sitting in the kitchen chatting with Ruth.

Chase had his laptop open, and beckoned to Rachel to come and sit beside him. He was obviously still in Silicon Valley mode. It usually took him a day or so to ease back down to ranch speed.

"I got your e-mail about the mine. Can we ride up there tomorrow and take a look at the damage?"

"Sure." Rachel accepted the mug of coffee Ruth offered her. "Did you see the pictures I took?"

"Yeah, BB passed them on to me." Chase frowned. "It looks pretty serious. I'm wondering whether we should just fill all the mine shafts we know about and demolish the main entrance."

"We can definitely do that, but it would be better to get

some idea what's going on below the surface before you close it up completely." Rachel hesitated. "We don't really know the extent of the mine works, or if there are other shafts. I'd like to do a comprehensive survey before anything else."

"Okay, how will we do that?"

Chase's ability to process information and move on was legendary.

"There are several ways to scope out the mine workings, but we'll need specialized equipment, which might be expensive," Rachel said.

"Let me worry about that. Can you deal with it yourself, or do I need to get someone else in?" Chase asked.

"I can probably handle it." Rachel considered her options. "I have lots of friends who work in mine engineering so if I don't know something, I'll be able to get help."

"Great. I'd rather keep it in the family," Chase said. "I don't want to scare off any potential guests. We still have guests on site for another few weeks before we close for the holidays."

"I suspect some of the mine goes under the Lymond Ranch," Rachel said.

Chase grimaced. "I wish that old fool Mark Lymond had sold the land to me. I made him a great offer. It would make things so much easier right now."

"Did Ruth mention that Mark's son is living there now?" Rachel asked. "We just got back from visiting him."

"Jackson's come home?" Chase raised his eyebrows. "He was always a nice guy. I wonder if it would be worth asking him if he's interested in selling the place."

"It's Cauy Lymond who's come back. I think his father left him the ranch," Rachel sighed. "He's not exactly Mr. Charming."

"I don't remember him very well." Chase squinted at his laptop. "He left school before graduation and went to Texas."

"So Ruth said. The place looked terrible, so I'm not sure how he's going to live there." Rachel took the refilled coffee mug Ruth offered her. "Billy said he couldn't see any signs of stock in the fields either."

"Then he'll be in trouble." Chase sipped his own coffee. "Maybe I should go up there and have a chat with him myself."

"Good luck." Rachel made a cross over her heart. "I wouldn't rush over there too quickly. He didn't seem very happy to see us."

"He was just shy," Ruth said, entering the conversation. "As Billy mentioned, I can be a little overpowering sometimes."

"A little?" Chase grinned at his grandma. "When you get an idea in your head you're unstoppable."

Ruth's answering smile was a little smug. "Got you lot all back where you belong, didn't I? Sometimes being as stubborn as a mule is a good thing." She patted Chase's arm. "Give Cauy a few days to get over us visiting him, and then go talk to him. After a week at that ranch he might just have changed his mind about staying."

Chapter Four

"Cauy?"

Cauy turned around to find a woman with streaked black and orange hair studying him intently. He'd been forced to come into town to get some groceries and had wandered into the Western wear part of the general store where a rancher could find almost anything he or she might ever need. When he was a kid, Cauy had loved coming down to the store with his dad. Not a lot seemed to have changed.

He cocked his head to one side to study the woman who had called out to him, and drew a blank.

"You don't remember me, do you?" she said, grinning at him.

"Nope." Cauy wasn't into playing games.

She pointed at her chest. "I'm Nancy Mulligan, Maureen's daughter. We were at school together."

He tipped his hat to her Texas style. "Er, hi, Nancy."

"You really don't remember me, do you?" She shook her head. "I'm devastated. I had the most horrendous crush on you for years, and you never even noticed."

Cauy frowned. Since the accident he'd lost some of his memories. "I—"

"Okay, so I was eleven, and you were like, fifteen, but we

could've made it work." She frowned. "Although maybe not, seeing as your dad wasn't exactly nice to my mom so the holidays would've really sucked."

"It's nice to meet you again," Cauy said cautiously. "Do you still work here?"

"Not anymore. I'm just helping out while Mom's at the wholesaler's. I share my talents between the Morgan Ranch and the Red Dragon Bar. You should come in one evening." She winked at him. "First drink is on me."

"I don't drink," Cauy said automatically.

She wrinkled her nose at him. "Not even water?"

"I'd hardly go into a bar for water."

"We have great local food as well." Nancy continued speaking, "Your dad used to come in a lot."

"I bet he did."

Something in Cauy's dry tone must've shown on his face because Nancy grimaced.

"Sorry. Not a good example at all. Is that why you don't drink?"

He opened his mouth to explain, and then shut it again. If Nancy did work in the local bar she probably knew all the town gossip. He didn't want his life out there again being picked over by carrions.

"Sorry, I'm terminally nosy, ask anyone," Nancy apologized, although she didn't sound very sorry. "It's an acquired habit after working in a bar for five years."

"It's okay." He looked around the store and made a desperate attempt to change the subject. "This place hasn't changed much at all."

"No, my mom hates to throw anything away so she keeps all the junk." Nancy shrugged. "Is there anything in particular you were looking for?"

"Just work gloves."

"Over there, beside the jeans." She pointed to the back wall with its old posters of rodeo stars in their Wranglers.

"You really should come into the bar one night just to say hi to everyone."

Cauy didn't reply and instead made his way over to the rack of gloves. Nancy followed him, and he had a sudden memory of a determined little girl on the blacktop at school always dogging his heels.

"Your hair is fair, isn't it?"

"Yeah." Nancy patted her head. "I just think that's super boring, and I got sick of all the dumb blonde jokes."

Cauy concentrated on the selection of gloves, stripping off his own to try on a likely pair.

"Wow, what happened to your hands?" Nancy asked.

He'd lived with the scars long enough to sometimes no longer notice them. Embarrassed, he shoved his left hand back into his glove, picked up the pair he'd just tried on, and headed to the front of the store.

"These will do fine."

Nancy followed him out and took up position at the cash register in the part of the store that catered to the tourist and local food needs.

He paid for the gloves in cash and stowed them in the pocket of his fleece-lined denim jacket. "Thanks, Nancy."

"You're welcome, Cauy." She handed him his change. "It's good to see you back. I hope you're going to stick around this time."

"We'll see how it goes." He managed a smile. "Can you tell me where the twenty-four-hour primary care place is situated?"

"Dr. Mendez's place is at the other end of this street." Nancy pointed. "Turn right and keep walking past the Red Dragon Bar. You'll find it just before you reach the gas station."

"Thanks."

Out in the street, the wind had picked up, making Cauy button up his jacket and bury his hands in his pockets. There were very few people about so rather than drive, he took the opportunity to stroll down the raised wooden sidewalk to check out the changes in his hometown.

There were several new businesses including a double-fronted coffee shop that smelled awesome, and a florist called Daisy's. Even the Red Dragon had been painted and freshened up. The primary care building's exterior was redbrick, but inside it was all bright lights and sterile efficiency. Cauy breathed in the hated smell of hospitals and straightened his spine.

"Hi!" A young woman greeted him from the reception desk as he paused uncertainly by the door. "May I help you?"

"Yeah, I made an appointment to see Dr. Mendez at eleven."

She clicked away at her keyboard and then smiled at him. "Cauy Lymond, right?"

"That's me." He handed her his insurance card and driver's license, which was from the state of Texas. If he stayed, he'd have to change that.

If he stayed . . .

She handed him a clipboard with a pile of paperwork attached to it. "Thanks for coming in early to fill out your new patient forms. Bring them back to me when you're done."

He retreated to the far corner of the waiting room, aware of several pair of interested eyes already fastened on him. Ignoring everyone, he put his head down, took off his gloves, and started writing. With his medical history, he might be some time. . . .

Rachel held the door open so that Mrs. Medeiros could enter the reception room.

"I'll come back in an hour to pick you up, okay?" She

had to shout as the old lady was hard of hearing and refused to admit it. "Get Julia to call me if you get out early."

She caught the eye of the receptionist, pointed at Mrs. M., and then at herself and her ear. Julia waved and Rachel stepped back into the hallway, colliding with a hard body.

"Ouch!" She rocked on her heels as her elbow was taken in a competent grip, which finally steadied her. "I'm really sorry."

She went down on her knees and started gathering up the boxes of drugs that had spilled onto the floor. Her gaze took in a familiar pair of muddy cowboy boots and faded jeans that fitted their owner really well. She went to get up, and he extended a hand to help her.

"Sorry about that," Rachel repeated. "I didn't see you behind me."

Cauy Lymond silently took the boxes and pill containers from her hands and replaced them in his paper bag.

"Not a problem."

"I was just dropping Mrs. Medeiros off for her checkup."

For some reason, Rachel kept talking, determined to get more than one incomplete sentence from her surly neighbor.

"As I said. No harm done." He tipped his hat to her. "If you'll excuse me."

"How about a cup of coffee?" Rachel blurted out.

He paused, his hazel eyes steady on hers. "*What*?"

"Would you like to have a cup of coffee with me at Yvonne's?" Rachel repeated slowly. "I've got an hour to kill, and I was wanting to talk to you about something anyway."

"Wanted to talk to *me*?"

"Yes, I realize you don't do talking, but that's okay. I'll talk, and maybe you can just listen."

He opened his mouth, and she poked him in the arm.

"Come on. Don't be a dope. I promise I won't bite, and once you've tasted Yvonne's baking you'll thank me."

He sighed and continued to look at her. "Okay."

"Great!" Rachel went to the main exit, and he followed her out, striding comfortably at her shoulder as she headed for the pink-and-black-striped awnings outside Yvonne's. "Did you like Dr. Tio? He's really cool, isn't he?"

"Dr. Mendez? He seems okay."

"I often come here when I've got errands to run in town. Yvonne has the best Internet outside Morgan Ranch." Rachel pushed open the door and inhaled the tantalizing smell of chocolate and coffee. "Have you met her yet?"

"No."

Jeez, he was back to one-word answers now, and she sounded like a chatterbox. Rachel went up to the counter where Lizzie was handling the orders.

"Hey, Liz. What's up?"

"Nothing much." Lizzie turned away from the cappuccino machine and did a double take at Cauy. "*Hey.*"

He nodded once, his face again hidden in the shadow of his Stetson. For the first time Rachel wondered whether Ruth was correct, and he was just shy.

"What can I get you?" Lizzie asked.

"Cappuccino for me, please," Rachel said, and looked at Cauy. "How about you?"

"Coffee, black, please." He took out a battered wallet from his back pocket. "And it's on me."

Rachel considered arguing with him and decided she'd rather keep him sweet.

"Thank you. But I *was* going to have a strawberry tart as well," Rachel confessed.

"I think I can stretch to that."

Rachel blinked. Had Cauy just made a joke and almost smiled at her? What was happening? Maybe Yvonne's place really was magical after all.

"Thank you."

"You're welcome." He handed over a twenty and then dropped the small change in the tip jar.

Lizzie winked at Rachel. "Go sit down, I'll bring the drinks over to you."

Rachel found a secluded spot near the back of the extended shop and sat down, unzipping her fleece and removing the knitted cap Ruth had made for her. Cauy followed suit, but of course left his hat on.

She had a feeling that if she waited for him to start chatting she'd be there all day. He reminded her of a lot of the hired hands on the ranch, men who did their jobs, were magic with the horses, but who didn't have a lot of time for the niceties of conversation.

"Did you work on a ranch in Texas?" Rachel asked even though Ruth had suggested otherwise.

He looked at her. "Nope."

"I suppose if you'd wanted to do ranch work you would've stayed home."

"I worked in the oil industry."

"Doing what?" Rachel asked.

He shrugged. "Whatever paid me a wage."

"Like?"

"General laboring, back filling pipelines, tending to the drilling rig, driving trucks, that kind of thing."

Rachel shuddered. "That doesn't sound like much fun."

"I was young and fit, and wanted my independence. It suited me just fine."

Lizzie came over with a tray and placed it in between them, interrupting their conversation.

"Black coffee for you, Cauy, cappuccino for Rachel, and two strawberry tarts." Lizzie smiled at Cauy. "The second one is on the house."

"Thank you." Cauy nodded. "It looks great."

Lizzie took the tray away with her. Cauy hesitated before slowly removing his gloves, which drew Rachel's attention to his hands. Both were scarred as if he'd been in a fire or something. She immediately averted her gaze, but not before she'd caught the hint of a challenge in his hazel eyes. Did he really think she was such an insensitive jerk that she was going to say something? She left blurting out stupid stuff to him.

Instead, she busied herself adding cinnamon to her cappuccino and cutting her strawberry tart in half.

"What did you want to talk to me about?"

Rachel looked up, her mouth full of strawberry, and hastily swallowed. So much for pleasantries. Cauy Lymond wanted to get away from her as quickly as possible. What was it about her that made staying in her company so awful? Most people liked her. She wasn't a bitch or the kind of person who liked to dominate a conversation.

"Slow down." She pointed at his tart. "You haven't even tasted it yet."

"I can do two things at once."

Cauy bit into the squishy center of the tart and stopped speaking, it was that good. It took all his concentration not to moan with delight. Rachel was right about one thing. He'd definitely be coming back to Yvonne's.

Rachel was smiling triumphantly at him. Damn, she was pretty. "See? Perfection in pastry."

"Yeah." He finished off the tart and licked his lips. "Now, what did you want to talk to me about?"

She made a face and rested her chin on her hand. Her short blond hair was ruffled from being under her hat, and up close her eyes were a startling blue. "Is it me?"

He blinked at her.

"I mean, that you don't want to talk to. Or are you like this with everyone?" Rachel asked.

"Pretty much like this." Cauy took a sip of his coffee.

"I suppose I should be pleased."

He didn't know what to say to that so he took another slug of coffee, which was also excellent, and waited her out. If he were honest with himself he'd have to say it was no hardship sitting opposite Rachel Morgan. There was a freshness and innocence about her that he'd lost a long time ago.

"Okay, I wanted to talk to you about the old silver mine."

He frowned. "The one on your ranch?"

"Yes, except I think it extends under your land as well."

"So what?"

She blew gently on the froth on her cappuccino and then licked it like a cat, making everything male in Cauy sit up and take notice.

"You remember the first time we met?"

"When you were trespassing?"

Rachel rolled her eyes. "Yeah, that time. I was checking out the fence line to see why some of it had gone down, and discovered some surface damage probably due to the last earthquake here in the summer."

"And?"

"It's possible the tunnels beneath the surface have become more unstable."

"So what?"

"Well, the ground could cave in."

"The mine is out in the middle of nowhere. What harm will it do if it does collapse into itself?" Cauy pointed out.

"I'm not sure." Rachel wrinkled her nose. "I just wanted to give you a heads-up that we might need to investigate further."

Cauy put his mug down on the table with a thump. "I'm not paying for anything."

"I haven't asked you to." Rachel sat up straight. "I just wanted—"

"And why did they send you to deliver this message?" Cauy interrupted her. "Did Chase Morgan think I'd be more willing to deal with you because you're so pretty?"

Her smile disappeared. "You think he sent his little sister to *kiss your ass*? Did it even occur to you that I might *know* what I'm talking about?" She got to her feet and threw a five-buck note on the table. "You really are a pain, Cauy Lymond. Have a great day."

She gave him one last scorching glare and then stormed out, slamming the door of the coffee shop behind her.

Cauy slowly exhaled.

This was why he didn't talk to people.

"Was Rachel okay?" Lizzie came to collect the cups, her expression concerned.

"She's just mad at me." Cauy handed her his empty plate. "I don't suppose you know what she does for a living, do you?"

"Rachel?" Lizzie paused. "She just finished college. Some kind of engineering degree, I think. You should check in with Ruth if you want to know all the details."

"Engineering," Cauy sighed, "Yeah, that figures."

So maybe she did know a "little bit" about what she was talking about after all. . . .

Lizzie returned to the counter. Cauy raked a hand through his hair and then replaced his hat. Why did he always seem to put his big foot in his mouth when Rachel Morgan was around? Now he'd have to apologize to her—again.

He finished his coffee and picked up the bag of prescriptions Dr. Mendez had provided for him. It was three years since the accident, but he still needed medications for his skin and his stupid brain. He'd weaned himself off all the painkillers as soon as he could—probably sooner than his doctors had wanted if he was honest, but he'd been afraid of becoming addicted, had seen too many peers succumb to managing their lives by medicating themselves into oblivion.

If he walked back to Dr. Mendez's place he would probably find Rachel there and get the apology over with as soon as possible.

"Hey."

He looked up into the face of an unsmiling cowboy with piercing blue eyes and let out a resigned breath.

"Let me guess. You must be a Morgan."

"Yeah, I'm BB. We were at school together."

"Did you come to tell me off for making Rachel mad, Blue Boy?"

The cowboy set his jaw. "I came to tell you to keep your nose out of my family's business, and to keep a civil tongue in your head."

"Trust me, I want nothing to do with anyone named Morgan." Cauy kept his tone courteous but ten years in the oil fields meant he wasn't going to be bullied. "And Rachel seems perfectly capable of fighting her own battles."

"She's my baby sister."

Cauy just held BB Morgan's stare.

A woman dressed in black came up behind BB and poked him in the ribs. "Are you fighting in my shop?"

"Not at all, Yvonne." BB tipped his Stetson. "Just saying hello to our new neighbor."

Yvonne didn't look convinced as she turned to smile at Cauy. "It's nice to meet you. Did you enjoy your coffee?"

Cauy stood up. "It was great, thank you. I'll definitely be back." He eased past BB Morgan, who didn't make it easy for him. "Have a nice day."

Unfortunately, the annoying Morgan decided to follow

him out of the shop. Ten paces down the raised sidewalk, Cauy swung around like a gunslinger confronting his opponent.

"Is there something else you want to get off your chest?"

"Yeah. My fiancée."

Cauy raised an eyebrow and stood his ground.

"Jenna McDonald," BB said.

"What about her?"

"Your father tried to trash her reputation in this town, so keep away from her."

"My father—" There were many things Cauy could say about his dad, but he wasn't going to give a Morgan the satisfaction of hearing them. "I have no idea what happened between them, but it's none of my business."

"Good." BB nodded. "Keep it that way."

He turned and walked back toward the post office, leaving Cauy to his own company. He was beginning to wish he'd stayed in bed.

His truck was parked at the far end of Main Street. He took the time to stow his bag of prescriptions and then walked back to Dr. Mendez's building. Rachel was just emerging through the front door, her head down low as she talked to a diminutive woman who was clinging to her arm.

Her gaze flicked toward Cauy, and then she ignored him and continued on her way. Keeping a wary eye out for any other Morgans, Cauy followed the pair at a discreet distance to an old SUV parked at the rear of the building. When Rachel struggled to get the old lady into the truck, Cauy stepped forward and helped out without a word.

While her passenger fussed with her seat belt and found a place for her enormous purse, Rachel turned to Cauy, her disdainful expression mirroring her older brother's.

"Did you want something?"

Cauy met her gaze head-on. "I wanted to apologize."

"For what particular thing this time?" Rachel asked. "Existing?"

He shrugged. "If that works for you. I was too quick to make assumptions. How about you let me know what's going on with the mine when you get new information?"

"Wow, three complete sentences at once." Rachel pressed a hand to her chest. "I'm honored."

Cauy knew he deserved her sarcasm, but it was hard not to smile. It reminded him of his sister Amy's ability to take him down a notch or two. Not that he felt very sisterly toward Rachel Morgan . . .

"I'll keep you informed, okay?" Rachel dug her car keys out of her pocket. "I've got to take Mrs. Medeiros home."

Cauy nodded. "Have a good day."

He waited until she drove off before leaving the parking lot to find his own truck. The wind was rising with that particular whine that set his teeth on edge and there was a hint of ice cutting through it. Keeping a wary eye out for BB Morgan, he zipped up his jacket and lowered the angle of his hat against the encroaching breeze.

He liked the way Rachel stood up to him. He liked the way she stared him right in the eye and told him to knock it off. How long was it since he'd had a conversation with anyone like that? His ex-wife, Lorelei, had tended to agree with everything he said, until one day she'd found someone she agreed with even more and divorced his sorry ass.

He didn't blame Lorelei for that. She hadn't meant to marry a man who no longer cared for the things she valued like big houses, cars, and fancy jewelry. He'd let her down. He'd let them *both* down, and she'd gotten half of everything he had left after his medical bills were paid.

He'd bet the ranch that Rachel Morgan wouldn't walk away so fast. She was young enough to have ideals, morals, and outrage to spare. He couldn't ever remember being like that, but he sure as hell admired it in others.

A fine mist of rain chased the cutting breeze, and he hastened to reach his truck and get the engine started. A nagging headache settled over his left eye. He'd have to call it a day and come back to the lumberyard tomorrow. Too many interactions made his brain hurt, and today had been a doozy.

Chapter Five

Cauy straightened up as a hint of sound shattered the quietness of the remote field he was working in to repair the fence. He couldn't quite believe that he'd been at the ranch for a week already. He looked over toward the copse of trees in the corner and tried to work out exactly what he was seeing. There was something big crashing around in there. Returning to his truck, he found his father's ancient rifle and retraced his steps moving on down the slope toward the green darkness.

A snuffling sound made him go still again. Wild pig? Mountain lion? He'd heard that the Morgans had recently captured some kind of wildcat on their land. He took another cautious step forward, his weapon raised, and heard a whicker of greeting. Two horses stuck their heads out of the foliage to stare at him. Neither of them had halters on nor looked as if they had been near a groomer for years, if ever.

Cauy backed up again, returned to his truck, and found a coil of thin rope and the remnants of his lunch. Treats in one hand, rope hidden behind his back in the other, he approached the horses.

To his surprise, as if keen for some company, they both

came willingly. He fashioned a couple of rough nooses and dropped them over the horses' necks and led them over to his truck. It was too far to walk them back so he'd have to attach them to the rear of the truck and drive real slow. They didn't seem to mind being taken along, which made him think that at some point they'd been broken to saddle and weren't completely wild.

He pulled up in front of his barn to discover another truck bearing the Morgan Ranch logo already parked there. With a resigned sigh, he killed the engine and got out. It didn't seem to matter what he said, the Morgans just kept on coming. . . .

"Good morning, son!"

Cauy considered the wrinkled old cowboy smiling at him. "It's Roy, isn't it?"

"Yup." Roy tipped his hat to Cauy. "The boss lady told me come on over and see if you needed a hand."

"I don't—"

Cauy barely got the words out of his mouth before Roy started off toward the two horses, and Rachel got out of the other side of the truck.

"Where'd you find these beauties?" Roy asked, running a professional-looking hand over the first horse.

With one eye on Rachel and the other on Roy, Cauy struggled to form a coherent sentence.

"Uh, out in the far corner of the ranch. I was mending fences."

"They look pretty good considering they've been out-side," Roy finished his appraisal, and straightened up, not without some difficulty.

"I haven't checked to see if they are branded," Cauy stated. "If they belong to Morgan Ranch, please take them."

"Your dad let a lot of things go the last year he farmed this place," Roy said, grimacing. "I reckon these are probably yours. You'd probably best get them checked over by the veterinary."

"But not by Jenna McDonald or BB might kill him," Rachel spoke for the first time.

Roy grinned. "BB wouldn't do that, but he might come along to make sure Jenna was okay."

Cauy cleared his throat. "Jenna McDonald is the vet? What happened to Ronald McDonald?"

"He retired to play golf. His son Dave and his niece have taken over the practice." Roy patted one of the geldings. "Call Dave. He'll come out." He looked over at the barn. "Anywhere safe and dry to keep these horses over the winter, Cauy?"

"The barn needs a bit of work," Cauy admitted.

"Then me and Rachel had better help you out." Roy turned to Rachel. "Get my toolbox out of the truck and find yourself some gloves." He turned to Cauy. "While Rachel's checking out the structure of the barn, why don't you find a safe place for those horses to graze?"

Recognizing defeat and reluctant to bundle an old man into his own truck and send him away with a flea in his ear, Cauy meekly untied the horses and led them down to the only field he'd managed to make secure so far. He still didn't understand how the Morgans could simultaneously hold his father in such low esteem yet be willing to help his son.

He'd been brought up suckling at the milk of his father's resentment of the Morgans, and it was a hard taste to get rid of. He guessed his father would've been shaking with rage right now, humiliated by being put in this position and more than willing to vent his anger on the next person who crossed him. Cauy wouldn't do that, but being managed didn't sit easily with him.

He'd left home to avoid all that crap, enjoyed his own life

without having to worry about parents or family or any of those things that weighed a person down. The Morgans seemed to thrive on being part of a family, and he genuinely didn't get it.

After a last pat for the horses, he returned to the barn where Rachel was studying the roofline.

"It's basically sound," Cauy said as came to stand at her shoulder, getting a whiff of lavender soap and warm skin that made him want to bury his face in her neck and just breathe her in.

"Yes, it is." She gave it another appraising stare. "How's the inside?"

He made a face. "Cluttered and dirty."

"Then we'd better get busy, hadn't we?" She walked over to Roy. "Let's clean out the interior so that I can take a look at the load-bearing walls and posts inside."

Cauy grabbed hold of her arm. "You guys really don't need to do anything, okay?"

They both looked at him as if he was nuts.

"We're right here." Roy made a gesture. "Why wouldn't we help out?"

"Because I don't need your charity."

"Charity?" Roy spoke up before Rachel even got her mouth open. "Where did you get that mealy-mouthed idea from? We're *neighbors*. In this part of the world, especially with winter coming, we *help* each other. Fifty years ago your grandfather Marvin helped dig out half the Morgan Ranch cattle that were buried in an early snowstorm. Let's consider this payback, so you can rest easy, youngster."

"And you do want somewhere to put the horses, don't you?" Rachel added, her blue gaze fixed on Cauy. "Even if we just accomplish that it's better than nothing."

Cauy took off his hat and shoved a hand through his

flattened hair. He knew what his dad would've done, but after the age of five he'd never wanted to be like him.

"Okay. I appreciate the offer. What do you want me to do first?"

As they worked Rachel let Roy direct Cauy's movements while she made sure the interior posts and walls were secure. After clearing out half the barn she could see the structure clearly. The floor was solid concrete and the drainage channels were usable. At some point the barn had been solidly constructed and well looked after. From what she'd heard about Mark Lymond, Rachel guessed he was the one who'd let everything go.

Even though Cauy was doing exactly what Roy asked him to do, Rachel sensed he really didn't want them there. His continued resistance stuck in her craw and made her want to stride over, knock his hat off his head, and kiss him silly.

She paused. *Kiss him silly?* Where the hell had that stupid idea come from? She glared at the back of his head. Maybe it wasn't such a bad idea after all. It would certainly shock him.

But what if he kissed her back?

How would he kiss—with that quiet stubborn certainty hidden beneath his remote expression, or would there be more? She'd never dated a man older than herself, and if Ruth was correct Cauy was almost thirty.

"Everything okay, Rachel?" Roy asked.

Flustered, Rachel took a step back and collided with the stone wall. "Yes, all good here. The structure looks great. All we need to do is make sure the drainage is working, and we'll be good to go."

"You mean Cauy will be good," Roy joked. "How about

I go back to the ranch and grab some basics for the horses while you finish helping our friend here?"

"Okay," Rachel said cautiously, her gaze colliding with Cauy's, who didn't look very keen on the idea of being alone with her at all. Irrationally, her urge to jump him only intensified. "I'll check the water flow."

While Roy went back to his truck she walked around to the rear of the barn and studied the rusted pipes before attempting to turn on the faucet connected to a rotting hose.

"I'll get that." Cauy reached past her, his shoulder brushing against hers, the warmth of him shocking after the coldness of the wind. "It's probably rusted in place."

She stepped back, stuck her hands in the pocket of her fleece-lined jacket, and watched him wrestle with the water pipe.

"You didn't need to stay." Cauy didn't turn around to speak to her. "I could've done this myself."

"It would've taken you at least a week to move all that stuff by yourself," Rachel pointed out. "Why are you so reluctant to accept help?"

"Maybe I'm just not used to it being offered to me." He swung around to face her, wiping his gloved hands on his jeans. The stubble on his chin was so long now it almost qualified as a beard. "I also didn't expect to be surrounded by Morgans."

"My family are good people."

He shrugged. "That's not what my father said."

"And your father was so well-liked and respected in this community."

"He had cause to dislike the Morgans."

"Because Chase offered to buy him out?"

"You heard about that, did you?" His wry smile was a surprise. "That's the only reason I'm standing here now. If Chase hadn't offered him all that money, my father would have sold the place and left me nothing."

"I don't get it," Rachel said slowly.

"My father would've done anything to thwart a Morgan. Even when it hurt him most."

"Then he was a fool."

"Can't argue with that." Cauy walked over to his truck. "I need something to loosen this up."

Rachel stood there like an idiot biting her lip and waited for him to return with a can of something in his hand. He tried to open the screw top and couldn't quite manage it with his gloves on.

"Give it to me." Rachel took the can and unscrewed it.

"Thanks. I could've—"

"Done it yourself, yeah, I know that, Mr. I Don't Need Anybody." Rachel carried on talking, aware that she was treading on dangerous ground, but kind of enjoying it anyway. "Have you ever *had* a real relationship?"

"Like with another human being, you mean?"

"Exactly."

He held her gaze. "Yeah."

"As in?"

"A wife?"

Rachel winced. "You're married?"

He looked around the desolate barn. "Like I'd be here if that was the case. She divorced me. I deserved it."

"Oh."

His smile was a challenge. "That's all you've got?"

"Did she divorce you because you insisted on coming out here?"

"Nope, but she would've hated it." He squirted stuff on the rusted faucet. "She left me about three years ago."

"Do you miss her?" Rachel blurted out.

"Nope." He gave the handle an experimental twist, and it screeched like a banshee in protest. He detached the rotting hose and looped it over his arm. "I'll get the new one."

He came back with a bright green hose and Rachel darted forward to help.

"I've got this," Rachel said as he again struggled to pull apart the packaging with his gloves on. "There's a tab right here."

"Thanks."

They were so close she only had to look up to be staring right into his eyes.

"What, no qualifiers about doing it all yourself?" Rachel said breathlessly.

The side of his mouth kicked up. "I know when to quit."

Her gaze fixated on his lips, and she inhaled the warm scent of his skin. Unable to stop herself she leaned in.

"What do you want from me, Rachel?" he asked so softly she barely heard him.

She knew he was giving her the opportunity to step back, no questions asked, but she stayed exactly where she was, her mouth an inch from his.

With a stifled sound he closed the gap between them and kissed her, the shock of his cold lips swiftly dispelled by the heat of his tongue as he took possession of her mouth.

He kissed with an intensity that stopped her breath and made everything inside her go quiet, and then hot, and needy. She grabbed for his shoulder to keep him exactly where she wanted him, and he dropped the coiled hose on her booted foot.

"Ouch!" Rachel yelped, and ripped her mouth away from Cauy's.

The shock of her loss made him rock on his heels until he realized she was hopping around like a demented chicken. He looked down at the hose and grimaced.

"Sorry."

"No problem," she gasped as she leaned back against the

wall and pressed her fingers against the toe of her boot.
"It'll be fine in a moment."

Seeing as she had good sturdy boots on, Cauy was pretty
sure she was going to be okay. He moved over to where she
stood and held out his hand.

"Do you want to go into the kitchen, take your boot off,
and check out the damage?"

"You mean like go inside your house with you, right
now?" She made a face. "I'm not sure I could take the risk."

"The risk of what?" Cauy asked. "I'm not the kind of
guy who presumes anything."

"Not you." The look she gave him was withering. "*Me*."

"Hey, it was just a kiss. No need to get bent out of shape
about it," Cauy offered. He wasn't sure how he'd ended up
kissing her and needed to get away before his body demanded he did it again.

"Sit down on that bucket over there then, and check your
foot out. I'll go and get the medical kit."

He skedaddled up to the house, Rachel's taste on his lips,
and his body humming with need. He tried to tell himself
that it wasn't about *her*. It was just that he hadn't had sex for
three years. Not that there hadn't been offers, but he'd never
been interested.

In the bathroom, he took off his gloves and washed his
hands before studying himself in the mirror. He looked
more alive than he had in weeks. He traced the scars on the
left side of his face half hidden by his stubble. He'd been
pretty once. The fact that he cared that he wasn't pretty any
longer annoyed him immensely. Rachel was too young and
innocent to stir his interest, and he'd better remember that.

She was also a Morgan. He could almost see his father
turning in his grave at that little kicker.

He grabbed the medical kit off the shelf. Maybe this was

just his body's way of letting him know he was ready to get laid again, and nothing to do with Rachel Morgan at all.

Yeah, right.

He returned to the barn and found Rachel sitting where he'd told her to, one boot off and her sock draped over it. She was gingerly touching her toes as if making sure they were all there.

Cauy went down on his knees and placed the medical kit on the floor.

"How's it looking?"

"Not too bad," Rachel said. "I probably shouldn't have taken my boot off because now my toes are swelling up a bit."

Cauy feared she was correct. "Even if they are broken, they don't do much for them these days. Either they buddy them up with tape, or put you in one of those stupid boots. The best thing to do is get the swelling down and go and see Dr. Mendez if things don't improve soon."

She grimaced. "Good job I didn't ride over."

"Yeah. Roy should be back with his truck soon so you can go home in that." Cauy got to his feet. "I'm just going to connect the hose and give the barn floor a good clean. Sit tight."

"Cauy?"

He braced himself. "Yeah?"

"Thank you."

"You're welcome."

He wasn't sure what she was thanking him for, the goddam kiss or his useless medical advice, but he wasn't going to inquire too closely. The truth was, he wanted to kiss her again, and that wouldn't be a good idea for either of them.

He attached the hose to the faucet, turned it on, and busied himself cleaning out the barn as if his life depended on it. The roar of Roy's returning truck made him look up and turn off the water.

"Come and give me a hand." Roy beckoned to Cauy to join him. "I've got a load of straw, a couple of buckets, and some feed for the horses in the back."

Cauy put down the hose. "I think you should start a tab for me."

"It's all good," Roy replied. "Where's Rachel?"

"She hurt her foot on the hose so I told her to stay put in the barn." Cauy came over and grabbed two bundles of straw. "Water's running, and the drains are working so I think we'll be okay to put the horses in."

"Good job." Roy took the buckets and bag of feed. "I'll take Rachel home as soon as we're done."

It didn't take long for Cauy to spread the straw and fill the feed buckets while Roy walked the horses up from the field. He kept an ear out for Rachel, but she seemed happy enough supervising from her perch on the bucket. She didn't look to be in much pain either, which made him feel a lot better.

Eventually, Roy stomped off for one last check on the horses, and Cauy went over to Rachel. She'd taken off her hat and her short blond hair framed the sharp angles of her face. She smiled as he approached, and he felt it right in the gut.

"Can you give me a hand to stand up? Then we'll be out of your hair."

He bent low and swept her into his arms.

"Eek! You'll put your back out!" She grabbed hold of him; one hand wrapped around his neck, the other on his shoulder. "There's no need to be so dramatic, cowboy."

He didn't answer, his senses too full of the feel of her in his arms to care about mere words. She smelled right.

She smelled like she belonged with him, and that was ridiculous.

"Come on, let's get you home." He started for the truck.

"My boot!"

He swung around and let her pick it up before resuming his journey. He took his time, enjoying the warmth of her body cradled against his, and the strength of her fingers against his skin.

Roy had left the passenger door open so he eased her up onto the seat. For a long moment, they remained locked together until he could persuade himself to let go.

"Thank you," she murmured against his throat, and he wanted to groan as her teeth grazed his skin. "Thanks for everything."

"Dropping the hose on your foot? Kissing you?" Cauy asked.

"Yeah. That." She smiled at him and kissed his nose. "Good times, eh? Sorry I'm such a klutz."

"I'm the one who dropped the hose," Cauy reminded her.

"True." She searched his face, her blue eyes watchful. "But I shocked you into it. If that hadn't happened, would you have kissed me again?"

"Maybe it was a sign that I shouldn't have kissed you in the first place," Cauy murmured, and then wanted to kick himself as the teasing light in her eyes disappeared.

"Maybe you dropped it deliberately." Rachel eased completely out of his grip and put her seat belt on. "Good-bye, cowboy. Have a nice evening."

Roy climbed into the driver's seat and winked at Cauy.

"See you tomorrow, Cauy. I'm bringing Ry over."

"Ry who?"

"Rowdy Yates Morgan. Haven't you met him yet?" Cauy shook his head. "He's the deputy ranch foreman, and he has a proposition to put to you."

"Great," Cauy muttered as the truck pulled away. "*More* Morgans."

Would he ever be rid of them, and did he even want to be? Rachel Morgan was way too alluring for her own good, and she seemed to like him way more than she should.

But then he liked her, too, and that was even more unexplainable.

Cauy went to check the horses in the barn and picked up the medical kit. The place was starting to look like an actual ranch again, which should make him happy, but all he could think about was Rachel Morgan. This wasn't how he'd wanted things to work out at all.

Chapter Six

Rachel wiggled her toes and eased her foot into her boot. The swelling had gone down and she was fairly sure her toes weren't broken. Ruth had taken a look and after a lifetime of experience doctoring cowboys on a working ranch had agreed with Rachel that there was nothing to worry about.

She'd slept well and eaten a huge breakfast with the rest of the family. She liked starting her day around the kitchen table while everyone talked about their plans. It made her feel so included. Her mom had never been great at sharing stuff and seeing as she'd obviously had a lot to hide, Rachel could kind of understand why now. But she'd always felt like an outsider—that if she didn't exist her mom would've just gone on happily without her.

Billy knocked on her bedroom door. "Do you want to help me in the barn this morning, Rachel?"

"Yes, that would be awesome. I'll meet you out there in a minute," she called out to him.

Part of her wanted to find out why Roy was taking Ry up to the Lymond Ranch, but she hadn't asked. Her brothers would be way too interested as to why she wanted to know, and Roy was something of a talker . . . Had he noticed there was something going on between her and Cauy? From his conversation on the way back to the ranch on the previous day she suspected he might.

When she'd kissed Cauy she'd touched his neck and traced the scar tissue that disappeared beneath his collar and up into his crisp curling hair. What had happened to him? Everyone said that working on the oil fields was a dangerous business, so had he been hurt? The mere thought of it made her stomach tighten.

She put on her thickest fleece, found her gloves, and went down the stairs to collect her coat and hat from the mudroom. The scent of bacon still wafted through the house, but the kitchen was now quiet as everyone had dispersed to their day jobs and Maria had gone off to school.

The air outside was so cold it hurt to breathe. She rammed her hat down hard on her head to cover her ears. Frost glinted on every surface and the gloomy gray sky made the landscape harsh and unwelcoming. Ruth told her it would get worse before Christmas, and that she should expect the snow to cut them off completely.

As she walked down to the barn, Rachel tried to imagine her mother living on the ranch, doing all the tasks Ruth so obviously enjoyed, and found it impossible. Annie had been such a fastidious city girl that she must have found ranching life really hard. She'd loved crowds, shopping, and going out, and none of those things existed out here.

Rachel found Billy in the tack room, hands on his hips as he surveyed the packed wall of saddles, bridles, halters, and reins. He turned to smile at her, the lines around his eyes crinkling.

"Hey, you. Chase wants this lot sorted out. The current crop of guests is a messy bunch. Do you want to help me?"

"Chase is very detail-oriented, isn't he?" Rachel said diplomatically.

"That's one way of putting it. His brothers aren't usually so kind." Billy's breath condensed in the cold air. "I must admit that I quite like seeing things in order myself, but don't tell the rest of the boys."

"Mom was really untidy," Rachel said, and then wondered why she'd mentioned it. Perhaps because her mother was very much on her mind right now.

"Yeah," Billy said, shaking his head. "To be honest, it drove me nuts."

"Me too." Rachel met his gaze. "Even when I was little I was always the one cleaning up after her." She paused. "I can't imagine her here at all. It's really weird."

"I should probably never have brought her here. We met in the city when I was at agricultural college." Billy sighed. "It never occurred to me that she wouldn't love this place as much as I did. But by the end she hated it."

"I'm sorry," Rachel said impulsively.

"What have you got to be sorry about? Wasn't your fault." He held her gaze. "I bet she was far happier in the city, wasn't she?"

"Yes, she refused to go on vacation to anywhere that *wasn't* a city or on the beach—not that we had much money for such things when I was small, and it was just us."

Billy grabbed a handful of lead ropes and started coiling them up. "That must have been tough."

Rachel picked up a bridle that someone had dropped on the floor, and checked the tab before rehanging it on the appropriate peg. "Before she met Paul she worked a lot. I hardly saw her."

Long hours on her own in small cramped rooms where she wasn't allowed to make a noise or play outside. When she wasn't at school, days staring out of the window with nothing to do but wait for her mom to come home. By the age of five she'd known how to make her own meals and sometimes even her mother's.

"I wish . . ." Billy started, and then stopped. "God, I wish things had been different. I wish I'd been a better husband

and worked out how bad she was feeling before she felt she had to run away to be herself again."

Rachel crossed her arms over her chest. "You're remarkably forgiving. She walked out on you, and your sons—and let's not forget she tried to drown a couple of her kids on the way out. Don't you hate her for that?"

Billy considered her for a long moment. "I've had to let that anger go, Rachel. It was killing me, and driving way too many destructive behaviors."

"So you've turned into some kind of saint now who forgives everyone?" Rachel only realized how angry she was when she started to shake.

"I'm no saint." He shrugged. "I'm just trying to be a better person."

"Well, good for you." God, now that she'd started talking she couldn't stop. "I wish I could be like that. I wish I could forgive her as easily for wrecking all our lives, for taking me away, for depriving me of all of this!"

"But you came back to us. You're here now," Billy reminded her.

"It's not the *same*. It's—" She finally got herself under control. "It's not *fair*."

Her mother's cool, dismissive voice resonated in her head. *Who ever told you that life would be fair, Rachel? Grow up.*

Billy took a step toward her, the concern of his face made her back up, and he stopped moving.

"It's okay to be angry with us, honey. We deserve it."

"It's *not* okay to be angry with your parents, and you know it." Rachel swiped at her eyes. "What if I'd gotten angry with Mom leaving me all the time, and she'd decided to walk out on me as well?"

For a long moment, Billy just stared at her, and then he reached out and pulled her into his arms.

"I'm sorry. I'm so sorry, love."

Rachel resisted the temptation to bury her face into his solid shoulder and bawl like a little child. Crying had never gotten her anything, and she wasn't about to start now. Being positive, staying happy, and never complaining were the only way to stay safe.

"Your mother and I were the ones who caused these problems, not you, and seeing as Annie is dead, it's on me now." Billy hugged her even tighter. "So if you want to talk, or vent, or just tell me to go to hell, I'm here for you. I'm going to listen and take whatever you need to say squarely in the face and live with it, okay?"

She drew back so she could see him. They were almost the same height and his eyes were the exact same shade of blue as hers.

"I don't *like* feeling angry. It's not me," Rachel confessed.

His smile was so sweet it made her want to cry. "You can't hurt her now, right? And she can't hurt you. I've missed being your father for more than twenty years. Give me the chance to at least offer you that comfort now."

"I'll have to think about it," Rachel offered. "It doesn't seem fair for me to rage on you when you've already suffered yourself."

"I deserved to suffer." His smile disappeared. "Don't ever forget that. You on the other hand had to deal with the fallout from the combustion of a marriage. It affected all of you in different ways, and we're still dealing with the after-effects now." He squeezed her shoulder and stepped back. "All I'm saying is that if you need to talk anything through while you're here, I'll be around, okay?"

"Thank you." Rachel swallowed a wedge of emotions threatening to block her throat. "I appreciate it."

"Then how about we get on with cleaning up this barn, and you can tell me how things are going over at the Lymond Ranch with the lovely Cauy?"

Gratefully accepting the change of subject, Rachel picked

up another bridle and then peered at Billy. "Why would you think I'd know anything about that?"

Billy winked at her. "Roy."

"Oh." Rachel returned the bridle and untangled a set of reins. "Cauy Lymond is . . ." She considered what to say next. "Infuriating." Yeah, that about covered it.

"He's certainly a man of few words." Billy hung another coiled rope on a hook. "Do you like him?"

Rachel tried a careless shrug. "What's to like? The man barely opens his mouth."

"Some women like the quiet ones."

"Not this woman. I like to chat. I need someone to chat back, and he thinks three sentences is an epic speech."

"You got three sentences out of him? Awesome. Roy thinks Cauy likes you."

"Really?" Rachel squeaked, and then tried to play down her enthusiasm. She was fairly certain Billy wasn't fooled. "Not sure how he can tell."

"Roy watches a lot of reality TV and always wins the sweepstakes for any dating game."

"*Roy* does?"

"Yeah, I know it sounds ridiculous, but it's a secret talent of his." Billy started on the untidy pile of saddle blankets, heaving them around without even breaking a sweat. "He seems to think Cauy has his eye on you."

"Like I'd care." Rachel replaced a fallen halter on its peg and hoped Billy wouldn't see her blushing in the dim light. "He's a loner, he's not even sure if he's going to stay on the ranch. He's made it perfectly clear that he's fed up with the Morgans trying to be nice and neighborly to him."

Billy chuckled. "I hope you're wrong about that."

"Why?"

"Because Ry's gone over there this morning with a proposal to tie our ranches way more closely together than ever before."

* * *

Cauy angled the phone against his ear as he attempted to maneuver around the horse's rear and get out of the stall.

"Yeah, I'm still here, Kim. Keep talking."

"What the hell are you doing?" Kim asked. "Sounds like you're in the middle of a circus or something."

"Something like that." Cauy shut the stall door and slid the bolt home. "Just mucking out the horses, then I've got to go into town, get some lumber, and stop by the feed store."

His lawyer snorted. "You don't sound like yourself at all."

"I'm not." Cauy returned the empty pail to the tack room and added grooming tools to his ever-growing list. "I've gone back to my roots, remember?"

"I thought you were just going to check things out and leave?"

"And go where? Lorelei got the house, the cars, and custody of the cats. I got a run-down family ranch."

"I've been working on that Morgan issue for you. Should I stop?"

"I assume you're billing me massive amounts of cash for what you've done so far, so you're hardly out of pocket," Cauy pointed out.

"Special rate for you, my old friend, but yeah, I'm making bank. You still want to make that claim for the Morgan land?"

Cauy contemplated the crisp black line of the Sierra mountains against the white sky and let out his breath. "I don't think I'm going to pursue that claim."

"So I should stop?"

"Yeah."

"Damn. It was fun raking up all that old family history. Speaking of which, your bro was asking me where you were yesterday."

Cauy winced. "Tell him I'm at the ranch, and to call me on my cell if he needs anything."

"Will do." Kim paused. "Anything else I can bill you for right now?"

"Not that I can think of, you bloodsucking leech."

Kim laughed heartily. "Okay, I'll send over what I've found out so far. Maybe you can review it and give me a final, definite no."

"Sure, but you'll have to print it out for me. I've got no printer, and I can't stare at a screen too long or I'll get a headache."

"Got it. Does FedEx deliver out there or will I need the Pony Express?"

"Cute. Now go and prey on some other poor client, and stop billing me for this call." Cauy smiled even though Kim couldn't see him. "Happy holidays, Kim."

"Right back at you, my favorite client."

Cauy ended the call and slid his cell back into his jeans pocket. He'd met Kim, a Korean-American, at night school when they were both studying for their degrees after a full day of real work. They'd hit it off immediately and stayed friends even when Cauy's life had changed so dramatically.

His time in Texas already felt like a dream. Being back on the ranch, relearning all the tasks he'd completed as a kid had a familiarity to it that soothed his soul. The idea of taking on the Morgans in the courts seemed wrong somehow. Being out here alone was healing him in some weird, unexpected ways.

Speaking of the Morgans . . .

"Here they come again," Cauy sighed.

Roy's truck bounced along the pitted track and came to a juddering stop in front of the barn. Another long, tall cowboy accompanied him.

"Morning, Cauy." Roy gesticulated at the blond next to him. "This is Ry Morgan. He works with me."

Ry Morgan had the same blond coloring as Rachel, but hazel eyes and a pleasant expression.

"Good to see you again, Cauy. Can I run something by you?"

Cauy took them up to the house and into the warm kitchen where he'd lit the range. The coffee was still drinkable so he poured them all a cup and sat down at the kitchen table.

"You know we're operating the ranch mainly as a dude ranch now?" Ry asked.

"So I gathered," Cauy said cautiously.

"Well, that brings some problems along with it."

"Okay."

"We need a constant stream of good horses for the guests, and at the moment that's proving to be a worry."

"How so?" Cauy asked despite himself.

"Sometimes new riders do stupid shit and damage a horse, or lose control and scare the horse so we need to retrain them. After the first season we had about six horses out of commission at any one time, and that meant we were short."

"I can see that might be an issue." Cauy nodded.

"Okay, so until we get permission to build our new barn, which will house an additional thirty horses, I'd like to ask you if you'd act as our backup barn." Ry sat back and stared expectantly at Cauy.

"I don't quite get what you want."

"We'd house an extra stream of trained horses here for when the others go down."

"Why can't one of the other ranchers help you with this?" Cauy asked.

"Because they're all working ranches and have a full workload already, and no space for spare mounts. You have a whole barn out there, which just needs cleaning out. We'd pay you for the space, obviously, and the inconvenience. You wouldn't have to do anything unless you wanted to."

"Who'd be managing the day-to-day care?" Cauy took a sip of coffee.

"We would, and the payoff is that once those horses are taken care of you could take advantage of the hands to restore your place at no cost to you."

"Whose idea was this?" Cauy looked from Roy to Ry.

"Mine." Roy put up his hand. "We've been wondering what to do about this problem for a while now—can't build over the winter—but will need space before a new barn is completed. When we cleared out your barn yesterday a little light bulb went off in my head, and I called Ry. What do you think?"

The idea of being surrounded by people made him want to shut the idea down immediately, but the potential of setting the ranch to rights more quickly made him hesitate.

"Can I take some time to think about it?" Cauy asked.

"Sure." Roy grinned at him while Ry simply looked calm. "We'd make it all legal and stuff. We're right next door and we're not planning on going anywhere."

"Thanks." Cauy rose to his feet hoping the other two would take the hint and leave rather than coming up with yet another idea to help him out. "I was just about to run into town and pick up some supplies, so . . ."

"Don't worry, son. We know when we're not wanted." Roy winked at him and struggled out of the chair. "We've got the last group of guests to get through the next few days and then we're done for the year." He sighed. "And this bunch have been a doozy. All guys for some reason, and all trying to prove who is the stupidest."

Ry shared a quick smile with Cauy. "He's right. This lot is the pits. Half of them think they're Billy the Kid, and the others have a way higher opinion of their riding skills than they should have after three days."

Cauy couldn't imagine wrangling with strangers on his own ranch. He followed Roy out to the truck alongside Ry.

"Are you okay with the dude ranch thing?" Cauy had to ask. "It sounds like a lot of work."

"Yeah, it is, but I love it, and it did save the ranch." Ry grimaced. "This particular group sucks. I'll be pleased to wave them good-bye and hope they never return." He shook Cauy's hand. "If you can see your way to helping us out over the next few months I'd be really grateful."

"Got it." Cauy stepped back as Ry got into the truck and slammed the passenger door. "I'll let you know as soon as possible."

Cauy cautiously considered the idea as he drove down to Morgantown. It wouldn't hurt him to help out, and he'd be getting something in return. His father wouldn't have liked it at all, but the longer he stayed at the ranch, the more Cauy doubted his father's account of how everyone in Morgan Valley had ganged up on him and tried to put him out of business.

His father's neglect of the once prosperous ranch was no one's fault but his own, meaning Cauy didn't owe his father's ghost any payback. He pulled into the parking lot between the lumberyard and feed store and considered where to start. He had a list of supplies as long as his arm so there was no point in rushing.

Most of the items he wanted were large and heavy so he might need some help. His attention was caught by a small gray pickup truck with the Morgan Ranch logo on the side parked right in front of the feed store. Was Ruth Morgan in there? Cauy backed up and decided to start at the lumberyard. He'd seen enough Morgans for one day. . . .

Devin Lassiter, who ran the lumberyard, was more than

willing not only to help Cauy with his list, but also to load his truck. Seeing as the guy had the body of a linebacker, Cauy mainly got to stand back and admire the ease with which Devin chucked things around.

"I'll call you when that roof tile comes in, okay?" Devin wiped his brow and replaced his baseball cap on his head. "Your account's all set up now so you're good to go."

"Thanks for your help," Cauy said, shaking Devin's hand. "I appreciate it."

"If you get stuck and need a list of local contractors, I've got one and they're all good workers."

"Thanks." Cauy locked his truck and turned toward the feed store as Devin went back inside whistling to his dog.

The Morgan Ranch truck was still parked near the front of the feed store, but Cauy didn't have enough time left to be shy. If Ruth was in there, he'd either try to avoid her or be polite until he could escape. He found himself smiling as he walked up the slope of the loading bay.

There was no sign of any of the family in the store, and he found all the stuff he needed. One more trip to Maureen's and he'd be set. He loaded up his truck and then went to the rear of the building to pick up a bag of chicken feed from the stack piled outside.

"Hey!"

He looked up to see Rachel waving frantically at him. She was crouched down beside one of the large metal bins. His feet took him in her direction before he made an actual choice to go there.

"What's up?" Cauy asked. "Are you okay?"

She glanced up at him. "Can you hold my legs?"

"What?"

She stood up. "There's something stuck in the bottom of this bin, and I can't reach it. If you held on to me I could get down there."

Cauy looked helplessly back at the feed store, but there was no sign of life. "Er . . ."

"Look, Em won't mind. She's busy helping someone pick out some chicks, and she's all alone in the store right now seeing as Ben's sick."

Cauy peered down into the vast metal bin, and the echo made him feel physically sick. "I can't go down there."

"I'm not asking you to. I'll do it, I just need you to help me." Rachel met his gaze, her blue eyes full of worry. "*Please*, Cauy, don't be a jerk."

He sighed. "It might be a raccoon, or a squirrel, or something that can get out all by itself if you just left it the hell alone."

"Or it might be stuck."

Cauy took another desperate look around, but he was on his own. "Okay."

"Great!" She started to climb onto the edge of the bin, meaning her denim-clad ass was now level with his face.

"Hold up." Cauy instinctively reached out to steady her, his hand on her calf. "Do you have gloves on, and something to wrap around the critter?"

"Did you just say *critter*?" Rachel grinned down at him.

"What's wrong with that?" Cauy raised an eyebrow.

"It sounds like something Roy would say right along with *varmint*." She put on her gloves. "Get me that feed sack, I can wrap the 'critter' in there."

"How about rather than going headfirst I lower you down, and then pull you back out?" Cauy suggested.

"I'm not sure I want to put my feet down there." She shuddered. "It looks kind of gross."

"So you'll risk your beautiful face instead, got it," Cauy muttered.

Rachel stared at him until he almost started to sweat. "What?"

"Nothing. Just hold on to my feet, okay?"

* * *

There were a couple of handholds on the side of the hollow metal bin, so Rachel used them to get lower. A flash of light from above indicated that Cauy had somehow directed his cell flashlight down her way, which was super helpful. A pair of frightened brown eyes stared back at her from the dankness at the bottom followed by a pathetic whine.

Rachel held her breath as she edged farther down and Cauy's strong hands closed around her ankles. She felt like an acrobat on a trapeze as she let go with her hands and grabbed for the creature, gathering it against her chest with one hand.

"I've got it. Pull me up!"

Cauy obliged, and she used her free hand against the wall to help steady her ascent. He grabbed her around the waist and turned her right-side up before carefully depositing her on the ground beside him.

"It's a dog," Rachel said.

"I can see that." Cauy gently touched the animal's head. "You should probably get it to a vet."

"Good idea." Rachel hesitated. "Is there any way you could come with me? I don't want to let this little guy go, and I can't drive with one hand."

Cauy sighed. "And the curse of the Morgans strikes again. . . ."

She frowned up at him. "What?"

"Nothing. It just seems like wherever I go in this town I trip over a Morgan."

He didn't sound mad, just resigned.

"If you're too busy . . ."

"It's all good. Come on." He was already walking toward his truck. "You'll have to tell me where to go."

Chapter Seven

"It's just in here." Rachel pointed to the open gate off the county road, and Cauy took the turn. "Keep going up the driveway to the top where the barns are."

"Got it."

Rachel peered anxiously down at the dog, who had barely made a sound since she'd rescued it from the feed bin. It had no collar or tag, so she had no way of knowing whether it had wandered off, fallen in, or been dumped there. Either way, the animal wasn't that old.

"This is the McDonalds' place," Cauy said.

"Yes." Rachel released her seat belt and opened the door. "Jenna's almost family. She'll see us without an appointment."

"Okay." Cauy got out as well, his gaze scanning the old wooden ranch house. "Do you want me to stay?"

Rachel had already started for the door but looked back at him. "You're going?"

He studied her for a long moment. "I guess not."

She went into the vet's office and straight up to the counter. "Hey, Meg, is Jenna around?"

"Yes, she's out back having her lunch. I'll get her for you." Meg paused as she noticed the dog. "Is that yours?"

"No, I found it."

"Go through to exam room two. I'll have Jenna meet you there." Meg held the door into the inner office open. "We're officially at lunch so she shouldn't be long."

Rachel went into the exam room and continued to clutch the dog to her chest. Cauy came in after her and closed the door.

"Do you want to sit down?" he asked her.

"No, I'm too worried." She continued her pacing.

A moment later, Jenna came through the door, her reddish-brown hair tied back in a ponytail and a smile on her face.

"Hey, Rach, what's up?"

Rachel held out the dog. "We found it at the bottom of one of the feed bins down at Em's store. Cauy helped me fish him out."

Jenna motioned for Rachel to set the dog down on the metal table and went to wash her hands.

"Well, it's actually a girl and judging from the size of her paws she's going to be a very big girl one day." Jenna gently ran her hands over the dog's flanks. "She's too thin, and probably dehydrated." She looked up at Rachel. "And that's just what I can tell from my preliminary exam. There might be other issues to consider."

She took the dog's temperature and frowned.

Rachel bit her lip. "Do you think she'll be okay?"

"I can't say that yet, but we'll keep her here, give her some fluids, and see if we can get her to take some nourishment. Then we'll take it from there, okay?" Jenna looked from Rachel to Cauy. "She's quite young, and she's suffered a traumatic experience."

"Is that why she's so quiet?" Rachel asked.

"Yes." Jenna patted Rachel's shoulder. "We'll do every-thing we can for her, okay?" She wrapped the dog in a soft towel and held her close to her chest.

"I know you will." Rachel found a smile somewhere. "Thanks, Jenna." She turned to Cauy. "Jenna's engaged to my brother Blue."

Cauy hesitated before tipping his hat to Jenna. "Nice to meet you, Dr. McDonald."

"Nice to meet you, too, Cauy." Jenna smiled. "It was kind of you to help Rachel."

He shrugged. "Well, as you might know yourself the Morgans can be quite persuasive."

"Bossy you mean?" Jenna asked. "Yeah, I know all about that. Are you passing through, or are you working at one of the ranches?"

Cauy grimaced. "Uh, I'm up at the Lymond Ranch."

"You're a Lymond?" Jenna couldn't quite conceal her start of surprise.

"Yeah. I'm Mark's son." Cauy paused. "I understand that you didn't get along with my father, but I suspect the blame for that lies with him."

Rachel stepped between them. "Cauy's nothing like his father, Jenna."

"I can already tell that," Jenna said, recovering her composure. "He's not shouting at me and saying I'm incompetent because women can't be vets."

Cauy winced. "I apologize."

"As I said, it's okay." Jenna opened the door. "Now, let me get this little gal settled, and I'll meet you out front, okay?"

Rachel followed Cauy out into the empty waiting room. Meg had disappeared so they were all alone.

"I'm sorry, Cauy," Rachel said softly.

"What for?" He took a seat and stared up at her.

"Making you bring me here. I forgot it might be awkward between you and Jenna."

He looked down at his scuffed boots. "Just don't tell BB, or he'll come after me again."

Rachel sat as well. "*Again*?"

"He warned me off."

"He's such an idiot sometimes," Rachel snorted. "Like Jenna can't take care of herself."

Jenna came into the waiting room wiping her hands on a paper towel. "Meg's getting her all set up. I can't detect a chip with my scanner so I'm betting she was either too young to be chipped or else her mother was a stray."

"Or someone dumped her down there," Rachel said.

"That's also a possibility," Jenna acknowledged. "But regardless of how she got there, we'll do our best to get her healthy."

Rachel smiled. "I'm sorry, I just hate it when animals are abandoned or left to fend for themselves."

"Me too." Jenna threw her paper towel in the trash. "I'll call you later today with a progress report, okay? Thanks for bringing her in. You did the right thing."

Rachel nodded and turned to the door, glad to escape. She went to stand by Cauy's truck. A few moments later he came out of the office and made his way over to her.

"You okay, Rachel?"

"Sorry, I get emotional about animals." She raised her gaze to the leaden sky. "My mom never let me have a pet. I was always finding strays and bringing them home, and she never let me keep them because we moved around so much." She tried for a smile. "I know she was right, but I always hated it."

Cauy reached out and drew her into his arms, one hand on the back of her head smoothing her hair. She fit perfectly against him and allowed herself to lean into his hard body for a much-needed hug.

"It's okay," he murmured against her hair. "It's okay to care."

She breathed in his scent and just let him hold her.

"Did your mom move around because of her work?"

"Yes, and in the beginning I suppose she was desperate not to be found by Billy or the authorities and brought home." Rachel looked up at him. "I didn't know why she was doing it at the time. I just hated constantly being uprooted."

"I can imagine."

"When she met Paul, things got a lot better, and we had a real stable home life," Rachel said.

"Paul's your stepdad, right?"

"Yes. He's a professor at Humboldt University. My mom met him when she was studying for her degree there."

"We all thought she was dead," Cauy said softly.

"And that Billy had murdered her. I know the story." Rachel eased out of his arms. "Although how anyone could imagine Billy hurting a fly I don't know."

Cauy shrugged, his gaze fixed on her face. "I suppose the cops will always go for the most obvious suspect."

"I guess." She looked past his shoulder. "Can we get in the truck? It's really cold out here."

He opened the passenger side for her and went around to get in himself. Warmth blasted out of the heaters as he turned the engine on.

"You don't like talking about your family much," Cauy said.

"Huh." Rachel shot him a look. "You don't like talking at *all*."

"I talk when I have something to say."

"Meaning I just chatter away like an airhead?"

"I didn't say that, and quit getting mad at me over something I didn't do."

Rachel opened her mouth to argue and then subsided in her seat. He had a point. She had no idea why she was pouring out her life story to him either.

"Hey." He tapped her cheek. "I didn't tell you to shut up either. I *like* hearing you talk."

Rachel just blinked at him. "I don't believe you."

"I'm still here, aren't I?"

"Yes." She considered him for a long moment, her gaze lingering on his faint smile. "I suppose you are."

Cauy resisted the urge to close the gap between Rachel and himself. She looked as if she'd be happy to go along with his idea, but you could never tell with a Morgan, and he didn't want to get his face slapped. There was just this *vibe* between them that sang so loudly he was amazed no one else could feel it.

Rachel cupped his chin and kissed him smack on the mouth. "Thank you so much for helping me out, I really appreciate it."

At first Cauy thought he'd spoken his thoughts out loud before he realized it was Rachel talking.

"Okay." He took his time leaning in, memorizing every freckle and line on her face, the way she was licking her lips . . . He wanted to growl and hold, and take, but none of those things were appropriate, and she deserved to be treated with respect.

The moment his lips touched hers he forgot rational thought and just experienced the unique, addictive taste of Rachel Morgan. He slid his hand around her neck, holding her close and took her mouth. She responded with a moan that drove him crazy, tightened his jeans, and made him want to strip her naked and ravish her properly. . . .

"Hey!"

A banging on the window made him wrench his mouth away from Rachel's and turn to see another far less friendly pair of furious blue eyes glaring at him through the glass.

"Get out of the truck!" BB Morgan knocked on the glass again.

"Hell, *no*," Cauy muttered. BB was a retired Marine. He'd beat the shit out of him. "I'm not going anywhere."

"Oh, for goodness' sake." Rachel flung open her door and stormed around to confront BB. "Go *away*!"

Jeez . . . now he'd have to get out, or he'd look like a loser.

"What are you doing kissing Cauy Lymond?" BB demanded. "Don't you have any sense?"

"I was *thanking* him!" Rachel stood her ground. "He helped me save a dog!"

"Then you shake his hand, you don't slobber all over him," BB said.

"What I choose to do has nothing to do with you, Blue Morgan," Rachel said.

"Yes, it does! You're my little sister!" BB turned to glare at Cauy, who had gotten out of the truck. "And this guy isn't for you."

"Says who?" Rachel had her hands on her hips, which in Cauy's memory of womankind meant that BB was about to get it. "I can kiss whoever I damn well like!"

"There's no need to curse," BB objected.

"Says the Marine who can't even keep his mouth zipped around his own daughter!"

"Um, guys?" Cauy stepped in between the two Morgans. "Maybe you want to take this somewhere else?"

Now they were both glaring at him, which was somehow better, but also precarious. He directed his attention at Rachel. "Do you want me to drop you back in town to pick up your truck?"

After one last scathing glance at her brother, Rachel nodded. "That would be very kind of you, Cauy."

"Okay, then, let's—"

BB interrupted Cauy. "Or you can stay here, Rachel, and I'll take you myself after I've seen Jenna."

"No, thanks." Rachel walked around to the passenger side of Cauy's truck, her nose in the air. "I'd rather go with Cauy."

"Rachel . . ." BB looked past his sister as the door to the vet's opened with a bang. "Oh crap. Hey, Jenna."

His fiancée didn't look very pleased to see him, which Cauy enjoyed immensely.

"What exactly are you doing, Blue?" Jenna asked.

"Cauy Lymond was kissing Rachel."

"Against her will?"

BB frowned. "Not that I could tell."

Rachel was blushing now, and Cauy fought an actual smile.

"Then why are you out here causing a ruckus?" Jenna demanded.

"Because—" BB stopped talking and held up his hands. "Okay, I'll shut up right now. Will that work for you?"

"Yes." She grabbed BB's hand. "Now, come on in, and leave these two consenting adults *alone*, okay?"

Cauy tipped his hat to the veterinarian in silent appreciation. She obviously had her Marine well under control, and he for one appreciated it. Rachel got in the truck. He backed out of the space and turned into the drive.

"I'm sorry about that," Rachel said in a very small voice.

Cauy shrugged. "I'd have been the same if I'd caught my sister kissing a Morgan."

"Sometimes they are just . . ." Rachel shook her head. "I didn't grow up here, and I don't know how to deal with them when they get all big brothery on me."

"Seems like you did a pretty good job back there."

"By getting mad?" She sighed. "I don't *like* losing my temper. BB's the worst of them, but he doesn't deserve that."

"Yeah, he does. Didn't you see the way Jenna laid into him? You did exactly the right thing. BB Morgan respects people who stand up to him. He always did even as a kid."

"They'll all want to talk about it at dinner tonight," Rachel groaned. "They *love* talking things through."

"Then come have dinner with me." Cauy couldn't believe he'd just said that. "I mean—"

"That's very sweet of you, but if I don't turn up for dinner, you know what will happen. They'll send out a search party with torches and pitchforks and your ranch will be the first point of call."

Cauy chuckled.

"Are you actually *laughing* at me?" Rachel asked slowly.

"Nope." Cauy slowed down as they entered the town and headed along Morgan Street past the post office and Yvonne's. "I wouldn't dare."

He parked up beside Rachel's truck and got out with her. "Let me know what happens with the dog."

"I will." Rachel scuffed her boots and avoided his gaze. "Well, I will if you give me your cell phone number. You do have one, don't you?"

"Yeah." He handed her his phone and she put her number in. He immediately texted her back. "Now we're all set."

"Thank you,"

"You're welcome." He hesitated. It was strange seeing Rachel at a loss for words. "If you really get fed up with all those Morgans you are welcome to come over. Ruth gave me enough food for a month so you won't starve."

"That's very kind of you, considering my brother threatened to punch your lights out."

"It's all good," Cauy reassured her.

For some reason, neither of them seemed able to end the conversation. The thought that he liked being around her, and that she brought light into his world, was both terrifying and appealing. He didn't need people. His wife had complained about that even when he'd been trying his hardest to fit in and give her what she wanted. And what could he offer now? A broken body, a whole mountain of baggage, and an outlook on life that made his mother despair.

"Bye, Rachel." He had to end it now. "Have a good evening." He nodded and got back into his truck, leaving her standing there alone before she too moved off.

He drove away. Better not to yearn for what he could never have—not that he wanted her. It was just that seeing her, even when she was mad at him, had become the highlight of his day. And kissing her? He took a slow breath reliving how that felt, and wanting so much more. . . .

Which was why he needed to keep driving. She was a Morgan, and he'd be the first man to admit she deserved better than a broken old crock like him. She loved to talk— he hated it—she was full of hope, and joy, and he . . . well, he wasn't. With that firmly in mind he drove back to the ranch, his thoughts on what to have for dinner and what sports channel to binge on after he'd eaten.

Chapter Eight

Chase opened his laptop and looked expectantly at Rachel. "So I've been doing some research into our mine problem."

As she'd been anticipating BB telling everyone about her kissing Cauy after dinner, Rachel had never been so happy before in her life to be lured into a technical discussion. BB had been unusually quiet and had gone off with Maria to check on her homework straight after they'd helped clear the table. Rachel suspected that Jenna had told him to keep his thoughts to himself. She hadn't even mentioned finding the dog because she'd believed BB would make a big deal out of it.

"Rachel?"

She took the chair next to Chase while HW groaned and got out of his seat. "I guess you won't be needing my input on this one, guys? Way out of my intellectual depth here."

Ry snorted. "Weird how Rachel and I are blond, and we can handle it."

HW gave his twin a casual pat on the head. "Good for you, Bro. I've got more important things to do like wash my hair."

"Dumbass," Ry muttered as HW sauntered away. "Sometimes I can't believe we're identical, let alone related." He took the seat on the other side of Chase. "So what's the plan?"

"I was hoping we could get some kind of camera down there that could roam around by itself and map the place," Chase confessed. "But, apparently, that's not possible."

Ry frowned. "Why not? They send those things down sewer lines and pipes all the time."

"No flat surfaces for the robot to run on, and problems communicating that far below the surface," Rachel said promptly.

"Yeah, that's right." Chase looked at her with approval. "So we're left with a few choices. The first one is fill in everything we find with concrete, which is kind of the traditional way."

"But we don't know the extent of the mine or the position of the tunnels yet so we could make things worse, and we might contaminate the groundwater system," Rachel pointed out.

"That wouldn't be good," Ry said. "What else can we do, Chase?"

"Well, we can monitor everything from above using"— Chase read aloud from his laptop—"'a wireless sensor network prediction technique based on multivariate statistical analysis of various parameters.'"

"What the hell does that mean?" Ry asked.

"Basically, keeping an eye out for sinkholes and the ground shifting using cameras and sensors on the surface," Rachel said.

"Okay, so why didn't they say that?" Ry looked at her. "Sounds just like Chase when he talks out of his ass."

Chase grinned at his brother. "Thanks." He turned to Rachel. "There is one more thing we can use to work out what's going on down there—ground-penetrating radar."

"Would that go deep enough?" Ry asked.

"If we use boreholes and lower the radar into the mine, then yes." Rachel nodded. "You can get some pretty good three-dimensional images these days. Can we afford to do that, Chase? We'd need some specialized equipment."

"It's okay by me. I'd rather have some idea what we're dealing with than not." Chase typed something on his keyboard. "I'll contact some people and cc you both on the e-mails, okay?"

"Sounds good to me." Ry pushed back his chair. "I'm off to town to see Avery. Does anyone need a ride?"

Chase looked up. "Dad's at his AA meeting. I'm not sure if he took his own truck so he might need a ride home."

"Okay. I'll check in with him." Ry nodded. "See you guys later."

Sometimes when Ry smiled he looked so like Annie that it hurt Rachel to see it. Not that her mom had been a great smiler. She'd worried so much about every little detail that she'd worn a permanent frown line on her forehead.

"He's a lot like Mom, isn't he?" Chase said without looking up. "More than HW, which is weird seeing as they are identical."

"I know." Rachel let out her breath. "It kind of freaks me out sometimes."

"Me too." Chase hesitated. "I remember Annie a lot more clearly than the others, and when she smiled . . . it could make your day so much brighter." He shut down his laptop. She'd noticed that none of them called Annie "Mom." "But man, when she got mad? Especially in the last year she was terrifying."

"So I gather." Rachel stared down at the table. "She didn't smile much when I was young."

Chase turned to her. "Before she married Paul?"

"Yes, we were always on the move, money was tight, and she was just so anxious. Even when I was small I knew that."

"That must've been tough for you."

"At least I had her." Rachel met Chase's blue gaze. "You guys lost your mother completely."

"But we had Ruth, and Roy, and Dad for at least a while, and this place. What did you have?"

"A mother on the run who, according to HW, didn't mean for me to tag along." Rachel couldn't believe she'd actually said the words out loud.

Chase reached out his hand to cover hers. "Hey, that's—"

"The truth, right?" Her voice cracked. "HW put me in the truck thinking Mom would bring me back and take him, her favorite child, instead."

"But she didn't," Chase reminded her gently. "She kept *you* and brought you up very successfully while forging a new life for herself." He paused. "It might sound a weird thing to say, but I kind of admire her guts. It can't have been easy."

"Yeah, you're right. She was pretty amazing." Rachel bit back a flood of memories and smiled instead. She'd learned early that expressing negative feelings didn't get you anywhere. "Let me know when you've got that equipment and we can take it from there."

She stood and put her balled-up napkin on the table. "Would you like me to pour you a cup of coffee, Chase? I'm getting one before I go upstairs to research ground-penetrating radar."

Chase stretched his arms over his head until his bones cracked. "Thanks, but I've got to go over to the guest reception. This last group of guests is causing January some scheduling issues. To be honest, I'll be glad when they've gone, and we have the ranch to ourselves."

"I thought you liked being a dude ranch?" Rachel was more than happy to change the subject.

"Most of the time I do, but this lot?" Chase grimaced.

"They just aren't working out too well. In the future I'm not going to book any more just-male groups. The dynamic is weird."

"Do you need any help?" Rachel offered.

"Thanks for asking, but the last thing I'd do is send you over there." Chase got to his feet. "I'm barely stopping Sam from taking them all out as it is."

Rachel smiled at the thought of HW's feisty retired military police girlfriend standing up to the dudes. Her phone buzzed and she took it out of her pocket to see a text from Jenna.

"See you later, Chase." She started to read as she left the kitchen, completely forgetting her coffee.

"Thanks for your input, Rachel," Chase called out as she climbed the stairs.

Dog remains in stable condition. One broken rear leg, probably from the fall, otherwise all good. More tomorrow, J x.

Rachel sent a text back. Thanks so much! Let me know how much I owe you!

Already taken care of, no worries. J x.

Rachel fired up her laptop and sat at her desk. At least the dog was okay. She stared at her cell. Maybe she should text Cauy and let him know. . . .

Would he want to hear from her? He said he liked it when she talked, but he might just be being polite.

"Cauy, polite?" Rachel said out loud. Sure, he could be, but he certainly didn't suffer fools gladly and had no problem drawing a line. He didn't back down from a bit of Morgan intimidation either.

She found his number and started typing.

Hey! Just wanted to let you know that the dog is doing okay!

She held her breath as the message flashed delivered, immediately regretting her cheery exclamation marks. And the message rhymed. Great.

Good to hear.

His immediate reply made her jump.

I'll let you know any further updates tomorrow.
Thanks again.
You're welcome.

Rachel considered what to do next. After talking to Chase about their mother she definitely didn't want to sit and brood.
What are you up to? Rachel typed.

Watching sports.
Oh, sorry to interrupt.
If it was that good I wouldn't have texted you back.

Rachel smiled at her phone. Vintage Cauy, dry and to the point. Idly, she checked her e-mail. There was one from her dad and Jane. She clicked on the link and stared at a photo of a blue crystal sea and old white pillars, which she assumed was Greece. In the pic, her father was standing behind Jane with one hand spread over her stomach grinning like a loon.

Rachel read the text.

Great News! Expecting our first child next year!

She stared at the picture for a long time, and then shut her laptop down. For once Morgan Ranch was silent around her. Ruth was helping Jenna furnish her new home, and everyone else was either out with the guests or in town.

Her phone chirped.

You okay?

Was Cauy actually checking up on her? Rachel silently shook her head.

Rachel?

She shot to her feet, grabbed her fleece, and went back down the stairs to the mudroom. Her sheepskin-lined coat, knitted hat, and boots were already warm when she put them on and went out into the inky black evening. She got into her truck and made her way out to the county road before taking a sharp turn back up into the Lymond Ranch.

It was weird to park at a ranch where there were no dogs coming out to greet you, no lights in the barn, and few welcoming lights in the house. Even as Rachel approached the back door it opened, and Cauy was standing there. Without a word, he stepped back and let her inside. It was warm in the kitchen. The remains of his evening meal sat in the sink, and the smell of freshly brewed coffee lingered in the air.

He watched her for a long moment and then held out his hand as she took off her coat and hat, placing them on the back of one of the kitchen chairs. Rachel found she couldn't sit down so she paced the kitchen, noticing for the first time that there were no family photos or personal items around.

"Why don't you have pictures?" she asked.

"Of what?" Cauy leaned up against the wall and watched her carefully.

"Of family, or friends, or, *anything*."

He shrugged. "I guess I haven't gotten around to it."

"You do have some then?"

"I'm pretty sure my mom left some behind. Why does it matter?"

"Because it *does*." Rachel turned to face him properly. "Pictures *matter*." Her voice was wobbling now, and he tensed like he was waiting for her to bolt. "Like pictures your stepfather and his new wife send *to all their friends* and just include you without mentioning it first."

"Pictures of what?"

"Their happy news. That they are having their first child, and that's kind of weird because my mother told *me* her husband couldn't have children, so who was *lying*, and why?"

Cauy shifted very slightly. "That sucks."

"That's all you have to *say*?" Rachel rounded on him.

"What else would you like me to say? One of them lied to you and, as far as I can tell, there's only one person who can answer that question, and it isn't me."

"Thanks for nothing." Rachel glared at him. "I suppose you're going to tell me you didn't ask me to come up here and start telling you stuff you didn't want to hear either?"

Cauy crossed his arms over his chest. "No. I'm not going to do that."

She made a dash for her hat and coat feeling so *stupid*, and *tearful*, and what exactly had she expected him to do?

"Hey." His hand closed gently around her elbow. "Rachel, just—"

He turned her against his body. For a second she stiffened as if ready to push him away, and then gave it up and flowed against him in one sudden wave. He just held her, his face buried in her hair as she cried as if her heart was broken. Reaching into his pocket, he found his handkerchief and pressed it into her hand.

She immediately stepped back and blew her nose.

"Thanks." Her brave attempt at a smile made something in his heart clench. "Sorry to get all emotional on you. I hate crying. I don't know what I was thinking."

He motioned her toward the two chairs in front of the TV he'd turned off when he'd heard her truck coming up the drive.

"I should probably go," Rachel said.

Cauy took his seat and waited her out until with a little sigh she came to join him.

"I feel like an idiot."

"Join the club." Cauy waited as she blew her nose again. "Would you like some coffee?"

She nodded, and he went to get her a mug and refreshed his own. It gave him something to do with his hands while his head tried to work out why Rachel Morgan had brought her problems to him. According to his ex, he was the world's worst person to confide in about *anything*, so how badly was he going to mess this up?

He brought her coffee and put the mug on the table beside her.

"You remembered how I like it," Rachel said. "Thank you."

"You're welcome." He resumed his seat and sipped his own coffee as if it had magical power to help him do the right thing.

"I suppose I should explain," Rachel said.

"Not on my account," Cauy hastened to say. "Unless you need to get something off your chest."

"I'd rather tell you than the Morgans." Rachel looked at

him. "They tend to be a mite overprotective of me and I don't want this to turn into a big *thing,* you know?"

"Okay."

It obviously was a big thing to have driven her to Cauy's place in tears, but he was willing to go along with her reasoning if it helped.

"I got a group e-mail with a photo of my dad and Jane in Greece." She looked down at her mug of coffee. "It was a general announcement that Jane was pregnant. They both looked thrilled."

Cauy nodded, channeling the therapist he'd had after his accident, who had just sat there and forced him to talk to fill the silence.

"I . . . didn't take it well," Rachel confessed. "Firstly that my dad hadn't given me a heads-up, but then he didn't tell me he was getting remarried until the actual day it happened either, so why am I surprised?" She paused. "I suppose you're going to say he probably didn't know how to tell me and didn't want to hurt my feelings."

"No," Cauy said. "I think he messed up. Big-time."

"You do?" She smiled at him through the remnants of her tears. "And then there's that whole other bit about me always wanting a sibling, and my mom telling me that Paul couldn't have children. Why would she lie about that?"

Cauy shrugged. "Maybe she was the one who didn't want any more kids. She'd already had five."

"And that didn't go well for her, did it, seeing as she walked out on four of them?" Rachel bit her lip. "Maybe *he* wanted kids all along, and she refused to have them."

"Sounds possible." Cauy took another slug of coffee.

"I never asked him because Mom said it would be too upsetting. . . ." Rachel winced. "I suppose you're going to tell me I should grow up and ask him now."

Cauy didn't say a word, and she carried on talking.

"But maybe wait until after this baby is born, right?"

Rachel seemed to be doing a great job sorting out her

problems by herself while he just sat there and nodded along. Maybe that therapist had been onto something. . . .

"I thought Jane was too old to have kids, or that she'd decided she didn't want them," Rachel sighed. "And as my dad was younger than Mom I suppose he's okay with it. Here's what's weird, Cauy. That baby isn't really related to me at all, is it?"

"Only through your family connection to Paul."

"Yes, that's right." Her smile was strained. "It isn't really anything to do with me. Paul, my stepdad, has moved on, and I've . . ." She sucked in a breath. "Become irrelevant."

Silence fell between them as Cauy tried to work out what to say. "Family can be complicated." Wow, that was profound. He tried again. "I didn't get along with my dad. We barcly spoke after I left home. But he still left me the ranch."

"Because you're his eldest *son*."

"I'm not sure if that's true." He took a quick breath. "My mom was seventeen when she married him. I was born six months after that."

It was Rachel's turn to stare at him without speaking.

"And before you ask, my mom won't tell me the truth," Cauy added. "She says it's not important. That there are two names on my birth certificate and that's all I need to know."

"Wow." Rachel put her coffee down. "Now I feel like such a whiner."

"I didn't mean for you to feel like that. I was just—"

"Sharing something personal to make me feel better?"

"Yeah." He held her gaze. "That."

She slowly stood and walked over to his chair. He leaned his head back to take all of her in as she framed his face with her hands and kissed his mouth.

"Thank you, Cauy."

With a stifled sound he hoisted her onto his lap and kissed her back. This time no one interrupted them, not even themselves, and it was glorious, and maddening, and . . .

Cauy cupped her ass and pressed her more firmly against the hardness contained in his jeans. She moaned into his mouth and rocked against him.

She slid her fingers under his T-shirt and he shivered as her nails lightly raked down his biceps.

"Is this okay?" she whispered.

His answer was his own attempt to get under the layers and touch her right back. He peeled off her fleece and unbuttoned her shirt while she yanked his T-shirt right over his head.

"Oh . . ." she breathed, stretching her fingers over his naked chest. "You're so *warm*, and hard, and . . ."

Cauy almost came in his jeans as she ran her fingers down over his pecs through the hair on his chest, catching one of his nipples with her nail. He slid his hand down the back of her jeans.

"Can I persuade you out of these?"

She undid the zipper and for a glorious few moments they both struggled to get her out of them, ending up with Rachel now sitting on the chair with Cauy on the floor between her thighs. He leaned in and kissed her mouth as he cupped her mound.

"Let me touch you."

She bit his lip. "What about you?"

He glanced down at his straining fly. "Later. Ladies first."

Rachel closed her eyes as Cauy flexed his fingers against her most tender flesh. He'd probably noticed she was already aroused as his thumb slicked through her wetness. He murmured her name as he learned her, caressed her, and slid one finger deep.

She came almost immediately, clinging on to him, and letting the new rush of emotions drive out old hurts as he moved with her.

"Yeah . . . that's it, honey, do it again." His appreciative murmur made her shiver as he slowly bit down on her neck and eased his finger into a driving rhythm that made her forget anything but the taste and smell of him, and the need for completion.

She gripped his shoulder so tightly she worried she'd do some permanent damage, but he didn't seem to notice, and letting go of him right now *so* wasn't happening. He was her rock in a storm of emotions, the calm center of her own personal blizzard.

She forced her eyes open. "I want you. All of you."

"Yeah?" He kissed her with a thoroughness that made every nerve ending she possessed sit up and take notice. "Then come to bed with me."

He eased free of her and brought his fingers to his lips, tasting her with a slow enjoyment that made her blush.

"Give me a second to make sure my bedroom is warm enough, and then I'll come get you."

"Okay." Rachel smiled foolishly at him. Unwilling to let him out of her sight, and almost too relaxed to want to move anywhere. "Get rid of all your other women, too."

He chuckled as he left the room, and Rachel forced herself to sit up. Where the heck had her underwear gone? She spied her panties and bra on the floor and started gathering up the rest of her clothes. The pocket of her jeans vibrated and she crouched down to check her phone.

It was her stepfather Paul's number. She struggled into her panties as she accepted the call.

"Rachel? Is that you?"

"Yeah. Hey." She tried to sound bright and cheerful. "I saw your news! Congratulations!"

His sigh echoed across the continents. "I'm sorry I didn't call you first. I intended to, and then Jane said she'd just e-mailed everyone because calling individually would be too expensive from here."

"She had a point." Rachel pulled on her shirt and buttoned it one-handed. "And it's okay. Having your first baby together is exciting."

His laugh was rueful. "It wasn't planned. Traveling messed with Jane's birth control, and now we're faced with being the oldest parents in the schoolyard."

"You'll be great." Rachel sat on the floor and pulled on her jeans.

"Only because I had all that experience with you," Paul said.

"Luckily, you never knew me when I was a small baby. Mom said I was awful." Rachel became aware of Cauy standing in the doorway and kept her back turned to him. "It was nice of you to call, but—"

"Rachel, you're still my daughter. I know you've got the Morgan family behind you now, but I'll always consider you as much mine as this new baby."

"That's very sweet of you." She smiled even though he couldn't see her. "I appreciate that very much."

"I always wanted to have kids, but your mother . . . well, she told me after we married that she'd had her tubes tied, and couldn't have any more, so that was that."

"I'm sorry," Rachel said.

"Nothing to be sorry about. I had you and your mom, and that was enough for me."

Rachel held the phone so tightly she thought it might crack.

"You still there, Rachel?"

She gathered herself. "You're breaking up a bit. Maybe you should go. Love you, Dad, and love to Jane."

She cut the connection and stayed where she was, all the time aware of Cauy's gaze on her. He still had his jeans on although he'd taken off his belt and unbuttoned them.

"You planning on going somewhere?"

She put her cell back in her pocket and stood. "No, that was my father, and—"

"Because that's okay." He found his T-shirt and put it on in one jerky motion. "Probably not good to make decisions when you're upset."

"I *was* upset, but that's not why I put my clothes on, I was talking to my *stepdad*, and it felt *weird*—"

He interrupted her again by handing over her jacket and hat. "Not a problem."

Rachel clutched her remaining garments to her chest as he marched over to the back door and looked at her expectantly.

"You're throwing me *out*?"

He shrugged. "Sounds like you've sorted things with your dad so your problem is solved."

Rachel stalked up to him and poked him in the chest. "I don't think I'm the one having regrets, buddy, but classy of you to put all the blame on me."

A muscle twitched in his jaw, but he didn't react to her deliberate taunt, which was annoying as hell. He was supposed to defend himself, get mad, and then sweep her off her feet into his bed and make love to her all night. But maybe he really did regret what they'd started, and she simply hadn't made the grade. She was the one who had forced her way into his house, cried all over him, and let him comfort her with *sex*. She'd taken everything and given nothing in return.

She rammed her hat on her head and struggled into her coat. He silently helped her find the second armhole, but she didn't say thank you.

"Good night, Cauy." She smiled at his T-shirt, not daring to look up into his eyes in case he looked either sorry for her or delighted she was finally leaving him in peace. "Thanks for listening. I really appreciate it."

This time he didn't stop her leaving, and she stumbled in the frosty night almost slipping on the ice in the yard. At least this time she wasn't storming out and slamming the door. That was progress, right? She took a deep breath and looked up at the clearness of the star-studded sky. Acting on her emotions never ended well and usually made her feel she'd let everyone down and was ungrateful. How many times had she tried to tell her mother how she felt only to be called out about how hard her mother's life was? Too many to count until she'd stopped complaining, and just done her best to keep her mouth shut and keep everyone happy.

She got into her truck and took it slow going down the slope, her tires struggling to find grip on the icy surface. She *was* glad her stepfather had called to straighten things out. If she'd just stayed put in her bedroom she would've received the call there, and none of what had happened later with Cauy would have occurred.

She allowed herself to think about how he'd touched her so carefully with his work-roughened hands, how easily he'd made her come. Did she regret that? Rachel sat up straight and slowly shook her head. She'd had sex before, but no one had taken care of her needs first. Most guys were way too selfish to even think about her pleasure before they took their own.

So she wouldn't regret that experience even if it was the last time she ever got to see Cauy Lymond half-naked. Her body disagreed with that, but she ignored those pitiful yearnings and focused on getting safely back to the ranch.

As the sound of Rachel's truck receded down the hill Cauy sank into his chair and put his head in his hands.

"Jeez, Cauy Lymond . . ." he breathed. "You complete and utter monumental *fuck*up."

The shock of seeing Rachel dressed when he'd come

back into the room had knocked him sideways, robbing him of speech and obviously his brains. He'd made assumptions, she'd gotten mad, and he'd let her walk out.

Again.

He *was* the *ass* in *assumptions*.

There was a pattern here that even he was aware of. He thought she'd changed her mind, had regretted letting him touch her, and was desperate to leave. But from what he'd allowed her to say she'd only covered up because she was talking to her stepdad, which was ridiculous, but made a weird kind of sense. He would probably have done the same if it had been his mom on the phone.

But why had he been so eager to rush to those conclusions? Was Rachel right and had he really been looking for a way out?

He couldn't answer that. Or maybe he just didn't want to face the truth. The thought of having her in his bed had been . . . Cauy sighed. *Awesome.* She was like the light. Having her in his hands and sinking into her warmth made him feel alive again. Thinking she was about to leave had gutted him.

All the reasons why touching her was a bad idea still remained. He licked his lips. The taste of her still lingered despite his hasty teeth brushing while he made sure his bed linen was clean and his boxers safely in the laundry basket. His dick was throbbing like a sore tooth. He'd been more than willing to take advantage of her emotional state so maybe it was right that he'd been stopped.

"Bullshit," Cauy spoke aloud. "You still want her."

There was nobody to answer him, but he already knew the truth. He'd have a cold shower, take himself off to bed, and try not to dream about what might have been.

Chapter Nine

"Can you come over, Rachel?" Rachel's stomach clenched as she listened to Jenna's message on her cell. "I wanted to talk to you about the dog."

Rachel finished her morning coffee and washed out her cup before going to find Ruth.

"Can we go shopping a bit later this morning?" she asked her grandma. "I need to go and see Jenna."

"There's no rush." Ruth shut the chest freezer and turned to Rachel, a huge leg of lamb clutched to the front of her apron. "Is there something wrong?"

"I found a dog in the bottom of one of the feed bins at Em's yesterday and took it to Jenna."

"Oh dear, I hope the little mite is okay." Ruth walked back with Rachel to the main kitchen. "Text me if you need anything. If it gets late, I'll just get Billy to take me instead."

"Thank you." Rachel bent to kiss Ruth's wrinkled cheek.

"Are you feeling all right yourself, dear?" Ruth's keen gaze swept over her. "You look tired."

"I'm fine," Rachel hastened to reassure her grandma. "I just stayed up too late reading research papers on mining and ground-penetrating radar."

It was the truth. She'd literally bored herself to sleep so she wouldn't think about Cauy.

"Tell Jenna I'm making her favorite vegetarian lasagna for dinner tonight if she wants to come over. I need to talk to her about the final details of the house as well." Ruth chuckled. "Sometimes I don't think BB's new place will ever be finished."

"It's certainly taken a while," Rachel agreed.

"That's because BB's so darn picky." Ruth placed the frozen lamb in the sink and cut into the plastic surrounding it. "I'm amazed Jenna puts up with it and him."

Deciding not to answer that, Rachel handed Ruth a towel to dry her hands and headed out to the mudroom to find her boots and outerwear. Her concern about the dog filled her thoughts as she drove to the McDonald place, which was not much better than thinking about Cauy.

Jenna was waiting for her in the cramped back office surrounded by cages filled with animals in various stages of recovery, piles of paperwork, and overstuffed filing cabinets.

"Hey, Rachel! Thanks so much for coming over." Jenna patted the seat next to her. "Come and sit down."

There was no obvious sign of the dog, and Rachel immediately feared the worst.

"So, what's up?" She tried for a calm tone. "Is the dog okay?"

"She's doing fine." Jenna paused. "The thing is . . . she's pregnant."

"*Pregnant*?" Rachel gaped at her. "But she's only a baby herself."

"Yeah, but females can reproduce from the age of five months, and I think she's less than a year old."

"Then I wonder if someone did dump her."

"It's hard to tell. But it's more likely she's been a stray all her life, and just fell into that feed bin when she was looking for food." Jenna paused. "The thing is, this is going to make her recovery slightly more complicated."

"In what way?"

"Well, the puppies will probably be small and need extra care and attention, and the mom will need to build up her strength considerably so she can feed them."

"That's all doable with good care, right?" Rachel asked anxiously.

"Absolutely." Jenna nodded. "The other thing I wanted to ask was do you have Cauy Lymond's phone number?"

"Why do you need that?" Rachel asked.

"Because he offered to pay for the dog's treatment." Jenna raised her eyebrows. "Didn't he tell you? It was very kind of him. I said I would be keeping any costs to a bare minimum because you are family, but he insisted on offering to help."

"That was . . . nice of him."

"Yeah, he seems like a good guy." Jenna studied Rachel's face. "BB seems to think you like him."

"I . . ." Rachel groaned. She'd already started to count on Jenna as a friend and an ally. "I kind of do, and then I also want to strangle him because he can be absolutely infuriating."

"Like most men," Jenna said, nodding. "Are you holding back because of me and my history with his father?"

"No!" Rachel paused. "Although *he* might be."

"He didn't let Blue scare him," Jenna observed.

Rachel glanced around the empty office and lowered her voice. "I just worry that maybe I'm pushing myself at him, and making a fool of myself, you know? He seems to like kissing me, and . . . other things, but—"

"Other things?" Jenna perked up. "Like what exactly?"

Rachel worried her lip, and Jenna spoke again.

"Look, we're practically family. I already like you a lot, and I'd love to help if you need to talk anything through."

"And you promise you won't tell BB?"

"Cross my heart and hope to die." Jenna traced the pattern over her blue scrubs. "After years of therapy, I'm *really* good at giving advice, ask anyone."

"Well . . ." Rachel let out her breath. Her other closest friend was currently working in a mine in South Africa so not very reachable, and there was something about Jenna that made Rachel *want* to confide in her.

The sound of whistling came through the back door and Jenna sighed. "That's Dave. How about I come around this evening for dinner at the ranch, and we can talk after that?"

"That sounds great," Rachel agreed. "Ruth said to ask you anyway."

Jenna glanced up as her tall, dark cousin came into the room. He looked as if he'd just gotten out of bed.

"Hey. Dave. Did you just wake up?" Jenna asked.

"Nope." He threw himself into a chair with a groan. "I've been up all night with a fricking horse with colic." He yawned so hard his jaw cracked. "Maybe you can take a look at him later, and make sure I didn't mess up."

"Of course I will." Jenna got up and Rachel followed her.

"I'd better go, Jenna. Thanks for everything and let *me* know about the costs for the dog, okay?" She didn't really want Cauy paying for anything at this point.

One of Dave's eyes opened, and he sat bolt upright. "*Hey.*"

"Hi." She smiled at him. "I'm Rachel."

He unfolded his large frame from the chair and shook her hand. "Nice to meet you. I'm Dave, and I'm good-looking, employed, and single, how about you?"

Rachel grinned. "I'm—"

"She's a Morgan, leave her alone, or Blue will skin you alive," Jenna said with a wink as she handed Dave a cup of coffee. "He's an okay person, really, but sometimes it's hard to tell."

"Thanks for the write-up, Cousin," Dave grumbled as he drained his coffee in one. "Maybe Rachel might like to find out what I'm like by herself." He put his mug down on the table. "Would you like to go out for a drink on Friday night at the Red Dragon?"

Rachel considered him. He *was* young, employed and very charming, and maybe she could do with an evening out with someone who genuinely seemed to like her?

"Can I call you?" she compromised. "I'm not sure of my plans."

"Sure." Dave smiled triumphantly at Jenna and helped himself to more coffee. "Watch and learn, Little Cousin, watch and learn."

Cauy answered his cell as he was walking down to the barn. He'd spent all night dreaming of Rachel and he half hoped she was on the phone.

"Hey."

"It's Jackson. Mom told me to call."

"*Hey*, it's good to hear your voice." Cauy stopped walking.

"You too, long time no speak, Bro. How's the ranch looking?"

"Like crap."

"Yup. After Mom left, Dad basically ran it into the ground. Are you going to sell up?"

Cauy looked around the frost-laced fields and the high black mountains that surrounded the valley. It felt like the whole place was holding its breath waiting for him to answer. "I'm not sure."

"Really?"

"That was my original intention, but . . ." Cauy's breath condensed in the frozen air. "There's a lot of our history here."

"Gotcha. After I've checked in with Mom, do you want me to come out?" Jackson asked.

"Yeah. I'd like that."

"Okay, I'll call you when I've finalized my itinerary. Stay safe, Bro."

Cauy carried on to the barn and started on the daily tasks of mucking out the horses before taking them to graze in the pasture. His younger brother was something of a talker. Years in the United States Air Force had made his delivery even more rapid. Despite not seeing each other much they were still close, and Jackson had pulled every string in the book to make sure he got leave to see Cauy after the accident.

Maybe with Jackson around Cauy wouldn't have time to obsess over Rachel Morgan and the rest of her family? Maybe he was just lonely. . . . His gaze swept the almost empty barn. He still hadn't gotten back to Roy about the proposal to use his barn for the Morgan Ranch guest horses. He tried to imagine a full barn and found the idea not unpleasant.

It would also mean he'd get on with the repairs to the old place faster, and with Jackson here they could come to a decision about whether to keep the ranch or get rid of it. But it also meant Morgans all over his personal space. . . .

One of the horses gently butted his shoulder, and Cauy got with the program. When Jackson arrived, Cauy would like to show him at least one piece of the ranch that proved things could be upgraded.

With that in mind, he took out his cell and sent a text to Ry. He figured Roy wouldn't be an early-morning texter.

> Agreeable to leasing you the barn. Let me know
> when we can meet and set terms. Thanks.

His cell buzzed in reply immediately.

> Awesome ☺ I'll be in touch. Ry

Cauy was just about to put his phone away when he received another text.

> Hey, this is Jenna. Wanted to give you an update on
> the dog. She's doing good, but is pregnant. Surprise,
> surprise!

Cauy blinked and read the message twice before replying.

> Okay. Let me know how that affects the estimate
> you gave me. It's not a problem; I'd just like to know.
> Thanks

Jenna didn't reply immediately so Cauy considered his options and decided to ride up to the old silver mine and check out the landscape. Despite years of not riding he'd found it easy to get back into it, and actually enjoyed the quieter view of life from the back of a horse. It gave him time to think and appreciate what was around him.

He couldn't imagine not being able to do this—get on a horse and ride for hours without even leaving your own family land. It was a privilege he hadn't appreciated when he was young, and all he'd yearned to do was get away from his father and find a new life for himself. Mark had never liked him. The more Cauy thought about it, the less likely he believed the man was his father.

Cauy clicked to the horse and set off at a gentle walk toward the rear of the ranch house. If he really wanted to find out if he was Mark's son he could do one of those fancy DNA tests. That might tell him something, but what if it did? Would he feel honor bound to give the ranch to Jackson? Mark had specifically left it to Cauy in his will.

Cauy snorted, almost spooking the horse. What if Mark had left him the dilapidated ranch as a final F-you? Maybe he'd hoped Cauy would go under with it. That sounded more like the man he'd known. A man he'd never been able to please, who had never praised him and constantly found fault. Yet he'd allowed the old man to influence his dislike of the Morgans.

Cauy leaned down to open the back gate and moved on up the slope, glad of his horse's warmth beneath him as the air grew colder. The silence was breathtaking. Even the sparse grass was frozen up here and glittered eerily when faint shafts of pale yellow sunlight managed to infiltrate the gloom.

He buttoned up his winter coat right to this throat, protecting the thin damaged skin there, and crammed his hat down low. Gloves were a necessity up here unless you wanted chilblains and the possibility of frostbite. Rachel hadn't said anything negative when she'd seen his scarred chest. . . .

"Snap out of it," Cauy muttered to himself as he reached level ground, and allowed the horse to lope. "She's not for you."

He reached the fence line that separated his land from the Morgans' and did a double take. A good twenty feet of the wire and posts had completely disappeared.

"Holy cow," Cauy murmured.

He took out his cell and had to take off his glove to punch in the numbers. No one answered so he left a message.

"Roy? There's a huge sinkhole close to the old mine. Come check it out as soon as possible."

He'd barely put his glove back on before his cell rang.

"I'm about half a mile away," Roy said. "I'll meet you there."

Cauy stayed on his horse and watched the two riders approach from the other side of the now disappearing fence. Roy pointed toward the mine entrance and, carefully skirting the hole, Cauy crossed over onto Morgan land and walked his horse down to where Roy and the other unknown cowboy were tying up their mounts.

"Hey!" Roy called out to him. "Thanks for calling."

"You're welcome." Cauy dismounted and tied his horse up as the other guy approached him with his hand out.

"Hi, I'm Chase Morgan. I used to be known as TC. Good to meet you at last, Cauy."

"Good to see you again."

Cauy shook yet another blue-eyed Morgan's hand. He hadn't seen Chase for years, but his dad had mentioned him in his last letter, none of it complimentary. Cauy's lawyers had also received a couple of optimistic inquiries while the will was percolating through the system about him selling the place, which hadn't endeared him to the man who was obviously used to getting his own way.

"If you'd sold me your ranch, this would be my problem now," Chase said.

Cauy blinked and then noticed Chase was grinning. Apparently, the oldest Morgan brother hadn't taken offense at the increasingly sharp replies from the Lymond lawyers.

"It's still your problem," Cauy replied. "It's the *Morgan*-ville silver mine and it's technically on your land."

"So you think I should just fill up my part, and leave yours alone?" Chase asked. "I'm not sure that's possible."

They started walking up toward the disappearing fence line and stopped well before the edge of the sinkhole.

"Wow," Chase said as Roy whistled. "That's something all right. Rachel told me this might happen."

"So what are you going to do about it?" Cauy asked.

"We're already on it." Chase's gaze swept the barren landscape. "As soon as the equipment arrives Rachel's doing a survey of the area so we can get some idea of the extent of the mine works." Chase paused. "With your permission, of course."

"She's not intending to go down there, is she?" Cauy asked.

"Nope, apparently, there's some new technology we can introduce beneath the surface to attempt to get a 3D image. Once we know exactly what we're dealing with, we'll consider how to fill the place in without damaging the water table."

Obviously, Chase Morgan didn't hang around worrying about a problem, he just went ahead and found solutions. Cauy tried to reconcile the slender nerd he'd known at school with the decisive tech millionaire who stood beside him.

"Sounds good." And now he sounded like a begrudging fool.

Chase nodded. "We'll keep you in the loop. You already know Rachel, right? So you can talk to her."

"Okay." Yeah, like he'd be doing that. Not.

Roy peered down into the hole. "I'll get some of that flashy orange tape you love, Chase, and stick it around the perimeter. We haven't got any rides scheduled up this way, have we?"

Chase consulted his phone. "Not that I can see. I'll put a note on the schedule and make sure everyone is aware of the issue at the team meeting tomorrow morning."

Team meeting? Cauy had a sudden image of the Morgan barn horses all gathered in a group huddle to hear what the great Chase Morgan had to say. He bit down hard on his lip and turned away. What a time for his sense of humor to return.

"You aren't running any cattle up here, are you, Cauy?" Roy asked.

"Nope. None to run."

Chase Morgan looked up from his phone. "We should talk about that."

Not if Cauy had anything to do with it. He'd had about enough of the Morgans taking over his ranch.

Chase obviously hadn't noticed Cauy's lack of enthusiasm as he kept talking.

"Ry says you're going to be our backup barn for the next few months. That's awesome."

"Yeah, well." Cauy shrugged. "Place is just sitting there three fourths empty."

"Getting permission to build the new barn has been hell," Chase confided as they walked back to the horses. "The fire regulations alone are enough to bankrupt me."

"Baloney." Roy snorted. "You just don't like being told what to do."

"True." Chase's unrepentant grin at Roy almost endeared him to Cauy, but he wasn't willing to be bowled over too easily. "Some people say I'm a mite over-controlling."

"*Some* people?" Roy raised his eyebrows. "Just your wife, your entire family, your business partners, and me."

"Hey, I'm trying." Chase gave Roy a playful punch on the arm. "January wouldn't put up with me otherwise."

"Best thing that ever happened to you," Roy said gruffly.

"Yeah." Chase's smile died. "One hundred percent true."

Cauy almost looked away from the obvious emotion on Chase's face. He tried to imagine what January Morgan was like and couldn't come up with anything.

Roy mounted up with a spring in his step that belied

his years. "I just had a thought. Maybe you should ask Ms. January if the historical society has any more information on the mine. You never know what might turn up."

"That's a great idea." Chase got into the saddle as well and tipped his Stetson to Cauy. He looked all cowboy on a horse. "Thanks for the heads-up about this, and I'll get back to you with an update as soon as I can, okay?"

"Thanks." Cauy nodded as he turned away. "I'd appreciate it."

He waited until the Morgans left before turning around and taking a good look at the entrance to the old mine. He hadn't been here since he was a kid when all the locals had visions of discovering gold, and came up here to try their luck. The fact that it was a silver mine and that they stood more chance of striking it rich in the running water of Morgan Creek hadn't deterred anyone.

The mine entrance was sealed up tight, and the discarded machinery and ironwork had been cleared away, leaving the place surprisingly bland and unexciting. Cauy turned back to his horse and mounted up.

He really should think of a name for the gelding, but he'd never been good at that kind of stuff.

Chase Morgan hadn't said a word about the hole being mainly on Cauy's land or even suggested Cauy needed to pony up some cash to help out. Cauy couldn't decide if that made him happy or mad. The Morgans all assumed that because the ranch was a dilapidated mess then so was he . . . Not that he'd done anything to dispel that impression, but still.

"The whole *family* is a bunch of control freaks." His words echoed in the silence. Yeah. That was it. In a nutshell.

Cauy grinned and clicked to his horse. Time to get back home and finish repairing the fencing on the second pasture. If the Morgan Ranch horses were coming, it would be needed.

Jenna threw herself down on Rachel's bed, and let out a sigh, and a discreet burp. "That lasagna was so good I'm not going to move for a week."

Rachel smiled down at her. "Ruth is an amazing cook."

"She's just amazing all-round. If she hadn't been helping me furnish this new house I think I would've murdered Blue by now." Jenna opened her eyes. "Sometimes he digs his heels in about the stupidest things, and we end up arguing, and I *hate* arguing, but sometimes you have to stick up for yourself, you know?"

"Yes," Rachel said fervently. "I know all about hating to argue but ending up doing it anyway."

"So what's going on with you and Cauy Lymond?" Jenna got right into it.

Rachel winced and sat on the end of the bed. "Nothing now."

Jenna nudged her with her foot. "Come on, tell me all about it."

"You promise you won't tell anyone?" Rachel asked.

"Not anyone by the name of Morgan, if that's what you mean. So you like Cauy, and I know he kissed you, so what gives?"

"I *asked* him to kiss me," Rachel pointed out.

"Okay, nothing wrong with that." Jenna nodded encouragingly.

"But that's the problem. It's always me." Rachel stared at Jenna willing her to understand.

"You mean you feel like you're stalking him or something?"

"No! But it feels like I'm always the one who has to do all the talking and the asking."

"From what I could tell, he's not exactly the chatty type," Jenna said cautiously. "But he's a grown man. If he didn't like you kissing him I'm fairly sure you'd know about it."

Rachel considered that. "But what if I'm . . . *imposing* myself on him?"

"In what way?" Jenna chuckled. "You didn't strip naked and lie in wait for him in his bed, did you?"

Rachel pressed a hand to her heated cheek. "Not *exactly*."

Jenna sat bolt upright. "*What* exactly?"

"I was upset about something, so I went over to his house, uninvited, and we talked it through, and then he gave me a hug, and he was being so *kind* that I kissed him, and things . . . *happened*."

"You slept with him?"

"Almost." Rachel sucked in a much-needed breath. "I would've, but we were interrupted, and then he decided I'd made a mistake when I was *emotional,* and bundled me out the door."

"Not naked?" Jenna breathed.

"No. I'd put my clothes back on, because, *reasons,* which was why he assumed I was already leaving despite the fact that he'd gone to tidy up his bedroom."

"Okay, so who would you say was at fault here?"

"Him for jumping to conclusions? I tried to explain what had happened, but he didn't want to hear me."

"Was he mean to you?" Jenna asked.

"Like angry?" Rachel paused. "It's very hard to tell with Cauy. He doesn't exactly give much away, but he didn't exactly shout at me. He just said maybe we'd made a mistake, and walked me to the door."

"So he didn't say it was all over, and he didn't want to see you again?" Jenna pressed.

"We're not exactly a couple. He didn't have to break up with me." Rachel sighed. "And *I* was the one who went over there without an invitation, cried all over him, and then let him give me . . ." She broke off, and whispered, "*Sympathy* sex."

"*You cried all over him and he didn't run a mile?*" Jenna raised her eyebrows. "That's pretty amazing, Rachel. And then he stayed around to give you *sex?*"

"We were in his house! He could hardly run away," Rachel objected.

"Maybe he really did wonder whether you had changed your mind when you had all your clothes on," Jenna mused. "Because sometimes men can be just as unsure as we are about whether someone really wants them or not."

"Cauy—" Rachel hesitated, remembering how fierce he'd looked when he'd put his T-shirt back on. "I think he was scared. I told him so as well."

"Scared of you?"

"Kind of. Scared of wanting me." Rachel sighed.

"Ruth thinks he's super shy."

"Trust me, he isn't. He just doesn't believe in wasting valuable words."

Jenna crossed her legs and looked over at Rachel. "What do you *want* to happen now?"

"I want him to come here, apologize, and explain," Rachel said.

"Do you think he's going to do that?"

"Probably not," Rachel grimaced. "But I can't keep chasing after him. Because whether he means to or not he makes me feel like I'm begging for some sign of affection, and I'm sick of being that person."

"I know exactly how you feel," Jenna said fervently. "So maybe this really is the time to make him come and get *you*. Has he ever done that?"

"He did come and find me and apologize once," Rachel admitted.

"Then maybe he'll do it again?" Jenna hesitated. "If he doesn't, then you'll know either way, right?"

"I suppose so." The thought of not seeing Cauy made her chest hurt. "I just hate all this uncertainty, you know? And I've *got* to stop storming out like a teenager when he says something I don't like."

"Finding love sucks," Jenna said.

"Until you find the right guy." Rachel smiled at her companion. "I don't think you have any doubts how BB feels about you."

Jenna blushed. "Yeah, took me a long while to believe him though. But that was more about *me* than about him."

Rachel lay back on the bed and stretched her arms above her head to stare at the cciling. Jenna had a point. Maybe she should work on herself. . . .

"Should I go out with Dave?"

"Why not?" Jenna grinned and flopped down beside her. "He's actually a nice guy under that goofy act. Smart, too."

"Well, duh, he's a vet," Rachel pointed out. "But would that be two-timing Cauy?"

"You just said you had no formal relationship with him to break up, so which is it?" Jenna asked.

Rachel vividly recalled Cauy's mouth on her and blushed. "Um . . . well, I did let him take . . . liberties."

"Liberties?" Jenna snorted. "Now you sound like Roy." She elbowed Rachel in the side. "Have a drink with Dave, keep it simple, and take it from there, okay?"

Chapter Ten

"Cauy, I'm sorry it's taken me so long to get back to you. Can you meet me in town around five at Yvonne's to talk about the horses?"

Cauy considered Ry Morgan's request, his gaze on the barn, and the pasture beyond where his two horses were grazing. He hadn't heard from Rachel for a few days, which wasn't surprising seeing as she was probably sick of him, and Jackson wasn't due to arrive until the Monday just before Thanksgiving.

"Sure. I have to go into town today to pick up my mail. I'll meet you there," Cauy replied.

"Great. See you soon."

Ry Morgan disconnected the call, and Cauy slipped his cell phone back into his pocket. The coldness in the air was making his damaged skin tighten up. He probably needed to speak to Dr. Mendez again and get some more lotion.

"Might as well make a day of it," Cauy murmured to himself.

He could also pop into the vet's and check up on the dog. He'd been by himself for two days, and the solitude was starting to get to him. Had he gotten used to hordes of

Morgans and townsfolk interfering in his life already? He went online and scored himself an appointment with Dr. Mendez at four, which gave him plenty of time to get everything done before he met Ry in the coffee shop.

He'd spent the last few days cleaning out the barn to make it ready for the new arrivals and every muscle he possessed was sore. But he also had a sense of achievement as the barn he remembered when he was a kid slowly came back to life. Why his dad had let everything go would always be a mystery. He'd been fiercely proud of the place when Cauy was a kid.

But he'd still never liked Cauy or the Morgans.

The parking lot at the vets was busier than last time he'd been there, and he guessed it was the afternoon session. When he went in, the four or five people already waiting greeted him like an old friend. After he signed in, everyone was more than happy to introduce themselves and tell him how they knew his family.

Eventually, Jenna appeared and waved at him to come through to the back. Tipping his hat to his assembled audience, Cauy left his seat to a chorus of good-byes and various invitations to dinner.

Jenna smiled up at him as she shut the door. "Having fun?"

He grimaced. "Just trying to be neighborly. How's the dog?"

"She's doing much better." Jenna took him through an untidy office and into a lean-to on the back of the property. "Come and see."

He viewed the dog and gently patted her head when she whined at him.

"She remembers you," Jenna said approvingly.

"I doubt it. Rachel did all the heavy lifting. I just gave her a ride."

"So I heard," Jenna said. "She'll be ready to leave tomorrow. Have you and Rachel discussed whether you're going to drop her off at the humane society or keep her?"

Cauy frowned and looked at the dog's big brown eyes. "I'm sure Rachel won't want to get rid of her."

"But Rachel's only visiting for the holidays," Jenna reminded him. "This dog is going to need a permanent home, and as she's going to have puppies she's not going to be very adoptable."

"Have you talked to Rachel?" Cauy asked.

"Not yet. I figured that seeing as you're paying the bills I should talk to you as well." Jenna looked at him expectantly. "Maybe you could check in with Rachel and let me know? I'd take the dog myself, but I'm about to move into a new house, and that's not the kind of insane environment any dog needs right now."

"Okay, I'll talk to her." Cauy nodded.

"Thanks." Jenna smiled at him. "I'd appreciate that."

Dr. Mendez decided Cauy needed to see a dermatologist in the bigger town of Bridgeport and set up an appointment for him. Cauy picked up a new month's supply of stuff from the pharmacy and stowed everything in the back seat of his truck. It was already getting dark, and the multicolored lights strung along the storefront of Main Street danced in the brisk breeze.

Cauy took a moment to gaze at the sight of his hometown, which hadn't changed much since he'd left. Sure, some of the shops were different, but the structures remained the same. Considering the property prices in California he suspected someone had fought hard to keep it that way. As a kid, he'd loved coming into town with his mom to pick up supplies from Maureen's, especially at this time of year.

"Crap. Supplies," Cauy muttered, and turned on his heel, bumping into someone right behind him. "Sorry, ma'am. I didn't see you there."

The short blonde woman smiled at him. "It's okay. I've got my steel-capped boots on, and you're much lighter than a horse." She looked at him inquiringly. "Can I help you with something?"

He let out his breath. "I was just thinking about the holidays. My brother's coming to visit, and I don't even think I have a spare set of sheets."

She chuckled and pointed down the street. "Maureen's has a bit of everything, and if that doesn't work you can try Bridgeport or one of the bigger cities. When's he arriving?"

"Monday."

"Then you've got the whole weekend to work it out." She gave him an encouraging smile. "Have a great day, now."

"Will do."

Living in Morgantown had him chatting to complete strangers now, and sharing his personal life. His mom wouldn't recognize him.

He continued down the street, stopping to look in the shop windows, aware that he was dawdling because he didn't want to arrive at Yvonne's too early. He could already smell the coffee wafting down the raised boardwalk, and his mouth was watering.

Coldness seeped into his clothes, and he gave up the struggle and headed inside the pink-and-black-decorated coffee shop where Yvonne was behind the counter by herself. For once the place was completely empty. She glanced up as he came in and smiled, which was almost as enticing as the smell of coffee. He hesitated by the door.

She beckoned to him. "Hi! Come on in. We're closing at six so you've got plenty of time."

"Thanks." He took off his hat and ran a hand through his flattened hair. "I'm meeting Ry Morgan here."

"So what can I get you?" Yvonne asked.

"A large black coffee, and . . ." Cauy studied the array of cakes. "A slice of carrot cake, please."

"Good choice. Carrots are healthy." Yvonne had a slight French accent, which Cauy couldn't help but enjoy. "Go and sit down. I'll bring it over."

Cauy found a seat, took off his heavy jacket, and draped it over the back of his chair. He really had forgotten he'd need all kinds of stuff for Jackson's visit. He couldn't expect Ruth Morgan to keep feeding him forever.

He took out his phone and started making a list. Tomorrow was the last Saturday before Thanksgiving so the shops would probably be packed. He needed to get out there and get stuff done anyway.

"Here you go." Yvonne appeared with a tray. "You're Cauy Lymond, aren't you?"

"Yes, ma'am." He nodded.

"Welcome home. I'm sorry I didn't get to chat with you last time you were in here. I got distracted by BB giving you a hard time about your father, but he's an idiot."

"My father?"

"I was thinking of BB but from what I've heard both of them are well-qualified for that title." She angled her head to study him more closely. "You don't look much like Mark."

"I'm told I favor my mother."

"Everyone liked her."

"Yeah. She's a peach." Cauy picked up his coffee and took a slug. "That is . . . damn fine."

"Thank you, I roast it myself." The shop door opened, and Ry Morgan came in. "I'll leave you to it, then."

Ry chatted with Yvonne before coming to sit opposite Cauy.

"Thanks for coming."

Cauy nodded. "No problem."

"The reason it took so long was because Chase insisted that we needed a proper legal agreement between us rather than a gentlemen's handshake kind of thing." Ry rolled his eyes and took out an envelope. "I got Henry Parker, our lawyer here in town, to draw something up."

"Thanks." Cauy took the envelope and quickly scanned the agreement. "It looks okay to me, but I'll get my lawyers to take a look at it."

"*Right,* your lawyers. Nice one." Ry grinned. He obviously thought Cauy was joking. "It's pretty straightforward. It just sets a time limit so we aren't there forever, and an estimated cost per horse upkeep and manpower. If you're okay with it sign all the copies and drop it back to Henry's office just across the street from here."

"Got it." Cauy picked up his coffee and took another sip. "Anything else?"

"Ruth's expecting you for Thanksgiving dinner at our place."

Cauy put down his mug and just stared at Ry.

"There's no point arguing." Ry tried to look solemn. "You don't want to break an old lady's heart now, do you?"

Cauy cast about frantically for an excuse. "My brother's coming to stay. He might have made different arrangements."

"Bring him with you," Ry said generously. "The more the merrier."

"I'll think about it," Cauy said, and started on his carrot cake. It was so good he slowed down to appreciate the flavors.

Yvonne brought Ry a cup of coffee and stayed to chat about her fiancé, who was obviously involved in the rodeo. When she went off to serve someone else, Cauy attempted to be sociable.

"You and your twin went into the rodeo business, right? I saw HW's name sometimes on TV."

"Yeah, he did good. Runner-up to the world champ in bronc riding a couple of years ago," Ry said without a hint of envy in his voice. "And Yvonne's engaged to Rio Martinez."

"The bull rider?" Cauy had always followed the rodeo.

"Yeah. He's on course to win his second world championship. I just hope he doesn't take Yvonne away from us."

"I'm not going anywhere!" Yvonne called out, and Ry gave her the thumbs-up as he drank his coffee.

"Did you say your brother's coming to stay at the ranch?" Ry asked.

"Yeah. Jackson. Do you remember him?"

Ry nodded. "He went into the United States Air Force Academy right after school, didn't he?"

"Yeah. He's just about to exit the Air Force after a ten-year stint."

"It would be nice to see him again too." Ry's cell buzzed. He really was a decent guy. He took his phone out of his pocket and read the text. "Damn."

"What's up?" Cauy asked.

"HW was supposed to be giving me a ride home, but he's stuck waiting for Sam at the airport."

"I can drop you back," Cauy offered. He might see Rachel and gauge how pissed off with him she really was. He needed to talk to her about the dog anyway. He'd settled up the bill with Jenna and needed to know what Rachel intended to do next.

"That would be awesome." Ry grinned at him. "You can confirm with Ruth that you're coming over for Thanksgiving as well."

When they'd both finished their coffee and said good-bye to Yvonne, Cauy walked with Ry back down the street toward the parking lot behind Dr. Mendez's building. It was now dark, and the lights were on in the Red Dragon Bar on the corner on the two main streets.

As they crossed the intersection the smell of beer and fried food cut through the sharp bite in the air. Cauy was just about to turn the corner when he saw a tall dark-haired guy laughing down at Rachel Morgan. She was wearing jeans and a bright cherry red sweater that almost came down to her knees.

"Who's that guy?" Cauy asked as casually as he could.

"That tall, goofy-looking dude?" Ry chuckled. "That's Dave McDonald, Jenna's cousin. He's also one of the local vets." Ry stopped walking. "Is that *Rachel* with him?"

Cauy nodded, his gaze fixed on the oblivious pair.

"Dave's a nice guy," Ry said slowly. "And I'm sure he'll settle down one day, but—"

Cauy was already moving in the direction of the bar before Ry had finished his sentence.

Dave was funny. He'd kept Rachel in stitches since he'd picked her up at the ranch. He held the door into the Red Dragon open for her to go past him into the warm interior. The dark-haired guy behind the bar glanced up at them and nodded to Dave.

"Hey."

Dave walked over, bringing Rachel with him.

"Hi, Jay. This is Rachel Morgan. Have you met her yet?"

"Nope. But I'm always pleased to meet a Morgan." Jay took Rachel's fingers in a firm grip and shook her hand. He was super fit with bulging tattooed biceps. "Welcome to the Red Dragon. What can I get you?"

Rachel looked inquiringly up at Dave. "What would you like?"

"You're *buying*?" Dave grinned at her. "I *knew* I liked you. I'll have a beer. Thanks."

Rachel turned back to Jay. "Two beers then, please."

"Will you be wanting food?" Jay expertly poured their drinks.

"Yes, please. I'm starving," Dave groaned. "But no beef. I've been around too many cattle today."

"We've got some great choices." Jay handed over a menu. "You can order at the bar, or take a table at the back."

Dave looked at Rachel. "Shall we go for a booth? More privacy."

"Sure."

Rachel picked up her beer and followed Dave toward the rear of the building. He found an empty booth and eased his lanky frame onto the seat. She picked up the menu and read through the offerings before passing it to Dave.

"There are some great vegetarian options."

"Like I'm going to eat grass." Dave shuddered. "I need to keep up my manly strength—especially now I've met you." He gave her a lascivious wink.

"Don't worry on my account. I'm having the chicken sandwich and fries." Seeing as Rachel felt no vibe at all between them she was more than happy to treat him like another brother. "The beer is good."

"Yeah, some local guys your big bro has invested in." Dave sipped his own beer.

"Chase?"

"Who else?" Dave raised an eyebrow. "You know any other local millionaires?" He sighed. "I wish there was a female version of him I could marry."

"Wow, way to make a girl feel special," Rachel teased him. "Is that why you asked me out?"

Before Dave could reply a blast of cold air from the opening door made Rachel look up as two cowboys came in.

"God, *no* . . ." Rachel breathed, and squeezed farther into the booth until she was right against the wall. "Why *now*?"

"What's up?" Dave started to turn his head, and Rachel grabbed his hand.

"No! Don't look, don't look!"

Dave regarded her steadily. "Then how am I supposed to know what's going on?"

"My brother Ry and Cauy just walked into the bar!"

"Sounds like the first line of a joke. What's the punch line?"

"Maybe your face?" Rachel hissed at him.

"Ry's not like that." Dave shook his head. "Now, if it was Jay, who was a Navy SEAL or Blue Boy . . ."

"It might soon well be Blue. Ry might bring the whole lot of them down here." Rachel grimaced. "Ruth promised me she wouldn't tell them I was going out with you."

"Why?" Dave sat up straight and pouted. "What's wrong with *me*?"

"Nothing. They're just a mite overprotective." Rachel took a hefty swig of her beer. "Is there another exit?"

"We're *leaving*?" Dave's puzzled expression almost made Rachel want to burst into hysterical laughter. "We just got here."

"But I don't want them to see us!"

"Why not?" Dave asked.

"Cauy doesn't even drink! Why on earth did he choose tonight to come in here?" Rachel chatted feverishly to herself as she found some cash to pay for the beers.

"Cauy who?" Dave inquired.

"Lymond!"

"Not Mark Lymond's son?"

"Yes! Keep up! Don't you ever speak to your cousin Jenna?"

"Sure I do, but I can't say I listen very hard." Dave sat back. "Hey, Ry."

"Evening, Dave, Rachel."

Rachel let out her breath and fixed a smile on her face.

"Ry, fancy seeing you here." She refused to acknowledge Cauy, who stood silently behind her brother.

Dave nodded to the two men. "Rachel and I are on a date, so now that we've exchanged pleasantries, can you guys move it along here?"

As Dave dumped both of them in it, Rachel couldn't help but look at Cauy, whose expression was grim.

"You're dating *him*?" Ry addressed Rachel.

She shrugged like she didn't have a care in the world. "So what if I am? I'm a grown woman. I can make my own choices."

"Okay, then." Ry took a step back. "We'll leave you to it. Cauy and I just came in here to celebrate our new arrangement for the barn. We won't disturb you."

"Thanks." Rachel smiled as hard as she could. "I'll see you at home."

Ry turned away. Unfortunately, Cauy didn't.

"Can I help you with something?" Rachel asked, and looked him dead in the eye.

He regarded her steadily back. "I just wanted to say hi."

She faked waved at him like a hyper teenager. The last time she'd seen him this close he'd been making her come. "*Hi!*"

"Jenna called me about the dog."

"Really?" He wanted one-word conversations? She could do that.

"I wanted to talk to you about it."

"Sure, drop me a text." She raised her eyebrows. "Anything else?"

"Not right now."

"Great. Speak to you soon, then." She turned away, faced Dave, and gazed worshipfully into his eyes. "So you were saying the chicken is good . . . ?"

It seemed to take a long while for Cauy to move off, but Rachel didn't let herself look over at him as Dave was chatting away like a champ.

"So what's going on?" Dave didn't even pause for breath as he changed the subject. "I feel like I'm missing something here. Like I'm the gooseberry in this particular pie."

"Oh, Dave." Rachel grabbed his hand. "I feel so awful for dragging you into all this. I'm not going out with Cauy or anything, but—"

"There's some shit going down between you. Even I picked that up, and I'm as dense as they come." He finished his beer. "Let's order the food, and I'll get another round in."

"You're not mad at me?" Rachel asked.

"Hell, no!" He grinned at her. "This is the best fun I've had all year!"

Cauy sat down and took off his hat to run a distracted hand through his hair. Even though there was music playing on the old jukebox he could still hear Rachel and Dave laughing like they didn't have a care in the world. They'd looked good together. Rachel was a tall woman and Dave topped her by several inches, which meant their kids would all be potential basketball players.

"Getting ahead of yourself there, Cauy," he murmured. "Slow it down."

"You okay?" Ry returned with the drinks, iced tea for Cauy and a beer for himself. "Sorry about that."

Ry settled himself opposite Cauy. "We're all a bit overprotective of Rachel and I'm not sure she appreciates it sometimes." His smile was rueful. "She went from thinking she was an only child to finding out she had four brothers, a living father, and a whole heap of secrets to come home to. That's a lot for anyone to take on."

"Yeah." Cauy sipped his tea. "I suspect she can take care of herself, though."

Not that she needed to. If anyone so much as looked at her funny he'd be all over them like a rash. . . .

Ry grinned. "Well, she certainly put us in our place." He glanced over his shoulder. "I wonder if she and Dave will become a couple? They looked like they were having fun together."

Cauy stared longingly at his companion's beer. After experiencing his father's rages he'd never been a big drinker, and he'd given it up completely after the accident. Nothing mixed well with ten different kinds of medication. He'd learned to love iced tea and stuck with it ever since. But the thought of getting drunk and going home to sleep it off was really appealing right now. He only had himself to blame for Rachel's decision to go out with other men.

"Are you sure you don't want a beer?" Ry asked.

"Nah, it doesn't mix well with my medication." Cauy managed a smile. "Thanks for the offer, though."

"Ruth said you were in some kind of accident in Texas."

"Yeah, but I'm doing great now." He gestured at Ry's empty glass. "Let me get you another one, and how about some food?"

He made his way up to the bar, spotting a few now familiar faces. Nate Turner was there with his arm around a beautiful dark-haired woman and Em and Ben from the feed store were choosing songs on the jukebox. If it hadn't have been for Rachel's presence, he might have enjoyed the experience of his hometown celebrating the start of the weekend. He normally avoided crowds, but this place wasn't doing a number on him at all.

He reached the bar and waited to catch Jay's attention. The owner had been joined by Nancy from the store whose

green and black hair was in pigtails tonight. She winked at
Cauy and came over.

"Hey, stranger. You made it."

"Hey. Can I have another of whatever Ry Morgan's
drinking, and can I order some food please?"

"Sure." She gave him the beer and then got out her order
pad. "What will it be?"

"Two hamburgers, medium rare, and fries."

"Ry always has that, he's so boring," Nancy complained.
"But don't tell Avery I said that."

As he paid for the food, Cauy remembered that Avery
was engaged to Ry. Sometimes remembering all the rela-
tionships was complicated. "Thanks, Nancy."

"You're welcome."

As he turned away he came face-to-face with Dave, who
grinned at him apologetically. "Sorry to drag you into a
thing with the Morgans."

"Not a problem." Cauy found a smile somewhere. Dave
was younger than him, better educated, and perfect for
Rachel, but for some reason he still wanted to punch his
lights out.

"Rachel's awesome. I *really* like her." Dave leaned in
close. "I'm thinking my wild days might be over."

"Great." Cauy had no idea why Dave had suddenly decided to confide in him, but he wished he'd shut the hell up.

"Do you think she's pretty?" Dave asked.

Cauy set his jaw. "If you have to ask me you're obviously
blind. She's beautiful."

Dave winked at him. "Yeah, she is, isn't she?"

Cauy had had enough, and after a brief nod he turned on
his heel and made his way back to Ry, the beer in his hand.

"Dave's an idiot," Cauy said, putting the beer down with
a thump, spilling some of the contents.

"Yeah, so what's new?" Ry mopped up the spill. "I bet Rachel will work that out pretty fast and move on."

The burgers were good, and Ry was easy company. Nate came over to introduce his soon-to-be wife Della to Cauy, and Ted Baker from the gas station also stopped by. If Cauy hadn't been worrying about Rachel he would've enjoyed the evening. No one pressured him to take a drink, which was cool, and no one said a thing about his father.

Eventually Ry checked his cell and wiped his mouth with his napkin. "I'd better get going. HW's still not back and there are chores to do. You still okay to take me home?"

"Yup." Cauy had studiously pretended not to notice when Dave and Rachel left a few minutes ago, hand in hand and laughing. . . . "Let's go."

They waved good-bye to Nancy and Jay, and went out into the relative quietness of Main Street. There were very few cars on the streets, and the temperature had dropped below freezing. Cauy headed toward his truck, which was parked behind Dr. Tio's practice, Ry at his heels.

Across the parking lot a couple stood next to an old beaten-up Jeep, heads close together, as Cauy's steps slowed. Dave swept Rachel into an extravagant over-the-arm dip and kissed the heck out of her.

Ry chuckled. "He really is an idiot."

"Yeah." Cauy unlocked his truck. "I second that."

Rachel finally got her breath back as Dave set her on her feet, and she clutched at his jacket. "What was that all about?"

"Cauy."

"What do you mean?"

"He came to get his truck." Dave was grinning like a loon. "I just gave him the best visual of us as a couple ever.

If he doesn't declare himself now, Rach, he's not worth the trouble."

She wiped clumsily at her mouth with her gloved fingers. "More likely he'll never talk to me again."

"His problem." Dave fought to open the obstinate passenger door of his Jeep and bowed elaborately to Rachel. "Now, let's get you home, my lady."

Despite the rattling state of his vehicle, Dave was obviously used to navigating the icy roadways up to the local ranches. Rachel had to endure him singing along to his favorite rap artist, but that was a small price to pay for being safe and warm. All she could think about was what Cauy would do . . . which was stupid because he'd probably do nothing.

Which was fine.

"Here we are." Dave came to a stop in the circular driveway of the ranch. "Do you want me to come in and face the Morgans with you?"

Rachel patted his arm. "Would you mind terribly if I just went in by myself? It's been a long day."

"Not a problem." Dave searched her face. "You okay?"

"I'm good, and thanks for a lovely evening."

He kissed her hand. "It was fun. Let's be friends."

"Sounds good to me." Rachel smiled at him.

"Do you want me to get out and kiss the living daylights out of you again?" Dave asked as she shoved her weight against the unhelpful passenger door.

"No, thanks, I'm good."

He pouted. "Rejected. Again."

"If I said I wanted a serious relationship with you, Dave McDonald, you'd run a mile."

"Probably." His smile was crooked. "But if you get sick of that other guy? I'd be more than willing to try round two with you."

The freezing rain had turned to sleet, and even so close

it was difficult to see the white painted exterior of the ranch house through the fog. Rachel wondered what it was like when it really snowed, and guessed that at some point she would find out. Her mother had hated being cold. . . .

Rachel stumbled up the slippery steps onto the porch and went in through the back door. Warmth hit her like a giant hug, and she wanted to purr like a cat. She took off her damp coat and hat, and hung them in the mudroom along with her boots. Chase had installed a brand-new heating system in the old house that kept them all warm as toast.

Hearing voices in the kitchen, Rachel made her way down the hall and came to an abrupt halt in the doorway. Sitting at the kitchen table looking as awkward as hell was Cauy. Ruth sat opposite him and Ry chatting up a storm, and pushing chocolate and cherry cookies at Cauy.

Ruth looked up and beckoned her forward. "Rachel! How did your date go, dear?"

"It was great!" Rachel eyed the coffeepot, wondering if she stood a chance of getting out of there before Ruth let her and decided it wasn't going to happen. "Dave's a really nice guy."

Ruth patted the seat next to hers, which placed Rachel right opposite Cauy. "Come and sit down. I made your favorite cookies."

"I can see that." Rachel added cream to her coffee, and took the seat Ruth pulled out for her. "Thank you."

"Cauy was just telling me that his brother, Jackson, is arriving on the last Monday in November." Ruth beamed at Cauy. "I told him to bring him along for Thanksgiving as well."

Rachel almost choked on her cookie. "They're coming *here*?"

"Yes, just like the old days when my husband was alive," Ruth said. "We did Thanksgiving, and the Lymonds did

Christmas." She glanced around the kitchen. "I'm not sure where we're going to put everyone, but maybe we'll use the guest dining room later in the day?"

"That might work." Rachel determinedly ate a cookie, and tried to ignore Cauy, which was kind of hard when he exuded such grumpy hotness.

"I'd better be going." Cauy finished his coffee and smiled at Ruth. He had a nice smile. It was a shame he so rarely used it. "It's getting late, and I have to go shopping tomorrow to prepare for Jackson's arrival."

"Where are you going to shop?" Ruth asked as she took his mug and plate.

"I'm not sure." Cauy smoothed a hand over his almost beard. He looked bone weary. "Probably one of the bigger towns."

Ruth nudged Rachel. "You could go help him."

"I doubt he needs help, Ruth, especially from me." Rachel tried to laugh it off.

"Actually, I'd love it if you could come along," Cauy spoke directly to Rachel for the first time. "I have no idea what I'm doing."

He stood and nodded to Ruth, and then Rachel. "Let me know, okay?"

He'd gotten as far as the steps of the porch before Rachel caught up with him.

"Hey!"

He turned to look at her through the swirling snow, one eyebrow raised.

Rachel crossed her arms over her chest, suddenly aware of the biting cold and that she hadn't stopped to put her boots back on. "Why did you say that about me coming shopping with you?"

He shrugged. "Because I could do with some help."

"But why *me*?"

"Why not? You know the area and the shops better than I do."

She almost stamped her foot. "But we're not talking to each other."

He looked around the empty yard. "Can't see anyone else I'm talking to right now."

"You know what I mean," Rachel growled at him.

"I don't want to fight with you." He held her gaze. "If I offended you I'm sorry."

Rachel let his words percolate for a long moment as she came slowly down the steps. She could take the olive branch he was offering and move on, or she could ask for a proper explanation, and maybe even a grovel.

"You were *horrible* to me. You kicked me out."

"Yeah?" Cauy took a step toward her until they were almost touching. His warmth seeped into her skin along with a hint of chocolate. "You weren't being so nice yourself."

She poked him in the chest. "You misinterpreted what you saw because you regretted what happened between us, and then used it to blame me."

He looked down at her; his brown eyes steady and his coffee-flavored breath condensing in the cold air. "Okay, maybe I did."

Rachel blinked at him. "You *admit* it?"

The corner of his mouth kicked up into a slight smile. "I might be slow, but I'm not a complete dumbass."

"So, we're *good*?" Rachel croaked.

"Sure."

Her gaze fastened on his mouth, and she leaned slightly toward him only for him to step back and tip his Stetson to her.

"Night, Rachel. Give my best to Dave. See you tomorrow."

She straightened and stomped back up the steps and into the house, slamming the screen door behind her as he drove away. Frustration carried her all the way to the kitchen where she sat down and grabbed another cookie.

"Men," she mumbled through a mouthful of chocolate.

Ruth handed her more coffee. "Any particular one?"

"Cauy Lymond." Rachel chewed vigorously.

"I thought you were going out with Dave now—at least that's what Ry and Cauy were telling me."

"Dave and I are just friends."

"Maybe you should tell Cauy that." Ruth patted Rachel's hand. "He didn't look at all happy when Ry was talking about Dave."

"Then maybe he should man up and ask me out *himself*," Rachel insisted.

"Didn't he just do that?"

"No, he asked me to go shopping with him because he doesn't know the area well, and he thinks I do—which is a mistake—that's not a *date*."

"At least he's trying."

Rachel stared at her grandma. "Why are you sticking up for him? He's totally annoying!"

"He certainly annoys you, which seeing as he hardly says a word is quite a feat." Ruth deftly removed the cookies before Rachel got any ideas about finishing the whole plate. "Maybe you should just tell him that you like him, dear, and take it from there."

"I *don't* like him," Rachel groused. "He's a big meanie."

Now she sounded like she was twelve . . . that's what he had reduced her to without even trying.

"I'm going to bed." Ruth untied her apron and reset the coffee machine. "HW's not back yet with Sam, so leave the lights on in here if you go up in case they need something to eat."

Rachel came around the table to give her grandma a big

hug. She smelled like chocolate and all the good things that made a house a home.

"Good night, Ruth."

"Good night, my love. Don't stay up too late fretting." Ruth patted her cheek. "See Cauy tomorrow and sort everything out between you while you shop."

Rachel didn't actually know that she was going, but she mumbled something that drew a soft laugh from her grandmother.

After washing off her plate and rinsing her mug, Rachel resumed her seat at the table determined to sort out her thoughts. The kitchen door opened, and Billy came in, his face breaking out in a smile when he saw her.

"Hey, stranger."

Rachel immediately felt bad about not spending as much time with him as she'd promised herself.

"Hey."

Billy hung his keys on the rack beside the door and sat down opposite her. "The roads were terrible up from town. The winter weather's closing in."

"So I noticed." Rachel shivered. "Good job the heating in this place works."

"It wasn't so good when your mom lived here. She didn't do well in the cold." His quiet gaze assessed her.

"It doesn't bother me," Rachel said. She took a deep breath. "Are you worried I'll crack and demand to be taken back to Humboldt?"

"Yeah, I suppose I am." His smile was rueful. "Stupid of me, right? You're not much like her at all."

"She certainly was . . . difficult sometimes." It was weird being able to say that out loud after years of having to hold it all in so that she didn't upset her mom.

"Yeah." Billy nodded. "Sometimes she had reason to be."

"It's weird to think that everything that went down that

last evening happened in this kitchen." Rachel couldn't seem to *stop* talking now. "But I get no bad vibes at all."

"That's Ruth. She healed this place for all of us." Billy's gaze swept the quiet, homey kitchen. "It still took me years to find my way back home."

"Do you think you'll stay here now?" Rachel asked impulsively.

"No place I'd rather be, and I've still got a lot of fences to mend," Billy said. "How about you?"

"I'm not sure yet." Rachel fidgeted with her mug. "I'd like to get out there, and see the world a bit before I settle down."

"You should." Billy smiled at her. "Get out there, spread your wings, and know we've got your back."

Now that Paul had sold her family home the thought of having the ranch to come home to *was* very appealing.

"Ruth told me your stepfather's wife is having a baby," Billy said.

"Yes. I *think* I'm okay about it." Rachel paused. "Dad called me all the way from Greece to let me know." Right in the middle of her getting it on with Cauy, but Billy didn't need to know that part. "I think it was a complete surprise for both of them."

"Still weird, though."

Rachel smiled at him. "Yeah."

"I remember when we found out you were a girl. We were so shocked." Billy rubbed a hand over his bearded jaw. "After all those boys I'd convinced myself that you were going to be another one. I think I actually cried when we found out."

"Just before she died, Mom told *me* that she didn't want another baby after the twins." Rachel stared down at her joined hands. "She said I was a mistake, and that when she found out I was a girl she cried too. But not in a good way."

Billy let out a breath. "Pregnancies were hard on her. I offered to get the snip after the twins, but she didn't want that. She did want you, Rachel. When you were born she fell in love with you just like she did with the boys."

The quiet certainty of his tone reached inside her and wrapped itself around her heart.

"Until she tried to drown me."

"She was not herself." Billy reached over and cupped her chin so she had to look at him. "She was ill, and the only person who failed her was *me*. Not you, not the twins or Ruth. I didn't realize what Annie was going through, and I will never forgive myself for that."

"She was a good mother to me." Rachel was not sure whom she was trying to convince. "And after she met Paul things improved a lot."

"I'm glad she met him, and I'm really glad he brought you up to be such an amazing person."

"Really? Don't you hate her for that?"

"I used to, but I realized it was pointless and that sometimes in life you just have to forgive people, move on, and do your best to fix your own crap." He smiled at her, his eyes very blue. "You can't live your life looking backward, Rachel."

She nodded, and he blew her a kiss. "That's my girl. What are you up to this weekend?"

Rachel groaned. "Thanks to Ruth it looks like I'm going shopping with Cauy Lymond."

Chapter Eleven

Cauy opened the door to find Rachel with her hand raised ready to knock.

"I heard your truck coming up the drive." He stepped back. "Come in."

"Are you sure that's a good idea?"

She stuck her hands in the pockets of her fleece-lined jacket and raised her chin. She wore a green knitted cap with a reindeer on it that made her look like a pixie, and he wanted to kiss her real bad.

Cauy shrugged. "If we keep our clothes on, sure. I wanted to show you where I plan to put Jackson so you can tell me what I need to buy."

"Okay." She wiped her feet on his threadbare mat and came in. "If you ask me, the whole place could do with a facelift."

"Yeah." Cauy led her out of the kitchen and along the main hallway that connected all the rooms in the house. He'd shut all the doors so it was definitely gloomy and un-welcoming. "Jackson will be sleeping in here."

He pushed open the door to reveal the chair and bed,

which were all he'd left behind after cleaning out his dad's stuff.

"Wow." Rachel came into the room and turned a small circle. "This is . . . depressing."

"Hasn't been touched since my mom left," Cauy agreed.

Rachel stroked one of the walls that still bore the marks of the tape he and Jackson had used to hang up their rodeo posters.

"It needs painting as well."

"I'm not sure I have time to do that."

Rachel nodded. "Then let's focus on the basics. Bed linen, drapes, a rug, maybe something to put clothes in?" She looked at Cauy, her eyebrows raised, and he wanted to kiss her even more.

"There's a walk-in closet in the corner."

"That helps." Rachel opened it and then recoiled from the towering stack of boxes. "What's in these?"

"I've no idea," Cauy confessed. "Probably Mom's stuff. I'll get Jackson to go through it with me."

"Good idea, especially if he wants to hang any clothes in there." Rachel went out into the hallway and paused beside the open door that led into his bedroom. "You're using a *sleeping bag*?"

"Only when I get cold."

Rachel rolled her eyes. "We'd better get you some decent sheets and blankets as well."

"Okay by me." Cauy hid a smile at the thought of her picking out his sheets.

"But don't get any ideas." Rachel pointed her finger at him. She didn't miss a trick.

"Yes, ma'am." He turned back toward the kitchen. "You ready to go? I need to gas up in town, and then we can be on our way."

* * *

Despite being old, Cauy's truck ran smoothly over the bumpy driveway that led down to the county road. He was also a good driver, and Rachel relaxed back into her seat.

"I meant to ask you about the dog," Cauy said, his attention on the roadway as he took the turn toward town. "Jenna wants to know what you want to do with her."

Rachel sighed. "I'd like to keep her, but I'm not sure how Ruth would feel about me bringing a pregnant dog to the ranch and leaving after the holidays."

"Ranchers always need dogs."

"Yeah, but puppies take a lot of looking after, and Ruth's got enough to do." Rachel looked out the window at the frost-covered pasture and fences. "Jenna said the humane society would be glad to have her, but—"

"I'll take her."

Rachel snapped her gaze back to Cauy's profile. "What?"

"I'll take her. I miss having a dog." He glanced over at her. "If that's okay with you?"

"That would be . . . *great*!" Rachel struggled for words, which wasn't like her at all. "That's *really* kind of you."

"My ex didn't like dogs so we had cats. Not the same thing at all."

"Your ex-wife?" Rachel asked.

He gave her a "who else" look, but she already knew she was fishing.

"Lorelei. She stayed in Texas and married a good friend of mine."

"Ouch." Rachel winced.

"Nah. They deserved each other. No hard feelings except she took half my money."

Rachel digested that information. "That's the price you pay for choosing the wrong person."

"People change. Stuff happens."

"Like what?" Rachel asked. It took a while for him to answer her.

"We eventually worked out we didn't want the same things anymore."

"You don't exactly sound cut up about it."

Cauy turned onto Main Street and slowed his speed as they went past the shops. "Would you want me to be?"

"Not really," Rachel said. "There's nothing worse than going out with a guy who sits there all night talking about his ex, and you just *know* he still hasn't moved on."

"As far as I know Dave's never been married so you're good to go."

Rachel gave him her sweetest smile. "Thanks for reminding me."

Cauy pulled into the small gas station and cut the engine. "I'll just be a minute."

Rachel got out with him. "I'm going to get some gum, do you want anything?"

"A bottle of water would be good."

"Okay, got it." Rachel went inside the tiny shop and spent a couple of minutes chatting to Ted Baker, who was a really nice guy.

As she came out with her purchases, a big old farm truck and rusty trailer pulled into the gas station with a shrieking noise that made her wince and backfired. Cauy reacted like he'd been shot, throwing his body backward and colliding with the pump, one arm thrown over his face.

Rachel ran over and touched him. "Are you okay?"

He slowly lowered his arm and stared at her like he'd never seen her before, his pupils wide and full of lingering horror.

"Cauy?"

He took two or three deep breaths and looked carefully around the gas station before his shoulders relaxed, and he unhooked the gas pump from his truck. Rachel stared at him uncertainly as the corrosive oily stench coming from the farm truck burned her throat and eyes.

Cauy walked past her to pay the bill and she got in the truck. Should she say something? Should she wait for him to explain why he'd reacted so violently? Rachel had the sinking sensation that even if she dared ask Cauy he wouldn't explain. And why should he? They weren't a couple or anything, so she had no right to question him.

She slowly put on her seat belt and set the bottle of water where Cauy would see it. He got in the truck, fired up the engine, and pulled off the forecourt.

"Are you okay?" Rachel had to at least make the attempt.

"Thanks for the water."

She wasn't surprised he hadn't responded to her concern. "You're welcome."

As he settled into driving she sensed it was the last thing he was going to say for a very long time.

Rachel waved as Cauy dropped her off in front of the house and disappeared off into the gathering darkness. They'd shopped up a storm, but he'd barely opened his mouth after they'd left the gas station. It had been a frustrating day. Rachel kicked the door and marched into the hallway just as Billy came down the stairs.

"Bad day?" he asked.

"You could say that." She took off her boots and coat, and followed him into the kitchen. "I went shopping with Cauy."

"You said you were going to." Billy handed her a large mug of coffee. "What went wrong?"

"He hardly spoke all day." Rachel groaned. "And I tried my hardest to get him talking. I even deliberately needled him, but he wouldn't take the bait." She fluffed up her hat-flattened hair. "I spent his money like water, and he didn't seem to care one bit."

"Sounds like a great day out to me." Billy winked at her.

"But why did he ask me if he was going to be like that?" Rachel sipped her coffee. "I even offered to go over there tomorrow and help him fix the place up, and he just said he'd let me know."

"Do you *want* to go over there?"

"Yes," Rachel said. "I'm trying to be mature about all this and not run away every time he goes quiet on me."

"Why?"

"I suppose you're going to tell me that I'm too much of a people pleaser and that I should stop it." Rachel drank more coffee, enjoying the warmth spreading through her system. "I can't help wanting people to be happy and get along."

"Are you?" Billy looked interested. "I was thinking more specifically about Cauy."

"Oh." She contemplated her half-filled mug. "I felt . . . worried about him."

"Because he wasn't talking?"

"No, because when we were getting gas this morning he lost it when an old truck and trailer backfired and almost threw himself to the ground. After that he clammed up on me and barely spoke at all." She sighed. "I tried to ask him about it but he didn't want to share."

Billy frowned. "He was in some kind of accident in Texas."

"And seeing as he worked in the oil fields it might have involved gas," Rachel finished his thought.

"Yeah." Billy pondered for a long moment. "The thing is, Rachel, you've got to let him tell you about that when he's ready."

"I *know* that. I just wish . . ." Her voice trailed away.

"That he'd gone ahead and told you," Billy said gently.

Rachel just nodded. There was nothing else to say.

"Maybe if he asks you to help out tomorrow he'll have something to share with you."

Rachel found a smile. "You never know, he might. But I wouldn't bet the ranch on it."

Cauy took out his cell and stared at the screen. Should he call her? Didn't she deserve some kind of explanation for him behaving like a first-class jerk the day before? But she'd seen him behave like a coward . . . how could he talk his way out of *that*?

His phone rang, startling him, and he accessed the call without checking who it was.

"Hi."

"Hey. It's Chase Morgan. Can you meet us up at the old mine this morning? We've got some new monitoring equipment to try out, and some of it will need to go on your land."

Cauy gripped the phone hard. "Sure. What time?"

"About an hour? I've got some work to finish up, and Rachel's busy downloading some specific software we need."

"Okay, I'll see you there."

Cauy ended the call and stared out over the frozen pasture. Soon he wouldn't be able to put the horses out to graze anymore and he'd need to purchase food, hay, and all the other necessities to keep them in the barn over a long, hard winter. In a few days the Morgan horses would also be arriving, and the place would be swarming with life and strangers again.

Things were changing whether he liked it or not. He either had to go with it, or go where? He'd lost his taste for adventure along with his Texas experience and wanted to stay on the ranch his family had owned for generations. He could almost see Mark's ghost hovering over him waiting for him to mess up.

Cauy zipped up his jacket and walked back to the house. He now had an excuse to see Rachel, on neutral territory, and maybe he'd find the courage to move things along with her as well.

"You got everything you need?" Chase called out to Rachel as she took another bag of equipment out of the flatbed of his huge blue Ford truck.

"Yup." She repressed a shiver. Up here on the lower slopes of the Sierras where the mine was situated the ground was starting to freeze hard. "I hope we can get the probes through the ice."

"Shouldn't be too difficult." Chase came up beside her, his face half-hidden between the sheepskin collar of his coat and his hat.

"Like you'd know," Ry murmured. "Chase is all theory and no action."

"Hey, I pay for everything so I do have some uses." Chase grinned. "Billy's coming up in half an hour to help after I get back."

"Great." Rachel looked at her two brothers. "Where's the map of the mine?"

Chase produced something from his pocket and unfolded it. "Here are the three versions we have all superimposed over each other so you can get a basic idea of where you might need to look. I've also loaded the same map onto your phone with basic geological information."

"That's really useful." Rachel took the map and held it tightly against the wind that was cutting across the barren plain. "I've already sketched out a basic plan for where I want to put the probes, and I've programmed them remotely to report back to Chase's laptop."

As she studied the map a truck pulled up on the opposite side of the fence line and Cauy got out. Rachel's heart gave a little anxious jump from just seeing him, which didn't bode well for her ability to get a coherent sentence out when he actually got close.

"Hey!" Ry waved at Cauy. "Thanks for coming."

Cauy didn't say anything as he joined the group, but Rachel felt his gaze on her.

"Damn." Chase checked his phone and started moving. "I got the time wrong. I've got to go on a conference call in ten minutes. You guys okay without me?"

"Well, yeah, although you're supposed to be giving me a ride back," Ry objected.

Chase half turned. "You can come with me now, or wait for Billy."

"I'll wait." Ry winked. "I've gotta let Rachel see that at least one of her brothers knows how to get his hands dirty."

Rachel wanted to kiss him for staying, but concentrated on the map.

"So what's the plan?" Cauy asked.

Still looking down, Rachel answered him. "I've got to set four ground-penetrating radar units up." She shoved the map at him. "I've marked the spots, and I also have them on my phone's GPS."

"Okay." Cauy studied the map, raising his gaze to assess his surroundings. "How far underground can these probes detect structures?"

"They wouldn't work too well on the surface. We need to drill some boreholes first and get them underground."

Ry grimaced and looked around the bleak landscape. "I hope we can break through."

"What size borehole are we talking about here?" Cauy asked.

Rachel showed him one of the GPR units. "Not much wider than this. The idea is to hopefully break through into the tunneling network and let the unit give us a 3D visual of exactly what's going on down there."

"Got it. Do you have drilling gear?"

"Yup." Ry gestured at the pile of equipment they'd unloaded from Chase's truck. He grinned. "I was waiting for my dad to tell me how to make it work."

"I know how to set up a drill rig," Cauy said.

Rachel grabbed his arm. "You don't have to do that, if you don't want to—I mean we just asked you to come up here because two of the boreholes are going to be on your land, and—"

She ran out of breath as both men looked at her as if she was crazy.

"I'm good, thanks." Cauy gently removed her hand from his elbow. "Why don't we start by marking out where those boreholes are going to be?"

By the time Billy arrived, they'd marked two of the potential drill sites with bright orange markers and were pacing out the third. It was bitterly cold and the sky and land blended into each other making everything gray and indistinct.

As the two men consulted about the drilling process, Rachel measured out the distance to the next marker going past Cauy's truck and onto Lymond land. She gave the sinkhole a wide berth and focused on the GPS on her cell phone. A strange thrumming sound traveled up through the soles of her boots, and she went still. Was there another earthquake happening? She looked back toward the others, who didn't seem to be feeling what she was feeling. A faint whooping sound rose over the horizon, and she turned toward Morgan Ranch as three or four horses ignored the warning tape and came thundering up the hill toward the mine.

Billy, Ry, and Cauy were moving toward the incoming riders trying to get their attention before they came too close to the fragile mine.

"Hey!" Billy shouted. "Where do you guys think you're going? You're supposed to be moving cattle!"

One of the riders slowed down and came to a stop beside Billy.

"Calm down, dude. We're just having some fun."

Rachel pointed at the fluttering orange tape. "This land isn't safe, and you shouldn't be up here unsupervised."

"Why not?" A second rider joined the first and looked down at Rachel. "We paid to come here, sweet cheeks, so we get to do what we like."

Behind her Cauy made a growling noise and stepped forward. Rachel grabbed hold of his jacket sleeve.

"Not on my ranch, you don't." Billy gripped the bridle of the first horse, and Ry took the second. "Either turn around and go back the way you came, or I'll take the horses, and you can walk."

"Like you could do that," the first guy joked. "Calm down. We just wanted to check out the mine."

"Which is dangerous, and is why you haven't been given access to it," Ry spoke up. He pointed at the huge sinkhole. "See that? You could've ridden right into it, and no one would've been able to stop you."

"Like my horse would do that," Idiot Number One jeered.

"Hey, you're right. The horse is intelligent enough to stop," Ry said. "The *problem* is you would've gone straight over his head and kept going down."

Idiot Number Three laughed and wheeled his horse around. "That would be cool to see, dude. Shall I try it?"

Billy whistled to the horse, which immediately stopped, turned on a dime, and came back to him.

"Whoa! Not cool, dude! Not cool at all!" Idiot Three bleated as he struggled to gather his reins and not lose his seat.

Rachel hid a smile as Billy petted the horse and stared levelly at the guy. "Try it again, and I'll get him to turn so fast you'll fall off on your ass."

"Jeez," Ry muttered, and looked at Billy. "How about we escort these gentlemen back down to the barn?"

He faced the four guys. "I'll give you a choice. Either ride down the slope to the house or get in the truck and let us take the horses."

"We'll ride." Idiot One looked like a thwarted toddler. "Thanks for nothing."

"You're welcome." Ry said, nodding, and then stalked over to Billy's truck. Rachel had never seen him so mad.

Billy hesitated, his keys in his hands, and looked between Cauy and Rachel. "You two going to be okay? I'll come back when I'm done with these fools."

Cauy nodded. "We're good."

Rachel blew out a breath as the truck moved away following the horses and riders. "That wasn't how I expected my morning to go at all."

"Bunch of jackasses." Cauy started walking toward his land. "Billy and I have figured out how to drill down. Let's get the rest of the markers in so that when he comes back we're ready to go."

"Okay." Rachel took out her phone again and studied the screen. Her heart was still racing after the confrontation, and the higher altitude was making it harder to breathe.

"You all right?" Cauy asked.

"I'm fine." She found the drilling spot and crouched down to place a flag there. "Just one more to do."

"Do you want to come and fetch the dog with me later?"

"Me?" Rachel's head shot up, and she almost overbalanced.

"Yeah. I thought you could help me settle her in."

Rachel got slowly to her feet. "I don't get you at all."

He raised an eyebrow.

"Yesterday you sulked for the entire day, and now—"

"I didn't *sulk.*"

"What would you call it then? Manly silence?" Rachel asked. "Because it sure looked like sulking to me."

"I didn't know what to say to you."

She blinked at him. "About *what*?"

"About me acting like a complete wuss in the gas station."

"I didn't see you acting like that. I saw someone *reacting* to what they perceived as a threat."

He opened his mouth as if to say something and then closed it. Rachel's faint hope died. Expecting people to share what was going on in their lives had never worked with her mother and obviously wouldn't work with Cauy, either. She was just supposed to quit asking questions, smile, and move on.

She looked blankly down at her phone. "Last marker to locate. How about we go find it?"

Cauy didn't move. "I hate how I overreact to shit."

She still couldn't look at him. "It's about fifteen meters that way."

"Rachel, I *hate* it." He shook his head. "I feel like a little kid cowering in the dark, and I freaking *loathe* it."

"Have you talked about it with anyone?" Rachel asked. "Have you—"

He cut her off. "I've talked about it until I'm sick of talking! I know *why* I do it, but that doesn't mean I like doing it."

"Okay." She looked past him. "Then let's not talk about it anymore."

Cauy watched her walk away from him, a ball of frustration growing in his chest. What the hell did she want him to say? Go all Oprah on her in the middle of this wasteland? And then what? What good would it do to rehash the worst moment of his life? Last time he'd tried sharing he'd ended up dumped and divorced while his ex cried on his best friend's shoulder about how frightened she was of him.

But he'd hurt Rachel. He'd seen it in her eyes, and that was even worse. . . .

He went after her, but she acted as if he wasn't there. Her gaze firmly fixed on the terrain as she counted down the distance. By the time she stopped they were out in the middle of nowhere upslope, and he couldn't see the mine workings.

"Here should do." Rachel stuck a flag in the tufted grass and straightened up. "Ruth gave me some coffee. Would you like some while we wait for Billy?"

"That would be great," Cauy said cautiously, and trekked back with her to the mine entrance where all the gear was piled up.

Rachel busied herself finding the right bag and produced hot coffee and cookies that she set on top of one of the piles of boxes.

"Here you go."

"Thanks."

He watched her closely. She was perfectly composed and smiling, but he'd learned enough to know that was just a front. He wanted to take her in his arms and kiss her until she melted against him and forgave him everything. But he knew in his soul that at some point he'd hurt her again, and he wasn't the kind of man who played with people's emotions.

He cleared his throat. "I feel like I always owe you some kind of apology."

"For being yourself?" She shrugged and sipped her coffee. "That's not really on you, is it? You don't owe me anything."

"I'm not good at sharing how I feel."

"I got that." She bit into her cookie and slowly chewed. "That's a good cookie. I'll have to ask Ruth to give me the recipe."

He tried again. "I've never felt that rehashing things and endlessly going over them makes anything better."

"I can understand that. I come from a family where all the secrets are finally coming to light, and it's totally shaken my worldview."

"How so?" Cauy asked.

"Finding out I had a living father and four brothers after thinking I was an only child for about twenty years was pretty mind-blowing. Realizing that my mother lied to me her whole life made me doubt who I was."

"That's tough." Cauy's curiosity overcame him. "Did you really have no idea?"

"Nope. My stepdad only told me that the Morgans were trying to find me when he ran out of reasons to keep me in the dark. My mother mentioned some stuff when she was dying, but I didn't really understand what she was talking about. After she died, my stepdad . . ." She paused. "Was obviously wanting to move on with his life. Giving me the Morgans probably made him feel a lot less guilty for finding a new woman to love."

Cauy instinctively reached for her, but she stepped out of his grasp. "It's okay. I didn't tell you that to make you feel sorry for me."

"I didn't think you did."

"Then we're good." She finished her coffee, all business again. "Billy should be back soon. Is there anything I can do to help you set up the drill rig before he gets here?"

Chapter Twelve

Rachel lay down on her bed and stared up at the ceiling. It had been an emotionally and physically tiring day. She was proud that she'd set up the GPR system and helped her family. For the first time she'd felt like she'd added some value rather than just endlessly taking. Watching the drilling and installing the equipment had kept her hands and mind busy.

But now it was almost time for dinner, and she'd showered and warmed up, and all she could think about was Cauy Lymond telling her to keep her nose out of his business. Maybe he really was emotionally unavailable. Or maybe he just didn't want to let *her* in.

Why did she constantly go after guys who weren't really into her? Did she really believe she could solve everyone's problems and make them love her? She'd have to ask Jenna about that.

Her cell phone buzzed, and with a groan she reached over to pick it up from the nightstand.

I'm planning on getting the dog. Let me know if you want to come and I'll pick you up.

Rachel stared at the message for at least five minutes. It would be far better for her sanity if she didn't respond, but she did feel some responsibility for the dog.

"Argh!" She rolled onto her back and put her hands over her face. "Life sucks!" She reluctantly texted back.

I'm just about to have dinner. Either come and join us (Ruth will love it), or pick me up in an hour.

Thanks, I'll be there in 10.

Cauy might send her all kinds of mixed signals, but his love of Ruth's cooking was a given. Rachel got up, groaning as her muscles protested, and made her way downstairs.

"Ruth, are you okay if Cauy joins us?" she asked her grandma, who was working with Billy to get the meal out on the table. "Because I kind of already invited him."

"That will be lovely. The more the merrier." Ruth beamed at her. "Billy said he was very helpful and knowledgeable today."

"Yes, he was," Rachel said. "Thanks for letting Cauy come. We have to go and pick up the dog from Jenna."

"The one you found at the feed store?" Ruth asked as she handed Rachel the silverware to put on the table.

"Yup. She's female and pregnant."

"Oh my." Ruth shook her head. "Where are you going to keep her, in your room, or in the barn?"

"I'm not keeping her. Cauy said he'd take her."

Both Billy and Ruth stopped what they were doing and stared at Rachel.

"That was nice of him, dear," Ruth said slowly. "But you're welcome to bring her here if you want."

"But I'll be gone a lot, and it didn't seem fair to load all that responsibility on you," Rachel pointed out.

"So you loaded it on Cauy instead." Billy grinned. "He's obviously quite taken with you if he agreed to that."

"Taken with whom?" BB walked into the kitchen and stole a roll from the table.

"Cauy Lymond with Rachel," Ruth said as she swatted BB with the tea towel.

"Seeing as she obviously likes kissing him I can't say I'm surprised." BB blew his grandma a kiss. "What's he done?"

"Agreed to take on that dog Rachel found."

"Oh yeah? Jenna was telling me about that. She said I should admit Cauy wasn't a bad guy seeing as he'd insisted on paying the whole bill." BB took his seat and sniffed appreciatively. "I'm going to miss your cooking when I move out, Ruth."

"You're only going to be a quarter of a mile down the road so you can come back anytime," Ruth said. "And when *are* you going to move out? Jenna says the house is ready."

"Trying to get rid of me?" BB winked at Ruth and lowered his voice. "I'm planning something around Christmas for Jenna, but don't tell her. If I succeed I'll be moving out before Maria goes back to school in the New Year."

"And if you don't?"

"I will. There isn't another option on the table." BB's smile was so confident Rachel had to admire him. "Maria agrees with me. Now all we have to do is convince Jenna and make me the happiest guy in the universe."

Rachel helped Billy place the roast beef, mashed potatoes, beans, and gravy on the table and took her place. True to his word, Cauy arrived on time along with a gaggle of Morgans and was seated across the table in January's seat. As usual, the conversation was loud, brisk, and a mixture of ranch business and personal stuff that sometimes had Rachel looking fourteen different ways at once. She still wasn't used to being part of a big noisy family.

Cauy ate his way steadily through two plates of food and answered every question thrown at him politely and succinctly. No one would ever accuse him of being chatty, but he wasn't rude. Even BB relaxed and stopped treating him like a threat. Rachel reminded herself that she'd only be at the ranch for another month or so before she got a new job, but she liked Cauy's smile, the way he used his hands, and the quiet, steadfast strength that emanated from him.

"Rachel?"

She blinked as he addressed her directly for the first time. "What?"

"I told Jenna we'd be there by seven. She said that was fine as she's finishing up some paperwork."

"Okay."

"Then you'd better eat your dessert fast and get a wiggle on." Ruth placed a huge apple crisp and a jug of cream in the center of the table. "I'll pack you up some food for Jenna as it looks as if she'll be missing her dinner."

Rachel got into Cauy's truck and put on her seat belt, placing the box of food Ruth had prepared for Jenna firmly between her booted feet.

Cauy didn't speak as he drove down to the vet's and turned into the empty parking lot. There were lights on in the main house so they headed in there.

Jenna was sitting in the back office, head down, writing when Rachel knocked and went in.

"Hey! You made it!" She came around to hug Rachel and eyed the box. "Don't tell me that's my dinner? Ruth is the best person ever!"

"Yes, it's all for you." Rachel grinned as she handed the box over. "It started off as a snack, and ended up as a three-course meal with extra sides so I hope you're hungry."

"Always." Jenna inhaled the scent of beef. "I've been out on call all day, and I barely had a chance to eat a thing." She turned to greet Cauy. "Hey. How are you?"

"I'm good, thanks." Cauy tipped his hat to Jenna.

"Let me go and fetch the dog." Jenna put on her white coat. "I've typed up a whole load of instructions for her, Rach, but if you have any worries or issues, just call me, okay?"

"Cauy's taking the dog to his house," Rachel said.

"Oh! Okay! That's awesome." Jenna smiled at Cauy. "Same instructions to you. Call me anytime."

Rachel followed Jenna out into the lean-to and closed the door firmly behind her.

"Jenna, have you got a sec?"

"Yes, what's up?" Jenna paused beside one of the big cages on the floor.

"It's Cauy. Do you think I should try and make him talk to me more?" Rachel asked.

"*Make* him?" Jenna snorted. "He's a man. Good luck with that."

"Then should I even *try* and ask him if he's interested in me or not?"

"You're not *sure*? From what I've seen and what you told me I would *definitely* say he's interested." Jenna checked the clipboard hanging on the front of the cage and detached a whole pile of papers. "The thing is, what are you trying to achieve here?"

"I just want to know where I stand."

"Fair enough." Jenna studied her. "And what if he books it?"

"Then at least I'd know, and I'd stop hoping. I think that's the worst feeling in the word, not knowing."

"Okay, so what are you looking for? Love, sex, marriage, all three?"

"I haven't thought of it like that." Rachel frowned.

"Then maybe you should," Jenna said. "Go in with a clear expectation of what you want and take it from there."

"If I have the nerve to actually do it," Rachel said gloomily.

"What have you got to lose?" Jenna sounded way too cheerful for Rachel's liking.

"Visiting rights to the dog?"

"At least you'll know," Jenna said.

"True." Rachel nodded. "I'll play it by ear."

"And remember, honesty is the best policy." Jenna unlocked the cage and the dog sat up expectantly. "Come on, my beauty. Time to go to your forever home."

The dog sat on Rachel's lap as Cauy drove them back to his house, her ears half-cocked, and her big wet nose snuffling everything in sight. It was good he wasn't a car nut because his window was now covered in dog drool. Rachel didn't seem to mind the occasional lick that was lavished on her either.

She'd fallen silent after they'd left Jenna's and had remained so, which was slightly unnerving. Maybe she'd given up trying to talk to him. He certainly deserved it. They arrived at the house and he killed the engine.

"You can bring her into the kitchen."

"Okay."

He opened the passenger door for her and then flicked on the lights in the mudroom and kitchen so Rachel could see where she was going. She kicked off her boots, came past him, and stopped dead.

"Wow, did you get the dog bed and crate for her already?"

"Yeah, well, I didn't want her coming home to a hard floor." He shut the door. "The crate was already here so I just cleaned it up, but the rest of the stuff I got in town the other day."

Rachel put the dog down in the cozy bed and stroked her head. "Look, you've got your own water and food bowls, your own blankie and toys!" She turned to smile at Cauy. "You've forgotten one thing, though."

He pointed at a cupboard by the sink. "I have food,

bones, and meds in there, and her leash is hanging in the mudroom."

"Not *those* things." She rolled her eyes. "Something way more fundamental."

"Like what?"

"What are you going to call her?"

"I'm not good with names." Cauy took off his coat, hung it over the back of the chair, and did the same with Rachel's. "I still call my horses Horse One and Horse Two."

"You can't call her *Dog*," Rachel objected. "Ry's already taken that one, and I'd get confused."

"Maybe you should pick something," Cauy suggested.

"She's your dog," Rachel said.

"But you found her." He smiled at her. She looked freaking adorable sitting there cuddling the dog, her blond hair shining in the light. "Help me out, here, please."

Rachel turned her attention to the dog and studied her intensely. "How about Hope or Grace—seeing as we found her and gave her a new life of opportunities?"

Cauy came over, crouched in front of the dog, and patted her head. "I like Grace."

And he sure needed some in his life . . . and had already been given more than he deserved.

Up close, Rachel's eyes were very blue and way too easy to just fall into. . . . Cauy recoiled as the dog jumped up and licked his jaw, sending Rachel down on her remarkably fine ass.

"Ouch!" She grabbed the dog again and laughed. "Just trample all over me to get to him, Grace, why don't you?"

"Fine by me," Cauy said. "I don't usually cause a stampede."

"Can I ask you something?"

Cauy nodded.

"Do you like me?"

"Yeah, of *course* I do." He gestured over at the chair. "Lady, I had you half-naked about a week ago."

"That was different. That was just sex." Rachel's cheeks heated, and she flapped a hand in front of her face.

He sat on the floor keeping the dog between them, his hand buried in her fur. "As in do I want to have a relationship with you?"

"Exactly."

He sighed. "Do you want the long answer or the short version?"

"Whatever works for you."

Cauy tried to gather his thoughts. "I didn't come back here to start a new relationship. I came to save the ranch, and this place sure needs a lot of help."

"So you're saying you don't have time for a relationship?"

"I suppose I am, and"—he hesitated—"I'm not great boyfriend material."

"Why do you say that? You're kind, and I find you very attractive or else I wouldn't be sitting here right now making a fool out of myself."

"You're no fool. I'm the one who screwed up a marriage." Cauy paused. "I suppose you could say I'm still gun-shy."

"Okay, so this isn't a good time for you. I get that." She fidgeted with the dog's collar. "It's not great for me, either. I need to get a job, and I'll only be here for another month."

Cauy chose his words with care. "Maybe we should admit the timing sucks and stay friends?"

"Maybe we should."

She held his gaze as he leaned in like an idiot; his gaze fixed on her lips, and he kissed her. She opened her mouth to him, and he delved inside, his tongue tangling with hers, and it was spectacular like the Fourth of July fireworks. She was the first to pull back.

"That was your *good-bye* kiss?"

Cauy shrugged. "I like kissing you."

"But you don't want a relationship right now, and neither do I." Rachel patted the dog as if her life depended on it, aware that her and Cauy's fingers sometimes met and intertwined in the dog's fur. She was reluctant to mention it in case he pulled his hand away.

"Exactly."

"Okay, we stay friends, you save the ranch, and I'll go off and find a new job." Rachel paused. "Then maybe one day when we're both older and wiser we'll get around to dating."

His fingers stilled in Grace's fur right over hers, and his thumb caressed her palm sending shivers of pure lust up and down her spine.

"Yeah, that's a great idea."

She waited. He didn't say any more, but his hand remained firmly in hers until she reluctantly eased her fingers free. She could do this. She was a mature, confident woman with thousands of choices ahead of her. If she and Cauy could realize it wasn't a good time to have a relationship why couldn't other people? It would save a lot of heartache if people were honest with each other.

She scrambled to her feet and went to wash her hands. "Do you want to show me how Jackson's room looks now?"

Cauy remained sitting on the floor with the dog. "You're quick to tell me when I'm avoiding a subject, but you're pretty good at it yourself, Rachel."

She turned to look at him. "I'm not avoiding anything. I told you how I see things, and so far you haven't disagreed, so I assumed we were moving on."

"You think it's that simple? That we can just turn off 'that'"—he brushed his mouth with his fingers—"and be friends?"

"You don't think you can handle it?" Rachel crossed her arms over her chest and hoped he didn't notice her very perky nipples. "Wow, and you're older than me, and much more experienced."

"Meaning I've learned that wanting someone like this"—he slowly let out a breath—"doesn't happen very often."

She was torn between delight at his admission and fear about what he was going to say next.

He looked her right in the eye. "It scares the crap out of me."

"Oh," Rachel said faintly. "Good. I think."

"All I know is that I want you, and for many reasons I can't have you." He moved the now sleeping dog off his lap and placed her in her crate with the door open before slowly standing to face Rachel.

She shrank back against the sink, but he kept his distance.

"It's okay. I'm a grown man, not a stupid teenage boy who doesn't keep his promises."

"I already knew that." Rachel sighed. At least she had her answer. "It's sad though, isn't it? That we can't get it together."

"Yeah." He shoved a hand through his hair. She couldn't help but notice he was as aroused as she was. "Now, do you want to see what I've done in Jackson's room or not?"

Chapter Thirteen

"Welcome home, Bro." Cauy clapped his brother on the back.

"Wow, what *happened*?" Jackson turned a slow circle taking in the ranch house and dilapidated outbuildings before bringing his attention back to Cauy.

"Dad didn't take care of the place after Mom left with you guys."

"I *knew* that." Jackson frowned. "But the last time I came out here things weren't this bad. Even then all Dad did was complain about the price of everything, and talk shit about the Morgans."

Jackson hoisted his kit bag on his shoulder and followed Cauy into the house. "At least it's warm in here." He dropped the bag in the mudroom along with his boots and came through into the kitchen. "Not much has changed."

His keen gaze swept the kitchen and alighted on the dog crate and its occupant.

"Who's this?"

Cauy went over to open the crate. "This is Grace. A friend of mine rescued her, and I agreed to take her on." He shrugged as Jackson made a fuss of the dog. "A ranch needs dogs."

"This ranch needs every bit of help it can get," Jackson said, ruffling Grace's fur. "How many cattle was Dad running?"

Cauy handed his brother a mug of coffee. "None."

"What the hell?" Jackson shook his head. He looked nothing like Cauy, being tall, dark and broad-shouldered. Serving in the Air Force had added confidence and strength to his sunny demeanor. "How about the horses?"

"I found two strays and brought them in." Cauy sat at the table. "I checked the farm office for the accounts. In the last year he sold off everything that wasn't nailed down."

Jackson took a swig of coffee. "Then what did he do with the money?"

"I have no idea. For some reason he named me as his executor. I can tell you straight out that when I checked he didn't have more than a hundred bucks in his bank account."

"Maybe he had another account somewhere?"

"If he did, I haven't found any evidence of it yet," Cauy said. "Basically, he left me the land and not much else." He paused. "I don't know why he left it to me when you were his favorite son."

"Jeez, I don't want it." Jackson held up his palm as if to ward Cauy off. "I'm happy to come back here and work as a rancher for a while, but I don't want this dung heap—pardon my French."

"You sure?" Cauy held his brother's gaze. "Because if you think it should be yours—"

"Nope." Jackson grinned at him. "It's all your problem."

"Damn, I thought you might say that." Cauy smiled back at his brother. Jackson was one of the most definite people he'd ever met and years in the military had only intensified his straightforward no-shit personality.

"I'll help out, I promise. I'd like to learn how to run a place like this so I can eventually buy my own." Jackson finished his coffee, and Cauy offered him more. "I'm not intending to re-up with the service. I've done my time."

"Ten years is enough," Cauy agreed. Like Blue Morgan, Jackson had joined up right out of school, and was roughly the same age as the Morgan twins. He was somewhat surprised his brother hadn't decided to become a career soldier but he wasn't going to ask questions. "You're more than welcome to stay here and help me put this place to rights."

"You're planning on staying? Mom seemed to think you might sell it off to the Morgans." Jackson shuddered. "Which Dad would've hated."

"I wouldn't sell to the Morgans." Cauy hesitated. "I kind of made that promise to Dad. I saw him just before he died."

"You *saw* him?" Jackson's mouth fell open. "Jeez, you two hardly spoke after you left home. Dad wouldn't even let Mom mention your name around here for years."

"Yeah, he got hold of Mom and said he wanted to speak to me." Cauy fidgeted with his coffee mug. "I didn't want to go, but after the accident and coming so close to death myself, I thought maybe I owed him something."

"And you promised not to sell the ranch to the *evil* Morgans."

"That was basically all he wanted to see me for." Cauy considered his brother carefully. "*I* was hoping he might tell me who my real father was."

Jackson just looked at him, and Cauy raised an eyebrow. "You knew?"

"I . . . wondered," Jackson said, grimacing. "He was so goddamn mean to you all the time, and for no reason at all."

"And if it's true, are you still sure that you don't want the ranch?" Cauy asked slowly. "If you are his only son . . ."

"No. It's yours."

"If I can make it profitable again, you, Amy, and Mom will get a percentage of the take."

"Awesome. You do the work and I'll sit around and be one of those trust fund babies you read about."

"Not sure how many of those there are in ranching, but you're welcome to try." Cauy heaved himself to his feet. "Let's get your stuff into your room."

Jackson looked up at him, his blue gaze searching. "How are *you* doing?"

"I'm good."

"You look a lot healthier than you did a year ago. I can hardly see any of the scarring on your face or neck."

Instinctively, Cauy reached up his hand to cover the damage. "Thanks."

Jackson stood and stretched. "My back is killing me. I hate flying."

"You were in the freaking Air Force!" Cauy held the door open for his brother, gladder of the company than he was willing to admit.

"Bro," Jackson said, winking. "That's exactly why I hate other people flying me."

A couple of hours later Cauy's cell buzzed, and he checked the text before going to knock on Jackson's bedroom door.

"Hey, do you want to earn your keep?"

Jackson opened the door. "What's up?" He'd changed into jeans and a plaid shirt and already looked like he belonged.

"Roy's coming over with the horses. I'll need some help getting them in their stalls."

"Roy who?"

Cauy paused to think. "I don't know his last name, but he's the foreman at Morgan Ranch."

"Oh, that Roy." Jackson whistled. "He's still alive? He must be about ninety." Jackson pulled on his boots and produced an Air Force baseball cap to put on his head. "Hang on. Why's he bringing Morgan horses *here*?"

"I agreed to rent them some space over the winter while their new barn is being built."

"That was . . . neighborly of you. Dad—"

"Dad would've let their horses die in the snow, yeah, I know, but I need the money," Cauy said. "Their hands are going to stick around and help me reconstruct the rest of the outbuildings."

"Got it." Jackson shivered as they left the warmth of the house and crossed over to the barn. "God, I'd forgotten how cold it gets up here in the winter."

"This is only the start of it." Cauy put on his gloves.

The roar of a big vehicle climbing the drive up from the county road caught his attention and he hurried into the barn. He flicked on the lights and paused to pat his two horses he hadn't turned out because of the upcoming turmoil.

"How many are you expecting?" Jackson asked, his chin buried deep in the folds of his fleece, muffling his voice.

Cauy eyed the remaining stalls. "This many."

"About a dozen, then." Jackson peered out of the barn into the fog. "There are two trucks with trailers coming in so that would be about right."

"From what I've seen the Morgan horses are all well trained. I'm not expecting any problems."

"Good, because I haven't got my cowboy on for about ten years," Jackson said. "And I don't want to look like a complete ass."

Cauy walked out to greet Roy, who was hopping down from his gigantic truck like a sprightly elf.

"Morning, Cauy." Roy nodded at him and then turned to Jackson. "You must be Jackson."

Jackson nodded. "That's me."

"Yup, I remember you. You look like your father." Roy

looked Jackson up and down and returned the handshake. "You've grown a bit."

Jackson grinned. "I should hope so seeing as I was only eighteen last time we met."

"You were in the same school year as the twins."

"Yeah, how are they doing? I see HW became quite the rodeo star."

"He's back home now. They all are. With the ranch changing and growing we've needed all hands on deck."

"Cauy was telling me about the dude ranch side. How's that going?" Jackson inquired as they walked toward the first trailer, where two guys were already letting down the ramp.

Roy jerked his thumb at the trailers. "Good enough that we had to train up another dozen horses and build a new barn."

Jackson chuckled and Cauy marveled at how easily his brother always got along with people. They weren't very alike, but had bonded over their shared resentment of the way Mark had treated their mother.

Roy nodded at the men who had gotten out of the second truck. "This here is Luis, Santiago, and Chester. They're going to be helping out today, and they'll be the hands coming back to take care of the horses every morning." Cauy shook hands with all three guys. "After they've finished with the horses, you can get them to help out with whatever you need doing around here—as long as they're back at my ranch by midday."

"Got it," Cauy nodded. "I appreciate the help, gentlemen."

He received smiles and nods in return, which suited him fine. The less talking he had to do the better.

Roy walked up the slope of the trailer. "Okay, let's get this done." He untied the first rope from the bar on the side of the trailer and led the horse down the ramp. "Any particular order you want us to put them in?"

"Nope. Just take any vacant stall."

With five of them working together it didn't take long at all to get the dozen horses into their newly prepared homes. Cauy and Jackson went round making sure every horse had fresh feed and water while Roy wrote the names of the horses on the whiteboards on each door.

With fourteen horses now in the barn the place warmed up considerably and Cauy was soon sweating. The Morgan Ranch hands weren't a chatty bunch, but they were efficient and worked hard, which made Cauy very happy. He even managed to have a quick word with Santiago about rebuilding the chicken house when he discovered the guy was apparently a great carpenter.

Roy capped his marker and turned to Cauy. "Looks good in here."

"It does." Cauy hesitated. "Would you guys like some coffee?"

"That's mighty kind of you, but we have to get back," Roy said. "I'll send Ry over to see how things are going this evening, but if you have any problems just text me, okay?"

"I will." Cauy shook Roy's hand again.

Roy pointed to the dilapidated shed beside the barn. "I suggest you start work on that one first so that Em from the feed store can deliver the winter supplies you'll need. Chase has already set up a separate account with her for Lymond Ranch."

"Good to know."

Cauy already had an account, but the Morgans insisted on thinking he was penniless, and he wasn't going to get into an argument about it. He'd pay his share.

Roy clapped him on the back. "Then we'll leave you to it." He started walking back to his truck and then turned around again. "My blasted memory. Chase said to tell you that he's got some really interesting images of the mine from the GPR units if you want to come over and see them."

"Thanks. I'll touch base with him."

"And Rachel was telling us about how well you were taking care of the dog." Roy winked. "She's *very* impressed with you."

Cauy raised an eyebrow and pointed at Roy's truck. "Didn't you say you had to go?"

Roy was still chuckling as he got into the driver's seat with Santiago, leaving Luis and Chester to take the second vehicle.

Cauy watched them leave and then went back to the house. Jackson followed him, a frown on his face.

In the kitchen Cauy gulped down the coffee like a lifeline, enjoying the immediate jolt to his cold system. Jackson joined him.

"Who's Rachel?"

Inwardly Cauy sighed. Jackson had always been the smart one of the family.

"Rachel Morgan."

Cauy could literally see Jackson work through the possible ramifications of that on his face.

"Chase has a kid?"

"Actually, BB has a kid, but Rachel is their sister." Cauy decided he might as well put it out there before Jackson drew his own conclusions.

Jackson choked on his coffee. "The baby who disappeared? The one Billy Morgan supposedly killed in a drunken rage along with his wife?"

"Yeah. That one. Apparently, Annie Morgan ran away with one of the ranch hands, ditched him, and went on to live her life under a different name. She took Rachel with her."

Jackson sat down at the table with a thump. "You're kidding me."

"Nope. You'll get to meet her and the rest of the family at Thanksgiving. We've been invited to dinner."

"How old is she?" Jackson was still focused on Rachel. "She must be in her twenties, right?"

"Twenty-three, I think." Cauy shrugged as if it didn't matter much to him. "She's the one who found Grace, and as she's only at the ranch for the holidays, I offered to keep the dog here."

"This is the Rachel who is very impressed with you?" Jackson asked, waggling his eyebrows.

"No, she was impressed that I had all the stuff ready when we brought Grace home the other night." Cauy helped himself to more coffee. "Speaking of which, I'm only letting Grace out in the fenced yard behind the house at the moment because I don't want her running off again."

"Got it." Jackson sat back, and Cauy heaved a small sigh of relief. "Do you mind if I go through the stuff in the farm office and try and make some sense of it?"

"Be my guest. You know that organization has never been my thing."

"There is also a pile of boxes currently taking up all the space in my closet."

"We can go through them as well if you like." Cauy checked the time. "I don't have anything planned for today." Like riding over and telling Rachel Morgan he'd made a terrible mistake and didn't want to just be friends . . .

Jackson finished his coffee and dumped the mug in the sink. He was never one to sit around worrying about possibilities. "Then let's get started. Maybe we'll find a few million bucks hidden somewhere."

"That would be good."

Jackson took Cauy's mug and rinsed it out. "*You're* short of money? What did you do? Piss it away?"

"Not exactly." Cauy winced. "Remember Lorelei got half of everything, and I'm still restructuring my company to reflect that."

"Basically, you're pulling the 'my money's all tied up'

defense and expecting poor old me to pay for everything?" Jackson joked.

"That's right." Cauy threw the dish towel at his brother's head. "If you find that million bucks, we won't have to worry about it, will we?"

Two hours later, they were knee deep in paperwork. Cauy was pining for a sight of the sky while Jackson was really getting into it.

"Hey, I had a thought."

Cauy turned to look up at his brother, who was sitting at the desk while Cauy sat on the floor. "That we should just make a huge bonfire and get rid of all this crap?"

"No, you'll need it for your accountant," Jackson tutted, and shook his head. "Is Kim still working for you?"

"He's my lawyer, not my accountant, but they work closely together, why?"

"Because I was just wondering whether Dad's hating the Morgans has anything to do with you. Didn't you say Kim was checking into some financial stuff about the Morgans for you?"

"He was, so what?"

Jackson held up a ledger. "Until Mom married Dad, the relationship between the Morgans and our ranch was cordial and financially productive. *After* they married, Dad took against the Morgans and refused to work with them anymore."

"What's that got to do with me?" Cauy asked.

"Don't be dumb." Jackson sat forward in the chair. "What if Dad knew or *thought* he knew that one of the Morgans, probably Billy, was actually your father?" Jackson chuckled. "That would certainly explain why he hated their guts."

As Cauy's whole world rocked and rolled, he put his hand on the floor to steady himself before shooting to his feet.

"I've got to get out of here," he croaked.

"You okay?" Jackson reached for Cauy even as he ran

past him. "I don't really believe that, dude, it was just idle speculation."

Cauy kept going as the implications of Jackson's suggestion hammered into his brain until he reached his truck, got in, and drove away as if the hounds of hell were pursuing him.

He drove upward, away from the county road and toward the boundary fence that bordered the silver mine. There was nobody up there except a few ghosts, and that was all the company he could deal with right now.

Turning off the engine, he braced his crossed arms on the steering wheel and stared out into the white wispy fog.

Rachel . . .

He fumbled in his pocket for his cell phone and then realized he'd left it charging in the kitchen at the ranch. When he got back—if he ever went back—should he call his mom and ruin her Thanksgiving by asking if Jackson was correct?

He tried to force himself to think. If Billy knew Cauy was his son he would never have allowed Rachel to get close to him. But what if Billy *didn't* know? Cauy was roughly the same age as Blue Boy. No one had ever suggested that Billy had been unfaithful to his wife. . . . The fact that Billy had gone to pieces after Annie and Rachel had disappeared didn't indicate he was the kind of man who was glad to get rid of his wife.

Cauy jumped as a truck with its headlights on full beam flashed its lights at him. Had Jackson come after him? He stayed in the truck as two people got out and came toward him. He couldn't see who they were in the glare of the lights, but he had a terrible suspicion he knew who it was going to be.

Those damn Morgans got *everywhere*.

Chase tapped on his window. "Are you okay, Cauy?"

Cauy didn't dare look to his left as he caught a glimpse of Rachel's worried face behind Chase's.

He reluctantly rolled down his window.

"Hey. I came to check the GPR units were still in place, but I can't see anything for the fog."

"We did the same." Chase's easy smile didn't make Cauy feel any better. "Do you want to come back and see the footage we've gotten so far? It's really cool."

"I wish I could, but my brother's just arrived, and we've got fourteen horses to deal with in the barn." Cauy kept his attention firmly on Chase.

"That's a shame," Rachel said. "I thought you'd enjoy it."

He couldn't even look at her.

Chase stepped back. "Never mind. You're coming over on Thursday, so you can see it then. Drive safely. This fog is getting thicker by the minute."

"Will do." Cauy gave a perfunctory nod. "See you then." He shut the window. He waited until the two figures got back in their truck, and then backed up and turned around. He had to go home. Jackson would want an explanation, but Cauy wasn't sure he had one to give.

Chapter Fourteen

"This is Yvonne's." Cauy held the door open so that Jackson could squeeze inside the busy coffee shop. "Take a seat if you can find one, and I'll get some coffee."

"Thanks." Jackson took control of the huge pile of mail Cauy had liberated from the post office. "Get me a slice of cherry pie while you're at it, okay?"

"Sure."

By the time Cauy got to the table, Jackson had already acquired a friend.

"Ry was here all on his own, and he invited me to sit with him." Jackson made space on the table for the two coffees. "I was just asking what we should bring with us to Thanksgiving."

Cauy hadn't even thought about that. Sometimes he felt like since the accident some of the civilized parts of his brain had never restarted.

"Trust me." Ry smiled. "We don't need anything. My grandma's a professional." He looked back toward the door. "But you can ask her yourself, if you like."

Cauy turned his head to see the trifecta of doom approaching the table—Ruth, Billy, and Rachel.

He cleared his throat. "Hey, Jackson, maybe we should move and let these good people have the table to themselves?"

Jackson gave him a funny look. "There's plenty of room if we just add another chair."

Ruth was all smiles as she sat down between Cauy and Jackson.

"How lovely to see you boys in town." She patted Jackson's arm. "And how are you? It's so nice to see you again."

"It's a pleasure to see you too, Mrs. Morgan." Jackson kissed her cheek. "I hear you've been looking out for my big brother."

"Well, he was all alone up there so someone had to take him under their wing." Ruth beamed at Cauy. "And he's been very helpful, what with the mine, and the horses, and Rachel's dog. . . ."

Jackson turned his killer smile on Rachel. "It's good to meet you. You obviously have great taste in dogs."

"Just got lucky, I guess," Rachel said. "It was nice of your brother to take her in."

Billy held out his hand. "Good to meet you, Jackson. I remember you from when the twins were at school."

"Yeah, I think you had the misfortune to coach our baseball team one summer." Jackson winced. "We were absolutely terrible, but we had a lot of fun."

"So are you planning on staying at the ranch?" Billy asked.

"I'll be there for a while. I just got out of the Air Force and I promised Cauy I'd help him set the place to rights." Jackson shuddered. "We spent all day yesterday sorting out the ranch office. You wouldn't believe the stuff we found." He half turned to Cauy and asked, "Shall I tell them how I freaked you out?"

"Please don't." Cauy glared at Jackson.

"What did you do?" Billy asked Jackson. "Cauy doesn't strike me as the kind of guy who gets freaked out."

Jackson leaned forward. "I was speculating about a family mystery, and—"

"You're not going to talk about it right now, are you?" Cauy said swiftly. "I'm sure the Morgans don't want to hear about it."

"Cauy, lighten up," Jackson said, patting his arm. "The whole idea is so absurd that maybe we just need to get it out in the open and disprove my stupid theory once and for all."

That was the trouble with Jackson, Cay thought savagely. He was stubborn as a mule, and thought "honesty was the best policy." All the Morgans were staring at them now and Cauy had a terrible sense of impending disaster.

Jackson carried on flapping his gums. "You know our parents married very young, and Cauy was born six months after the wedding?"

Ruth and Billy nodded, their amusement replaced by cautious interest.

"Dad never liked Cauy, and we always wondered whether Mom had only married Mark because she was pregnant by another man."

Silence fell, broken only by other people's happy conversations and the clink of coffee cups and plates. Cauy wished he could fold himself up small and disappear under the table.

"What did your mother say about that?" Ruth finally asked.

"She wouldn't tell us anything. But Dad hinted at it all the time." Jackson looked from Cauy to Billy. "Seeing as Dad only started hating the Morgans *after* his marriage I wondered whether there was some connection." He shrugged his broad shoulders. "I'm not sure why Cauy freaked out at the very idea, but there it is."

Cauy's gaze was inevitably drawn to Rachel's so he had

an excellent view of when she put two and two together and came up with the same answer he had.

"You wondered if . . . Billy was Cauy's *father*?" Ruth asked faintly.

"Yup." Jackson nodded and looked expectantly around the table.

"Not possible." Billy sat back, his blue eyes clear and unwavering. "I swear I never looked at another woman when Annie was my wife." He turned to Cauy. "I did hear rumors about Anita back then, but she was my friend, so I ignored them and wished her happy when she chose to marry Mark. Does that make you feel better, Cauy?"

Rachel shot to her feet and stomped out of the café.

Jackson raised his eyebrows. "What did I say?"

But Cauy didn't have time to answer his stupid brother; he was already chasing Rachel down.

"Stupid, stupid, idiotic stupid, stupid MEN!" Rachel muttered as she strode along the boardwalk toward the parking lot. "STUPID!"

She had reached her truck before she heard someone calling her name and swung around, still snarling, which certainly made Cauy Lymond back up fast. *"What?"*

He held up his hands. "Okay, I can understand that sounded bad, but—"

She took a step toward him. "I. Don't. Care. Go away and bother some other poor woman, why don't you? You told me you were worried Mark wasn't your father so why didn't you add the last bit?"

"I didn't even *think* about that possibility until Jackson opened his big mouth!" Cauy shot right back at her.

"Are you sure that's why you decided not to have sex with me?" Rachel demanded.

"Hell no! *You* were the one who walked away from that.

I had *no idea* Jackson was going to come up with that stupid story and blurt it out at Yvonne's!"

"It doesn't matter anyway." Rachel shook her head. "It's just a symptom of the whole. I am *done* with you and your stupid, infuriating ability not to *talk* to me!"

She stamped her foot so hard she almost bit her tongue.

He stood there silently, and she wanted to smack him real bad.

"Go. Away, Cauy."

He squared up to her. "What do you goddamn *want* me to tell you?"

She blinked at him as snow began to fall. "*Everything!* Don't you get it?"

"*Why?*"

"Because you *can't* live all inside yourself! You can't deliberately cut yourself off from any emotion and feeling."

"Okay." He moved so fast she was up against the side of her truck before she even reacted, his hard body covering hers, shielding her from sight. He leaned down, his hat blocking the snow, and one arm braced over her head.

"After my accident, I wasn't doing too well. I was badly burned, I had headaches and flashbacks that made me feel like I was right back watching the damn oil burst out of the well at high pressure—except this time it was in slow motion, and I still couldn't stop it happening."

He drew in a deep, shuddering breath.

"I had nightmares. So I went to see a shrink and talked, and talked, trying to make things right. I took every pill they threw at me, and life became a blur of pain and hospitals, and desperation. I lost myself somewhere."

Rachel struggled to bring her hand up to his scarred cheek.

"I don't *want* to talk about it anymore. I want . . ." He buried his face in the crook of her neck. "I came back here to start again."

Rachel slid her hand around the back of his neck and just held on to him, her heart racing and her mind furiously trying to decide what to say. Did he have a point? When did talking things through lose its value if you wouldn't or couldn't change the past?

There was so much she wanted to say to him right now about all the other stuff, but how *could* she when all she really wanted to do was hold him tight and tell him that everything was going to be all right?

He eased slightly away from her so that he could look down into her face.

"You're smart, and bright, and full of positivity and I just can't stop coming back to you." He kissed her hard. "You're the best thing in my life right now, and I don't want to ruin it."

"How about we just *try*?" Rachel whispered. "Maybe you won't?"

He stared at her for a long moment and then kissed her until she forgot how to breathe. Melted snow dripped down her neck and she shivered.

"This won't work," Cauy groaned. "Come home with me?"

"What about Jackson?" Rachel asked.

"After airing our dirty laundry in public he can damn well walk." Cauy grabbed her hand. "Come on."

His truck was close by, and fifteen minutes later they were at his ranch. He kept hold of her hand as they went through the kitchen and the dog woofed a welcome.

"But I haven't said hi to Grace!" Rachel said.

"Later. No more interruptions."

Cauy kept going until she was in his room and could admire his new bedding up close and personal. He locked the door and turned back to her, his expression so damned hot that she almost melted on the spot. As if in a dream she walked into his arms and kissed him, her hands tugging at his jacket, his fleece, and his T-shirt until with a stifled groan he pulled everything off over his head.

His hands were equally busy, and soon she was down to her bra and panties with him just in boxers. He held her so close she could feel every throbbing inch of him against her stomach.

"Don't stop now." She bit his ear. "I'd rather not have Jackson knocking on the door."

The arm around her hips tightened, and he walked her backward toward the bed.

"Nice sheets," Rachel gasped.

"Yeah." He followed her down and straddled her. "Even better with you on them."

He kissed his way down her throat to her breasts and lingered there, teasing her nipple through her bra with his teeth as his callused hands explored even lower. Rachel couldn't stay still, her fingers tangling in the curls at the nape of his neck and scratching slow circles on his scarred shoulder that made him shiver.

"I want you." He reared over her, his gaze intent. "I can't promise you anything right now, but—"

"Stop talking." She grabbed hold of his head and brought him back down to her.

"First time you've ever told me to shut up." He nuzzled her throat and kissed her so slowly she wanted to die of lust. His hand slid beneath the cotton of her panties, teasing and testing her most intimate flesh until her hips bucked insistently against the palm of his hand.

He eased himself lower until her thighs were spread wide and removed her already damp panties. Knowing how good she was shortly going to feel, Rachel let out a purr of pure anticipation. He groaned as he flicked his tongue against her and slid one finger deep making her come so fast she almost couldn't deal with it.

She shoved hard on his shoulder until he raised his head, his gaze so steamy she wanted to come again.

"Do you have protection?" Rachel asked.

"I don't, but I bet Jackson does." Cauy back crawled off the bed. "Don't answer your phone."

He was back so fast she barely had time to unhook her bra and throw it onto the rug to join the rest of their scattered clothes. He straddled her and ripped the foil packet open with his teeth before shoving down his boxers.

Rachel leaned in and wrapped a hand around his thick length, but his fingers closed over hers.

"Next time, okay? If you keep touching me I'll come in your hand."

She reluctantly released her grip and lay back watching him fumble to cover himself. He met her gaze, his smile crooked.

"Out of practice."

"How long is it since you've done this?" Rachel asked.

"Three years at least." Cauy lowered himself over her. "Not sure I remember what to do."

Rachel guided him closer and moaned as he thrust deep. "I think you've still got it."

He didn't speak, he was too busy gathering her close and rocking himself even deeper until there was nowhere else for him to go. As ripples of sensation fired off all her nerve endings, Rachel focused on the amazing feeling of being stretched and full, of the heat and stiffness buried inside her, of *Cauy* . . .

"Mmm . . ." She rolled her hips allowing him to sink even deeper, and he groaned in her ear.

"That's . . ."

He eased back, setting off another round of interesting sensations and set up a steady rhythm that made Rachel cling to him and take every single thing he offered. His hand slid between them and gently caressed her bud, and she dug her nails deep into his skin as she climaxed again.

"Yeah, that's my girl, give it up for me," Cauy growled in her ear. "Take me, take all of me."

She didn't care what he thought or what she looked like anymore. She was all *need*, and want, and *heat*, and somehow Cauy was incredibly and amazingly the answer to it all.

Cauy slid his other hand under Rachel's fine ass and held her exactly where he wanted her, his strokes shorter now and more demanding as the desire to come overcame everything else in his universe. He'd never expected to have sex again—especially not like this. He was adrift in the essence of Rachel, her taste, her smell, the intimate feel of her clasping his cock, and he never wanted to separate his body from hers again.

"Cauy, *please* . . ."

He wasn't sure if she was urging him on or was as desperate for completion as he was. He no longer had the control to do anything but accept his body's rush to climax and take her along with him on the ride of his life. He thrust one last time and held still as he came so hard he thought his head might explode. Just when he thought he might survive, Rachel climaxed again. He fully expected to die, and didn't regret a single thing.

When he'd finally finished thrashing around like a teenager, he eased himself free and rolled over to deal with the condom.

"Bathroom's through there if you need it." Cauy gestured to Rachel, who was still lying back with a dazed look on her face, which did all kinds of great things for his ego.

"Okay."

She got up and he heard the shower turn on. He followed

her in a leisurely fashion and stepped in behind her as she started to shower.

"Room for one more?"

She turned to him and pressed her whole body against his, wrapping her arms around his waist, and just stayed there as the water poured over their heads. He didn't even mind. . . .

Cauy was just turning the water off when they both froze as a truck came up the driveway, its tires crunching on the gravel.

"That's probably Mr. Big Mouth himself," Cauy muttered. "What do you want to do?"

Rachel sighed against his chest. "I'd better get dressed in case BB bursts in here to defend my honor."

Cauy slid a hand into her wet hair, cupping the back of her head. "You can stay if you like."

She smiled at him, and he wanted to pick her up and take her right back to bed.

"I've got a lot to process in my head. You probably do as well."

"I thought we were done talking."

"We are." She looked up at him, her gaze half-shy and half-concerned. "So we just let this happen if we want it and pretend the rest doesn't matter?"

"Always with the hard questions." He kissed her. She tasted like him and his shower gel, which was somehow perfect. "That's why we're done talking."

She wrinkled her nose. "Don't overanalyze, just go with the flow?"

"Why not? We can't seem to keep our hands off each other, and I like this better than arguing." Cauy held his breath as she searched his face.

"That's true."

There was a knock on the door.

"Hey, Cauy?" Jackson shouted. "You got a Morgan in there?"

"Give us five minutes!" Cauy yelled back.

Cauy handed Rachel a towel, and she hastily dried herself and slipped into her clothes. Watching her cover up all that glorious skin he'd so recently explored made him want to cry. She vigorously rubbed her short hair with the towel and was good to go. Except that he didn't want her to go, especially when she looked like the most sexually satisfied woman in history.

Cauy scrambled into his clothes as well. "I'll give you a ride home."

"Thanks."

He unlocked the door and warily looked out. There was no sign of Jackson, but the smell of coffee wafted down from the kitchen.

He took Rachel's hand. "Come on."

They walked down the hallway toward the kitchen door, which was ajar.

"*Jeez,*" Cauy croaked as he came to an abrupt stop in the doorway, making Rachel walk right into his back. "Er, *hi.*"

Ry, Billy, and Ruth all sat at his kitchen table drinking coffee with Jackson, who was making agonized "forgive me" faces at Cauy.

Behind him, Rachel made a stifled sound and half turned back. Cauy grabbed hold of her elbow and brought her fully into the light. If he was going to get it, she was going to have to watch.

Ruth smiled at them both. "Oh, there you are, Rachel. Now let's go home."

Chapter Fifteen

The next morning, Rachel braced herself as she entered the kitchen, but Ruth was the only person still around. She hadn't *deliberately* slept in after her encounter with Cauy, but she hadn't set her alarm. The last thing she wanted was a roomful of Morgans giving her their opinions about the current state of her love life. She was pretty certain that Ry would have told HW and maybe even the rest of them.

Rachel helped herself to coffee, and took scrambled eggs and bacon out of the still warm cast-iron pan on the stove. Working on the ranch had definitely increased her appetite.

"Would you like some pancakes to go with that?" Ruth asked.

"No, thanks, I'm good." Rachel sat at the table and ate while Ruth put on her specs and read the local paper.

"That was funny," Ruth said conversationally as she turned the page.

"What was?" Rachel asked.

"Last night when you came into Cauy's kitchen and found us all camped out there waiting for you."

Rachel groaned and covered her eyes. "I'm never going to live this down, am I? Why did you *all* have to be there?"

"Well, Ry was driving, and Jackson needed a ride after

Cauy left him behind," Ruth said. "Where else were we supposed to go?"

"Ry could've dropped you off first and left Jackson at the front door. Or you could've stayed in the truck."

"Where's the fun in that?" Ruth winked at her. "I thought Cauy was going to pass out when Billy looked at him." She chuckled. "Why on *earth* did Jackson think Billy was Cauy's father?"

"Because he's an idiot?" Rachel sipped her coffee. "Who asks someone *that* in the middle of a coffee shop?"

"Jackson was always a straight hitter." Ruth offered Rachel more coffee. "And at least it's out in the open now, and you're not worrying about it."

"True," Rachel reluctantly agreed. "Which, considering the circumstances, is a good thing."

"There *was* some mystery about who fathered Anita's baby," Ruth mused. "I'll have to ask Roy if he remembers anything about the men who worked on the ranch back then. It *was* odd the way Mark suddenly took against us after his marriage."

"Was Mark really not nice to Cauy?"

"I never remember him saying a good word about the boy, and I wasn't surprised when Cauy took off when he was sixteen." Ruth took out a notepad and a pen. "Would you be willing to go into town and get me a few things I forgot yesterday? I've got to start the pies today for Thanksgiving."

"Sure!" Rachel was eager to do anything that got her away from her siblings on the ranch.

"And maybe you can drop Cauy's mail off to him on your way back? Jackson left it all in Ry's truck."

"I'm sure I can do that as well." Rachel waited as Ruth kept writing. "Aren't you going to say anything about me and Cauy?"

Ruth looked up. "What would you like me to say?"

"Are you . . . annoyed with me?"

"Why would I be? He's a nice boy, I know the family, and that's all there is to it."

"But I'm only here for the holidays." Rachel wondered why she was offering up her own objections rather than waiting on Ruth's. "Am I being unfair?"

"That's between you and Cauy, dear." Ruth ripped the sheet of paper off the pad and slid it across the table to Rachel. "After sitting here at this very table and listening to all the nonsensical reasons your brothers have had for falling in love, or not falling in love, I've heard just about everything under the sun. They all worked it out in the end, and I suspect you will too."

"Oh," Rachel said. "Actually, I was hoping for some advice."

"Do you love him?" Ruth held her gaze.

"It's not like that," Rachel hedged. "We just like each other a little bit."

"And does he make you happy?"

"I think so. I'm trying not to overanalyze it at the moment."

"Then enjoy it until he doesn't, and then come and talk to me again." Ruth patted her hand.

"Thanks, I will." Rachel tucked the list in the pocket of her shirt and stood up. "Is there anything else you need in town?"

"No, Yvonne's bringing Rio with her to Thanksgiving dinner, and she insisted on bringing several desserts and her delicious bread rolls. I only have to make the pies and deal with the turkey and sides."

"For about twenty people," Rachel reminded her. "I'll help as much as I can."

"We'll manage." Ruth stood up and put the newspaper away. "We always do."

Impulsively Rachel went around the table and hugged her grandma tight.

"Thank you, Ruth."

"For what? Making you do all my chores?"

"No, just for being you, and for making me feel so welcome here." Rachel hugged her even tighter.

"It's your home. It always has been," Ruth said. "Don't you ever forget that."

"I'm sorry, Bro," Jackson said again. "I didn't think things through."

Cauy eyed his brother, who was sitting at the desk in the farm office working through another pile of paperwork. Cauy had gone out into the freezing wind to tend the horses, only to find that the Morgan Ranch hands had got there before him, mucked out all fourteen horses, and put them out to pasture for a couple of hours.

He'd spent a few minutes talking to Santiago about renovating the large feed shed. Santiago had written down a list of supplies necessary to get the roof back on and fix the old door. He intended to start work tomorrow after they'd cleared out the junk, and Cauy was looking forward to helping him.

Cauy had left them to it, confident that things would get done, and went back to the house to have his breakfast. He'd dreamed of Rachel rather than his usual nightmares, which was a pleasant change. He almost wished she'd stayed the night but that might still be a step too far. He reminded himself that he wasn't going to think about anything too deeply and should just enjoy the moment.

"Isn't it a good thing I asked Billy if he was your father?" Jackson looked hopefully at him. "Otherwise you might have been committing all kinds of indecencies with Rachel."

"I wasn't—" Cauy sighed. "Hell—"

"She's really hot," Jackson said, nodding. "I can see why you like her."

Cauy had no intention of discussing Rachel with his gabby brother. "How's the paperwork coming along?"

Luckily, Jackson was easily diverted into talking about money. "I've straightened up the last couple of years so you can turn those over to your accountant. They are all online now and in some kind of order. The deeper Dad got into the booze, the more discrepancies I noted." He sat back. "There's money there somewhere, but I can't find it yet."

"Maybe he drank it all." Cauy perched on the edge of the desk to look over Jackson's shoulder at the old written account books.

"Possible, but unlikely." Jackson stretched out his arms. "I still think he stashed it away in another bank somewhere."

"Then keep digging."

"Will do. Is there anything that needs doing with the horses right now?"

"Nope, the Morgan Ranch hands have seen to pretty much everything."

"Nice." Jackson grinned.

"I'm going to measure up the old food storage shed so that we know what length timber to cut," Cauy said. "But I can get that done myself."

"I thought I might go into town and buy some wine, or something to take with us to the Morgans," Jackson said.

"That's a great idea." Cauy stood up.

"Maybe flowers for the table?" Jackson frowned. "Is there a florist in town?"

"Yeah, right close to the coffee shop. I think it's called Daisy's."

"Then I'll stop off there if it's open, or maybe I can do it online."

Cauy paused at the door. "How come you know about all this stuff?"

Jackson shrugged. "Lots of different postings mean you

have to get your manners on. Let me know if you need anything in town before I go. Like condoms or anything."

Cauy winced. "Yeah, I'm sorry about that, I wasn't anticipating—"

Jackson threw a cardboard carton at him, and Cauy reflexively caught it.

"There you go. I'll get some more."

"Thanks." Cauy stuffed the condoms into his pocket aware that he might be blushing, which was totally unacceptable. "I owe you."

Cauy was busy hauling stuff out to the trash pile when he heard a truck stopping outside the house. He threw the rotting timber onto the ever-increasing heap and went to see who had arrived.

Rachel stood at his back door petting Grace, who had been running around the fenced part of the yard. Just seeing her made him stop and stare like a fool. Why she'd taken a chance on him he would never understand, but he intended to enjoy the moment.

As if sensing his stare, she turned around and waved. Her smile hit him low in the gut, and he was instantly hard. He walked toward her and swept her into his arms for a kiss that instantly turned hotter than hell. He backed her up against the wall and hitched her up until the zipper of her jeans met the bulging fly of his, and pressed himself close.

"Cauy . . ."

Her arms wrapped around his neck and adjusting his stance he picked her up and carried her inside, stopping at least twice to grind himself against her like some horny teen. She didn't seem to mind, her booted heel jabbing his ass like she was spurring him on.

When he reached his bedroom, he locked the door and deposited her on the bed, his mouth locking back over hers as she undid his belt and plunged her hand inside his jeans to fondle him.

"Jeez . . ." His breath whooshed out as she shoved down his boxers and took him in her mouth, drawing him deep and holding him there while he struggled to get his balance and keep up. His fingers tangled in her short blond hair as he enjoyed every pull of her mouth on his heated, hard flesh.

When he thought he might come, he gently eased her away, and helped her out of her jeans and panties, cupping her mound in his palm and finding her more than ready for him.

He sat on the bed, found a condom, and covered himself before drawing her down to straddle his lap.

"This okay?" he murmured against her lips.

"God, *yes*."

She bit him as she rocked her hips taking him deep, rising and falling over him, her breasts in his face as he frantically tore off her jacket and sweater and lavished her skin with his mouth.

It was wild, it was hot as hell, and they were coming together, and that was the best thing of all. . . .

Rachel shuddered through her climax, her nails digging into Cauy's neck and shoulders and his mouth swallowing her screams. She'd never had sex like this before. It was addictive.

She slowly raised her head to find him smiling at her.

"Hi."

"Hi yourself." She kissed his nose. "Is Jackson here?"

"No, he's in town." Cauy kissed her back, his mouth lingering until she started squirming on his lap making him catch his breath. "Want to go again?"

"I have to get back and help Ruth," Rachel sighed. "There's a lot to do feeding the family and the last guests."

"Okay." Cauy gripped her around the waist and eased her free of him. "Shower?"

"Not enough time." She breathed in his scent. He'd been working outside and smelled like wood smoke and the barn with a side of ice. "I only came to deliver the mail Jackson left in Ry's car."

"Thanks for doing that."

Cauy moved off the bed and went into the bathroom. She heard water splashing, and when he returned, he'd obviously washed up. She gathered her clothes and went to set herself to rights. There were red patches on her throat and chest from his stubble. According to her phone, she'd only been at the ranch for twenty minutes, which was kind of amusing.

When she reappeared, the bedroom door was open, and Cauy was whistling in the kitchen. She paused to appreciate the cheerful sound. Had she ever heard him whistle before?

"Can I get you some coffee?" Cauy called out as she came into the kitchen.

"Yes, please." Rachel headed for the back door. "I'll just get your mail."

On her return to the house, her cell buzzed. She took it out of her pocket to read the text message from Chase and frowned.

"What's up?" Cauy asked as she came through the door.

She sat at the table and took the coffee he gave her. "Chase says he thinks someone has gotten into the mine."

"What?" Cauy's smile disappeared.

"Some of the images from last night show inconsistencies." Rachel sighed. "He wants me to go up there and check around the sensors to see if there's been a cave-in or something."

"I'll come with you." Cauy finished his coffee in one hit. "What about Ruth?"

Rachel was already texting. "Chase is on it. She says just go ahead and report back."

Rachel was happy to go in Cauy's truck, which was better suited to the terrain than hers, and had the added benefit of heated seats, which worked sporadically but were better than nothing. The high ground around the mine was as bleak and desolate as the moon surface.

When she got out of the truck at the first GPR unit the coldness made her cheeks hurt and her breathing ragged. Luckily, she didn't have to stay out there for long.

"This one looks okay."

Cauy nodded, and they drove to the second marker, which was similarly undisturbed.

"Let's stop at the mine," Rachel suggested.

"Sure." Cauy parked close to the entrance and got out, his expression darkening as he came around to her side of the truck. "What the *hell*?"

Rachel stared at the broken bottles and silver tracks of frozen beer that littered the closed entrance to the mine. The wooden panels had been kicked or attacked and the bottles thrown at the barrier.

"Someone obviously tried to get in here," Rachel stated.

"Yeah, and I bet it was those Morgan Ranch guests who came up here the other day."

Rachel glanced at him. "We don't know that for sure."

"Who else could it be?" Cauy asked.

"Someone from town? I gather it's still something of a draw to thrill seekers."

"True, but the most obvious answer is the guests." He crouched down and began to pick up the shards of glass.

"Watch your hands," Rachel warned. "Can I take one of the buckets from the back of your truck to put the glass in?"

"Go ahead."

They picked up the glass, and Cauy continued his search around the mine entrance.

"Lots of hoofprints and one set of tire tracks." He stopped and looked back at Rachel. "If they didn't succeed in getting in here, where else might they have tried?"

Rachel's gaze went to the sinkhole and she walked over to peer into its depths. There was no sign of anything down there let alone a vehicle.

Cauy turned on his flashlight, but the high-powered beam picked up no trace of any activity or disturbance.

"Too obvious?" Rachel asked.

"Too dangerous." Cauy turned off the light. "Let's go and check the other two GPR units, and see if there's anything up with them."

The third GPR was fine, and at the fourth marker, the one farthest away from the mine itself, there was no obvious sign of surface damage. Rachel got out of the truck and turned a slow circle, her hands deep in her pockets and her chin buried into the warmth of her knitted scarf.

"Cauy, look at this." She bent down and picked up a few cigarette butts, and a spent lighter. "Someone was out here."

He joined her, his quiet gaze scanning the barren fields and frosted fence line before he set off down the slope following a faint trace of footsteps in the ice. Rachel went after him. He reached a hollow sheltered from the wind that was cut into the side of the hill, and stopped again.

"The ground is very flat here. Maybe man-made." Cauy stamped his booted foot and then looked up the slope. "And the lines are . . . not natural." He studied the sparse bushes growing up against the side of the slope and suddenly dove into them.

"Hey!" Rachel glanced wildly around and then followed him in, holding her arm across her face to avoid the branches springing back as he forged ahead of her.

"Wow."

Rachel peered around Cauy's shoulder. "What is it?"

"I think it might be another way in to the mine."

Rachel reached out to touch the broken planks of wood and Cauy grabbed her hand.

"Don't get too close."

She frowned at him. "I'm not stupid. I was just trying to work out if anyone had moved the boards recently."

"There are footprints around here. If they did get in, this might be what Chase picked up on the GPR unit and camera." He turned back. "Come on. Let's go and tell him what we've found."

Cauy heeled and toed his boots off in the Morgans' spacious mudroom and hung his coat up. Rachel had disappeared upstairs. She'd told him to go through to the kitchen when he was ready, and she'd join him. She'd already sent a text to Chase on the ride over so he was expecting them.

Cauy carefully stretched his fingers and studied the damaged skin. He'd forgotten to put the cream on last night, and it showed. But the problem was more than skin-deep. Shrapnel from the explosion had embedded in his left hand breaking his fingers and wrist in multiple places. Flinging up his left arm had saved his sight so he'd learned to live with it. But today the pain was jagged and set his teeth on edge. The cold seemed to infiltrate every tiny crack and nagged like the worst kind of toothache. He'd have to take some medication later, and he hated that.

"You okay?"

He turned to see Chase coming down the stairs, his laptop under his arm.

"Yeah. What's up?"

Chase waved at him to go first. "Nothing much. I've taken the rest of the week off, and I intend to enjoy the time with my family. It's cool that Jackson was able to join you for Thanksgiving."

"You just reminded me"—Chase found his cell—"I need to tell him where I am in case he gets lonely."

Chase snorted. "No chance of that here. There's always someone getting into your business."

"Have you thought about building yourself a separate house like BB is doing?" Cauy asked.

"January likes it here in the old house." Chase shrugged. "That's all I need to know. And we do have an apartment in San Francisco, so we can get away for some privacy."

"Lucky you." Cauy went into the kitchen. "Jackson wouldn't know a boundary if it slapped him in the face."

"So I heard. To be honest, I'm amazed you let him live after that clunker." Chase sat at the table and opened his laptop. "Let me show you the images the GPR units recorded last night."

By the time Rachel arrived smelling like a bunch of flowers from her shower, Cauy was convinced Chase was correct, and there was definitely something going on in the mine. He let Rachel relay what they'd discovered out near the main entrance and the new hidden unmarked entry point on Lymond land.

"Thanks for checking it out," Chase said as he shut down his laptop. "I'll put more cameras up there and see if we can catch a glimpse of these guys."

"Rachel thinks it might be people from the town, but I'm more inclined to believe it's your current guests," Cauy stated.

"It could be either." Chase rubbed his hand over his face and groaned. "The last few guests are leaving the day after Thanksgiving only because they couldn't get flights and we offered to let them stay another night. If we hold off actually accusing anyone of anything, maybe the problem will take care of itself."

"I suppose so." Cauy wasn't convinced, but waiting a couple more days wouldn't hurt. "The boards on the second entrance looked newer than the ones at the original level. I'll have to check the Lymond records and see if my father left any notes about finding that entrance or doing anything with it."

"That's a good point." Chase exhaled. "Maybe he was using it for storage or something. I'd hate it to be any of our guests. We really don't need that kind of bad publicity for the ranch right now when we're just getting started."

"I'm more worried about someone going in there and causing a cave-in. That environment is very unstable," Rachel piped up.

"Agreed." Chase nodded. "Let's get through Thanksgiving and take another look on Saturday, agreed?"

Cauy and Rachel both nodded.

"Great. I'll let everyone else here know what's going on so that they can keep an eye out for any suspicious behavior from the guests."

"Maybe we could pay BB to patrol the cabins every night and scare the crap out of anyone who ventured out?" Rachel suggested.

"Not a bad idea, but we do already have cameras here at the ranch," Chase reminded her. "Which I can also access to see if there's been any shenanigans going on. Mind you I'm way more likely to see Ry and HW sneaking around trying to get it on with their lady loves." Chase grinned with all the smugness of a happily married man. "They're both so sad."

"I think Sam's planning on moving into town soon," Rachel said. "HW doesn't know yet."

"She's a brave woman," Chase said, shaking his head. "He's not going to be happy about that."

Cauy cleared his throat. He really didn't want to know every single detail about the Morgans and their complicated private lives. The only Morgan he was interested in was sitting right next to him, her thigh touching his. He half rose from his seat.

"I have to go into town and get some supplies. Do either of you need a ride?"

"Sorry, Cauy. We got off topic there for a moment." Chase smiled at him. "Thanks for all your help, and we'll see you and Jackson tomorrow for Thanksgiving."

Rachel stood as well. "I'll walk you to the door."

Cauy didn't argue with the first great suggestion she'd made in a while. He followed her to the mudroom where he'd put his jacket, hat, and boots.

"This place hasn't changed much," Cauy said as he took his jacket off the hook.

"Did you come here when you were a kid?" Rachel asked, leaning back against the dryer, her arms folded under her breasts, drawing Cauy's gaze.

"Once or twice, when my dad didn't know where I was going. He would've beaten the crap out of me otherwise." Cauy studied the old stairs. "Which room are you in?"

She waggled her eyebrows at him. "Wanna see?"

"Not if you want me to keep my clothes on." Cauy set his Stetson on his head.

"Didn't we just do that?" Rachel blinked at him. "Like an hour ago?"

"Yeah." He glanced down at his jeans. "So?"

Reaching out a hand, she traced his straining zipper with one fingertip, and he forgot how to breathe.

"I like that," Rachel said.

"Which particular thing?" He wrapped his fingers around her wrist, bringing her whole hand into contact with his now aching dick.

"This would do nicely," she purred.

He stepped in close, trapping her against the dryer, his whole body aligned with hers. He hadn't felt this desperate since he'd first discovered sex as a teenager and wanted it all the time.

"I'd like to take you up those stairs, strip you naked, and make love to you all day," Cauy murmured against her lips.

"Okay," she sighed.

"You're not supposed to encourage me. We're standing in your grandma's mudroom."

"Not a problem for me." Rachel licked his lower lip and then bit down on it, sending a shot of pure lust straight to his groin. "I think I'm a bit besotted with you."

"Yeah?" For one wild moment he considered picking her up and taking her to her bedroom before his hard-won common sense reasserted itself over his hard-on. "Your brothers would kill me."

"True, but it would probably be worth it." She put her hands on his chest and pushed him away. "Go home then, and I'll see you tomorrow."

Cauy put on his coat and boots and did exactly what she said. She might not mind him facing the Morgan brothers, but he'd rather stay alive and try again another day.

Chapter Sixteen

"So I hear you and Cauy are *involved*."

Jenna gave Rachel a meaningful look as they set the table in the guest center for Thanksgiving dinner. Ruth had decided her kitchen was too small to fit everyone in, and had moved operations to the dude ranch dining room and bar, which was four times the size of her kitchen. The family was currently decorating the place with Thanksgiving-themed colors, flowers, and googly-eyed fake turkeys.

"Whoever told you that?" Rachel passed her a basket of orange napkins.

"Everyone." Jenna laid the napkin flat on the table, and with three quick twists of her wrist created something that looked like a bird, and stuck it in a glass.

"The Morgans can't keep a secret to save their lives," Rachel complained.

"I think that after years of *keeping* all the secrets, they try and be honest with each other—maybe a little *too* honest," Jenna admitted as she deftly folded another napkin. "But I'd rather that than everyone lying to each other."

"Cauy and I agreed to . . . go with it for now," Rachel admitted as she attempted to copy what Jenna was doing with the napkin and failed miserably.

"Go for what exactly?" Jenna asked as she corrected the crumpled napkin and slowed down so Rachel could copy her more easily.

"Sex mainly." Rachel still couldn't get the darned bird right.

"And you're okay with that?"

"I . . ." Rachel paused. "It's the best I can get at the moment. Cauy's busy resurrecting the ranch, and I'm supposed to be getting a proper job somewhere else. Neither of us is looking for something permanent."

"So it's a temporary hookup kind of thing?"

"I suppose it is," Rachel said slowly.

Jenna didn't sound judgmental so why did Rachel want to defend herself anyway? Her connection with Cauy went far deeper than a hookup. Maybe she was scared to try to define what it was because whenever she did that she found out the other person didn't agree with her. In fact, Cauy had specifically stated that he didn't want her to obsess over something they were both enjoying. Maybe he did see it as just a hookup.

She'd never just had sex for the sake of it before. Somehow it felt weird. . . .

"That's a lovely dress, Jenna, is it new?" Rachel attempted to change the subject.

"Yes." Jenna smiled as she smoothed a hand over the patterned yellow silk that went perfectly with her red hair. "Blue gave it to me and insisted that I wear it today."

"Do you think he actually chose it?" Rachel tried to imagine the retired Marine in a dress shop.

Jenna laughed. "I think he probably had some help. Yvonne and January have definitely been whispering with him about something. Are you *sure* you're okay with how things are going with Cauy?"

Rachel glanced at Jenna, who had managed to make

another twenty napkins look pretty while she'd been laboring over one.

"Yes, I am." She summoned a smile. Trust Jenna to stay on topic. "Really. It's not as if we have to decide anything right now. He'll be living at the ranch, and I'll be back here again so this isn't a do-or-die moment."

"*Is* Cauy going to stay?" Jenna asked. "Did he tell you that?"

"Considering how much work they are doing on the place, I assume he is." Rachel made another lame-assed napkin bird and quickly stuck it in a glass before Jenna noticed.

"At one point, Chase was trying to buy the place."

"I gather Cauy and Jackson's father didn't want to sell it to a Morgan."

Jenna made a face. "Mark Lymond wasn't a nice man. I shudder to think what being his kid was like."

"Especially as he didn't think one of his kids was his own," Rachel added as they moved on to the next table, which would house the hands, the dude ranch staff, and the remaining guests. "The way Cauy talks about him sometimes makes me wish he was alive so I could go and thump him with his own shovel."

"He was quite intimidating in real life. He carried a lot of anger inside him," Jenna said as she rearranged the table decorations to match the others. Delicious smells were already emanating from the kitchens, and Rachel's stomach rumbled. "I was quite afraid of him."

"Cauy's not like him at all."

"I know he's not." Jenna grinned at Rachel. "Otherwise I'd be telling you to run away as fast as you could."

"Rachel?"

Rachel turned to see Blue beckoning imperiously to her from the dining room door. She raised her eyebrows, pointed at her chest, and then at Jenna's back, and he mouthed, *You*, and put a finger to his lips.

"Excuse me a minute."

Rachel left Jenna happily making swans out of a new set of napkins and followed her brother out into the reception area.

"What's up?" Rachel asked.

"Come with me." He took her hand and led her into the private offices on the other side of the building.

He unlocked the door of Chase's office, snapped on the lights, and ushered Rachel inside, closing it behind him. A box of flowers with Daisy's name on it sat on the desk, sweetening the air.

"I just wanted to give you a heads-up." BB leaned against the door, one hand in the pocket of his best jeans.

"About what?" Rachel asked.

"Don't rush off after lunch, okay?"

"I was planning on eating so much I wouldn't be able to move for a week, so there's no danger of that." Rachel studied him carefully. "What's wrong?"

"Nothing's wrong." He fingered the collar of his new checked shirt as if it was too tight. "I'm just making sure I've got all my bases covered."

"Covered for what?"

He grinned at her. "My home run, of course." He opened the door and bowed elaborately as Rachel went past him. "What time is lover boy getting here?"

"If you mean Cauy, then in the next half an hour or so, why?"

"Just checking." He winked at her.

Rachel paused to stare into his blue eyes. "What are you up to?"

"Nothing much."

She didn't believe that for a second. "Are you going to finally give Jenna the keys to the house and carry her off?"

"Like I'm going to tell you that."

Rachel sighed. "Big tease."

"Yup. Just keep your wits about you and don't be surprised by anything that happens."

"I always do around you Morgans," Rachel muttered.

He gave her a side hug. "Hey, you're a Morgan too."

For the first time she actually believed him.

They walked back into the reception area where Ruth and Billy were just arriving carrying boxes of additional food.

"Do you need a hand?" Rachel called out.

Billy nodded. "Head out to my pickup. The food is all stacked in the back." He carried on after Ruth. "Relax, Mom, you know I'm a qualified chef, right? I can help out all day if you need me."

Rachel went out into the bitter cold and grabbed a box of what smelled like pumpkin pie. It was way heavier than she had anticipated, and she was struggling to balance it against her chest when it was taken out of her hands.

"Let me get that for you."

She frowned at Cauy, who had relieved her of the box. "I'm perfectly capable of carrying pie. It's the least I can do seeing as I intend to eat as much of it as I can get in my mouth."

"There's plenty more boxes out there to take in."

"Then why don't you go and get them?" Rachel inquired sweetly.

"Okay."

He dumped the box back in her arms making her rock on her heels, and disappeared again leaving her struggling to get through the door. So much for girl power . . . She took the pies into the large industrial kitchen and dumped them on the table.

Billy looked up with a smile. "Thanks, sweetheart."

"You're welcome," Rachel gasped, and turned back to the door, her knees wobbling, and not just because she'd seen Cauy. She managed to avoid getting slapped in the face as the door swung inward to reveal Cauy and Jackson both carrying stacks of foodstuffs.

"Just put everything on the table for now," Billy said. "And thanks for helping out. The bar's open in the dining room, and Ruth's already setting out some appetizers, so go enjoy yourselves."

"We'll keep going until the truck's empty," Jackson said. "And then we'll really deserve a drink. Thanks for having us over, Billy, we sure do appreciate it."

Cauy wore his usual thick sheepskin-lined coat, brown hat, and jeans that looked slightly better than his weekday ones. Not that she cared what he looked like with his clothes on after seeing what lay underneath . . .

"Hey, Rachel!" Jackson said, grinning at her. "Happy Thanksgiving."

"Right back at you." Rachel picked up a smaller item from the pickup bed and returned to the kitchen. The last few Thanksgiving dinners she'd had at home had been over-shadowed by her mom's illness and her stepdad's increasing commitment to working all the hours he could manage. In retrospect she wondered if he'd been spending all his free time with his soon-to-be new wife. After her mom's death, she and Paul had either eaten out, or pretended they'd for-gotten, and just gone on as if it was any other day.

The Morgan Ranch celebration was a different matter altogether. Ruth liked to gather up anyone she came across who was either a stranger in town or on their own. This year, among others, she'd invited the new local dentist, Mr. Lam, Dr. Tio Mendez and his grandmother, and Nancy from the Red Dragon Bar.

Rachel got busy, welcoming people to the ranch, setting them up with drinks and appetizers, and generally making everyone feel at home. The fact that she was accepted as one of the family still confounded her sometimes, but she couldn't deny that it made her feel warm inside. She no longer felt like an outsider and that was a small miracle in itself.

Jackson was soon happily introducing himself to everyone, but Cauy settled at the bar, his back to the room, and chatted with Nancy, who had taken on the unofficial duty of bartender-in-chief. Occasionally she'd sense he was watching her, but after talking to Jenna, she didn't want him to think she would hang on his arm like a lovesick fool. . . .

"Hey."

Coming out of the kitchen where Ruth and Billy were performing miracles of culinary excellence, she found him propping up the wall.

"Hey." She smiled up into Cauy's eyes. "Are you having a good time?"

"I'm doing okay."

"You don't like crowds, do you?"

"Can't say I'm a fan." He leaned down and kissed her. "You look happy."

"I am happy." She leaned against the wall so she could look up at him. "I'm starting to think that I might really belong here."

His brow creased. "You're a Morgan. Of course you belong here."

"But I didn't know that," Rachel pointed out. "If Chase and the others hadn't tried to find Annie I might *never* have known about all this," she said, gesturing at the window. "All this stark, beautiful wildness my mother hated so much that she disappeared and never came back."

"You're here now." He cupped her chin. "And you look damn fine to me."

"So do you." She hesitated. "You *are* going to stay, aren't you?"

He didn't speak for so long she held her breath.

"Yeah."

To her dismay, he didn't sound particularly convincing.

"I like the idea that you'll be around when I get back."

"Waiting for you?"

"Yes. Preferably naked in bed."

His brown eyes crinkled at the corners. "I think I can manage that."

She wanted to put her hands on him right now, to tear off his shirt and lick him like her favorite Popsicle.

"Don't look at me like that." His voice deepened, sending spasms of lust straight to her lady parts.

"Like what?" Rachel breathed her reply.

"Like you want to devour me."

"But I do." She raised her gaze to his face. "Is that a problem?"

"Right now?" He glanced around the hall. "Yeah, because this place is crawling with Morgans, and if I kiss you, things might get out of hand fast."

"We could slip away." Rachel took his work-roughened hand and placed it over her breast. "For a few minutes. No one would miss us."

He shifted his hand until his palm cupped the weight of her breast and his thumb grazed her covered nipple. "You're driving me insane here."

"Good." She took his other hand. "Come on."

As she passed the kitchen, she stuck her head in the door. "How long until we sit down, Ruth?"

"About half an hour, why?"

Yvonne had now joined the melee in the kitchen, and was taking out a multitude of desserts and breads from her pink boxes.

"I thought I'd go over to the house, call my stepdad, and wish him a happy Thanksgiving. I wonder if he's celebrating it in Greece?"

"That's a kind thought, dear." Ruth nodded at her. "While you're over there, get Cauy to bring the crystal bowl filled with cream out of the refrigerator, and bring it back with him. I forgot it."

"Cream?" Cauy murmured against her neck. "Things are getting better by the minute."

Was the man who'd once ordered her off his land and barely managed to sling two sentences together making a joke? Had she changed him? Had he changed her or was it something about Morgan Valley that soothed the soul and brought out the best in people?

Still blushing that Ruth had guessed Cauy was going with her, Rachel headed out the back door of the visitor center, avoiding the guests, Cauy at her heels.

"How's Grace doing?" Rachel asked as her breath condensed around her in the cold air. The trees were free of leaves now, and the pasture a regimented glittering white carpet that rolled away toward the menacing darkness of the Sierra foothills.

"She's doing great. I put a dog door in so she can get in and out to the fenced yard. She was curled up in front of the fire when we left."

"Lucky Grace." Rachel took Cauy's hand and hurried him up the stairs.

"What about my boots?"

"No time for that." Rachel rushed him along the corridor. "And we don't want anyone coming into the house knowing we're up here, doing this."

"We don't?" He hauled her in close using the front of her sweater. "So we keep our boots on?"

"From what I remember, you can get naked very quickly when you need to." Rachel wrapped an arm around his neck. "And so can I."

"Naked it is, then." His smile was as hot as hell. "Race you."

The house was warm as toast and within a minute or two

Cauy fell back on the sheets and let Rachel crawl all over him. She licked his collarbone, enjoying the salty-sweet taste of his skin, and then went lower, skimming down over his rather nice abs to her ultimate target.

His ragged groan as she licked him from root to tip made her want to smile. He gave her no time for that, flipping her onto her back with a strength that always surprised her considering how lean he was.

"My turn."

Soon she was gripping the sheets and writhing around like a needy fool as he carefully brought her to the crest of a climax before protecting himself and sliding home deep and true. She drew her thighs up and planted her heels in his muscled ass, urging him on.

He slowed down, taking his time until she was almost reduced to begging, before he finally relented and took her over into pleasure so bone deep that she lost her sense of self. She traced the raised lines of the scars that fanned out from his throat down his left arm and over his back.

"I'm not as sensitive there," he murmured in her ear, surprising her with the admission.

"I didn't notice." Rachel shaped his shoulders with the palms of her hands and slid them down to his wrists. "I just hang on and pray I'll survive."

"Me too." His chuckle warmed her as he kissed her throat and slowly levered himself off her. "I suppose we should be getting back."

Rachel studied him as he sat on the side of the bed putting on his shirt and boxers. He was as lean as a greyhound with no excess fat on him at all, and she wanted to pull him back down to her, and just stay there forever.

"Are we just hooking up?" Rachel asked.

He turned to look at her. "Why would you think that?"

She sat up and drew her knees to her chest. "Because all we do is have sex."

"Mainly because we both choose the worst times to get it on, and then we have to rush." His faint smile was wry. "I'll take you out on a real date if you like."

"Like one when we talk to each other, and all that good stuff?" Rachel asked dubiously.

"Sure." He gathered up his clothes. "Do you think it will be okay if I use the bathroom?"

"It's next door so you shouldn't bump into anyone," Rachel said, pointing in the general direction. "Go ahead."

He paused at the door and looked back at her.

"You still okay about this?"

She thought about not making love with him ever again . . . and couldn't imagine it.

"I'm good." She blew him a kiss. "Go get cleaned up."

He waited another beat before nodding and leaving her alone in the unusually quiet house. She lay back on her bed and studied the ceiling. She wanted him, she liked him, and she didn't want to give him up, so why was she still so unsettled? He hadn't asked for a commitment, and she hadn't asked for one back. They were both in agreement about that at least.

But why *couldn't* it become more? The thought burst into her head. Couldn't they talk and grow together and even be separated for a while, and it not make the darned bit of difference? Her mother had scolded her for building elaborate dream scenarios out of nothing and being upset when they didn't materialize. Wasn't that what she was doing right now? Trying to make Cauy into something or someone he had never wanted or asked to be?

Rachel let out a sigh and rolled over to the side of the bed. The water had shut off next door so Cauy was probably finished. Her body was humming with satisfaction, but her mind wasn't quiet. She reminded herself of all the reasons why a relationship with Cauy wasn't in the cards. She imagined his face if she suddenly turned up at his place saying she wasn't leaving town, and would stay and live with him forever.

He'd run for the hills . . . and she'd probably get as bored and resentful as her mother had been.

She snorted at that image and found her smile again. She wasn't going to build castles in the air and watch them come crashing down again. She'd take what she'd been given, live in the extremely pleasant moment, and be thankful for it.

Cauy adjusted his grip on the huge crystal bowl Rachel had given him to bring over to the guest dining room and glanced at his companion as they walked across from the house. She'd been quiet since she'd come out of the bathroom, and that always worried him. Had he missed something? She'd asked him if he thought of her as a hookup, and everything in him had rebelled at that idea.

She was much more than that. She was a revelation.

Cauy stopped walking. "It's not just about the sex."

"Where did that come from?" Rachel blinked up at him.

Cauy carried on talking. "What you said earlier. The sex is great, but I don't think of you as just a booty call."

"Thanks." She smiled, but it didn't quite reach her eyes. "That's good."

"Unless that's what you want?"

She frowned. "I'm the one who likes talking things through, remember?"

"Got it." Cauy nodded. "And I meant what I said about taking you out on a proper date."

She pressed her gloved hand to her chest. "Be still my beating heart."

He found himself smiling. She was laughing up at him again so that was much better. He loved her smile and the way she lit up from inside. Somehow it made *him* feel more alive, like there was hope for the future, and all that other stupid sentimental stuff he'd given up on.

"There are a lot of extra cars here," Rachel said as her gaze went past him to the crowded circular driveway. "How many people did Ruth invite? This looks more like *fifty* than twenty, and some of these cars are either rentals or have out of state plates."

She held the door open so that Cauy could go first with the crystal bowl. The roar of conversation and the sight of so many people milling around made him want to retreat, but he had to keep going, Mrs. Morgan needed the cream.

"This is weird," Rachel muttered.

Cauy delivered the cream and went back to find Rachel. "What is?"

"All these people."

"Your grandmother is a generous woman."

"I know that, but—" Rachel grabbed Ry's arm as he went past her. "What's going on?"

Ry shrugged. "Don't ask me. BB's up to something, but he's not telling me anything, although I think Chase is in on it."

Ruth banged on the table loud enough to create a pause in the chatter. "Will everyone take their seats, please?"

Cauy noted that the four remaining guests had been corralled at the table with the ranch hands who certainly wouldn't allow the guys to get away with any bad behavior. It was the same four guys who had appeared at the mine before, which set all Cauy's hackles up.

Rachel took Cauy's hand, led him to the Morgan family table, and pulled out the chair next to hers. He took a quick survey of her brothers, but no one seemed to object to his presence so he sat down. Yvonne, Billy, and Ruth appeared and placed platters of carved turkey at the end of an enormous buffet table filled with food.

"Everyone help yourselves!" Ruth said. "Family hold back, and no fighting in the line!"

Chapter Seventeen

Rachel eyed the last bit of stuffing and turkey on her plate, and visualized putting it in her mouth. Nope. It wasn't happening. She barely had room for any of the desserts that were now on the buffet table, and she had to try the pie Cauy had gone to fetch for her.

She looked over the chattering crowd on the far table and barely recognized anyone. Something was definitely going down, but she had no idea what, except that BB Morgan was in the thick of it.

"I got you all four different kinds of pie," Cauy said, setting a plate in front of her. "I wasn't sure which one you'd prefer."

She stared up at him admiringly. "Good thinking."

He shrugged and sat beside her helping himself to coffee. "Your two older brothers are out in the hallway whispering to some old guy with a white beard."

"Santa?" Rachel asked, the spoon halfway to her lips.

"Wrong day," Cauy said. "He wasn't wearing the red suit, either."

"Maybe its BB's Realtor, and he's going to hand over the keys of the house officially to Jenna?"

"Didn't BB build it himself with Chase's money?" Cauy finished his coffee.

"Not all of it. He definitely got a loan."

"Maybe it's the bank manager come to repossess the place."

"Funny," Rachel said, mock-frowning at him. "On Thanksgiving?" She put down her spoon. "Oh my gosh, he's changed."

"Into what?" Cauy inquired, his gaze still on Rachel.

"*His dress uniform*," Rachel said, gasping and grabbing hold of Cauy's hand. "Where's Jenna?"

Blue Boy Morgan cleared his throat and stood at the front of the gathering. "Can I have your attention, please?"

Everyone immediately stopped talking to stare at him. Chase stepped up behind him, one hand on Blue's daughter Maria's shoulder.

"Jenna? Can you come up here, sweetheart?"

Rachel held her breath as Jenna slowly turned toward her fiancé, her face a picture, and made her way to the front.

Blue took her hands in his and stared down at her.

"I hope you're going to like this idea of mine, but it's also okay if you don't." He took an audible breath. "I love you, Jenna."

"And I love you too," Jenna replied.

"The house is ready for us and Maria to move into."

A slight frown marred Jenna's brow. "Yes, I know that."

"So I was hoping you'd be agreeable to us moving in there tonight?"

Jenna glanced around to where Maria was nodding in agreement.

"Tonight?"

"Yeah. Right after we're married." Blue turned to the man standing behind Chase. "Pastor Muller's open to performing the ceremony right now, if you're willing. Chase has agreed to be my best man, and Yvonne, January, Nancy, and Maria want to be your attendants."

Jenna's mouth fell open. "You . . . organized all this *without telling me*?"

It felt to Rachel like the entire room held their breath waiting for BB's answer.

"Yeah, I did. I even got your parents and sisters to come out here." He nodded at Ry, who opened the door into the kitchen to reveal all of Jenna's adopted family waving awkwardly at her. "We already did the paperwork, but you told me the idea of getting the wedding organized was stressing you out, so I decided I'd try it this way." He paused. "What do you think?"

Jenna slowly turned around taking in all the faces, including her parents, and then settled her gaze back on Blue, who looked more nervous than Rachel had ever seen him before.

"*You* did all this?" She pressed her hands to her chest, her voice trembling. "For *me*?"

Blue nodded and stood stiffly to attention as if expecting an official reprimand.

"Oh, thank *goodness*! I was *dreading* organizing the darned thing." She threw herself into Blue's arms. "You couldn't have done anything more likely to appeal to me in my whole life!"

Everyone stood and cheered as Jenna rushed around kissing and hugging her family, and Ruth attempted to sort out a space for the wedding to take place.

Rachel sank back into her seat and wiped away a tear. "That was quite something."

Cauy gave her a skeptical look. "You'd be okay if a man organized your wedding for you?"

"No, *I* wouldn't, but Jenna was getting stressed with her mother and sisters all telling her what to do, where to hold the wedding, whom to invite, and all the other stuff so she was in despair of ever getting it done. This works perfectly for her." Rachel happy-sighed. "She gets to enjoy her moment, and then moves into her own house with the people she loves. Blue *really* gets her."

"Amazing, but apparently true," Cauy murmured.

"I *wondered* what the flowers were doing in Chase's office."

"Come again?" Cauy asked.

"BB took me aside this morning and gave me a heads-up that something was happening after lunch. There was a florist box of beautiful, fragrant flowers from Daisy's on Chase's desk. I *assumed* they were to decorate the Thanksgiving table, but those flowers were pink and yellow. They must be for the wedding."

"Okay."

Rachel smiled at Cauy. "Sorry. I'm just sorting it all out in my head. I forget you can't keep up if I utter too many sentences."

Jackson sat down on the other side of Rachel and smiled at her and Cauy. "This has been some Thanksgiving. Great food, great company, and now a surprise wedding."

"That's the way we Morgans roll," Rachel deadpanned. "Just a regular day here at the ranch."

Jackson grinned and leaned in closer. "Is that Nancy Mulligan at the bar?"

"Yes. Do you want an introduction?" Rachel asked.

"That would be very kind of you." Jackson stood and Rachel realized he was determined to make it happen right now. "The wedding's going to start soon and I'd like to get it done before then."

"Sure." Rachel walked over to the bar and waved at Nancy, whose hair was pumpkin orange and yellow. She wore a long pink sweater that reached her knees and black leggings with daggers and skulls on them.

"Hey, Nancy, do you remember Jackson Lymond? He's moving back here for a while."

Nancy slowly looked Jackson up and down. "I *vaguely* remember you, but as I had a terrible crush on your brother I can't say I looked too closely."

Jackson grinned, apparently not bothered by her withering appraisal. "You had a crush on Cauy? That's hilarious. Does he know?"

Rachel touched Jackson's arm. "Maybe you'd better keep that to yourself? I think Cauy's about done with you sharing his secrets with the world."

"Oh, Cauy knows, I told him when he first got back to town." Nancy made a face. "He still wasn't interested, but that's okay."

"He's obviously blind," Jackson said. "No offense, Rachel."

"None taken." Rachel barely managed to conceal a grin. Jackson certainly had a way with words. She was amazed that he'd lasted ten years in the Air Force. "Nancy works at the Red Dragon Bar in town. You should pop in and see her one evening now that you're reacquainted."

"That's a great idea." Jackson smiled at Nancy. "I look forward to it." He shook her beringed hand. "Nice to meet you again."

"Nice to meet you too, er, Jack."

"Jackson." He held her hand for just a fraction too long and stared into her eyes before walking back into the throng of people and organizing the chairs.

Rachel turned to Nancy. "Do you really not remember him?"

"Oh, I remember him very well. He was on every team, won every debate and all the awards as the star quarterback of the football team." Nancy winked at Rachel. "It's good for his ego *not* to be remembered for a change."

Rachel chuckled as she turned back to find Cauy also sorting out chairs. Chase came up and touched her shoulder.

"Jenna wants you to come out back and see her."

"Is she okay?" Rachel asked.

"She's doing great. You'll find her in my office sorting out her flowers."

"Thanks." Rachel went through the lobby and into the business space at the back of the building. Females who were all laughing and having a great time surrounded Jenna. Rachel arrived just behind Sam.

"Rachel! Sam!" Jenna's face brightened when she noticed Rachel hesitating by the door. She still wore the yellow silk dress and someone had pinned a short veil over her hair. "Come in! BB ordered extra flowers so I wanted you, Sam, and Avery to join my girl posse."

Sam snorted. "I'm not exactly girly, and I rarely wear a dress, but I'll happily stand up with you for this."

Rachel smiled so hard her face hurt. That Jenna had thought to include her in her impromptu wedding felt like being encircled in loving arms.

"I—I'd love to," she stuttered, "that's . . . so sweet of you."

Jenna pointed at the box. "You and Sam can decide which flowers you want to carry. BB picked my favorite colors and asked Daisy to make up a variety of designs. They're *beautiful,* aren't they?"

Rachel tried to picture her brother in a flower shop and again failed miserably.

She went over to the box, and Sam followed her.

"Isn't this great?" Sam asked as she randomly took one of the small posies of flowers tied with a pink ribbon. "If I ever get hitched to HW I'd like a wedding where everything is already done for me."

Rachel took the last posy that had tight pink rosebuds in the center. "You could elope to Vegas. They can handle all the arrangements for you out there."

"That's an awesome idea." Sam broke off one of the flowers and stuck it behind her ear. "HW likes Las Vegas. He can go watch Rio compete in the bull riding on the same visit."

"Should I give HW the heads-up on this plan?" Rachel asked jokingly.

"Not yet. He hasn't groveled enough for my satisfaction," Sam said, winking at her. "Maybe in a year or two I'll broach the subject."

Jenna's stepdad appeared in the doorway. He wore a beautiful pinstripe suit and a yellow tie matching Jenna's dress, which made Rachel suspect BB's influence had been far wider than she'd anticipated.

"Everyone ready?" he inquired, his fond gaze on Jenna. "Mrs. Morgan says you can come out anytime you like."

"I'm good to go." Jenna took a deep breath, picked up her flowers, and placed her hand on her stepfather's arm.

Rachel took up her position beside Sam, and followed the others out into the hallway and back to the dining room. Chairs were lined up in rows creating an aisle, leading to the front of the room where the pastor stood with Blue and Chase. Music started playing, and Rachel noticed a harp player had been installed in the corner. BB really was an organizational genius. Was there anything he'd forgotten?

Maria led the way, her dress a pink version of Jenna's, and scattered flower petals. Jenna's gaggle of girls followed, and lastly came the bride, who was smiling so hard she almost levitated.

Rachel caught sight of Blue's face as he watched Jenna approach, and wondered how it felt to have that much intensity and love laser-focused on you. Jenna had overcome her own insecurities to truly believe that Blue loved her. Could Rachel ever do the same, or find a man who would make her feel that way? She looked for Cauy in the crowd and found him at the back, his gaze right on hers.

When Jenna reached Blue and smiled up at him, it was like watching the sun emerge. Blue touched her cheek like she was made of fine china, his emotions plainly visible on his normally inscrutable face. Rachel had to swallow a lump in her throat as she stepped back to sit beside her grandmother.

Ruth took her hand, her own trembling, and Rachel took strength from that as the pastor married the couple and pronounced them man and wife. Blue picked Jenna up, swung her around, and soundly kissed her. Everyone cheered, and Rachel allowed herself the luxury of a few tears.

A handkerchief appeared under her nose, and she gratefully took it.

"I never understand why everyone cries at a wedding," Cauy said.

"Because we're happy?" Rachel blew her nose and tucked his handkerchief in her pocket.

"Yeah, that." Cauy continued to look down at her. "You okay?"

"Yes," Rachel sighed. "It was just so *lovely,* and unexpected, and Jenna is *so* happy."

Someone was handing around glasses of champagne, and Cauy gave one to Rachel. She took a hasty sip even before the first toast was made. By the time everyone had been accounted for she had downed the whole thing. Cauy stood quietly at her side raising his glass of water for every toast.

At last, Blue stood on one of the chairs and grinned at everyone.

"Thanks for making this such a special day for me and Jenna, and if any of you want something to do this evening? You're more than welcome to come by and help me move Jenna's stuff into the new house."

"Haven't you got better things to be doing this evening?" HW hollered, his arm around Sam.

"This evening? No." Blue winked down at his wife. "Tonight, definitely."

HW groaned as Jenna blushed. "Then I suppose I'd better go warm up my truck."

Cauy walked out of the guest center with Rachel at his side and paused to look up at the cloudless night sky. They'd just waved off the happy couple and some of the guests were starting to leave. Out here, away from the city lights, the stars seemed brighter, and more numerous, and the air so much purer. He shivered and buttoned his jacket against the sharp teeth of the breeze.

"It's going to snow tonight," he murmured. "I can feel it in my bones."

The thing was, the ache wasn't just a physical thing anymore. It was tied in with his need for companionship, for being *part* of something—a need he thought he'd banished forever.

Rachel sighed and leaned against him. "It's been a wonderful day. I'm glad you were here to share it with me."

He wrapped his arm around her shoulders and held her close as they both stared out across the frozen fields. The horses were all tucked up in the barns, and only Ry's dog and the barn cats were visible snuffling around in the fading light. He felt . . . *weird*, and unsettled, as if he couldn't deal with all these good things happening in his life.

"I have to get back," Cauy murmured. "Grace will need feeding."

"Okay." Rachel didn't move away, and he did nothing to make her.

"You could come with me?" Cauy couldn't quite believe he'd made that offer, but now that it was out there he had no intention of taking it back. One thing he was learning was that time moved on, and you had to keep up or give up.

"I wish I could." Rachel turned and cupped his bearded chin. "But I can't leave Ruth and Billy with all this mess to clean up."

"Okay." He kissed her cold nose, and then her warm lips. Her eyes were so blue. . . . "I'll give Grace a kiss from you."

"You do that." Her smile was as beautiful as the crystalline valley and resonated with him at some deep level that made him just want to stay in the moment and take it in. Jeez, he was getting fanciful in his old age. Time to disengage before he really said something he'd regret.

"Did Jenna mention when she expected the puppies to arrive?" Rachel asked.

"She had no idea." Cauy smiled. "Jackson and I have both helped birth puppies before, so I'm not worried."

"Where is Jackson, by the way?" Rachel looked around.

"Still inside yakking himself to death. That guy has never met a stranger."

"He's certainly nothing like you."

"I used to wish I was like him," Cauy confessed. "Because my dad liked him so much more than me."

"Your father was a fool." Rachel held his gaze. "*Everyone* knows that."

"Everyone called Morgan, maybe." Cauy felt ridiculously comforted by her unwavering support, and also terrified. She was so open to him that he feared for her—for the damage he might do—for not being the man she deserved. He gave in to the temptation to kiss her one more time.

"I'll go find Jackson, and then we'll be off."

"I'll come in with you."

She kept hold of his hand as they walked back into the guest center where the Morgan family and staff were attempting to restore order. With a smile, she left him to it and went into the kitchen. Jackson saw him and grinned.

"Hey, Bro. You ready to go, or should we stay and help these fine people clean up?"

"I wish we could stay, but I need to get back to Grace and check the horses," Cauy said.

"Okay, let me get my jacket."

Jackson then spent another ten minutes saying good-bye to everyone while Cauy kept it to as few specific people as possible. Eventually, he just leaned against the wall and waited his brother out.

Billy came out of the kitchen and walked over to him. He was wearing a Happy Holidays apron, which should've looked ridiculous on him, but somehow didn't.

"Are you leaving?"

Cauy repeated his excuse. "Yup, I have to get back to the dog."

"I hope you had a good day." Billy looked him over.

"It was awesome. Thanks for inviting us."

"You're welcome." Billy nodded. "Rachel had a good time as well."

Cauy straightened, wondering what Billy was going to say next.

"I can tell she's very fond of you, Cauy."

Cauy didn't know what to say to that so he concentrated on holding Billy's gaze and looking responsible.

"She's had a rough few years, so I wouldn't want anyone hurting her."

"I hear you." Cauy accepted Billy's pointed remark head-on. He deserved the reminder, and he'd take heed of it. "I would never deliberatcly hurt her."

Billy nodded. "Keep it that way."

"Yes, sir."

Cauy let out his breath as Billy turned and went back into the kitchen. Rachel's father looked like a sweet guy, but there was a strength to him Cauy recognized—one survivor to another. He wouldn't take an insult to his only daughter lightly. Cauy could see where Rachel got her courage.

"You okay?" Jackson came up beside him. "You look like you're about to bolt."

"I'm good." Cauy levered himself off the wall. "Let's go home."

Chapter Eighteen

Rachel stacked the last clean glass back on the bar shelf and heaved a sigh of relief. It was getting late, and all she wanted to do was fall into bed and sleep off the mountain of food she'd eaten. Cauy had definitely enjoyed sharing Thanksgiving with her and the Morgans, although she sensed that large gatherings were still an effort for him.

What exactly had happened to him in the accident and its aftermath? She wondered whether she'd ever have the right to ask him that question. It was all very well Billy saying she should wait for Cauy to tell *her,* but sometimes it sucked waiting. She took the used bar towel through to the laundry in the kitchen and washed her hands in the sink. Ruth had gone on ahead, leaving her and Billy to finish up.

"Are you all done, Rachel?" Billy asked as he cleaned the kitchen table one last time.

"Yes. I think we can go now."

Billy smiled at her. "It was a good day. I'd forgotten how much I enjoy running a kitchen."

"Seeing Blue and Jenna get married was awesome." Rachel went to look for her jacket. "They both looked so happy. Did you know what was happening?"

"Actually, I did, but I was sworn to secrecy." Billy took

off his apron. "And as I've been focused on regaining my children's trust there was no way I was going to let that secret out."

Rachel handed him his jacket. "It's snowing out there, so wrap up."

"You too." The denim made his eyes look even bluer, if that was possible. "The Lymond boys had a good time."

"Yes, they did." Rachel linked her arm through her father's as they turned off the lights and stepped into the reception area. "It was kind of Ruth to invite them."

"You and Cauy are getting along well now."

"As well as he'll let me." She half smiled. "It's like prying open a clam."

Billy chuckled and then shuddered as Rachel opened the front door, and the cold wind hit them full-on. "Damn. I'd better go check everything's okay in the barn. I doubt any of the boys remembered. Why don't you go on home?"

Rachel considered the softly falling snow, which made the whole landscape an unrelenting and unrecognizable white. "I'd rather stick with you. I can't even work out which way *is* home."

"I'll keep you safe." Billy patted her hand. "With two of us we can get it done faster."

Luckily, Billy knew where he was headed, and all Rachel had to do was hang on to his arm and stick close to his side. The lights of the barn came into view really fast, and she blinked at them through the snow. It was amazing how the snow distorted everything.

"If it gets really bad, we'll string up some rope guidelines between the house and the barn," Billy said as he stepped onto the cement floor and shook the snow out of his hat. "It's real easy to get turned around out there when there's a storm coming through."

Rachel was getting that big-time. She followed Billy

down the center of the barn as he checked each horse, staying to pat heads and feed treats as she went.

"That's not right." Billy halted near the other end of the barn near the tack room.

"What isn't?" Rachel turned from petting her horse, Petunia.

"There are two horses missing." He pointed at the empty stalls, his expression grim. "Do you have your cell phone on you?"

"Yes, of course." Rachel got it out of her pocket. "Who do you want me to call?"

"Let's start with Roy. If anyone knows where those horses are, it'll be him."

By the time Billy and Rachel got back to the house, Roy had arrived in his truck, and Chase was also in the kitchen. The twins were helping Blue move Jenna into the house. Rachel had called them, and they promised to keep an eye out for the horses and come back to help as soon as they'd finished.

Rachel accepted the cup of hot chocolate Ruth offered her and cradled the mug in her cold hands. Chase was texting on his phone, and Billy was explaining which horses had disappeared to Roy, who was sitting at the table next to Ruth.

"Bonanza and Rawhide?" Roy asked. "Those two yahoos Carlson and Sean were riding them this week."

Ruth looked up. "And they were both here at the wedding. I didn't see them leave." She prodded Chase. "Call Sam. Ask her to check if those boys are all tucked up for the night in their cabin; she's right next door to them."

"Will do." Chase started texting again. "I've alerted Nate Turner and asked Jay to keep a lookout in town in case anyone rides in or drives through with our horses."

"Didn't Sam go with HW?" Rachel asked.

"No, she was too tired and went to rest up," Ruth said. "January's in bed as well. She felt a little queasy after all that rich food."

"Pregnancy does that to you," Chase murmured as he focused on his screen. "I advised her not to eat too much, but she told me to shut it."

"January's breeding?" Roy slapped his thigh. "Good Lord."

"Scratch that." Chase looked up, his expression horrified. "I wasn't supposed to mention it. She'll kill me."

Ruth chuckled. "As if I hadn't guessed already."

"Don't ask her any leading questions, okay?" Chase looked imploringly at his grandmother. "Or she'll know I blabbed. She wants to tell you herself and didn't want to upstage BB's wedding."

Rachel hid a smile at her oldest brother's inability to keep a secret. Even in the middle of such drama it was cool to know she was going to be an aunt in the new year.

Chase's cell buzzed, and he returned his gaze to the screen. "Sam says she had to knock hard enough to raise the dead. Two of them are there, and two of them are missing."

Billy whistled. "Then I suppose we have to assume that those two idiots are somewhere out there in a snowstorm."

"With two of our good horses," Roy added.

"I'm more worried about the liability issues of losing two guests at the moment," Chase groaned. "We're going to have to look for them, aren't we?"

"I darn well wouldn't," Roy muttered. "Serves them right."

"They are still our guests, they're on our land, and we are unfortunately still responsible for them even if they are complete dickheads." Chase stood up. "I'll notify all the local ranches to keep an eye out as well." He looked over at

Roy. "You know this land like the back of your hand. What's the best place to start searching?"

Roy looked at Billy and Rachel. "I'd start at the silver mine. The two fools were very interested in that."

"And Cauy and I found that new entrance," Rachel said. "Maybe they've gone up there?"

"Fools if they have." Ruth shivered. "It's even colder up there than it is here, and apart from the mine, there are very few landmarks to get your bearings from."

"And what about that great big sinkhole?" Roy said gloomily. "Let's just hope they haven't ended up down there."

"Rachel, do you want to go with Billy and Roy?" Chase asked her directly. "I'd appreciate your expertise on this matter if they have gotten into the mine itself."

"Sure," Rachel said, nodding. "I still have my protective gear. I'll go find it."

By the time she returned, Billy had loaded up Chase's big truck, and Ruth was handing out coffee to go. Rachel got into the back seat of the truck, and Billy looked over his shoulder.

"I sent a text to Cauy seeing as the guys might be on his land."

"Okay." Rachel put on her seat belt. She was currently wishing she hadn't drunk so much champagne.

"You're the only one who knows exactly where that second entrance is." Billy swung the truck around in a circle and set off, the bright headlights illuminating the swirling snow and not much else. "Do you think you'll be able to find it again in this weather?"

"I'll do my best." Rachel grimaced. Her sense of direction had never been great. "It's relatively close to the fourth GPR unit."

Billy nodded as the truck began to climb, its engine laboring. "We'll head up to the main entrance to the mine and take it from there."

Cauy sifted aimlessly through the pile of mail he'd picked up from the post office, separated out the junk, and tossed it in the trash. Jackson had gone to bed, leaving him in peace for a while. There was a letter to each of them from their mom and a thick envelope from Kim, Cauy's lawyer, which probably related to his research on the Morgans.

Cauy propped Jackson's letter up against the desk light and opened his own. Just seeing his mom's handwriting made him smile. She wrote about her dogs, her daily life, what Amy was up to, and all the regular mom stuff. Apparently, she was going out with friends for Thanksgiving, which he would've known if he'd opened his mail earlier. He'd called to wish her a happy Thanksgiving, but she hadn't picked up.

"Bad son," Cauy murmured to himself, and folded up the letter. "I'll call her again in the morning."

He opened the envelope from Kim and scanned the cover letter, which didn't offer many specifics, but contained an estimate of costs that made Cauy wince. He'd learned to be careful with money at a young age, and he'd never really grown out of it. During the legal transition of the ranch into Cauy's name Kim had dug up some land dispute between the Lymond and the Morgan families in the late nineteenth century, which had never gone to court, and shared it with Cauy.

According to Kim at the time, the Morgan family had pretty much owned the valley, the new township, and the mine, and anyone with sense knew they would not get justice in Morgan Valley if it was against the founding family. Kim argued that Cauy could still put a claim in for the land, even though he might not win, and maybe get an out-of-court financial settlement.

"'Chase Morgan can afford it!'" Cauy read out loud, noting the exclamation mark his lawyer had added for emphasis. "I'm sure he can, but I'm not sure I want to do that to Rachel's brother."

He spread the sheets out and studied the two maps Kim had provided. The oldest map showed the boundary line with the mine completely on Lymond property. Had his ancestors wanted all the profit from the mine to go to them? Of course they had.

Cauy stacked the papers and put them on the side of the desk. He'd look through them again and give Kim a definite no after the long weekend. Even if he hadn't been involved with Rachel he wouldn't be pursuing the claim. Living here and accepting the help the Morgans had so willingly offered him had changed his mind and freed him from his father's brainwashing. Let them keep their land, and he'd tend to his own.

His cell buzzed and lit up with a text from Chase.

FYI 2 horses and 2 guests missing from ranch.
Believe might be at old mine or new entrance on
Lymond side of fence.

Cauy stared at the text and then glanced out of the window where the snow was still falling before texting his reply.

I'll go up there right now. Thanks

He put on his warmest gear, poured hot coffee into his flask, and set off, leaving a note for Jackson on the kitchen table. He hoped his tires would manage on the icy road and the barren fields close to the mine. He drove slowly, worried that the horses might appear at any moment when the visibility was down to almost zero. It was one of those times when he was really glad he'd stopped drinking.

As he drew closer to the mine, the dazzle of another set of stationary headlights hit his windshield, making him blink and slow down even more. He cautiously parked up on the flat expanse in front of the mine and got out of the truck into the howling wind.

Roy lifted his hand and shouted, "Cauy!"—his voice almost snatched away by the gusting breeze. He was sheltering in the overhang of the mine. "Over here!"

Cauy rammed his hat down, lowered his chin, and set off. It was only a few feet, but it felt like miles as if his boots were loaded down with lead.

He recognized Billy by his white beard and then saw Rachel.

"We found the horses!" Roy pointed at the side of the blocked-in entrance. "Tied up all safe and sound."

"Great. Where are the riders?" Cauy asked.

"We're not sure." Roy grimaced. "Can't see them in the sinkhole, which is one good thing. Rachel thinks they might have gone to the other entrance."

"That's possible," Cauy agreed. "Especially if they set out before it snowed and are now stuck there. How about I go down and check it out, and you guys take the horses back to the ranch?"

Rachel leaned into the conversation against the wind. "That's what I said. I was just waiting for you to turn up so we could go."

Cauy frowned at her. "You don't need to come."

"I'm the only person here with any experience in structural integrity. If they *have* gotten into the mine, we'll need to make sure it's safe before we go in after them."

Cauy held Rachel's gaze and admired the resolve in her eyes. He might not like it, but he sure as hell respected her.

"Okay. Good plan." He accepted defeat. "How about Billy and Roy take the horses back, and then come and check in on us at the second entrance? They can either pick us up, or help us get the guests home."

Billy glanced at Rachel, who gave him a quick, reassuring nod. "We'll do that. I don't want to risk leaving the horses out here much longer in this wind."

"I'll help you tie them to the back of your truck," Cauy offered.

Ten minutes later he had Rachel in his passenger seat, and she was using the coordinates on her phone to guide them to the fourth GPR unit. Cauy didn't think his truck would make it down the slope to the actual mine entrance, and Rachel had cautioned him not to get too close anyway. To his relief, the wind had eased a little, as had the snow. He'd heard enough shrieking and moaning to last him a lifetime. He was beginning to understand why the townsfolk had abandoned Morganville, and the mine, and settled farther down the valley.

Rachel shivered. "I can see why my mom hated it in the winter."

"This isn't the worst weather I've seen out here either," Cauy commented. "We've had blizzards that blow for days and pile the snow up several feet high so you have to dig a path between the house and the barn to get to the animals."

"So Billy was telling me." Rachel leaned forward and pointed. "The GPR unit is right here."

"Got it." Cauy saw the flicker of orange tape just before he ran it over. "I'll park up, and we'll walk down the slope."

Rachel zipped up what looked like a long puffy ski jacket and drew the hood over her knitted hat.

Cauy frowned. "Are you sure you'll be warm enough in that?"

"It's full of down and works really well for skiing, so I think I'll be okay." She turned to smile at him. "Are you ready?"

The last thing he wanted to do was get out of his nice warm truck and trek off into the snow, but he really had no choice.

"Sure. I'll bring my flashlight." He stuck his coffee flask in his other pocket and tried to pretend it was a normal working day.

"Jeez . . ."

He stepped down and his breath seized in the cold. He hurriedly covered his mouth with his scarf and waited for Rachel to join him. He grabbed her gloved hand in his and set off down the slope, taking his time over the uneven frozen ground, his flashlight illuminating their path.

"Look." Rachel poked him in the back. "The entrance is open."

Cauy walked slowly up to the gaping hole, his heart hammering, and peered inside. The air smelled old and metallic. Nothing about it made him want to go in there. At least the overhanging ridge provided some shelter from the wind.

"Let me look." Rachel came alongside him, and he held the flashlight high for her. "I can see a tunnel, and there's a light. It must be them."

She turned to Cauy. "Let me go first, okay? And follow my exact footsteps. This place is not stable."

"Got it." For once he had no intention of arguing with her.

She knelt, took off her backpack, and opened it to reveal a hard hat with a light, an orange safety jacket, and some kind of tool belt.

"Very professional looking," Cauy quipped to disguise his gathering unease. "I've just got my coffee."

She put on the backpack. "Let's take this really slowly, okay?"

He eased to the side and gripped the door frame as she took her first step inside, the lamp on her helmet a softer glow than the white beam of his flashlight. He forced himself to move over the threshold and immediately froze. Along with the fetid air came the smell of beer, and ancient history. Something about the structure of the passages made the wind whistle and creak like a living thing.

Rachel took another two steps, her head moving as she scanned the narrow passageway and the wooden supports. Even as she paused a trickle of dirt dropped from the ceiling followed by a groaning sound. She moved on and then turned to look back at Cauy.

"Are you coming?"

He tried to move forward, but he couldn't. The idea of going deeper into that hellishly small space was doing his head in.

"Cauy, are you okay?" Rachel asked.

He managed to shake his head.

"Okay, how about you stay right by the door and watch out for Billy while I go and get these two idiots?"

He backed up as fast as if he'd seen a rattlesnake and leaned against the solid rock of the opening, his gloved fingers hanging on like a baby bird to the side of a nest. He turned his face toward the outside positively enjoying the freezing snow melting on his face and the slap of the wind. Rachel would think he was a coward, but there was nothing he could do about that. The mere thought of being trapped was more terrifying than anything else in his current existence.

* * *

After one last concerned glance back at Cauy, Rachel went forward. Part of her was thrilled with actually being inside the old structure, while her professional side was busy assessing the risks. The mine timbers were aged pine and looked remarkably strong, but the packed soil between them had shifted, changing the ratio of the weight and undermining the overall balance. Someone had chalked an arrow on one of the walls along with a series of numbers that meant nothing to Rachel.

As she eased along the passage the distinctive smell of weed curled around her, and she wanted to roll her eyes. Instead, she turned on Cauy's big flashlight and took a left at the tunnel junction, ending up in a small hollowed-out turnout.

"Don't shoot!" One of the guys cackled and giggled as her flashlight swept over him. "Ouch! You're hurting my eyes."

Rachel lowered the light. "What the hell are you doing in here?"

Idiot Number One held up his hands. "Having some fun. Do you wanna join us, sweetness? My name's Carlson, and this is Sean."

"I know who you are—you're the idiots who left two horses out to die in a snowstorm and broke into a dangerous mine."

"What snowstorm?" Carlson asked, grinning at her. "It was fine when we left."

"The whole county is out looking for you including the sheriff's department, so maybe you could get off your asses and come on out?" Rachel said.

Sean pouted. "I love my horse, Bonanza. He's a badass."

"And you left him outside in a snowstorm," Rachel snapped. "If we hadn't found him he would probably have frozen to death."

Sean staggered to his feet and weaved unsteadily toward Rachel. "He's okay, right?"

"I don't know. He's currently on his way back to the ranch to be inspected and treated."

"Then how am I supposed to get back?" Sean demanded like it was her fault.

Having dealt with her fair share of stoners at college, Rachel knew she wouldn't get much sense out of them.

"We have a truck." She glanced over at Carlson, who was finishing up his joint. "Are you done?"

He flicked the ash on the floor. "No need to get all riled up, babycakes. We're coming."

Rachel took a moment to check that there were no smoldering ashes or other combustibles lying around and escorted Sean to the door. She kept hold of his arm as he stumbled along the tunnel giggling whenever he almost fell.

Cauy was waiting at the exit, so she handed Sean over to him without comment and went back to make sure Carlson was coming. His voice echoed in the cavernous interior.

"Wow, it really is snowing."

Rachel waited for him to catch up with her and walked him toward the exit. Cauy glanced briefly her way.

"I just saw lights coming down the hill so either Roy's back or one of your brothers has brought his truck up here to help. I left my spare flashlight outside to guide them toward this entrance."

"Great, then we can offload these two idiots."

"Hey!" Sean said. "I heard that."

Cauy stepped outside, one arm holding a swaying Sean in place. Rachel nodded to Carlson to come through the opening. As Carlson stepped forward, he lost his footing and crashed heavily against the doorjamb, giggling and snorting as he attempted to right himself. Rachel staggered

as he crashed into her, almost sending her to the ground.
She used her strength to shove him outside.

Even as he half fell to his knees, the mine gave an omi-
nous creak, and the wooden lintel above the entrance snapped
in half.

"Rachel!" Cauy shouted, and dived toward her, taking
her completely down to the floor like a sacked quarterback.

Even though his body covered hers, the roar of the wall
coming down was deafening, and they were both covered in
a layer of rocks and dust.

Coughing and choking, Rachel tried to push Cauy off
her, and finally succeeded in rolling him onto his back. It
was only then that she realized he wasn't conscious, and
that there was a pool of blood gathering on the floor beneath
his head.

Rachel took off her backpack, found her spare flashlight,
and set it on the ground. Her fingers were shaking so hard
it was difficult to check Cauy's pulse and release the tabs on
the small medical kit she always carried with her. His hat
had disappeared somewhere under the pile of debris, his cell
phone was smashed, and he'd obviously been hit in the back
of the head with something sharp.

Rachel rolled him into the recovery position on his side
and examined the back of his head. She couldn't see a punc-
ture wound, but pressed a medicated pad to where his hair
was most bloodied and hoped for the best. Within a minute
his eyes opened, and he groaned.

"What happened?"

Rachel decided to keep it simple. "You hit your head.
I'm just cleaning the cut before I stick a Band-Aid on it."

He blinked at her, and his eyes finally focused. "We're in
the mine."

"Yes, well, as to that . . ." She smiled brightly. "I'm sure
it's all going to be fine."

He eased away from her and sat up, swaying so hard she braced herself to catch him again. He slowly turned his head to where the exit had been.

"*Shit.*"

"Yes. Exactly." Rachel nodded. "Carlson tripped and fell into the doorjamb, and brought the lintel down."

Cauy continued to stare at the pile of rubble while Rachel finished cleaning up the blood on the back of his head. She sprayed some antiseptic onto his skull, and he didn't even flinch.

"I have to get out of here."

Rachel went still, then put her medical kit away before crawling around to face Cauy. He looked perfectly composed, but there was a tightness around his mouth that worried her.

She tried to sound soothing. "I'm sure that as soon as Billy and Roy see the guys standing out there, they'll work out what's happened and get some help up here."

Cauy shook his head. On closer inspection his whole body was shaking. He grabbed his phone and stared at the shattered screen. "Storm's gotten worse again. They probably won't come. We're trapped."

Rachel found her cell, which had been protected, in her backpack. "Cauy, it's okay. We can do this."

"Rachel." He grabbed hold of her hand. "I goddamn *can't*. Don't you understand?"

She gripped his fingers hard. "The rest of this space looks structurally secure so we're safe enough."

"*Safe?*"

"Yes, all we have to worry about is making the exit wall secure when they dig us out from the other side."

"What if the whole damn ridge has come down?" Cauy asked.

"It didn't sound like it did to me." She held his gaze.

"Let's see if my cell phone's working, and we can get hold of Billy or Chase."

As soon as she turned on her phone, the text icon lit up and her phone buzzed with messages from Billy and Ry, whom she assumed had seen what had happened. She picked one at random and replied, but the message wasn't delivered. She tried again.

We're both okay. Exit is blocked. How bad is it on your side?

She waited hopefully for Billy's reply, her hand still locked in Cauy's.

There was still no answer so she had to assume they were on their own until someone dug them out. At least someone out there knew where they were.

Rachel glanced dubiously at Cauy. The vibe he was giving off was not good, but there was nothing she could do about that right now. She turned slightly so he couldn't read her screen. Could she pretend?

"Billy says the storm has picked up, and they'll have to wait until tomorrow to try and get through to us." She took a deep breath. There was no point in sugarcoating the issue. "It's a good thing we've got each other, right?"

Cauy visibly shook himself. "Yeah, or else I would be curled up in a ball screaming my lungs out right about now."

"You don't like small spaces?" Rachel opened her backpack and took out two thin heat-retaining blankets they used at the end of marathons. If she kept calm maybe she could help Cauy through this. She was totally convinced that when Billy realized what had happened he'd get them out.

"Not since I got buried." Cauy shuddered. "When the oil well exploded I ended up under a huge pile of burning debris. Between the choking fumes, the fire, and the shards of metal flying around I was lucky to be alive."

"So this is much better then." Rachel continued to search her backpack.

Cauy raised an eyebrow. "Like how?"

"No fire, no flames, just a piddly little rock fall that knocked you out."

"*Piddly*?" He held her gaze. "Is this your way of making me feel better?"

"Is it working?"

He considered her. "Well, I'm not curled up screaming, so yeah, I suppose it is."

"Good." She handed him her small flashlight. "Do you want to come and explore with me?"

He recoiled as though she'd thumped him. "Are you *nuts*?"

She shrugged. "I've always wanted to come down here. I suspect that after this fiasco, Chase is going to fill this mine to the brim with cement regardless and pretend it never existed." Cauy was still staring at her as if she might explode at any moment. "If you don't want to come, you can sit here and keep an eye on my cell phone."

She waited a second, but he didn't move. She wasn't surprised. At least he didn't look so shell-shocked, and he hadn't fallen to pieces when she'd told him the bad news about their delayed rescue.

"There might even be another way out," she tempted him.

"Not working, Rachel, but nice try."

His faint attempt at a smile made her want to high-five him. He was so much stronger than he realized.

"Okay, I won't be long. I'm not even sure this section connects back into the main mine workings. It could've been an exploratory tunnel."

"Don't go too far."

"I won't." Rachel stood and adjusted her hard hat, glad that she'd had it on when the rocks came down. "I'll see if those idiots Carlson and Sean left anything behind that we can use. I guess this wasn't the first time they came in here."

She pointed at the silver blanket. "These are great for retaining heat. If you get cold, you can either sit on it, or wrap it around your shoulders."

"I'm not cold."

"Yeah, it's actually quite warm in here so that's one good thing." She smiled at him. "I'll be as quick as I can."

Cauy watched Rachel saunter down the mine corridor like she was sashaying down Main Street and wanted to shout at her, to tell her not to be so damned stupid, to sit down, and—

And what? Rock and cry along with him? He breathed out and forced himself to take stock of his situation just like his therapist had taught him. Yeah, sure he was currently trapped inside an old abandoned silver mine, but as Rachel had so kindly pointed out, he wasn't buried alive, burning, or suffocating.

Things could be a lot worse.

Or the mine could just collapse right on top of them, and they'd never recover the bodies. . . . He felt the weight of it above him like a pressure in his head.

Cauy groaned and rubbed his hands over his dust-encrusted face. He'd stopped the rocks from hitting Rachel and kept her safe. That was a good thing. If the mine *did* come down he'd know very little about it. His breathing eased a little, and his heart rate was no longer at running-away-from-zombies level.

Taking the silvery blanket, he spread it out on the floor and sat on it, noticing the instant difference to his already frozen ass. The Morgans would get them out of here. All he had to do was spend the night in the mine. . . .

Worrying about that ceiling coming down.

Cauy frowned at himself. Talk about negative thinking.

He was the poster boy for that. Did he *want* Rachel to think he was a complete wuss?

"Too late, bud," Cauy murmured to himself. "I think she already knows."

Rachel reached the spot where she'd found Sean and Carlson and shined her flashlight around until she located the lamp they'd obviously been using. There were also two sleeping bags, one of Ruth's patchwork quilts, and two couch pillows that should've been left in their cabin. If she could persuade Cauy to take a few more steps into the mine they could probably bed down here for the night in relative comfort.

But would he come this far? If he wouldn't, she could simply take everything and make them a bed closer to the exit. In the corner of the alcove there was a metal file cabinet that looked completely out of place in the mine. Rachel approached it and tried the rusting drawers, but they were locked. She couldn't believe Sean and Carlson had lugged the thing up from the ranch, and wondered who had. There were cigarette butts and bottle caps beside the rickety chair, but they looked older.

Rachel left the space and went farther down the passageway. The silence and warmth settled around her. How long was it since anyone had mined down here? The tunnel narrowed, and she decided to turn back. There was no point risking her safety when she'd already been lucky enough to survive one unexpected cave-in.

She walked slowly back to where Cauy was sitting with his back to the wall like a nervous gangster. He'd found his flask of coffee and set it out on the ground in front of him. She sank down beside him.

"I'm so glad you brought this. I left my flask in Chase's truck. I only have water in my backpack."

"Help yourself."

Rachel took a couple of big glugs and savored the searing heat of the coffee as it went down her throat. "That's good. Are you having some?"

He took the flask from her and had a quick drink. "I'll save some for the morning."

"Good idea." She kept her voice light and encouraging. At least he was anticipating them having a morning, which had to be good, right? "Sean and Carlson left some sleeping bags and stuff back there that we can use. Would you like to come and check them out?"

"I can't." He stared down at his booted feet. "I know it sounds stupid, but I need to be the closest I can get to the outside world."

"Not a problem. I can bring their stuff in here." Rachel went to get the quilt and sleeping bags. She also brought the high-powered lantern and set it on the floor near the remains of the exit. It brightened things up considerably. "I think they finished all the weed."

Cauy's reluctant laugh warmed her soul as she sat beside him on the blanket and wrapped the other one around both their shoulders.

"There's something else odd back there."

"Like what?" Cauy asked with some effort.

"Some kind of filing cabinet, a desk, and a chair. They look like they've been there for ages. When Chase arrives in the morning, I'll make sure he clears them out before the mine is filled."

Rachel surreptitiously checked her cell, but there were no new messages or replies to her. It looked like they really were on their own. . . . It wasn't the first time she'd been down a mine, but she'd never imagined she'd end up sleeping in one. Not that Cauy was going to sleep. She had a sense he was way too uptight even to lie down, but she was going to make him try anyway. Some of her can-do positive attitude would really come in useful right now.

She fake-yawned. "How about we put the quilt underneath us and join the two sleeping bags together so that we can get comfortable?"

"Comfortable?" Cauy looked at her as if she was mad. "Down *here*?"

She shrugged. "Might as well." She grabbed the heavy quilt. "Can you help me?"

Cauy spread the quilt while she zipped the two bags together and placed the pillows at the top.

Behind her, the wind prowled the old mine like a living thing, making the structure sway and groan. Every time there was an extra loud crack, Cauy flinched.

"Come on." Rachel patted the bedding.

She took off her boots, got into the sleeping bag, and scooted across so Cauy could join her. Eventually he did, removing his boots and lying alongside her, his whole body rigid. She rolled onto her side, put her head on his shoulder, and manhandled his arm around her shoulders.

His heart was beating so fast she was surprised he was able to stay still. She smoothed a hand over his open jacket and petted him, hoping he'd relax just a fraction.

"It's okay," she murmured.

"No, it damn well is not."

"Hey!" Rachel poked his chest. "This is the first time I've ever gotten to snuggle with you without worrying about anyone interrupting us."

"Bullshit."

"It's true! We're all alone and horizontal with our clothes on."

He turned his head to look down at her. "If you think I'm capable of getting it on in an abandoned mine your optimism is misplaced."

Rachel pouted. "Then I suppose we'll just have to talk to each other. Unless you want to go to sleep?"

He went quiet and then sighed. "I think I'd rather listen to you talk."

"It doesn't work like that," Rachel said. "Even I can't talk all night. You'll have to contribute. How about we start with you telling me how you ended up injured?"

"You want me to revisit the worst day of my life, while I'm trapped in a *freaking silver mine*?"

"Yes, Cauy Lymond." Rachel looked right into his eyes. "I do."

Cauy held Rachel's gaze, astounded at her nerve, and considered his options. He could go and stand by the door and paw pathetically at the rocks. He could retreat farther into the mine and go nuts, or he could stay in the warm sleeping bag with an incredibly nosy woman in his arms. There really was no contest.

"I was called in to investigate a drilling rig that was malfunctioning," Cauy began speaking, and suddenly he didn't want to stop. "It was a holiday weekend, and that particular crew were new and untried. I shouldn't have let them out there by themselves, but as far as I knew there hadn't been any problems either with that particular rig or that crew."

Rachel eased closer against his shoulder. He couldn't see her face, which somehow made it easier to talk.

"By the time I got to the site, things had gotten long past being a problem and gone into critical meltdown. I didn't know that. I stepped up to the drilling platform and the whole thing blew up in my face." He touched the scars on his throat. "Literally. I was blown backward in the air, and that's the last thing I remember before coming to buried under a pile of burning metal covered in crude oil."

Rachel shivered and stroked his chest. "That must have been terrifying."

"Yeah. I thought I was going to burn to death. Luckily, one of the guys saw which way I'd fallen, and I was far enough away from the actual rig for them to dig down and recover me."

"Thank goodness they found you," Rachel whispered.

"I didn't think that way for a long time." He swallowed hard. "I was a mess. Half my body was burned. I needed skin grafts and all kinds of pain medication just to keep me alive. There were times when it was so hard to keep going that I almost *wished* I'd died. If it hadn't have been for my mom and family I don't think I would've made it."

"What about your wife?"

"She . . . didn't do well with sickness and hospitals. They weren't really her thing."

Rachel's indignant snort almost made him smile. "Her thing? If that was my husband stuck in a hospital it would *become* my thing."

"She liked life to be happy and stress-free."

"Well, she sounds like an idiot," Rachel said.

"That's harsh. Some people can't deal with the darker side of life. When I came out of the hospital I was no angel." He hesitated. "I was angry a lot of the time, I had endless appointments and medical stuff to take care of, and she just couldn't handle it."

"I still don't like her," Rachel sniffed.

"You would've. She's a very happy person to be around."

"As long as *she's* happy, you mean?"

"Not everyone is cut out to look after someone who has changed so dramatically. I wasn't the man she married. That's on me."

"Marriage is about all those things. For richer, for poorer, in sickness and in health," Rachel argued. "You couldn't help what happened to you."

"She begged me not to go out to the rig. I was supposed to be attending some function with her, and I bailed at the last minute. She thought I should've let one of the other guys deal with it, but I was never that kind of boss, and she hated that. She blamed me for going."

"*Still* not liking her much," Rachel muttered.

"Did you forgive your mom for walking out on her sons and husband?" Cauy asked.

"That's different!"

"How so? I could say the same things about your mom. Everyone who met Annie out here liked her a lot, and no one could believe she'd up and leave like that."

"She was . . . ill. She had postpartum depression after having me."

"And she acted out of character. She broke up her marriage, and I broke up mine. Both of us changed."

"They are not the same at all." Rachel struggled to sit up and face him. "Your ex-wife didn't have the depth to care for you when you were sick, my mother . . ." She paused. "My mother walked out on her family and never looked back."

"Lorelei didn't look back either. She married my best friend the day after the divorce came through."

Rachel winced. "That sucks."

He held her gaze. "I deserved it."

"*Why?* Why do you keep saying that?" Rachel demanded.

"Because I frightened her."

Rachel went still and just stared at him until he stumbled on. If the mine was going to collapse around him he might as well get everything out and really alienate her forever.

"As I said, I was in pain, I had terrible headaches and blackouts. One night I woke up to her screaming and fighting me." He took a much-needed breath. "She said I tried to strangle her—she had marks on her throat." He shuddered.

"She moved out that day, straight over to my buddy's house. He wanted to set the cops on me, but she wouldn't allow it."

"Because at some level she *knew* you didn't mean to hurt her." Rachel touched his cheek. "She *knew* it was an aberration."

"She *should've* called the cops. She was probably just too scared of me to do it," Cauy insisted. "I was *way* out of line. That's when I knew I couldn't get better all by myself, and went to see a shrink. I also weaned myself off almost all the painkillers."

"So you tried to make things right," Rachel said. "Did you tell her that?"

"Of course I did, but she wasn't into listening to me anymore." He sighed. "And Rod was very happy to cosset her, and insist that she'd never have to deal with me again. She liked being protected. Nothing wrong with that."

"Some best friend." Rachel shook her head. "You certainly know how to pick 'em."

"When I married her I was trying to fit in—to be like everyone else," Cauy confessed.

"What do you mean?"

"I was never good at parties or all that other stuff, but Lorelei loved to socialize so I tried hard to be the man she wanted."

"So maybe, in the end, Lorelei did you a favor?" Rachel met his gaze.

Cauy let that thought sink into his head. "Yeah. Maybe she did in a weird ass-backward way. After the accident things changed for me—my *priorities* changed. *I* changed. I wasn't willing to pretend to care about all those superficial things anymore."

"Okay, I don't hate her now." Rachel patted his cheek. "And you know what? If she'd really been scared and wanted to get back at you, she *could've* called the cops, taken you to court, and would probably have gotten even more in the divorce settlement."

"She didn't do any of that," Cauy pointed out.

"*Exactly.* So she used what happened to get out of a marriage that no longer appealed to her, took what she was owed, and moved on."

Cauy just stared at her until she frowned at him. "What?"

"You are relentlessly optimistic about everything, aren't you?"

She shrugged. "I try to be."

"It's weird."

"It's the way I learned to survive."

Cauy took off his jacket, folded it up, and put it against the wall behind them. Rachel did the same with her puffy coat. Then he gathered her up against him again and sat back against the pillows.

"Why do you think you have to be positive all the time?" Cauy asked.

"You're asking me questions now?" Rachel groaned. "The world really is about to end."

Cauy took a look at the thousands of pounds of rock above their head and devoutly hoped she was wrong about that.

"Why does being positive make you a survivor?"

"Because my mom needed me to be that way." Rachel rubbed her cheek against the sleeve of his fleece. "Are you sure you don't want to try sleeping?"

"Stop avoiding the question," Cauy said firmly. "Your mom's happiness wasn't dependent on you."

"It felt like it was. When I was little, and there was just the two of us, I always felt like everything was my fault somehow—that I was this massive inconvenience to her. I worried that if I didn't behave just right she'd leave me. I used to store food under my bed and keep my clothes packed just in case she didn't come home one night."

Cauy's hand drifted into Rachel's hair. "But she took you with her. If she *really* thought that, she could've left you behind with the others."

She stiffened in his arms and buried her face against his shoulder.

"Mom didn't mean to bring me."

Cauy eased a finger under her chin so she had to look up at him. "Come again?"

"She didn't intend to take me. HW snuck me into the back of the guy's truck she left with."

"*Why*?"

"Because she loved HW best, and he thought if he left me with her she'd bring me back and take him."

Cauy took a while to process this, and then shook his head. His heart literally hurt for her. "Wow, that's messed up."

"As soon as I found out what really happened I realized why I'd always felt like Mom hadn't wanted me around. She did improve once she met Paul, and she was able to settle down. Things were way better then."

There she went again, making the best of a bad situation. Cauy cuddled Rachel closer wanting to do something, *anything* to comfort her for a hurt that could never be healed. She was nothing like him at all, but he admired the hell out of her.

"I don't mind if you complain about stuff," Cauy murmured. "In fact I appreciate it."

"Liar." She playfully punched his arm. "You're a terrible sulker."

"I like to think of myself more as an inarticulate loser."

She chuckled, making his shoulder vibrate. "Okay, I can go with that. How come Jackson is so chatty then?"

"Probably because unlike me, he never doubts who he is or where he comes from," Cauy said.

She sighed. "You and me, both."

Cauy glanced over at the pile of rocks blocking the door.

"I still can't quite believe this is happening. I must be the unluckiest guy in the universe."

Rachel smoothed her palm over his stubbled chin. "You might as well lie down beside me and relax. It's going to be hours before they start digging us out. I'm sure we could find something to do to while the time away."

"Relax?" He gulped as she ran her thumb down the zipper of his jeans. "You have to be kidding me."

She blinked at him. "That wouldn't make you feel good?"

"Not when I'm worrying about several tons of rock falling on my head, no."

"You're sure?"

He removed her hand. "Absolutely. I'll take a rain check."

"Okay." She sighed and rubbed her face against his shoulder. "I'm actually quite tired. It's been a busy day."

"Then sleep. I'll let you know if we're in imminent danger." He eased down on their makeshift bed and arranged her more comfortably against him, liking the way it felt so natural to hold her.

"I'm not worried about you sleeping with me and strangling me, you know," Rachel murmured sounding half-asleep already.

"I haven't slept with a woman since that night," Cauy acknowledged. "But I'm in a far better place these days."

"I know that, and I trust you." She kissed his chest. "I'm really comfortable right here."

"Good." He smoothed a hand through her hair wondering how on earth she could say such a thing when they were stuck in a freaking mine. "Go to sleep."

He'd told her the worst thing about himself, and she'd tried to make him feel better about it. That was the kind of person she was. Her outward composure and confidence had been earned the hard way, and he respected that—and wished he could be the same. His struggles had turned him inward. Rachel had used her stressful past to reach out to others in a positive way. He could learn a lot from her.

He already had.

Her cell phone was still sitting on the top of the sleeping bag so he went to move it to a more convenient place. The screen flashed up her messages, and he noted the network icon was missing. Her last two texts showed as undelivered, and nothing new had come in.

So she hadn't quite been straight with him after all . . . but he didn't have the heart to blame her. If she hadn't calmed him down he'd probably still be at the rock face scrabbling to get out. Keeping one arm around Rachel, he turned to pick up her backpack and hooked it into his lap before stowing the phone safely inside. There was a large folded map in the bag labeled HISTORIC MORGAN MINE, which he took out to study.

He might as well try to work out how this arm of the mine connected to the main one. Just in case they needed another way out . . . He had to suspect that someone in the Lymond family had used this place recently, and that the dude ranch guests had just discovered the entrance and taken it over for their own purposes.

Unfolding the map he squinted at the faint markings, and used his finger to trace a line from where he thought he was up to the main entrance. There was some kind of connection, but it wasn't exactly straightforward. The question was, had that route been blocked as well? With the recent earthquake activity, and the nearby remains of the creek that had powered the stamp mill it was highly likely. He still wasn't sure he could venture deeper into the darkness without pissing his pants. But what if the rescue tomorrow morning went wrong? What if they caused the cliff above to come down and bury the entrance under a mile of rock?

Cauy forced himself to breathe. Worrying about what hadn't even happened yet would get him nowhere. Rachel was an engineer; if anyone could get them out safely, it would be her.

He carefully refolded the map and leaned back against the wall, his eyes half closing despite him. Rachel was right. It had been a very long day. . . .

Chapter Nineteen

Rachel woke up to a faint buzzing sound in her ear, and irritably swatted a hand around her head. That was the thing about living on a ranch. There were flies everywhere.

There was a grunt, and she opened her eyes to see Cauy squinting down at her.

"Was I snoring?" He yawned. "I can't believe I actually fell asleep."

"I'm sorry I smacked you. I thought you were a fly." She smiled up at him. Despite everything it was remarkably fine to wake up next to Cauy Lymond. "What time is it?"

He still wore a watch so he angled his wrist toward her. "Six in the morning I guess—unless we slept through another day."

"I doubt that." Rachel settled back into Cauy's embrace. "I don't think we're going to be rescued before it gets light."

"*If* we're rescued."

"You think the Morgans would leave me here?" Rachel snorted. "You, maybe, but not their precious little sister."

"I suspect they'd do anything to rescue you," Cauy agreed.

"And, at least they know where we are," she reminded him.

"I was looking at the map in your backpack." Cauy

gestured to her bag. "There's definitely a link between this branch of the mine workings and the main one—or there was."

"It looked clear as far as I went, and the trajectory was definitely upward," Rachel said. "Do you want to see if we can get out by ourselves?"

Cauy frowned at her. "Can you imagine what your family would do to me if they broke in here and found you'd disappeared?"

She pouted. "So you wouldn't even attempt to come with me and find out?"

"Not unless my life depended on it."

"Okay." She sighed. "But would you freak out if I just went and took a look before the cavalry arrive?"

"I can't exactly stop you, can I?" He removed his arm from around her shoulders and she immediately felt bereft. "You're a grown woman."

Belatedly she remembered the rules of their no-strings-attached relationship. Last night she thought they'd gotten past that, but she should have known never to assume.

"You're right." She eased away from his side and got out of the sleeping bag. The temperature was frigid, and she hastily put on her coat and boots. "I'll go and take a look."

"You probably think I'm a coward," Cauy said slowly.

Rachel glanced back at him as she zipped up her coat. "Not really. If I'd been through what you have, I'd probably stay put as well."

"I *feel* like a coward."

"Then that's on you." Rachel held his stare. "I promise I won't be long. I'll take the map with me and borrow your big flashlight, okay?"

Cauy nodded as she consulted the map and made some preliminary plans. He'd made it clear that he wasn't responsible for her choices, and she had just returned the favor. What he made of that was up to him.

She folded the map until it showed the relevant section and set off, her hard hat on her head and her backpack in place. The tunnel went by the hollowed-out section where she'd found Sean and Carlson, and snaked upward. Her booted foot hit what felt like old metal railings or possibly just the remaining pins. She doubted any valuable metal had been left in the abandoned mine.

She used the flashlight to examine the passage, and continued upward as it narrowed and grew steeper. It definitely felt like she was in a connecting tunnel. She put her hand on the wall and held still as the space suddenly widened in front of her and the cold breeze intensified. Fresh air was flowing into the works from somewhere.

The map indicated a straight line that appeared to go up toward the main entrance, but the tunnel appeared to end. Rachel turned in a slow circle noting the wooden crates, an abandoned pick, and a couple of old glass bottles half buried in the dirt from the roof. Puzzled, she rotated again and then focused the light upward and saw a large hole with what looked like the remains of a ladder attached to the side.

"Straight up indeed," Rachel murmured, her voice echoing in the cavern. "I don't think either of us are going up there."

She turned and made her way back, pausing every so often to check out the structure of the workings and the construction of the tunnels. It was truly amazing to see how carefully the mine had been erected, and how long it had remained intact. She could even see the marks of individual pickaxes. There was no water damage and, apart from the odd fall of soil, the issues at the top of the mine didn't seem to have impacted this level.

There was something about the silence of the place that appealed to her. Was it because she was a Morgan and her ancestors had mined here? Was that why she'd instinctively gravitated toward an engineering career before she'd even known about her heritage? She reached the alcove where she'd found the ranch guests and considered the filing cabinet anew. What on earth had possessed someone to use this space as his or her office?

If Chase was willing to remove the filing cabinet before permanently shutting down the mine they might find out. Seeing as this branch of the mine was on the Lymond side, she suspected it might actually belong to Cauy.

She arrived back to discover that Cauy had rolled up their temporary bed and put on his coat and boots. He'd also rediscovered his hat, dusted it down, and set it firmly on his head.

"Anything happening?" Rachel asked as she took off her backpack.

"I haven't heard a thing yet."

He glanced back at her from his position by the entrance where he appeared to be gingerly clearing rocks away.

She joined him and hunkered down at his side. "We can shift some of this stuff. Don't touch anything close to the actual exit wall. Some of those rocks are still holding that wall up."

"Got it." Cauy placed another sizeable chunk of rock to one side. "I figured it might help to clear a path. How was the tunnel?"

She sighed. "The map was surprisingly accurate, but it ended in a hole in the ceiling with a vertical climb out and no usable ladder."

"Then let's hope they can get us out this way," Cauy said.

"I'm sure they will," Rachel assured him.

He was amazed at how calm he was, and attributed that entirely to the woman at his side. She'd done more to cure him of his fears than a year of seeing a shrink or trying to pretend nothing was wrong. She'd even told him to suck it up and not project his insecurities on her, which he'd deserved.

How could he let her walk away from him?

Cauy went still. Where had that thought come from? He had no right to expect anything from her. She deserved so much more, but he wanted her, he wasn't going to lie to himself anymore.

If they got out of the mine—*when* they got out—he would take the time to think things through and work out how to ask her if she'd be interested in taking things further with him. She'd probably laugh, but he had to ask.

"Are you okay, Cauy?"

He looked over at her. "I'm good, thanks."

Her smile warmed his soul. She'd done the unthinkable—made him believe that not only could he have a future with her, but that she might like him just the way he was.

A rumble of sound vibrated through the outside wall of the mine. Cauy tensed as Rachel jumped to her feet.

"It's got to be them!" She grabbed Cauy's hand and kissed his cheek. "We'll be out of here in no time!"

Cauy doubted that, but even he was surprised at the scale of the operation Chase Morgan had organized, and the speed of their deliverance. Chase had obviously called in the best of the best. Without anyone asking him he found himself bundled up in a blanket being transported to Morgan Ranch. Mrs. Morgan sent Rachel up to bed and put Cauy in the best parlor tucked up on the couch with a bowl of hot soup and crusty bread.

He fell asleep almost immediately and woke up to find Mrs. Morgan sitting opposite him knitting something fluffy. He blinked at her for a puzzled moment before everything came flooding back.

"Mrs. Morgan." He struggled into a sitting position. "Is Rachel okay?"

"Please call me Ruth." She looked up from her knitting. "Rachel's sleeping now. January's keeping an eye on her. How are you feeling?"

"A little tired," Cauy acknowledged. "Being stuck in a mine wasn't exactly high on my to-do list."

"So I should imagine. I checked that cut on your head, but it seems to be healing nicely all by itself." She smiled at him. "Rachel said you were very brave and protected her when the wall came down."

He shrugged. "I did my best. She kept me sane while we were trapped in there, so I think we're even."

Ruth shuddered. "I can't imagine how that must have felt for you."

He held her gaze. "If Rachel hadn't been there I would probably have freaked out. She was . . . amazing."

"Rachel's certainly good at keeping everyone happy," Ruth agreed.

Cauy swung his legs over the side of the couch and set his feet on the rug. He had a sense that he needed to be upright for this conversation.

Ruth returned her attention to her knitting. "All her life, Rachel has believed it's her job to support everyone, make the best of everything, and put herself second. Sometimes it breaks my heart."

Cauy nodded. "I hear you." He carefully drew the quilt to one side, his sense of relief of being out of the mine rapidly evaporating. Was Ruth subtly trying to tell him that Rachel didn't need another set of problems to deal with? Problems like *him*?

"I think I'd better be going home now." Cauy cleared his throat. "Thanks for everything, and please give Rachel my best."

She raised an eyebrow. "I didn't say any of that to make you bolt, young man."

"I know." He found a smile somewhere. "I just need to get back. Jackson will be worried."

Ruth stood as he did and put her hand on his sleeve, her

gaze concerned. "Cauy, you're a good man. I hope you stay and make the Lymond Ranch a huge success."

Cauy nodded. "Thank you. I'm not planning on leaving anytime soon."

Rachel would be leaving. Not him. She deserved to fly.

He'd make sure of it.

He turned to the door and went into the mudroom where someone had put his jacket, boots, and hat. It occurred to him that he didn't have his truck or a working cell phone. He was reluctantly turning toward the kitchen to see if he could beg a ride when Billy came toward him.

"Ruth says you're leaving, Cauy. I can give you a ride home. I've got to go into town."

"That would be awesome." Cauy took a quick look up the stairs as they went by, but there was no sign of Rachel. But what could he say to her now? "I'd call Jackson, but my cell phone is broken."

"It's not a problem."

Billy got into his truck, and Cauy opened the door on the passenger side. It was only afternoon, and yet it felt like another endless day. It was still blowing a gale and the snow had turned to sleet, which made everything miserable and churned up the muddy roads.

Kind of how he felt inside, like someone had kicked him down the stairs.

Cauy braced himself in case Billy wanted to offer him some advice about Rachel, but the rancher talked about the weather, his cattle, and the departure of the last guests, and how glad everyone was to see them go.

It didn't take long to reach home. Jackson's truck was parked next to the barn, and all the house lights were on. Grace barked from inside as he got out of the truck, and the cold hit him afresh. Billy got out too and came around to him.

Cauy held out his hand. "Thanks for getting us out of the mine."

"That was all Chase's doing." Billy smiled as he shook Cauy's hand. "I just happened to be in the right place at the right time to see what went down and act on it."

"I'm grateful for that." Cauy hesitated. "And if there's anything I can do for you or your ranch, please feel free to ask. I'm not my father, and I have no intention of adopting his old prejudices."

"I think we've all worked that out already." Billy clapped him around the shoulder and winked. "Stay safe, Cauy."

Cauy went into the house to an enthusiastic welcome from Grace, who pranced around him like he'd been gone for a week. Jackson came into the kitchen and looked him up and down.

"You okay, Bro?"

"Perfect. You?"

"I'm good." Jackson raised an eyebrow. "Dude, you were stuck underground in a mine. I think you could elaborate a little."

Cauy shrugged. "I'm fine. I got out alive. There was no fire, no oil exploding under high pressure, and all I got hit with was a piddly piece of rock on the back of my head."

Jackson leaned against the doorframe. "Are you sure that knock on the head wasn't serious? You sound weird."

Cauy forced a smile. "I'm just tired."

"I can imagine." Jackson straightened up. "If you need to talk to me about anything, you know where I am."

"Got it."

Cauy took off his hat and jacket. He'd left his boots on the mat outside. If he *had* anything to say he trusted Jackson, but there was nothing left to share. He had some thinking to do, but he already knew the answers. Mrs. Morgan had just pointed out something so obvious that even he had realized it was true. Now he just had to find a way to live with it.

* * *

"I saw the paperwork Kim sent you on your desk, Cauy. I hope you don't mind that I read it."

Jackson had paused from eating an enormous piece of chicken pie to address Cauy, who sat opposite him at the kitchen table. He'd taken another nap, and Jackson had woken him up to eat at seven.

"Are you going to take it up?"

"Nope." Cauy chewed vigorously but the food still choked him. "No point in riling everyone up around here."

"Especially if we want to stick around." Jackson nodded. "It made interesting reading though."

"I barely made it through the cover letter," Cauy admitted. "Although seeing how much Kim charged me for each sentence I probably should get my money's worth and read it through."

There was a knock on the back door, and Grace started barking. She'd definitely perked up in the last couple of days.

Jackson raised his eyebrows. "Are we expecting anyone?"

"No." Cauy put down his fork. "But I bet you a hundred bucks it's a Morgan."

Jackson went to open the door while Cauy kept hold of Grace's collar.

"It's Roy." Jackson stepped back to reveal the diminutive ranch foreman. "You owe me a hundred bucks."

"No way," Cauy snorted. "He's basically a Morgan." At this point he was just glad it wasn't Rachel. He still hadn't figured out exactly what to say to her. "What can I do for you, Roy?"

"Evening, Cauy." Roy tipped his hat, wiped his feet on the mat, and closed the door behind him. "Chase told me to bring that old filing cabinet we found in the mine up to you. It was under Lymond land so he reckons it must be something to do with your family."

"Or he just wants to get rid of it," Jackson added. "Do you want a hand taking it out of the truck?"

"Yes, please. I'm not as strong as I used to be." Roy winked at Jackson. "I'm afraid it will flatten me if I try to do it alone."

Cauy had half risen from his seat, but Jackson waved him back. "I'll get this. Where do you want me to put it?"

"The new feed store would be best," Cauy said. "I don't want anything rusting here in the house."

"Yeah, we've got enough junk. I found Mom's old Christmas tree in my closet today. We should put it up." Jackson nodded at Roy. "I'll just get my coat."

Chapter Twenty

"So Cauy was okay when he left?" Rachel asked Ruth as she ate her lunch at the kitchen table. She'd slept round the clock and was ravenous.

"He seemed to be, why?" Ruth sipped her coffee.

"I meant to tell him to get checked out by Dr. Tio. He did lose consciousness for a minute, and that can't be good for someone who's had previous head trauma."

Ruth studied her over the rim of her mug. "Cauy's an adult. I'm sure he can make that decision for himself, Rachel."

"Yes, but he doesn't like to admit there's anything wrong with him, so—"

"Maybe you should let him make his own mind up."

Rachel put down her fork. "Are you trying to say I'm interfering?"

Ruth's blue gaze met hers. "What do you think?"

"Oh, don't do that answer a question with a question thing." Rachel sat back. "It drives me nuts. Can't you just tell me what you're getting at?"

"From what you've told me, you and Cauy aren't going out together, are you?" Ruth asked.

"Not officially . . ." Rachel said. "But—"

"So it's not up to you to tell him what to do. That's all I'm saying, my dear."

Rachel folded her arms across her chest. "He *likes* me telling him what to do."

"Are you sure about that?" Ruth sighed. "You don't have to fix him, Rachel. He's not your problem."

Rachel stared at her grandmother as a thousand replies formed in her mind. "I don't *want* to fix him."

"If you say so, dear." Ruth smiled at her. "Now, what are you planning to do for the rest of the day? Now that the last guests have departed we can finally just be family again and start preparing for Christmas."

Ruth carried on talking as if eager to distract Rachel from her blunt appraisal of her tenuous relationship with Cauy. She liked him just the way he was. After the night they'd spent together in the mine she was fairly certain he was as keen to have a *real* relationship with her as she was.

She finished her meal, took a last gulp of iced tea, and wiped her mouth on her napkin. "I have to take Grace to the vet's today. She needs more shots, and Jenna wants to check how the puppies are doing."

"Shouldn't Cauy be doing that?"

"I made the appointment, and I forgot to tell him, so this one's on me." Rachel made sure she had her cell phone in her pocket. "The next one will definitely be up to him."

Ruth nodded. "Give Jenna my love, and ask her if she wants to come over for dinner and tell us how life is in her new house."

"I'll certainly mention it to her." Rachel stood and dusted toast crumbs off her chest. "It's odd not having BB and Maria in the house anymore."

"I know," Ruth agreed. "And it's certainly a lot quieter."

Rachel put her silverware and plate in the dishwasher, washed her hands, and went to put on her warmest outerwear. A chill was definitely settling over the whole valley and she'd have to get used to it. The stark splendor of the white fields against the towering black Sierra mountains spoke to her soul. Wherever she went in the world, she now knew this place would always remain in her heart.

She got into her truck and drove the short route to the Lymond Ranch singing Christmas carols at the top of her voice. Maybe getting stuck together in the mine had been a good thing for her and Cauy after all. . . .

She parked outside the house and got out to the sound of Grace barking from the fenced-in yard. The henhouse had been repaired and was currently full to bursting with feathered occupants huddled together against the winter cold.

"Back door's open! Come on through!" Jackson called out to her.

She went inside to find him sitting at the table eating cake and drinking coffee. He wore a thick flannel shirt and had bunny slippers on his feet.

"Hey, how are you feeling, Rachel?"

"I'm good, thanks." Rachel bent to pet Grace, who had come bounding in through the doggie door in the mudroom. "Is Cauy around?"

"He went into town about an hour ago to get a new phone. He just sent me a text saying he's on his way back. Would you like some coffee while you wait?"

"That would be great." Rachel glanced out of the window to where Cauy's truck usually stood. "What are you up to?"

"Still going through the family finances," Jackson said, grimacing. "I can't believe how disorganized my father was, and Cauy's not much better. He's not used to having to think about every dime because he has all these people to do stuff for him."

He handed her a mug of coffee and a carton of cream. "For light relief, I decided to clear out the closet in my bedroom and found the old Christmas decorations my mom used to put up. Cauy's going to check the lights when he gets back so we can put the tree up."

"That's cool," Rachel said. "Do you need any help? I'm just sitting here doing nothing."

Jackson looked her up and down. "If you mean it, could you help me shift a couple of the boxes into the farm office? I can't get deeper into the closet until these two are out of the way, and they are too big for me to manage on my own."

"Sure!" Rachel took off her jacket. "I'd love to help."

It was better than sitting there biting her nails waiting for Cauy to come back, full of a weird mixture of hope and fear.

Jackson carried on talking as they walked down to his bedroom. "They're not heavy. Just awkwardly shaped. I don't want to bring a whole pile of crap down on top of myself while I manhandle them out. I think one of them is full of stuff for the tree."

When they reached the closet, Rachel immediately saw what he meant. The two biggest storage containers were at the bottom of a huge stack of boxes. "Maybe we should move some of the smaller ones on the sides before we start."

"Okay."

They worked together for several minutes to reduce the piles, and were able to slide out the first box and then the second without incident.

"Phew!" Jackson said. He checked the weight of each cardboard container. "How about you take the one on the right?"

Rachel bent down to gather the box in her arms and discovered that it was a lot lighter than she had anticipated. It was just awkwardly large to hold. She followed Jackson across into the office and waited as he cleared a space on the desk. Several papers fluttered to the ground, and Grace pounced.

Jackson groaned and relieved Rachel of her box. "Can you get that back from Grace? Cauy will kill me."

"Sure!" Rachel sat on the floor and picked up the rest of the pages while Grace wrestled and growled at the one she'd found. "She's only got the envelope. Does he really need that?"

"Probably not," Jackson said. "I'll just go and get some scissors. Mom taped these up good."

Rachel gathered the rest of the scattered papers on her lap and was attempting to set them in some sort of order when the word *Morgan* caught her attention. Forgetting all about good manners, she read the first page of the document, her sense of outrage growing with every word. Cauy and his lawyer were joking about screwing Chase out of a fortune?

She stared at the wall. Was that why he'd really come back? To take down her family?

"I found the scissors." Jackson came back in and halted as he noticed she was still sitting on the floor. "You okay?"

"Yes." She stood and fixed a smile on her face. "I couldn't help noticing this letter is about Cauy suing the Morgans for land."

"Oh yeah, that." Jackson cut through the tape. "Kim's really good at discovering the dirt. That's why Cauy pays him so well."

The back door slammed, and Rachel started toward the sound, the papers clenched in her hand. Cauy was just taking his coat off as she entered the kitchen. He looked exhausted. Everything in her wanted to rush into his arms and make him better.

"Hey." He nodded but made no effort to come any closer. In fact he looked downright wary. "What's up?"

"I came to take Grace to the vet."

"Okay," he said, nodding. "Do I need to come with you?"

"That's entirely up to you." Rachel raised her chin. "I wouldn't want anyone thinking I was telling you what to do or anything."

"Is something wrong, Rachel?" Cauy asked slowly, his gaze on her face.

"You tell me." She held up the pile of paper. "Your lawyer seems to think you have a legal case to grab some of Morgan Ranch."

"Yeah, that's true, but I—"

"So why haven't you gotten around to mentioning it while my family have saved your ass on several occasions including getting you out of the very mine your lawyer thinks you should have ownership of?"

He opened his mouth to answer her, and then seemed to think better of it. She, on the other hand, couldn't *stop* talking.

"And what about me? I thought we'd reached some kind of understanding the other night, some kind of . . . bond."

"Rachel . . . as to that." He met her gaze. "I'm sorry."

Her heart actually hurt. "Sorry for what exactly? Raising my expectations, or making me look stupid?" She was proud her voice wasn't shaking. "Or did you just get a good laugh out of deceiving my whole family?"

A muscle flicked in his jaw, but he didn't defend himself. Rachel gathered her resources.

"You might not be Mark Lymond's real son, Cauy, but you sure as hell act like him." She bent down and gathered Grace in her arms. "Have a great day."

She managed to grab her coat as she left, and made it to her car without losing it entirely. She settled Grace in the seat beside her and started the engine. So there it was. Someone she thought cared for her had let her down again and thought only of himself. Ruth had been right. Cauy didn't need her at all. Was she cursed? Or was there something seriously wrong with her that made everyone take advantage of her even when she tried her best?

Rachel backed carefully out of her space. Whichever one it was, she was no longer going to sit back and take it.

* * *

"What the hell is going on?" Jackson stormed into the kitchen and loomed over Cauy. "I couldn't help overhearing Rachel tearing you off a strip, and you just let her?"

"Yeah." Cauy sank down onto the nearest chair. He wanted to crawl into bed and hide for a week to lick his wounds. "It's none of your business."

"Why didn't you just tell her you have no intention of pursuing that case?" Jackson plonked himself down beside Cauy. "Have you got a death wish or something?"

Cauy fixed his brother with his hardest stare. "Can you just drop it?"

"*No*." Jackson stared right back. "You *love* her. Why did you send her away?"

"I don't . . ." Cauy couldn't even finish the lie. "I *can't* . . ."

"Can't what? Be straight with her?" Jackson demanded. "Do you want me to go after her and tell her the truth?"

"Goddamn it, no!" Cauy was shouting now. "Why the hell do you think I sent her away in the first place?"

"I don't know, Bro." Jeez, now Jackson was bringing out the sarcasm. "Please enlighten me."

"Rachel's too young for me, and she needs her own life, not getting stuck with someone who's *had* their life and just wants to stick around on a ranch and grow old."

"You make it sound like you're ninety!" Jackson wasn't backing down. "What are you? Six years older than her? Seven? That's *nothing*, Cauy."

"She's just gotten out of college. She has her whole life ahead of her," Cauy insisted. "She doesn't need to be stuck here with *me*."

"Maybe she wants to be stuck with you. God knows why, but maybe she does!" Jackson shoved a hand through his hair. "So you let her think you're a land-grabbing asshole to get *rid of her*? Jeez, Bro."

"I did it for her," Cauy growled. "It's for the best."

"*Right*." Jackson stood and looked down at him. "Just for the record. You *are* an asshole, but not for the reasons you think. I'm going to set up the Christmas tree. I don't need your help, okay? Just sit here and reflect on your stupendous stupidity in sending the woman who obviously loves you away!"

Jackson slammed the door as he left, making Cauy wince.

He'd done the right thing. Trying to explain everything wouldn't have worked. Rachel would've refused to give up on him because that was fundamental to who she was. Her accusation about the lawsuit had offered him the perfect way to make her hate him and move on with her life without having to worry or feel responsible for him.

The fact that he needed her and wanted her was enough reason to send her away. She deserved to be put *first* for a change. Cauy buried his face in his hands and took several deep breaths. He'd survive. He'd done it before. He was doing this *because* he loved her, not because he didn't. Why couldn't Jackson see that?

The fact that it was tearing *him* apart didn't matter either. Rachel had to come first even if it left him in the dust.

Luckily, Jenna had been called out to attend to a horse with colic so Rachel only had to deal with Dave at the vet's. As he was somewhat of a one-man show even though her heart was breaking, she only had to smile and nod along as he examined Grace and took the cast off her leg.

After insisting on paying the new bill and setting up a separate new account for Grace, Rachel headed home. She'd already decided she wouldn't return the dog to Cauy. Having to see him again regularly—even if it was just to talk about the dog—would be too much to deal with right now.

When she reached the ranch, she sat down on the steps with Grace and introduced her to all the other dogs that milled around the ranch, and then took her inside. Billy was sitting at the kitchen table reading something on his laptop. He looked up when she came in, and smiled at the dog.

"Who's this?"

"This is Grace." Rachel didn't have to make the dog go over to Billy. All animals loved him.

"Cauy's dog?"

"Mine now—that is, if you and Ruth don't mind keeping an eye on her after I've gone," Rachel said as Billy ruffled Grace's big ears.

"Does Cauy know about this?" Billy asked slowly.

"He'll work it out." Rachel filled the dog's bowl with water and showed Grace where it was. "He's not stupid."

"What's wrong?"

Rachel sat at the table and let out a breath. "Why would you think something was wrong?"

"Because you're my daughter and I've learned to read your face over the past few weeks, and you're not happy. Did something happen with Cauy?"

Rachel was debating what to say when Chase came in and sat beside her. He pointed at the dog.

"Where did that come from?"

"It's the dog Rachel and Cauy found at the feed store," Billy said helpfully. "Rachel's taking charge of her now."

Chase frowned. "Did Cauy kick her out?"

"Me or the dog?" Rachel tried to make a joke, but didn't think she'd quite pulled it off. "I bet he'll miss Grace more than me."

"What happened?" Chase turned the full power of his immense focus on her.

"I was just asking her the same thing," Billy said.

"I went over to Cauy's to pick up Grace and take her to the vet's. While I was there I discovered that Cauy had set his lawyer to investigate what he described as an illegal land grab by the Morgan family almost a hundred years ago."

"What?" Chase blinked at her.

"Apparently, the Lymond family claimed that about one eighth of *our* ranch, including the silver mine, belongs to them," Rachel said. "And Cauy's lawyer said that even if he can't prove it, Cauy should take you to court to screw you out of a lot of money that you can well afford."

"Wow. Weird that he hasn't mentioned it." Chase looked at Billy. "I thought you said he was all about putting the past behind us and moving on?"

"That's what he said when I dropped him home the other night," Billy confirmed. "I wonder what's going on?"

"Maybe he just wants money and revenge for his father," Rachel said darkly.

"*Money*?" Chase snorted. "He doesn't exactly need any himself, you know. He owned an oil company in Texas that was just bought out by one of the big guys."

"*What*?" Rachel sat up straight. "He said he worked as a laborer and then a roustabout!"

"He certainly started that way, but he made his money later." Chase gave her an exasperated stare. "Don't you *google* the guys you date? I thought everyone did that these days for safety reasons."

"Usually I do, but"—Rachel was babbling now—"I wasn't really officially going out with Cauy, so I didn't. Are you sure he's rich?"

Chase tapped away on his keyboard and turned the screen so she could see it. There was a picture of Cauy obviously taken before the accident, and a whole long biography about him and his oil companies.

"Holy cow, he's almost as rich as you are!" Rachel

breathed. "He said Lorelei got half of everything, and I was feeling sorry for him!"

"So he doesn't need our money, which brings us back to the idea that he's doing this to revenge a man who might not actually be his father anyway," Chase pointed out with his usual calm logic. "I'm not buying it."

"Neither am I," Billy chimed in.

Rachel looked at them both and shook her head. "So where does that leave us?"

Billy glanced at Chase. "Are you quite certain Cauy admitted he was going to go through with this court case?"

Rachel ran the painful encounter back through her head. "He didn't argue that he wasn't. Probably because he knew he didn't have a leg to stand on."

"Then maybe he just said it to get rid of you?" Chase suggested.

Billy cleared his throat and turned to Rachel, who was staring open-mouthed at Chase. "You'll have to excuse your big brother. Sometimes he opens his mouth before he thinks things through and sticks his boot right in it."

Chase looked startled. "Sorry, did that sound rude? It just seemed to be the most logical conclusion. I didn't mean to imply—"

"There's no need to apologize. You're probably right." Rachel groaned. "He could've just let me down easily."

"Maybe he thought he did." Chase nodded, and then scowled as Billy elbowed him in the ribs. "*What?*"

"Perhaps you should just shut up now and let me handle it?" Billy raised his eyebrows. "I'm sure January needs your help somewhere else."

"She'd call me if she did." Chase closed his laptop. "Okay, I can see I'm not wanted. Let me know if there's anything further I can do to help Rachel, okay?"

"Help?" Billy shook his head as Chase left the kitchen. "With help like that who needs enemies?"

"I know he was trying." Rachel rested her chin on her hand and sighed heavily. "I don't think there is anything left *for* you to say, is there? Cauy Lymond wanted me to think the worst of him, and he accomplished his goal."

"Yeah, he did." Billy hesitated. "The real question you have to ask yourself, Rachel, is *why*?"

Chapter Twenty-One

"Where's Grace?" Jackson came into the kitchen where Cauy was sitting at the table and looked around. "She didn't get out, did she?"

"Rachel hasn't brought her back." Cauy pretended to focus on reading his mail.

"You let her kidnap *our dog*?"

"She's not our dog. Rachel took Grace to the vet to get the cast removed," Cauy explained. "She found the dog. I was just doing her a favor looking after it."

"So Grace won't be coming back?" Jackson frowned. "I bought her a Christmas present."

"Then you can go over to Morgan Ranch and give it to her, it's not exactly far."

Jackson came to sit next to Cauy. "You do know we've been invited for Christmas dinner?"

"I wouldn't count on it." Cauy pushed his coffee to one side. He'd drunk way too much and had a headache. He still hadn't reconciled what he'd said to Rachel with how his heart was currently feeling. It felt *wrong*, like he'd completely misread everything. "Rachel's probably told them what a bastard I am, and they'll close ranks to defend her."

"And you already know what I think of that stupid

strategy," Jackson muttered. "Maybe I'll go and leave you here to stew in your self-righteous juices."

"Nice image," Cauy said as he rose to his feet. "Let's just hope the Morgans don't leave us a dozen horses to take care of by ourselves as well."

"If they do, it'll totally be your fault." Jackson looked up at him. "Can I borrow some of your tools to get into that old filing cabinet?"

"Sure, help yourself." Cauy stretched and checked the time. "I've got to see to our horses anyway so I'll come out with you."

It seemed weird walking anywhere now without Grace padding along beside him. He'd kind of hoped Rachel would bring the dog back but hadn't been surprised when she'd chosen not to. He'd cut her off and set her free, so why did it still feel as if he'd cut out his own heart as well?

"Cauy, are you coming?" Jackson shouted at him from the newly roofed feed store.

"I'll just get my tools."

It took them a while to figure out how to get into the rusted drawers, but they eventually worked it out, prying the top one open and dumping the whole thing on the newly laid cement floor.

"Eew." Jackson wrinkled his nose. "It smells like booze."

"That's because someone was stashing their whisky in there." Cauy bent down and fished out two empty bottles. "There's another one here that's on its side with the lid not properly closed. It's leaked all over the rest of the stuff."

"Any gold?" Jackson asked hopefully.

"In a *silver* mine?" Cauy crouched beside the drawer and stirred the rest of the contents with his gloved finger. "Looks like old accounts books to me."

"What date?"

"Early twentieth century, I think." Cauy used the light on

his new phone to illuminate the gloom. "Not sure I want to lean in too close in case I catch something."

"I'll check them out later," Jackson said. "Let's get the second drawer open."

Cauy helped Jackson lower it to the floor. It was heavier than the last one, but there only appeared to be one item inside. It was a large metal box with a key sticking out of it.

"Wow," Jackson said. "Treasure!" He patted the table. "Bring it up here into the light."

"Knowing our luck it will be lumps of coal," Cauy muttered as he heaved the heavy rust-encrusted box onto the table. Jackson had to use the pliers to persuade the bent key to turn in the lock, but he managed it eventually.

"Whoa," Jackson breathed. "*That's* where Dad was keeping his money."

Cauy stared at what appeared to be gold coins. "You're kidding me. What idiot puts their money into fake gold coins?"

Jackson was examining them. "I don't think they're fake, Cauy. You remember how Dad was always going on about those old coins his father handed down to him? He must have decided to carry on the collection."

"So you think they're worth some money?" Cauy asked dubiously.

"Yeah, I'll check them out on the Internet, okay?" Jackson grinned at him. "We're rich! Well, I am. You are anyway."

"Any money we recover from them should go straight back into the ranch," Cauy stated. "We need stock, and—"

"Don't be such a tightwad." Jackson held up his hand. "I'm not planning a gambling trip to Vegas or anything. Just let me just enjoy the moment, okay?"

"Sorry, my sense of humor's not working too well these days." Cauy stepped back.

"And whose fault is that?" Jackson picked up the metal

box and started back toward the house. "I'll clean them up and get back to you as soon as possible."

"Great." Cauy turned to the barn, the smell of rust clinging to him. Whatever happened with the coins he'd make sure Jackson got half the profits. He'd start on the horses. It would give him something to do and stop him worrying about how Rachel was doing.

About three horses in, Cauy heard a truck pull into the yard and poked his head out into the frosty air to see Roy and some of the Morgan Ranch hands coming toward the barn.

"Evening, Cauy!" Roy came straight for him, an elderly man by his side. "Have you got a moment?"

"Sure." Cauy braced himself as he showed Roy and the stranger into the newly reorganized tack room, which was slightly warmer than the open-ended barn. The guy looked a little long in the tooth to be a new ranch hand. "How can I help you?"

Roy pointed at the man next to him who on closer inspection looked vaguely familiar. "This here is Shep Gardin. He used to work on our ranch, and now he has his own place about a mile up the road next to the Turners."

Cauy tipped his hat to the elderly man, who was regarding him intently. "It's a pleasure to meet you, sir."

Shep turned to Roy. "He could be."

"You think?" Roy grinned, displaying the gap in his teeth. "I thought so as soon as I saw him. He's *like* Anita, but he definitely doesn't have her coloring."

Cauy patiently waited them out until Shep turned to him.

"My son Benjamin."

"Yes?" Cauy asked cautiously.

"He worked at the Morgan Ranch with me. Went to school with your mother, and was walking out with her."

Cauy glanced at Roy. "As in *going* out with her?"

Shep nodded vigorously. "Very sweet on her. She was a lovely girl. We approved."

"I think Ben might have been your father, Cauy," Roy said. "You have a look of him. It took me a while to work it out, and then I asked Shep what he thought, and found out he'd also been wondering. He saw you in Doc Mendez's waiting room a couple of times, and once at the veterinaries'."

Cauy focused on Shep. "What happened to Ben?"

A quiver of emotion rushed over the old man's face. His kind brown eyes were the same color as Cauy's. "Tractor and trailer rolled over on him when he was seventeen. He died instantly."

"I'm sorry for your loss." Cauy said the words automatically.

If Shep was correct, it might explain why his mother had seen no alternative than to marry someone else to give her child a name.

"We can do that fancy DNA testing if you want," Shep said gruffly. "But you do have a look of my boy."

"I'd be happy to do that as long as my mother doesn't object," Cauy said. He held out his hand. "It's good to meet you regardless, sir."

Shep's shy smile reminded Cauy of his own before the accident. "That would be wonderful, son. You'll have to come and meet my Marjory. She'd be thrilled."

"Now, don't rush the boy," Roy admonished his friend. "He's got a lot to think about already."

Shep nodded and stepped back. "Thanks for introducing us, Roy. Now, seeing as I'm here, let me help out with the horses."

Rachel whistled to Grace and came out of the barn. It was still early in the morning, and the sun had managed to climb over the Sierras without adding any warmth to the valley. She wasn't sleeping well and had woken up when it was still dark, and decided to spend an hour mucking out the horses. Grace had enjoyed chasing the barn cats and hanging out with the other dogs. She'd spent most of the night whining, which hadn't helped Rachel sleep any better. She'd been that way ever since Rachel had brought her home three days ago. At some point in the night Rachel had felt like joining in. . . .

"Grace!" Rachel called out again, and the dog finally emerged from the barn, ears flapping as she galloped toward Rachel.

Rachel was just about to put on her leash when a truck came through the gate and pulled into the circular yard. She instinctively grabbed hold of Grace's collar. The dog was still young, and not well trained enough to always come back when she was called.

Rachel went still as Cauy emerged from the truck muffled up in his thick sheepskin coat, brown cowboy hat, and a scarf. She didn't want to speak to him, but pride made her stand her ground, and wait for him approach her.

"Morning, Rachel." He tipped his hat to her, but she couldn't see his eyes beneath the lowered brim. "I brought Grace's stuff over. I thought you might need it."

With an excited yelp Grace tried to bound forward. Rachel released her iron grip and let her go. Cauy sank to his knees and grabbed hold of the dog, running his hands through her fur, and murmured sweet nothings in her ears as she tried to lick his face. Grace's tail was wagging so hard Rachel was surprised she hadn't taken off.

She knew how good Cauy's work roughened hands felt, and for a terrible second yearned to launch her own body at him and be given the same welcome. She'd fallen in love with him and there was nothing she could do about it. Instead she watched in silence as man and dog bonded again. Eventually he looked up at her, his smile crooked.

"Sorry. It was just so good to see her again."

"So I gathered." Rachel crossed her arms over her chest. "She misses you."

"Yeah?" Cauy gave Grace another pet and reluctantly got to his feet, his gaze lingering on the dog. "I'll put the stuff on the porch."

"There's no need," Rachel said.

Cauy went still. "Excuse me?"

She gestured at Grace, who was jumping up at Cauy demanding more attention. "She wants to be with you. Take her home, okay? Just let me know when she has the puppies." She half turned back to the barn. "Thanks for coming, Cauy. Bye, Grace."

"Rachel, wait," Cauy called out to her. "I didn't come here to steal your dog."

"She's not my dog." Rachel forced herself to face him with a smile. "She's obviously yours. Look how happy she is just *seeing* you."

"I don't want to take anything—"

"Anything else away from me?" Rachel interrupted him. "You can't own something that was never yours in the first place. You can't make something or someone love you." She found another smile. "And I'll be leaving soon so it's much better if she stays with you."

"You're definitely going?"

She raised her chin. "Not until after Christmas. You'll have to put up with me until then, but I promise I won't embarrass you or anything."

"That's not what I meant, and you know it," Cauy said fiercely.

"Then why don't you take your damn dog and leave?" She raised her eyebrows. "Unless you're claiming *this* part of the ranch is yours as well?"

He stared at her for a long moment, and then abruptly turned away and headed for his truck. He held the passenger door open and Grace jumped up without a backward glance. In less than a minute he'd disappeared from view, the roar of his truck taking a long time to die away in the stillness.

Rachel leaned back against the barn wall, her knees shaking. She hated confrontations, but he'd deserved everything she'd thrown at him.

"Nice."

She jumped as a voice behind her spoke, and turned to see HW smiling at her. Because of what he'd revealed about her mother's choices she hadn't pursued as strong a relationship with him as she had with his twin and her other brothers. He was far less open than they were and often regarded her like she was a ticking bomb.

"Which part?" Rachel asked.

"All of it." He came to lean against the wall next to her, his blue eyes and blond hair a mirror of her own. "You owned him big-time."

"I don't want to own him," Rachel muttered.

"Yeah, you do."

"Like you'd know anything." Rachel faced him. "Cauy Lymond wants half our ranch. He's the last person in the world I want to have feelings for at the moment."

"You still have them though."

Rachel frowned at him. "Have you been talking to Jenna or something? I really don't need another Morgan telling me how I'm feeling right now."

"Just trying to help." HW didn't take the hint and gracefully disappear, but continued to study her. "You're like me."

"In what way?"

He shrugged. "We both find it difficult to believe we are lovable. Mom did a number on both of us."

"She *loved* you."

"Only on her terms." HW glanced at her. "That's exactly how she was with you, too, wasn't she?"

"I . . ." Rachel felt like she'd been sucker punched. "That's not—"

"Yeah it is," HW insisted. "We both try and make everyone else happy because we're afraid we're not good enough, that we'll be left behind. Don't tell me I'm wrong. I've *watched* you do it."

"Like you'd know anything." Heat gathered in her chest, and her hands fisted at her side.

"Hey, I know it all." He stepped away from the wall and spread his arms wide. "Go on."

"Go on what?"

"You're dying to get angry at something so why not me? You obviously don't like me very much."

"Why would you think that?" Rachel squared up to him.

"Because you don't talk to me like you talk to the others."

"That's not true!"

"You don't talk to me because I was the one who messed up your life." HW's blue eyes clashed with hers. "You think I don't like you."

"You don't," Rachel snapped.

"I like you fine." He paused. "You think I resent you for being the one Mom took with her when the opposite is actually true."

"You liar!" Rachel gaped at him. "You *wanted* her to take you!"

"When I was five, yeah, I did, but you know what? I'm glad she didn't because I wouldn't be the man I am now if she had."

"You'd be like me you mean?" Rachel was way past being polite, and well on the road of sharing a few home truths. "The kid who was never good enough—never you?"

He frowned. "What the *hell*?"

Rachel marched up to him and poked him in the chest.

"She loved you best. She *died* wishing you were there with her. She told me to go *away*!"

HW grimaced and reached for her. "Jeez, Rach, I'm sorry, I didn't *know*, I didn't mean to—"

"It's okay." She stepped out of his reach. She'd never told anyone what her mother's final words had been before, not even her stepfather. "You just reminded me that I did the right thing walking away from Cauy. I refuse to beg anyone to love me anymore."

"Okay, I hear you." HW studied her carefully. "You done now?"

She nodded and let out a very shaky breath.

"Good. One day you *will* meet someone who makes you feel that way, I promise you. Look at Sam. She loves me despite all my shit. If Cauy Lymond doesn't have the intelligence to appreciate *you*, he's an ass."

"I know that." Rachel nodded. "Thank you."

This time she didn't avoid HW when he drew her into a hug. Of all the people in the world *this* man, *this* brother truly understood what she'd gone through with their mother. She'd never forget that. They shared something none of their other siblings would quite understand, and she was finally at peace with that.

"She did love you, Rachel," HW murmured into her hair. "If she hadn't, she would've abandoned you somewhere, or brought you back. Hell, I was *counting* on her bringing you back. I've always thought that having you with her finally made her seek help for her depression. She didn't give up on you. If she'd come back . . ." He sighed. "I think things would've gotten worse."

"Thanks for nothing," Rachel mumbled against his chest, and was rewarded by the rumble of his laughter.

"Right back at you." He put his hands on her shoulders and

eased her back until she had to look up into his eyes. "We've both said what we needed to say. Can we be friends now?"

"I'll think about it."

HW grinned. "That's my girl." He wrapped an arm around her shoulders. "Now come on, let's go and get some breakfast before Ry eats everything on the table."

Chapter Twenty-Two

"Yeah, Mom, that's great, but—" Cauy desperately tried to cut in on his mother's Christmas spiel as she commented on every person living or recently deceased she'd interacted with, and assumed Cauy knew them too. It was early Christmas morning. It was snowing, and Grace was tearing around the house, a big red bow around her neck, desperate to go outside.

"I wanted to ask you something personal," Cauy said.

"About what?" Anita finally ran out of breath.

Cauy managed to push Grace out into the fenced yard and sat opposite the Christmas tree Jackson had set up in the kitchen. The ancient colored lights flicked on and off, but there was a suspicious smell of burning he'd have to investigate as soon as he got off the phone.

"It's about Mark." Cauy held his breath. "Sort of."

His mom sighed. "I knew you'd never let that go now that you're back at the ranch. What is it now?"

"Do you remember a guy called Ben Gardin?"

Silence crackled in the air between them for so long that Cauy thought she'd cut the connection. It had been almost three weeks since he'd had the conversation with Roy, and he had finally decided to ask his mother for the truth. Three weeks since he'd been near Rachel and the Morgan Ranch as well . . .

"Mom?"

"Yes. I knew Ben."

"So you probably know what I'm going to ask you next," Cauy said. "I met a guy called Shep. He asked me to send his regards to you."

"Ben's father?" Anita asked. "He was a lovely man. Ben was just like him."

Cauy gripped his phone harder. "Is it possible Ben was my father?"

This time the silence went on even longer, but he could hear his mom breathing so he waited her out.

"Yes, it's possible."

Cauy briefly closed his eyes. "Okay. Thanks for being up front with me."

"Ben died before the end of our senior year."

"So I heard," Cauy said gently. "That must've been awful for you."

"It was." She sighed. "I don't really want to talk about it, okay?"

"Understood." Cauy nodded even though she couldn't see him. He'd tried to introduce her to video calls but she hated technology. "Are you okay for me to make contact with the Gardin family?"

"If you're going to stay at the ranch, I can hardly stop you. It's a small place. Word would get round eventually."

"I intend to stay here." Cauy hesitated, reluctant to push his luck. "Considering what we just discussed should Jackson inherit this place?"

"He told me he doesn't want it," Anita said. "And you know Jackson. Once he makes his mind up he's pretty stubborn."

"What about Amy?"

"You can ask her when she comes out to see you in the

summer. She'll have finished her nursing degree by then and will probably have an opinion of her own."

Knowing his feisty little sister, Cauy had no doubt of that.

"I'm thinking that after I'm gone I'll set up a trust so that Jackson, Amy, and their kids each get a share of the ranch. What do you think?"

"What about your own family? Jackson said you'd met someone wonderful."

"I'm not planning on getting married again anytime soon, Mom, so don't get your hopes up," Cauy said. "Things didn't work out between us. She deserved better than me."

"That's a shame, darling," Anita said. "But are you sure about that? Jackson said she was the perfect woman for you."

"She is." Cauy pictured Rachel's face when he made love with her. "But—"

"But nothing, Cauy," Anita interrupted him. "The moment Ben knew I was pregnant, he wanted to marry me. I said no because I was afraid of what people would think. I regretted that decision for the rest of my life. If I'd agreed maybe I could've somehow prevented what happened to him."

"Mom . . ." Cauy fidgeted with his phone.

"If she really is the right woman for you, please don't let her slip through your fingers, love."

"What if she's young and has her whole life ahead of her whereas I'm a washed-up fool?" Cauy asked.

"Do you love her?"

"Yeah. I do."

"Does she love you?"

"I think so," Cauy said.

"Then don't squander that love, please, Cauy. Don't do what I did, and let your fear hold you back."

In the background her doorbell chimed, setting off the dogs. "I have to go, darling. Give my love to Jackson, and tell him to call me later."

Cauy kept talking. "What if this woman is a Morgan?"

Anita's chuckle was both a delight and a surprise. "Then more power to you. That would certainly stick it to Mark Lymond."

She ended the call, leaving Cauy sitting there staring blankly at the Christmas tree.

"What's up, Bro? Merry Christmas." Jackson grinned at him from the doorway. He wore an Air Force blue T-shirt and PJ pants with rockets on them. "Were you talking to Mom? How's she doing?"

"She said for you to call her later." Cauy put down his cell phone and went to disconnect the Christmas tree lights. "She also said it's highly likely Ben Gardin was my father."

"Cool!" Jackson got a beer out of the refrigerator and toasted Cauy with it. "That's awesome news! What time are we supposed to be at the Morgans?"

"Are you still going on about that?" Cauy asked.

"I saw Ry in the Red Dragon yesterday, and he assumed we were coming." Jackson frowned. "What's the problem?"

Cauy considered, his gaze drawn to Grace, who had come in from the yard and was happily shaking wet snow everywhere. *Could* he turn up at the Morgans? *Should* he?

"I'll call Mrs. Morgan and check in, okay?" Jackson took a package off the tree and crouched beside Grace. The package squeaked loudly, and Grace bounced around like a crazy thing. "Here you go, girl, plastic squeaky steak! Enjoy!"

Cauy left them to it and went into the farm office. He closed the door against the assault of squeaky noises and sent a text to Kim.

Are you around?

Dude! It's Christmas! Kim replied immediately. **Of course I'm working!**

Cauy smiled. Have you got a moment to draft a letter for me?

Sure, what do you need?

Cauy sat on the edge of the desk and typed in what he wanted. Can you fax me a copy to this number when you're done?

Will have it to you in an hour.

Thanks, Kim. Cauy sent the fax number.

Wait until you see my bill . . . LOL

Cauy's smile died as he ended the call. Whatever happened next, at least he could tell his mom that he'd tried . . .

"What do you mean Cauy and Jackson Lymond are coming to eat Christmas dinner with us?" Rachel stared openmouthed at her grandmother.

They were setting the tables in the guest dining room. It was a tradition that all the hands and Morgan Ranch staff were invited to Christmas dinner. It was snowing outside, but the large room was warm as toast with a log fire burning in the massive rock chimney.

"*I* invited them." Ruth raised an eyebrow. "It's called being neighborly."

"To the man who wants to extort cash out of your grandson on a frivolous lawsuit?"

Ruth handed Rachel a bunch of silverware. "I doubt Cauy will go through with it."

"Why doesn't anyone believe he meant it?" Rachel

complained. "It's like you all think he's a nice guy or something."

"He *is* a nice man. Maybe too nice, and too quick to take a hint." Rachel straightened the table center arrangement, which Avery had designed to resemble a cowboy boot filled with Christmas presents. "I think he'll do very well with the ranch."

"Who else did you ask?" Rachel attempted to change the subject.

"Dr. Tio Mendez and his grandmother, Nancy and Maureen from the shop, and Shep and Mary Gardin."

Rachel put the last fork in place. "Who are the Gardins?"

"Didn't Roy tell you?" Ruth handed her a stack of linen napkins. "Shep's son Ben might well have been your Cauy's father."

"Firstly, he's not my Cauy," Rachel said. "And secondly, how come no one let me in on this stupendous piece of gossip?"

"Possibly because every time one of us mentions Cauy you get all defensive and growly."

"Gee, I wonder why," Rachel said. "It's not like he broke my heart or anything."

"Did he really?" Ruth paused to look searchingly at her.

"Yes, I think he did." Rachel found a smile. "But that's okay. You can't make someone love you, right?"

Ruth put down her basket of napkins. "Cauy's a good man, Rachel, but he's not an easy man. He's already dealt with a lot in his life, and I suspect those scars will always be with him."

"You think I don't know that?" Rachel asked.

"I think you believe it's your job in life to make everyone feel better," Ruth said. "And maybe you should be thinking about putting yourself first for a change."

"That's exactly what HW told me." Rachel held Ruth's gaze. "But you don't understand Cauy at all if you think he needs holding up. He's one of the strongest men I've ever met. He's managed to close himself off so completely that he truly believes that's who he is, and how it will always be."

"And you can't stop him from believing that."

"I'm not trying to." Rachel took a deep breath. "It's up to him, isn't it? If he truly wants a relationship with me he's got to reach out. I can't climb those walls or break them down all by myself." She patted Ruth's shoulder. "It's okay. I get that. I'm sad that he's not prepared to go that extra mile for me, but I'm not going to hang around waiting for him to change. I deserve more."

"That's my girl." Ruth's eyes were full of tears, which almost made Rachel well up. "Strong and sassy."

Rachel wished she felt the words more, but she was convinced that if she kept saying them that in time she would.

Chase came in with a new load of wood for the fire and halted at the sight of Rachel and Ruth embracing.

"Everything okay?"

"It's all wonderful." Ruth was the first to speak. "How is January feeling this morning?"

Chase made a face. "Still puking. But she says she'll be fine for lunch, and I believe her. It's amazing how quickly she perks up after she's emptied her stomach."

"Thanks for the graphic detail," Rachel said, grimacing. "Is there anything else at the house that needs bringing over?"

Chase shook his head. "I did want to ask you about something, though, Rachel. Do you have a minute?"

Rachel tensed as he took her through to his office. "This hasn't got anything to do with Cauy Lymond, does it?"

"No, why should it?" Chase gave her a funny look. "Raj, the guy who helped me out when you were stuck in the mine, contacted me a couple of days ago with a government job opportunity based in Sacramento."

"You don't need a job," Rachel quipped back.

"But you do." Chase clicked something on his laptop, and the printer went into action. "I told him about you and the kind of job you were looking for. I've forwarded you his e-mail, but I thought you might like a printout as well." He picked up the sheets of paper and handed them to Rachel. "They're looking for an engineer to work closely with the registry for historic California mines."

"The what?" Rachel looked down at the paperwork.

"Like as a consultant and adviser. You'd get to visit abandoned mines and tourist attraction ones, make sure they follow safety regulations, and issue reports on the overall state of each mine." Chase closed his laptop. "Is that something you might be interested in? The pay isn't great, but it would be a good place to start your career, and it's relatively close to home. They might even let you telecommute."

"Thank you." Rachel looked up at him. "I don't know what to say."

"There's no rush." He smiled as he headed for the door. "Look through the information, and get back to me or Raj after the holidays."

"It was really kind of you to find out about this for me."

He shrugged. "What else is family for?"

"I've never had anyone look out for me before." Rachel had to say it. "It means the world to me."

Chase turned to look at her, his expression suddenly serious. "You're part of our family now, Rachel. Never forget that and know we'll all be doing our best to make those lost years up to you."

She nodded and clasped the paperwork to her chest as he opened the door and went out. She might have been unlucky in love, but at the Morgan Ranch she'd discovered a family who loved her and wanted her to stick around.

She swallowed hard. Having that sense of home made the thought of leaving so much easier. Whatever happened over the years to come she would never ever be a stranger here. She folded up the paper and went to put it in her coat pocket in the coatroom.

Seeing Cauy again might not be quite so difficult when surrounded by all her family. And, if he put a foot out of line, having four big brothers might just come in handy. . . .

Cauy braced himself against the wave of laughter and conversation coming from the Morgan dining room, fixed a smile on his face, and followed Jackson in search of their hostess. Of course, the first Morgan he saw was Rachel dressed in a yellow fluffy sweater and skinny black jeans laughing with Jenna beside the fire. She looked beautiful and like she didn't have a care in the world, which was exactly what he wished for her in his less selfish moments. The rest of the time he just wanted to wrap his arms around her and hold her forever.

Carefully avoiding catching her eye, Cauy kept his gaze on Jackson, who was now shaking Billy's hand and laughing, which wasn't helping Cauy's nerves.

"Thanks for inviting us," Cauy said to Billy. "Especially considering the circumstances."

"Would that be you claiming half my ranch, or you making my daughter mad?" Billy asked.

"I hope to settle all those matters shortly, sir." Cauy swallowed hard and held Billy's gaze.

"Good." Billy nodded and turned away. "Ruth's in the kitchen if you want to speak to her."

"Not bloody likely," Cauy murmured to himself. He had the sense that if he wasn't careful, all the Morgans would seek him out and demand answers he wasn't yet ready to give. He spotted Dr. Tio sitting with an elderly lady in the corner and went over to them. Hopefully, that would give him time to steady his nerves before dinner got underway.

Of course, when they were called to the table, some

sadist had decided to sit Cauy opposite Rachel and a whole row of formidable Morgan men. He looked around for Jackson, who was comfortably situated between Nancy and her mom, and having a great time.

Ruth finally emerged from the kitchen with Yvonne and Avery at her side to say grace. She got them started passing the massive plates of turkey, ham, and all the trimmings around the table.

Cauy didn't feel much like eating and took the minimum he could get away with to avoid looking either rude or weird. He jumped as someone leaned over to fill his water glass and the ice clinked.

"I assume you don't want wine, Cauy?" Rachel asked.

He finally looked at her, and couldn't look away. She was always beautiful to him, but today—after not seeing her for a while—she was his whole world.

"No, thanks," he managed to reply. "Water's good."

She put down the water jug. "How's Grace?"

"About to have her puppies anytime now according to Jenna. I brought her with us. She's in the house if you want to see her."

"Thanks, I'd like that." Rachel took some turkey and passed the platter to her left, stopping to chat with Billy, which gave Cauy the chance to concentrate on his plate again.

She didn't attempt to draw him into anything resembling a conversation, and he knew he deserved it. Her ability to conceal if she was hurt and present such a calm front to the world was both an amazing advantage and a massive road-block to understanding how she really felt. He had no doubt in his head that she would survive without him. She was a strong woman.

But every so often, when she thought he wasn't looking, she'd sneak a glance at him like she couldn't help herself.

He only noticed because he was doing exactly the same thing to her.

The meal seemed to take forever, but even the Morgans couldn't eat everything in the universe. Eventually, Ruth stood up to thank everyone for coming, and to recall the highlights of the year. Roy then thanked Ruth to great applause on behalf of all the guests.

As Roy sat down, Cauy rose to his feet and waited for the conversation to die down, leaving a sea of curious faces staring at him. He'd never felt so exposed in his life. He cleared his throat and turned to Ruth.

"Mrs. Morgan? There's something I wanted to say to you." He took the folded paper out of his pocket. "I know there has been some speculation that I intended to sue the Morgan Ranch for a parcel of disputed land. I wanted to set the record straight today." He handed Ruth the letter. "This is from my lawyer, and states that I have no intention of ever litigating about this land, and that my heirs will never do so either."

Ruth glanced down at the letter. "Well, that's mighty fine of you, Cauy. I never thought you'd go through with it anyway, but thank you."

"You're welcome."

Cauy sat down to a smattering of applause and faced a row of Morgans. Rachel was staring at him as if he'd done something terrible. He met her gaze. Now came the hard part.

"Would you like to come and check on Grace with me?"

She considered him for a long moment. "Okay."

He followed her out into the lobby, and they both collected their jackets before braving the weather and heading for the ranch house that looked like the image on a Victorian Christmas card. Cauy's boots crunched in the snow and his breath condensed as he followed her lead. Someone had threaded colored lights through the spindles on the porch and swept away the snow from the wooden planking. The whole place looked magical.

Rachel held the screen door so that it wouldn't bang on Cauy and stepped into the quiet house, shedding her boots in the mudroom and unzipping her jacket.

"Where did you put Grace?" she asked.

She turned only to find Cauy was right there. She took a step back and hit the wall. He stared down at her, one hand braced above her head.

"I never meant to take your family to court."

"So they all kept telling me." Rachel suddenly found it hard to breathe.

"I only told you I did because I wanted you to think I wasn't worth your time and energy."

"Well, it worked." Whatever he was trying to do she wasn't going to make it easy for him.

"It didn't work for me," he sighed. "I thought I was doing the best thing for you—setting you free to find some nice guy, who was new, and unspoiled, and—"

"Not you. I get it," Rachel said. "But *why*?"

"Because that's what you deserve."

She raised her chin. "Who made you the judge of what I deserve?"

"I'm not an easy guy to live with."

"So you're high maintenance. So what?"

He shifted his stance slightly so that he was even closer and leaned in. "So maybe I'm not good enough for you."

"Says who?"

"*Me*, goddamn it!" He tenderly kissed her brow, and then her nose. "I suck."

"I know that." She shivered as he kissed her cheek. "You're an awful, terrible human being."

"Yeah."

"Whom I like despite desperately trying to convince myself otherwise."

"Then will you consider forgiving me for trying to push you away from me?" Cauy asked.

She eased out of his half embrace. "It depends."

"On what?"

He looked wary now, which she was enjoying much more than she should.

"What made you change your mind and try and make things right with me?"

"A couple of things." He rubbed his hand over his mouth. "Firstly, my mom told me that if I really loved you I shouldn't waste my time telling you, and secondly—"

"Back up." Rachel held up her hand. "Did you just say that you *love* me?"

He met her gaze, his brown eyes clear. "Yeah, I did."

"*Really*?" He nodded, and she scowled at him. "Yet you still blew me off?"

"As I was trying to say before you interrupted me, I didn't think I had that right."

"To *love* me?"

His mouth twisted. "Look at me, Rachel. I'm never going to be perfect."

"What makes you think I've ever wanted perfect?" she asked.

"Because that's what you *deserve*."

She rolled her eyes. "We're back to that, are we? What if I want you, just the way you are. What if I love *you*?"

"Then I'd be the luckiest man on this planet." He reached for her, but she held up her hand. "What?"

She was trembling so hard she thought she might pass out. "I want someone who will always be there for me— someone who will always put *me* first. I *deserve* that."

"Yeah, you do." He nodded slowly. "I want to be that man."

"You do?"

He pressed his palm to his heart. "I want to be here for you whenever you need a friend, or a lover, or just someone to shout at." He formed his hand into a cup. "I want to hold you here, in my heart and soul like a bird that will fly away from me sometimes, but always return. Do you *get* that? Do you want that?"

"That's the most beautiful, poetical thing anyone has ever said to me," Rachel whispered.

He shrugged. "It's how I feel."

"And it's the most sentences I think you've ever spoken to me in one go."

This time she let him take her hand. "That's good, right?"

She collapsed against him, and he closed his arms around her and held her tight. She'd missed the taste and sheer strength in him so badly. . . .

"Are you going to let me kiss you now?" Cauy asked hoarsely.

With a strangled sob, she flung her arm around his neck and raised her mouth to his. Their kiss was both a promise, and a welcome home—a commitment, and a revelation.

"I love you, Rachel Morgan," Cauy murmured between kisses. "I tried to let you go, and I don't think I can do it again."

"You won't have to," Rachel assured him as she kissed him. His hands were roving her body, pressing her against the hardness in his jeans and making her want . . .

A frantic barking echoed down the hallway, and Cauy's head shot up.

"That's Grace."

He ran down to the kitchen, Rachel in hot pursuit, to discover Grace lying on her side in the dog basket panting hard. Cauy crouched beside her and then turned to Rachel.

"The puppies are coming. Do you want to fetch Jenna?"

She leaned in and kissed him one more time before rushing to put her boots on. There was still a lot for her and Cauy to work out, but one thing she was certain of—he would never go back on his promise to her.

Laughing up at the falling snow, Rachel retraced her steps to the guest center. It was Christmas Day, her forever family surrounded her, Cauy had expressed his love for her in complete sentences, and she was about to become a doggie mamma.

What more could any woman want?

Kate's Christmas Cracker Candy for Rachel

(With thanks to Angela James of Carina Press
for the original recipe)

40 saltine crackers
½ cup of butter (I like to use salted butter.)
1 cup sugar (I like to use light brown sugar lightly
   packed.)
2 cups chocolate chips (I like milk chocolate,
   but dark is also good.)

Preheat oven to 400 degrees F.

Place the crackers side by side in a jelly roll pan lined with foil or silicone.

Melt the butter in a pan and add the sugar. Bring to a boil, stirring constantly for 3 minutes. Do not let it burn; reduce heat a little if necessary.

Spread over crackers with a spatula.

Bake in oven for 5 minutes.

Sprinkle chocolate chips over surface; you can get creative and try different kinds of chocolate, or add caramel. Cover with foil and leave for 5 minutes to melt.

Spread the melted chocolate over the caramel.

Add toppings (pecans, mixed nuts, sea salt, sprinkles, peppermint, etc.).

Cover and place in the refrigerator or freezer to set for a couple of hours. (That's where I keep mine.)

Break it up, and eat! Repeat.

Connect with Us

Visit us online at
KensingtonBooks.com
to read more from your favorite authors, see books
by series, view reading group guides, and more.

Join us on social media

for sneak peeks, chances to win books and prize packs,
and to share your thoughts with other readers.

facebook.com/kensingtonpublishing
twitter.com/kensingtonbooks

Tell us what you think!

To share your thoughts, submit a review,
or sign up for our eNewsletters, please visit:
KensingtonBooks.com/TellUs.

More by Bestselling Author
Hannah Howell

__Highland Angel	978-1-4201-0864-4	$6.99US/$8.99CAN
__If He's Sinful	978-1-4201-0461-5	$6.99US/$8.99CAN
__Wild Conquest	978-1-4201-0464-6	$6.99US/$8.99CAN
__If He's Wicked	978-1-4201-0460-8	$6.99US/$8.49CAN
__My Lady Captor	978-0-8217-7430-4	$6.99US/$8.49CAN
__Highland Sinner	978-0-8217-8001-5	$6.99US/$8.49CAN
__Highland Captive	978-0-8217-8003-9	$6.99US/$8.49CAN
__Nature of the Beast	978-1-4201-0435-6	$6.99US/$8.49CAN
__Highland Fire	978-0-8217-7429-8	$6.99US/$8.49CAN
__Silver Flame	978-1-4201-0107-2	$6.99US/$8.49CAN
__Highland Wolf	978-0-8217-8000-8	$6.99US/$9.99CAN
__Highland Wedding	978-0-8217-8002-2	$4.99US/$6.99CAN
__Highland Destiny	978-1-4201-0259-8	$4.99US/$6.99CAN
__Only for You	978-0-8217-8151-7	$6.99US/$8.99CAN
__Highland Promise	978-1-4201-0261-1	$4.99US/$6.99CAN
__Highland Vow	978-1-4201-0260-4	$4.99US/$6.99CAN
__Highland Savage	978-0-8217-7999-6	$6.99US/$9.99CAN
__Beauty and the Beast	978-0-8217-8004-6	$4.99US/$6.99CAN
__Unconquered	978-0-8217-8088-6	$4.99US/$6.99CAN
__Highland Barbarian	978-0-8217-7998-9	$6.99US/$9.99CAN
__Highland Conqueror	978-0-8217-8148-7	$6.99US/$9.99CAN
__Conqueror's Kiss	978-0-8217-8005-3	$4.99US/$6.99CAN
__A Stockingful of Joy	978-1-4201-0018-1	$4.99US/$6.99CAN
__Highland Bride	978-0-8217-7995-8	$4.99US/$6.99CAN
__Highland Lover	978-0-8217-7759-6	$6.99US/$9.99CAN

Available Wherever Books Are Sold!

Check out our website at
http://www.kensingtonbooks.com